RECURRENT NIGHTMARE

She was dressed in red tee shirt, yellow shorts, and sandals. I wasn't paying much attention, really, just watching her look over the side at the wake, when, before I could even cry out, she suddenly climbed up on the rail and plunged in, very near the stern.

I screamed and heard her howl of terror as the propwash caught her, sucked her under, and the prop cut her to pieces.

There was little I could do, but I ran back to Hanley, who just nodded sadly.

"Take it easy," he said gently. "She's dead, and there's no use going back for the body, it won't be there. We *know.*"

"How do you know that?" I snapped.

"Because we did it the last four times she killed herself, and we never found a body then, either."

By Jack L. Chalker
Published by Ballantine Books:

THE WEB OF THE CHOZEN

AND THE DEVIL WILL DRAG YOU UNDER

A JUNGLE OF STARS

DANCE BAND ON THE *TITANIC*

DANCERS IN THE AFTERGLOW

THE SAGA OF THE WELL WORLD
Volume 1: *Midnight at the Well of Souls*
Volume 2: *Exiles at the Well of Souls*
Volume 3: *Quest for the Well of Souls*
Volume 4: *The Return of Nathan Brazil*
Volume 5: *Twilight at the Well of Souls:*
           The Legacy of Nathan Brazil

THE FOUR LORDS OF THE DIAMOND
Book One: *Lilith: A Snake in the Grass*
Book Two: *Cerberus: A Wolf in the Fold*
Book Three: *Charon: A Dragon at the Gate*
Book Four: *Medusa: A Tiger by the Tail*

THE DANCING GODS
Book One: *The River of Dancing Gods*
Book Two: *Demons of the Dancing Gods*
Book Three: *Vengeance of the Dancing Gods*

THE RINGS OF THE MASTER
Book One: *Lords of the Middle Dark*
Book Two: *Pirates of the Thunder*
Book Three: *Warriors of the Storm*
Book Four: *Masks of the Martyrs*

DANCE BAND ON THE
TITANIC

Jack L. Chalker

A Del Rey Book

BALLANTINE BOOKS • NEW YORK

A Del Rey Book
Published by Ballantine Books

Portions of this text were originally published in various magazines and anthologies: "Dance Band on the Titanic" was originally published in *Isaac Asimov's Science Fiction Magazine* and *World's Best Science Fiction 1979*; "In the Wilderness" was originally published in *Analog*; and "In the Dowaii Chambers" was originally published in *The John W. Campbell Awards Nominees, Vol. 5*.
Grateful acknowledgment is made to the following for permission to reprint previously published material:
A.C. Projects, Inc.: letter from John W. Campbell, Jr. to Jack L. Chalker. Copyright © 1985 by Perry Chapdelaine and George Hay from *The John W. Campbell Letters, Vol. 1*. Reprinted by permission of A.C. Projects, Inc.
The Mirage Press, Ltd.: annotated bibliographic material by Jack L. Chalker from *A Jack L. Chalker Bibliography*. Copyright © 1984, 1985 by Jack L. Chalker.
Random House, Inc.: "No Hiding Place," edited by Judy-Lynn Del Rey from *Stellar 3*. Copyright © 1977 by Random House, Inc. Reprinted by permission of Ballantine Books, a division of Random House, Inc.
Stuart David Schiff: "Stormsong Runner" by Jack L. Chalker from *Whisper II* by Stuart David Schiff, Doubleday, 1979. Reprinted by permission.

Library of Congress Catalog Card Number: 87-91885

ISBN 0-345-34858-3

Manufactured in the United States of America

First Edition: July 1988

Cover Art by Darrell K. Sweet

This book has to be dedicated to
Ben Bova, Harry Brashear, John W. Campbell
Jr., Judy-Lynn del Rey, Martin L. Greenberg,
George R.R. Martin, Mark Owings, Stuart David
Schiff, George Scithers, Suzy Tiffany, and Bob
Tucker, all of whom had something to do with
these stories in one oblique way or another.

CONTENTS

ACKNOWLEDGMENTS

INTRODUCTION: THE WRITING GAME

WHENEVER ONE OF THOSE LITTLE FORMS COMES IN for credit or information or whatever, under "occupation" I invariably write "novelist" in the blank because that's what I do. Not "writer" or "author" (except the latter on immigration forms when going to other countries since it gets you nicer treatment), because I am basically a novelist. I think long; I'm generally much more comfortable with novel lengths and beyond than with the short form. This might be because I'm a veteran ham and former teacher and don't like to be restricted to short takes, but whatever the reason, I am far more comfortable with unrestricted space.

I'm probably best known as an author of series, although some of my editors say "serials." I have only three sets of related books that I think of as series—that is, each novel is complete by itself but all concern the same characters in the same basic universe—and these are the *Well World* books, the *Dancing Gods* books, and the *G.O.D., Inc.* books. Even the *Well World* books don't quite fit; there are five of them but there are only three novels, the second and third volumes being one continuous narrative and the fourth and fifth another. These were broken up due to the vagaries of the publishing industry—it's more profitable to sell two $3.50 paperbacks than one $4.95 paperback—on direct order rather than by my design or preference.

There are also serials, which means one humungous book broken up into a bunch of smaller books for the same reasons as above. These include *Four Lords of the Diamond*, *The Rings of the Master*, the *Soul Rider* books, and the *Changewinds* books. Most of those individual volumes do not read independently but are part of a continuous narrative. An aside: *The Rings of the Master* is not my title; my title was *The Malebolge Rings*, but editors ordered that changed since they argued that readers wouldn't know how to pronounce Malebolge and still make it a great sounding title but would read it instead as Male-bolge in which case it sounds idiotic. You *do* know how to pronounce it, don't you? Well, do you at least know why you *should* know?

The difference between writing short fiction and writing novels, even half a million word novels, is at least as great as the difference between being a champion billiards player and a world-class pool player. Both billiards and pool are played on the same sized table with the same cues and balls, but while the object of one is to put specific balls into specific pockets, the other game doesn't even *have* pockets. Very few champions at one can be equal champions at the other. When I grew up in Maryland, bowling meant duckpins; that other game that was scored the same but had the huge balls and the equally huge scores was tenpins and was played by ham-handed dolts who couldn't appreciate the subtler duckpin game. A world champ tenpin bowler is lucky to get eighty in ducks; a duckpin champ often can't break a hundred in tens. They are scored the same and look somewhat the same (although you get three balls per frame in duckpins and it still doesn't help) but they are totally different games requiring totally different skills.

By the same token, there are born novelists and born short fiction writers in the sense that authors tend to be far better at one form than the other. The watchword of the short story is economy; it is built around a central idea or concept and has no room to stray from it, and if characterization is required it must be developed with an economy of words during the course of getting to the object of the story itself. This is one reason why most short fiction masters do, at best, mediocre novels. The novel is not a big short story; it is an entirely different form requiring pacing, a broad structure, interrelated sub-plots, and often a multiplicity of themes. A good novel is not an expanded or "long" short story but must be crafted differently to work. The short story author trying a novel all too often tries building it along a short story structure (that is, around a single theme or idea that can not justify the length) or gets lost in all that verbiage and pads and plods.

Now, a novelist is used to thinking of multiple themes and tracks and painting on a broad canvas; when writing short, the novelist tends to feel restricted, limited, the mind seeing endless possibilities for going this way or that and feeling uncomfortable with the limitations the short form imposes and the comparatively large amount of time it takes to craft a work that is generally no longer than a single chapter. Often he or she feels like a mural painter asked to engrave the Sistine Chapel ceiling on the head of a pin. The short story is extremely difficult to do well, since a tremendous amount must be accomplished with just a few well-chosen words and with little or no margin for error.

There are, of course, rare individuals who do both equally well, but even for them, the one who is essentially a novelist will gravitate to the long form quickly while leaving the short form only for those ideas that must be developed but can not stand the extra length. The short story writer may have one or two novel successes but, after that, failures. In earlier days, the short story was king and there were literally hundreds of markets for it; these days, outlets for short fiction are few and far between while the novels have large markets and it's the novelists who make the real money. Writers must eat; novelists eat better. This is something of a tragedy, because any talk of the superiority of one form over another is nonsense. Both are art, just as billiards and pool and duckpins and tenpins are all valid sports, and both accomplish different and equally important ends. I wish there were more opportunities for short fiction writers these days because I miss the real bulk of fine writing produced in the form of decades past, but it's tough for a short story writer to be living on beans while watching the novelist dine on Dom Perignon and caviar. Now, it *is* true that short fiction writers win more awards, but that's because there are fewer markets and far less competition and only the best get published, but it's damned tough to eat awards.

Thus, every short story writer I know today is a profitable hobbyist—they get paid for short stories but they do something else for a living. The lucky ones also write for their "real" money, but they tend to write for Hollywood and often under mysterious pseudonyms so you, the readers, and The Critics won't find out. It's astonishing, though, to find the number of familiar names bylining episodes of *He-Man: Master of the Universe* and *Challenge of the Go-Bots*. Hollywood is not all *Twilight Zone* and *The Hitchhiker*, but it pays well. It is even more amazing to discover some of the familiar (and mostly male) names behind those flowery pseudonyms on popular romance novels.

I originally started in the short form, as you'll see, but with only encouragement and no sales. Of course, I wasn't very ambitious in the writing game when young, and rarely aggressively tried to sell anything that I wrote. I never got a form rejection slip—it was always one of those nice letters of encouragement (one of which is reproduced elsewhere in this book), although once I actually got a bill (see my introduction to "No Hiding Place").

I've been an editor, a publisher, and a packager of SF and fantasy, as well as a bibliographer and creator of novelties. I've been around this field and in this atmosphere since I was thirteen, even though my first original fiction sale wasn't until I was almost thirty. When I did turn to writing seriously, starting with a novel, I sold it the first time out. Since then, I've had a couple of ideas that never became books either because editors didn't like them or mostly because editors demanded massive changes that made the ideas no longer interesting. You might call these (all two of them) the Lost Novels, although elements of them are in several other stories of mine—all the good parts—and two parts of one are here.

As I write this, I have thirty novels, book-length or longer, under my belt, but this book you hold contains my entire professional short story output. Short fiction comes hard to me; it's far more work than it seems and for far less money than it should pay considering the sweat and labor. There is also the concern of the marketplace. A writer writes to communicate with a vast and largely anonymous public. A short story might take weeks or even months to craft well, go to a magazine, then be published there and have a store shelf life of just under one month. Then, unless the story is anthologized or continually reprinted, it's gone. Again, at this writing, only one of these stories is currently or even recently in print, while every single book-length work I have ever written is in print and available—and earning money and communicating. Thus, I turn to short stories only when a concept or idea demands the short form.

I don't write merely because I hate to get up in the morning; I write because I have things to say, and I hope I reach the people capable of understanding them. Publishing this way is a scattershot approach, but it reaches a vast audience and is no more scattershot than teaching. Novels sell well and have very long lives; short stories sell relatively poorly and even some of the greatest lapse into obscurity very quickly. I get paid an awful lot of money for my novels because they sell so well; I get paid a pittance for short fiction in comparison because the sales aren't heavily influenced by the short story names inside a magazine or anthology. If I want to both communicate broadly and long and live in a very comfortable manner, novels are the way to do it. I once had a winner of many Nebulas and Hugos dispute that on a panel and brag that one short story of his made fourteen thousand dollars including a TV sale. But it was his *only* story that made that kind of money, the sum was made over a period of years, and if that same sum were offered for a novel of mine, my agent would laugh and then say, "Now, seriously..."

I am constantly besieged by requests to do another *Well World* book or another *Four Lords* book or sequels to many of my independent novels. Many if not most of my readership get to know and like the characters, themes, and worlds that I have created, which is gratifying, and want more. On the other hand, I have seen talented careers go down the toilet as good authors, lured by money and an automatic market, write volume twenty-five of a good three-book series. Now, some have lots of money and a few even have fan clubs or conventions devoted to those series, but they are not writing the good books they are capable of, and all the time and energy devoted to those hack series of endless novels means they are really at a self-imposed creative dead end.

Since attaining some degree of fame and financial security, I have rigidly held to the principle that a story takes as long as it takes and that's it. If it takes only 6000 words, that's how long it takes. If it takes 40,000 words, that's okay, too. If it takes 100,000 or 500,000, so be it. I have had offers from some editors to expand some of the stories herein into novels, but I have been unable to justify it. I could lengthen them, but I could not *improve* them or add anything by so doing. Indeed, while I'm certain there must be some, I can not offhand think of any examples of a really fine short story that was expanded to novel length where the longer version was preferable or superior or added anything except money to the author's pocket.

And yet, the few stories here are important to me. My sometimes collaborator on nonfiction works and occasional alter-ego, Mark Owings, calls these "the good stuff." They range from my earliest surviving attempt at fiction writing ("No Hiding Place") to my own personal favorite of all the words, long and short, that I've written to date, ("Dance Band on the *Titanic*"). I do a number of readings of "Dance Band" since it's not only my personal favorite but also reads well aloud in under an hour, and I find in every audience that there are at least a few people who had read the story initially and remember the story fondly because it touched them in just the ways it was intended to—only nobody remembers that I wrote it. I very much dislike the idea of communicating anonymously; I spend far too much time cooped up alone in my office with a CRT screen and keyboard to deny the little recognition due me when a story works.

If anyone wants to know why I don't spent more time on short fiction, the low pay, relatively short public availability, and anonymity even when the story works are the main reasons. Another is the tendency to be type-cast (see my notes on "In the Dowaii Chambers") so that the people for whom the story is intended simply do not read it. And, of course, I have discovered time and again that people read and like a short story but do not remember the author, while those who purchase novels know exactly who they are reading. And, then, there is also you out there—you don't buy short story collections very much (and I expect even this one will be among my smaller sellers) or anthologies, either. This is not the way to encourage more short fiction output nor support such work.

And that brings me to the subject of you.

For someone who grew up in this field, I often wonder just who you all are. Few SF critics even bother to review my works at all, although I'm generally vilified when they do. One SF editor who began as I did in the fanzines and who wanted to be a Big Name Writer but had only one good story in him, stood up at a gathering of SF writers out west a few years back and vilified and mocked me as well as a couple of other very successful SF/fantasy writers by name. I and the others he mocked were not there; I myself was three thousand miles away at the time. I'm told a number of people in the audience laughed and applauded. I figure it must be tough to be eaten alive by the knowledge that, no matter what a person's accomplishments, he is a failure at what he dreamed of doing most while others attained his goals, so that he has to do things like this to people he wishes he was. I always thought it sadder still that so many in that professional audience were in the same state of frustration and envy as he. When great success eludes some writers, they try to settle for critical acclaim; when even that fails, there is nothing left but bitterness.

The fellow spent seven years gratuitiously attacking me in person and print. Not long back he dropped dead, and I received a number of requests for tributes to this beloved figure. He was a good editor and nobody should die that young, but he was a sad case and an asshole when he died and death did nothing to expunge that. I loathe hypocrisy and attack it in my writings; I could not indulge now. One still might learn from it, though. He's still being praised as a great editor, and perhaps he was, but that wasn't what he wanted to be or to be remembered for. Such is life.

Still, I've also received some wonderful letters and comments from some of the giants of our field, the very authors I held and still hold in awe and wonder as a reader of their works, telling me how much pleasure I have given them. Those are worth more than a hundred good reviews or a thousand Hugos.

I've won a number of regional awards, but the only major one wasn't an SF award at all but a prestigious mainstream award—the Gold Medal of the *West Coast Review of Books*. Somebody out there buys incredible numbers of my books in this and many other nations and languages, yet I've never been nominated for a Hugo or a Nebula for my writings, even in the popular vote awards. That's not any angle to nominate me, it's just a commentary. It appears that my vast readership out there comes primarily from outside the established SF readership. Mainstream critics have generally liked me, while SF critics who bother at all tend to either hate my guts or dismiss me as inconsequential. I have some theories on why and we'll get to them in a moment.

But when you remember that neither Cary Grant nor Alfred Hitchcock, among a host of others, ever won an Oscar, and Steven Spielberg can't even get nominated, you realize that in the end those awards mean very little. It is, after all, hard to take most critics seriously anyway. They tend to be, on the whole, failed writers or frustrated ideologues left behind by their contemporaries' intellectual growth.

One critic said he'd read *Web of the Chozen* and *A Jungle of Stars* and that was enough. For somebody with my output, that's like judging Shakespeare entirely by *Coriolanus* and *Henry VIII*. It is probable that the vast majority of you who read this book won't like all the stories in it. I would be almost disappointed if you did, since I think they represent a very broad range, from simple gimmick tales and technological problems to some pretty complex and downright artsy stories. There was no attempt in writing them to create this range; these stories were created in the deep corner of my mind that I cannot consciously touch, and they are as they are because they had to be that way.

Tom Disch, another critic, one of the failed writer's school but so beloved of the *literati*, called the *Soul Rider* books "better-written Gor novels." That got me to thinking of a comment the late Judy-Lynn del Rey said to me when I tried something very fancy in a book. "Jack, take it out or you'll regret it. The science-fiction readership is smart but terribly naive and unsophisticated. They're incapable of divining complexities not spelled out for them. All you'll do is wind up with them not understanding a word you're saying and crucifying you for it."

I took her advice on that one but not on many other books since. From the mail and comments I get, I'm not at all sure she was right in her evaluation, but she sure was right about the SF (as opposed to mainstream) critics. For example, let's say I was around in 1923 and studied and discovered a tremendous amount about the beliefs and personalities of an obscure and laughable right-wing revolutionary group in Germany whose leader had just tried to revolt in a beer hall and been slammed in jail. I note, for example, the virulent anti-Semitism that the Vienna-bred leader has and promotes to his followers, and I see it going down quite well with the German population who always used Jews for scapegoats.

So I sit down and write this near-future SF novel about how this (disguised) leader and his party somehow manage to rise from the ashes and take over control of a major industrial nation, and, after the usual purges and dictatorial set-ups, begin rounding up the millions of Jews in his country, as well as gypsies and anybody else he didn't like, maybe fourteen million people or more, confiscating everything they had to the cheers of the population, and sending them all—men, women, children, no difference—to slave labor camps where vast numbers are eventually gassed and the party leaders in charge make lampshades from the skin and sift the ashes of the crematoriums for gold from the fillings, etc., while feeling no particular guilt, going back to their homes, listening to Beethoven and Brahms, and arguing the aesthetics of Impressionists over chess and fine wine.

Many would have laughed and sneered and accused me of writing voyeur fiction—I certainly couldn't have been published in a "proper" way and might well have been banned. At best, I would have been attacked by critics within this field as someone indulging in sado-masochism, sexual depravity, you name it, and perhaps even attacked as advocating what I was trying to expose.

Well, I'm a historian, specializing in ideologies in theory and practice, so I read all the obscure theoreticians, and I look at the dogma of religious sects and the like, and then I create my models, set them up, and let them run. Interestingly, if I choose an Ideologically Correct set of victims there's nary a peep from anybody. To give one example, when I have super-women dominating men who are kept as sex objects for breeding purposes, that's okay, but when I use *women* in the subservient role, that's Gor. But, you see, for the purposes of exploring dangers and dangerous minds and people, women work better right now than men because women are the large group just attaining a solid role in the work-place, just attaining full rights, and just getting their concerns addressed—it's women's rights, not men's, that are under the most constant assault. New Eden was a construct of three blended ideologies using their common denominators. These are real and have some power and each has literally *millions* of followers right now (no exaggeration). One is middle eastern, one is Oriental, and the third is an established American religion. A lot of people delved beneath the surface and addressed the hard points I was trying to make. That was who I was writing for from the start.

Our world today is full of people willing and eager to surrender their minds to rigid leadership. The United States is awash in cults and cult leaders and those who drank Kool-Aid with Jim Jones were people very much like your neighbors and mine. It sometimes seems that whatever part of the upper-middle-class young the religious cults don't snare, the radical left and radical right do. The current intellegensia seems hell bent on stuffing any and all new drugs into their systems without regard for consequences to their minds and bodies, while at the same time dismissing all medical claims to the contrary and still pushing macrobiotic foods, telling how bad habits like smoking and a lack of jogging are for you. Go some time, if you dare, to that part of your city where the young girls dress scantily and try to make tricks on the street corners so they can turn the money over to their pimps and get their fixes in this modern, liberated day and time and then tell me how outlandish New Eden is.

Forget the American/European ethic and look at where the bulk of human population is in this world and see how most of them live and what they believe. Even the ones living in relative affluence do not live in the same reality as you and I. We have enough advocates for the western bourgeoisie; I like to deal with the bulk of humanity you never think about but is all around you.

Tom Disch saw only the surface and thought they were variants on Gor novels.

But, you see, the *literati* of today's SF are in fact very surface-oriented. Their themes are simplistic, their messages obvious. That's not what it's all about. You see, New Eden isn't Ideologically Correct. It does not clearly and obviously convey the Right Political and Social Messages as We Have Determined Them. The funny thing is, the messages of that big novel are (unusually for me) more or less Ideologically Correct, but I approach human problems as highly complex things requiring hard and complicated work made all the more difficult by imperfect analysis and solutions. Figuring out the messages requires work. Far too many critics mistake an ability to use and understand big words for intellectual activity. This is a familiar retort of the educated idiot; true art, for them, is measured not by its message and content but by its inaccessibility to the masses.

I'm sorry, but the world and the human race isn't at all simplistic and God help me if I ever wind up being consistently Ideologically Correct. Once you surrender your common sense and reason to a snobbish intellectual elite, you're on the road to surrendering everything. This sort of elitist outlook has been with us for as long as commercial publishing and it is composed of the "intellectuals"—self-styled—who, by their insistence on conformity to *their* standards and *their* ideology and *their* agenda, are in fact the very antithesis of intellectual.

This attitude, it's always seemed to me, stems from a need on the part of some people to be superior in something to everybody else. In its own way it's no more different than the whites of the Confederacy and the prewar South who didn't need slavery economically (and, in fact, most didn't own slaves in the antebellum South) but desperately needed some race or class to look down on. The plantation owner's grandfather was probably a convict sent to Georgia and so superiority of blood, in the European sense, was denied him.

This intellegentsia of today, in fact, consistently identifies more with European things, with the European sense of social class. Come to think of it, the bulk of critics in Britain and on the Continent are products of a class structure but are not upper class themselves. It is a bit sad to think of someone becoming a critic as a wedge into a class structure. Much contemporary European intellectualism has been aimed at redefining class structure to include the intellectuals rather than eliminating the structure, no matter what their self-deluding rhetoric claims.

Some of this is Lenin's fault. Lenin forever perverted Communism by writing that Marx was wrong; that the proletarian masses were too ignorant to revolt and required an educated, intellectual elite to guide them and teach them the true path. And thus the *bourgeoisie* became the Party, led by the very bourgeois Lenin and Trotsky; the aristocracy of blood represented by the Romanovs became the Commissars; and the masses remained where they were. The Russian Revolution did not eliminate class, it merely redefined it, as has virtually every *political* revolution of the nineteenth and twentieth centuries.

I once wrote a book called *The Identity Matrix*. It contained, by the way, the only definition of freedom that is meaningful—*freedom is the right to be wrong*. All other concepts of freedom go back to that premise or they are false. Any other idea is simply a demand for a choice of oppressors.

The Identity Matrix was, unusually for me, very well reviewed and well received by editors and by academia as well as by a number of mainstream reviewers. Science fiction critics, however, reviewed it in the main as a sex change novel and found it wanting. If it was a book about man becoming woman, I would agree, but it's not. That *is* what happens on the surface, but it's not what the book is about. The book is about mind control and about containing scientific genies in bottles. The SF reviewers don't like what the lead character becomes in the end; the more astute reviewers understood that this was not a woman but rather an individual whose mind had been completely edited and rewritten up to three times by a bunch of men. If you couldn't figure that out, then you couldn't understand the book. SF reviewers, in the main, failed to understand the book. It wasn't obvious.

I just finished reading a pile of British reviews of my *Dancing Gods* books. Since the British reviewers in general hate my guts, I was very surprised to find that almost every one of them was quite favorable. (One accused me of being too "American" but that's what I am—those same reviewers would howl if I dismissed, as I never would, Amis and Greene and many others as too British.) Still, I was suddenly struck by a common chord in all those reviews. They liked the characters, they liked the fantasy, they had fun with the books as intended, but *not a single one of the reviewers understood that the* Dancing Gods *books are satire*. Not one. And it's very broad and obvious satire, too. The Books of Rules are, of course, the codified cliches of all epic fantasy series. And not a single one of those British reviewers considered that. Not a one. In fact, one of them complained that "Chalker's fantasy world, alas, is too much like all the others." Makes you wonder, doesn't it?

Even Robert Heinlein isn't immune. He wrote a novel called *Friday* which was quite complex, but at its heart was a character who was not a woman of the future but rather an artificially created, even programmed, creature made by an idealistic old man as the old man's image of what such a woman should be like. Things proceeded logically from this premise, but in the dozens of SF reviews of the book I have found not one critic, like the book or hate it, who could grasp that simple subtlety.

One wonders about the validity of any criticism by someone who requires cartoons and diagrams. One certainly can't respect their intellect, which is well below that of the average reader if these examples are typical, and, alas, they are.

But, of course, being ideologically incorrect and accessible to the masses isn't enough. I have other crimes to answer for. For example, I write relatively fast compared to most novelists.

Well, that's the way I am. Some painters paint in a flash, others take months. Michelangelo painted all the great frescos surrounding the Sistine Chapel dome in one to three days each. He must have been some kind of commercial hack artist. I have never found any correlation between literary merit and speed, pro or con. I once sat down with the late Will "Murray Leinster" Jenkins, and we did some figuring and finally determined that he'd averaged one story or novel every two weeks from January, 1915, until our count in April of 1971. Some of it wasn't very good, of course, as he'd be the first to admit, but the percentage of good to bad wasn't much different than for those authors who produce a novel every two years for ten years, and some of his stories are genuine classics that revolutionized our field and are acknowledged today as works of genius. John Russell Fearn and R. Lionel Fanthrope wrote about the same amount during roughly the same period and produced nothing worth remembering or acclaiming. Speed is irrelevant. Some people work fast, some more slowly. Me—I cheat. Some people wait and take two years to write one 500,000 word massive tome. I take the same two years but break the 500,000 words up into four parts and get credit for four books. And I often write something entirely different to clear my mind during that period as well.

Of course, some writers are actually much faster than I am but appear to be slower and more deliberative. There is one fellow out in California who's a highly celebrated SF novelist and winner of every award around who does two good novels a year. He also happens to be a physics professor who both teaches and does research. I submit that by definition he is a much faster writer than I could ever be, considering the amount he writes while doing what for most people would be more than a full-time job. When *I* was teaching, one or two books a year was the best I could manage and at that time nobody called me fast, either, but I was writing faster than I am now. It's all relative. Writing is now and has been for a decade my sole occupation and source of income. The odds are ten to one that *most* major writers today write at surprisingly fast clips; it just depends on what else they're doing. It shows how phony such critical commentaries can be, though, when you think it through. Of course, thinking is simply not something the bulk of contemporary SF critics are all that good at doing.

Some people seem upset with me simply because I'm popular and successful, as if this had anything to do with it. There are some very fine writers who are neither and never will be, and others who are who don't deserve to be. Again, there is little correlation between the two. Whether there *should* be is beside the point; there never has been and never will be.

Also, thanks to you out there, whoever you are, I don't have to spend any thought at all trying to please or match the kind of "standards" that the self-styled critics of any age have always tried to impose on an ignorant and benighted public that's usually far from ignorant and far more discerning than any of these elitist guardians of art. Nor, of course, are high sales and popularity relevant, either—if they were, the highest literary artists of the eighties would be Judith Krantz, Jackie Collins, Harold Robbins, Janet Daily, and maybe Danielle Steele, and our greatest artist would be Jim "Garfield" Davis.

Success itself is anathema to many critics. I recall how they all fawned over Gene Wolfe until Wolfe committed the serious compound sin of writing a five-volume serial novel and then having it be popular and successful. All of a sudden Gene wasn't their darling any more on anything at all. Did his big project now make all the works they once liked somehow bad? Regardless of whether or not you liked the five-volume work, it did not negate any past or future accomplishments nor make something good bad—yet that is indeed the inference. Makes you wonder, doesn't it?

The art, the universality, shows through if and when it's there, and mere craft and mediocrity comes to the fore as well. Lillian Hellman was the toast of the *literati* of her day, even though she hung around with that writer of cheap thrillers. I checked five big bookstores last week. Not a single word of Hellman's was available (except her introductions to Hammett collections) but every word of that writer of cheap thrillers, Dashiell Hammett, was there. The recent revival of *A Watch on the Rhine* was very dated even as a period piece and highly stilted and awkward. It didn't hold up and it folded before dwindling, bored audiences. Now go read or even watch *The Thin Man*.

The incredibly influential critics of the Algonquin Round Table called Hellman an artist for the ages and barely tolerated Hammett's presence while tolerating his writings not at all. They were the arbiters of taste, the ones who said what art was. Quick, now—name the members of the Algonquin Round Table. Some of you might have managed to name one or two since a couple were wonderfully quotable, but I bet you're stuck now, and the rest of you never heard of them in the first place. But I'll bet all of you have heard of Dashiell Hammett.

So, I find myself on the outside looking in, yet with all of you out there really getting a charge out of what I write. I hear from you in letters and meet you occasionally out there in the real world. I'm at peace with myself and at war with pretension, elitism, snobbery, and paternalism. Hopefully the comments here and elsewhere in this book will clearly show that one needs perspective in this business. Hammett shorted himself out worrying about the fact that he wasn't producing great art, only potboilers, and that's a shame. It seems to me that art is possible in a tightly restricted society (El Greco comes to mind, as well as Michelangelo and Da Vinci) but it has a better chance when the artist can create what he or she wants to create. I have that freedom, and I'm not going to surrender it to anyone for an award or a good review. I'll certainly take an award or a good review, but those are not factors entering into what I write. You make it all possible. I often wish I could yank Hammett forward in time and show him those stores and liberate him. What other great books we might have!

A recent critic of our field who's also a well-known writer suggested that Picasso was a true artist while Norman Rockwell was nothing more than a brilliant technician and that the standard was that Picasso could

do what Rockwell did but Rockwell couldn't do what
Picasso did. This is nonsense. Each was creating from a
different background and perspective and each set different goals for himself. Both attained those goals. Picasso had the luxury of family money which allowed him
time to develop; Rockwell was forced to come up
through the commercial art marketplace. There is really
no evidence to support the concept that either could
have done what the other did, but much evidence to in-
dicate that neither *wanted* to. The false implication of the
statement above is not that Picasso was one thing or
Rockwell was another, it is the implicit argument that we
must choose—Picasso or Rockwell. I am forced to respond, "Why must we choose when we can have both?"

Another writer and critic recently was excited by the
assertion that our field could produce a book fully as
great as *Moby Dick*. I never thought that this was in
doubt. I mean, we have already done it. The book is
called *Moby Dick*, and it meets every standard for fantasy I ever heard of. It is, indeed, the fantasy element
that makes it great. Ahab's madness is not that he lost a
leg and wants that whale; Ahab's madness is that he
knows *just* what supernatural forces he is facing and is
conceited, even mad, enough to believe that he can beat
them with a harpoon.

That article, in a major SF magazine and by an author
who is not major, is asking the question of whether SF/
fantasy can ever produce art to stand with the classics.
Considering that about half the classics that have already
stood the test of time are fantasies, it's an ignorant concept. It also implies a number of pretty idiotic ideas.
First, that nobody in our field has achieved such status,
which betrays true ignorance, and, second, that all of the
writers of the past in this field were somehow inadequate, with not a single artist among them, an assertion I
find particularly insulting especially from a writer in this
field writing in an SF magazine. But the third and most
revealing assumption he makes is that he and the writers
he mentions in his piece are, according to him, the first
and perhaps the only ones at the long end of the evolu-

tion of SF and fantasy capable of achieving this level of greatness.

There are only two things I can guarantee you about this field, assuming the human race survives and there is at least one society left where writers can write freely, and the primary guarantee is that we will see not just one but many truly great works of literature published in SF or fantasy (more likely the latter—it doesn't date like even the best SF).

The other absolute guarantee is that those works will not be written by anyone who sat down to create a great work of literature by design.

I remember the time of the New Wave in the late sixties, a movement that's never completely died in Britain. I also remember Roger Zelazny being appalled when he read himself labeled as a New Wave writer. (Aside: the last thing a failing movement does before collapsing is try to find a couple of successes to embrace for legitimacy's sake). "But the New Wave is style over substance!" Roger noted. "My aim is substance with style." He achieved it—and that's why he's so successful and still very much around. It's also why the New Wave collapsed.

Moby Dick is just a whaling story with a supernatural McGuffin at its center, but it's the character studies, the gritty atmosphere of the period, and the universality of its characters seamlessly *mated* to that story and that supernatural menace that makes it great. *Moby Dick* is not a great novel because of its style. It's not even very good taken that way. *Moby Dick* is a good, but not great, novel with its substance and without style. What makes it great is *substance with style*.

Consider, for example, another character study with a supernatural McGuffin—*Hamlet*. Hell, the plot's old. Shakespeare ripped it off, really. Why does his version alone survive to great acclaim? *Substance with style*. But which is most important? Shakespeare always had style. Even *Henry VIII* and *Coriolanus* have style. But they would have vanished into the obscurity of most of Shakespeare's contemporaries had they not been dragged along by the strength of so many truly *great* plays. Plays with substance.

At this writing the big new thing in SF circles is something called "cyberpunk." The leader of this new movement, anointed by the critics against his will and finding the term uncomfortable, is an affable young writer named William Gibson. His current status is really based more on a first novel than a career but one suspects he will have a decent career, maybe even a spectacular one, judging from how he's managing his instant superstar status. *Neuromancer* is actually well within the old line mainstream of our field. The plot is about equal dollops of Budry's *Michaelmas* and the motion picture *Tron* with a bit of the movie (not the book) *Blade Runner* thrown in. One local veteran SF fan called it "A standard computer thriller but written as if it were done by MTV." So, in other words, what we actually have is something *old* being done in a new way—with a new and unique style. *Substance with style*.

Others lumped into this movement include a couple of pretty damned good writers like Greg Bear and Bruce Sterling, neither of whose works are very much like Gibson's or each other's until the critics get to work building a unified cyberpunk field theory that is as much fantasy as any of their books and not nearly as well constructed. They are smart enough to take the labels and use the acclaim (which will be fleeting) to build their careers.

Now whole bunches of would-be writers will try to imitate Gibson and many will get his style down fairly well, but virtually none will have any substance.

SF writers are supposed to predict, so here's a prediction that you can check out. The cyberpunk worshipers, like the New Wavicles, will have (somebody else's) style and yet be lousy or incompetent storytellers. They will sell a few stories to the critics building inevitable anthologies of cyberpunk stuff and to the cheapest-paying paperback publishing houses whose editors are trying to ride a trend, but they will then vanish into well-deserved obscurity. Norman Rockwell did create art; a legion of painters perfectly imitating Rockwell did not.

The same goes for those imitators of van Gogh, Rembrandt, da Vinci, and, yes, Picasso. So did N.C. Wyeth —who was dismissed in his time as a cheap commercial illustrator and is only now being appreciated—as well as his son Andrew and grandson Jamie.

In other words, producing art means being uniquely yourself. Hack work means attaching yourself to someone else's success and, by imitating their style or structure, attempting to some share of glory. Gibson, Bear, and Sterling each do unique things and follow their own, not each other's, compass. Those who have now jumped on the cyberpunk bandwagon will do neither, yet that is just what this fellow is talking about when he talks about a new school of writing. Indeed, the very *concept* of a "school" of writing is at the heart of the problem, whether it be New Wave, cyberpunk, or anything else. This fellow is urging the writers of the present and future to become imitative hacks. Some will follow, will be hightly praised by the critics, and maybe win awards, but they won't be artists, and their works won't last.

The eventual problem that Gibson and Sterling in particular will have down the pike is that such critical movements have short lives. If they continue along the same paths that are now bringing them acclaim, they will be dismissed as "formula" and "old hat." If they take risks and do things stylistically different than their prior work, they will be viciously attacked for selling out or deserting the movement. Ask Zelazny or Ursula LeGuin, to name just two, about that. If they shrug it off and continue to write as and what they must, they will continue to be artists.

And there's the more insidious problem. If you want to make a career of writing and you aren't independently wealthy, you find yourself eventually between a rock and a hard place, between commercial and artistic considerations. It's a delicate balancing act and sometimes you don't make it with a particular work, which falls more to one side or the other. Another thing that a writer faces is that stylists rarely make it on style alone. Substance, or just telling a good story, wins over style every time. If you can attain both, you have a potential for something greater than its parts, but if you must lean, then you must lean on story first or you will not make a living in this business. I make no bones about being a storyteller first and foremost; it is an honorable and ancient profession. Good storytellers are occasionally executed but they never starve. Poets starve.

And yet, I am an artist, a creator of things that never were and some that never could be. I interpret, I create, I entertain, and I teach. Whether or not I'm a *good* artist is up to you and your children and grandchildren. I am not pretentious, and some of these self-styled arbiters of taste and art can't stand that. Dostoyevsky wrote fast and furiously to cover his gambling debts before his bookie broke all his bones. Dickens, Dumas, Shakespeare, Twain, and many other "commercial hacks" of their day wound up being recognized as the great artists they were because they still communicate to us today. The critics of his day vilified Dickens as a weaver of tripe, a teller of episodic serials designed to sell handkerchiefs. He did, after all, write a chapter a week like clockwork and send it up to Fleet Street to be published. Even the length of the work was set by the popular reception to earlier chapters. They saved their praise for true *artistes* like Edward Bulwer-Lytton (you know, the fellow who actually started a novel "It was a dark and stormy night" and who once set Pontius Pilate in a novel fifty years after he was governor of Judea), after whom annual contests in bad writing are named.

My own role models have been writers like Evan Hunter and Louis L'Amour who have been producing three books a year for decades, some of them really fine works of art. Within the SF/fantasy field, there's Jack Vance, Poul Anderson, Anne McCaffrey, and many others.

The fact is, most of the selections of the Book-of-the Month Club since I started writing novels are out of print and unobtainable now, probably permanently. All my books are in print and all are still selling. No artist can ask for more than that. And, with the publication of this volume, all my short orphans will be gathered together as well for new eyes to see.

Cliff Simak once said that for years he was going to write the Great American Novel; he started it time and time again, each time doing a bit and then sticking it in a drawer while he wrote some science fiction novel or story. One day, after many years of this, he realized that he didn't *want* to write anything but science fiction and he resented the straitjacket other literary forms placed on him. He never touched that manuscript again—but he wrote a whole lot of really classic science fiction.

Like most successful authors with mainstream and academic followings, I am often asked, "Now that you're famous and financially comfortable, are you going to write some serious fiction?" I generally reply, when I stop laughing, that I write quite a lot of serious fiction. The fact that the vast bulk of it is science fiction and fantasy is because of the tremendous freedom those forms give the creative writer. I find it fascinating that so many "serious" mainstream writers tend to move into our corner of the field (where the publishers rush to deny it's SF or fantasy lest the critics get the wrong idea) because of that freedom: Romaine Gary, Kingsley Amis, Doris Lessing, John Updike, Phillip Roth, Bernard Malamud, and Gore Vidal immediately spring to mind. Some wrote/write SF and fantasy all the time and simply pretend they do not: Kurt Vonnegut, Nevil Shute, and the like. Still others whose works cover a great range began in this field and never entirely abandoned its trappings nor turned their backs on it: Tennessee Williams, John D. MacDonald, Donald Westlake, and many, many more.

I was doing a book signing with Frank Herbert and Anne McCaffrey down in Sydney, Australia in late 1985 where Frank and Anne got into an argument over which one of them had the first bestseller listing for a book strictly labeled as science fiction. Somebody in line asked why that was important, and Frank turned and snapped, "It's time we put some honesty up there where it belongs."

I really liked Frank. I already miss him.

And that brings us to this book, the Unknown Writings of Jack L. Chalker. I think I've gone on long enough here; you'd better read a story or two before we go any further. I'll pop in again with more commentary, but I compulsively keep sticking my own nose in my own affairs anyway.

I have set this collection up in more or less chronological fashion, in order of *writing*, not publication, with notes on my career at that time, with one exception which will be explained when we get there. Also here, in addition to my published short fiction, is the essay "Where Do You Get Those Crazy Ideas?," done at the request of Del Rey books but never used, and two never before published stories, including "Moths and Candle," along with, of all things, its very distinguished rejection slip. That's the one I saved until the end. Along the way, before each story, I've added comments on it from the perspective of time. I'm glad to have them all in print and available again and preserved. I hope, when you finish, you'll be glad you came along for the ride.

Jack L. Chalker
Westminster, Maryland
September, 1987

INTRODUCTION TO
"NO HIDING PLACE"

"No Hiding Place" is the oldest piece of my fiction I will
admit to, predating even the earliest fanzine versions of *A
Jungle of Stars*. I think I had the rough idea for the plot and
the alien's own physique down pat by the time I was fourteen, and I remember doing an early draft of this in 1958 or
1959. It doesn't survive, perhaps mercifully, but I remember
more about it than I'd like to. I also remember it was the first
story I dared submit to anyone, and it was, of course, rou-
tinely bounced, although the Scott Meredith Agency offered
to whip it into professional shape for a fee of only $100. Back
then they might as well have asked for a million for all the
money I had.

I didn't touch the story again until I fell into a creative
writing course in my senior year of college. You know the
kind—a dozen students and a professor whose dissertation
was on "Verisimilitude in the Parenthetical Expressions Used
in First Chapters of Edward Bulwer-Lytton Novels," or
something like that. Everybody was to write a story and then
have copies made for the professor and all members of the
class, one a week, and then it would be the subject of fierce
discussion in which the eleven other students would trash it
to earn brownie points from the professor. Most of the stu-

dents took the course because they really thought it was a step toward professional writing; I took it because I needed the English credits and it was held at three in the afternoon.

Using "No Hiding Place" was an easy way to do virtually no work at all. The original still survived then, but I was much older and more experienced and had done a great deal of nonfiction writing and editorial work. I took out the old brown manuscript, read through it, then completely reworked the plot and theme into its current structure. It took me about three days, most of that retyping, to get it into shape. At that point I had no thoughts of publishing it; it was just an easy three credits, and it got me dumped on by the class—and the only "A" that professor gave in that class and course that semester. Maybe I misjudged the man . . .

A couple of years later I found it in my desk and sent it to a couple of magazines in operation at the time. In return, I got letters from some editors, and that was an education in itself. There were also no outright rejections; every editor it went to liked it, but each had a totally different suggestion for rewriting it. I didn't push; it wasn't very important to me then to sell professionally. I also didn't accept any of their suggestions for rewriting. I remember that one wanted to make it some grandiose epic space-time chase with a strong hero protagonist; Ted White, then editing *F&SF* I think, had a whole raft of hoary SF cliches he wanted me to insert, including excerpts from the Encyclopedia Galactica, which might explain why White isn't still editing SF. I still have the letters around someplace.

The fact is, while this is a Campbellian Problem Story, it is deliberately unconventional in approach in that it has no hero and indeed no organic center. The center is, in horror story fashion, not a person but a house, and the only character we get to know at all is the villain, who, although scary and imposing, is at heart just a soldier doing his duty. It is the unusual manner in which the story is told, more the format for the old classic horror stories than SF, that really bothered the editors; they wanted a good guy chasing Treeg through it all and interacting with the innocent victims who get in the way, and they wanted to know about the big war and the background of the conflict when that conflict is simply part of the McGuffin, irrelevant to the story in more than that usage. Since the editors, in their own way, were really bothered by the unconventional approach to a conventional story,

I figured I'd wait until unconventional structure was more accepted. The story went back in the desk drawer until that time came.

That time turned out to be 1977, when Judy-Lynn del Rey, who was just launching Del Rey Books and who had a few of my books in her title list, asked me for a short story or novelette for her original anthology series *Stellar*. She wanted all her current authors in there, but particularly the new kids on the block. I, frankly, didn't have the time to work up a story for her and mentioned this to Mark Owings, one of the few people outside academia or publishing who'd read "No Hiding Place" years before. Mark surprised me by remembering it in detail (although he is legendary for his photographic memory), and I hunted it up, retyped the first page to remove the professor's comments and the "A," made a Xerox copy so the age of the paper wasn't so obvious, and sent it off to Judy-Lynn, who sent back a contract and a check.

The story was published in *Stellar #3* (Del Rey, 1977)— one of the few in that series not picked up by the SF Book Club (more on this trend later). More interesting, it was bought by an editor who was often accused of insisting on old style and old techniques and not open to new ways of doing things. Yet those other editors who'd previously had a crack at the story were often in the forefront of "experimental" fiction, and to a one insisted on the injection of fifties standards to buy it; Judy-Lynn bought it and published it without a word changed.

Judy-Lynn took her lumps in her ten-year reign as well. She was usually vilified by The Critics, didn't win an award until after she died, yet she was the most influential editor and publisher in this field since John Campbell said it was okay to be a good writer first. She made SF a mainstream commodity, put large numbers of SF and fantasy authors on the real bestseller lists, and showed that SF was the equal to any other literary *genre*. Every time she would publish something odd or off-the-wall or by a supposedly avant garde writer (such as Phil Dick's *A Scanner Darkly*) people would sit up and say, "Huh?" She spent her whole career insisting only that people write good SF and fantasy novels rather than bad ones. Some crime, huh? Only after she died did they vote her the Hugo she deserved. Her husband, Lester, refused it, noting that it would have meant a lot if they'd voted for it while she was still alive but it was insulting to

vote it to her because she died. She deserved her Hugo, but
Lester was right; I would have felt the same way.

Looking over this story now, from the perspective of all
those years, I find it no weighty philosophical piece, but still
a good, fun problem story that reads well and entertains, and
that's always the best reason for bringing a tale back into
public view. Maybe the editors were right, though. It's a
pretty gruesome old dark house story and might make a good
splatter film—if only I had a hero and a heroine . . .

No Hiding Place

1

IT WAS A SLEEPY LITTLE RIVER TOWN, SITTING ON THE silt bed beside the mighty Mississippi. The town of New-townards, Louisiana, was a waystop for the steamers and barges that plowed the mighty river; it had been a refueling and rest stop on the waterway to New Orleans or up toward Vicksburg since 1850. It was a very small place, and the town hadn't changed much in the century-plus since the first river steamer piled on wood for the long journey north.

The people were a quiet sort, with little ambition and with that sense of peace and tranquillity that only an isolated community atmosphere can give. This isolation gave security of sorts as well, for the town had not been settled by the almost legendary Bayou folk of the sur-rounding lush, tropical swamplands, but by hardy capi-talists who picked their location on the river for profit.

The Bayou people had become more legend than real by the twentieth century. No one alive could remember seeing any of the quiet, backward swamp folk for a long, long time, and even those who claimed experience with the mysterious backwater people were only half believed. Certainly the Bayou's secretive inhabitants were no longer any threat to the community welfare and, at best, were merely the poor people out in the sticks.

A town like Newtownards was a difficult place to keep a secret. The art of gossip had fallen into disuse simply because there was nothing the locals could whisper to each other that wasn't already common knowledge. Crime, too, was a rarity, and the town kept only two local policemen, two old war veterans whose major duty was checking the more deserted areas for hoboes and other itinerants who might be drifting through and looking for a free place to sleep. For anything more serious, a state police barracks ten miles to the south kept watch on several small towns in the swamp, which was a favorite hiding place for escaped fugitives. But since Newtownards had little to offer men on the run, being the most public of places, the only troopers who had visited the place officially came for ceremonial functions.

The town, as did all small communities, had its history, and it was especially colorful. Rackland's Maurauders had ridden through, back when the country was split and Grant was mapping his strategy, and had set up an observation post in the town's one mansion—deserted Hankin House, empty since the founder of the town and builder of his castle had fled, insane. Colonel Rackland's valiant party used the hilltop to look for any signs of Farragut's ships heading up the river toward Vicksburg, and for any signs of Yankee soldiers lurking in the swamps to the west. There, too, they had met the fate that had haunted Hankin House since 1850, when, after only three months in his new home, Josiah Hankin had suddenly gone mad and attempted to kill everyone nearby, while babbling of a horror in the house.

The old juju woman had come after that. She had originally warned Hankin not to build on the knoll, for, she said, a demon lived within the hill and would take all who disturbed its rest. She had not seen the thing, of course. But her grandmother's people, in 1808, had declared the hill a sacred place of worship, where weird, bacchanalian rites had been carried out by ex-slaves who lived in the Bayou. Now, the juju woman had warned, Josiah had paid the price, and so would all others who disturbed the demon who lived in the hill.

Yes, Hankin House was the town's true pride. In an open society, people, being human, still must talk of something, and the locals had talked about the old house for better than a century. The townspeople didn't really *believe* in *Obi* and voodoo demons living in hills, but they remembered, too, that Josiah had been the first, not the last, to meet a strange end.

Colonel Rackland and two of his men had died by fire in that house, without a single part of the house itself being even singed. The lone survivor of his command had come down the hill a white-haired, raving maniac. Fearful townspeople had investigated, but found nothing but three bodies and a still, ever so still, empty house.

The house was vacant, then, when Farragut finally *did* move his force up the Mississippi. It had remained a still, silent, yet expectant spectator while the town wept at the news that at a place called Appomattox the world had ended. The house had slept while pioneers traveled the mighty river in large steamboats, moving beneath the hill on which the house stood.

Then in March of 1872, on that very same day that U.S. Grant was taking the oath of office for his second and tragic presidential term, Philip Cannon bought the house. Cannon had profited from the war, and even more from its aftermath. But his shady past seemed to be so very close behind him that he was always running, running from his past, his shadow, and himself.

He was running west when the ship he was on docked for fuel in Newtownards, and he had seen the mansion sitting majestically above the town. "Fit for a king," Phil Cannon thought, and despite the anxiety of the towns-people, he located the last Hankin relative, paid her off, and the house was his.

Cannon spent lavishly, building up, refurbishing, until the twenty-two-year-old house looked as if it had been built the day before, a shining monument to Josiah's

taste for Gothic architecture and to Phil Cannon's desire
to feel like a king.

And Cannon loved it. He became, by virtue of the
smell of money, a very big man in Newtownards, and no
one asked about his past. People with noble pasts seldom
go to live and work in a tiny town in the midst of a
swamp.

Then, one day, almost exactly two years after Cannon
had moved in, the big man failed to put in an expected
appearance with his usual pomp, strutting as he always
did with his little saloon-girl on his arm.

It was not just the townspeople's dislike of the unexpected, nor their concern for the legends, that made
them immediately investigate. Many had shady dealings
with Cannon and they grew panicky at an unscheduled
disappearance. So, a group of businessmen walked up
the road to Hankin House and knocked. When they received no answer, they tried the door and found it un-
locked.

The crystal chandelier Phil Cannon had imported
from Spain tinkled as the hot wind blew off the river and
through the open door into the main dining room.

The found *her* head, eventually, taken off her slender
shoulders as if by a giant razor. They never did find Phil
Cannon's.

As was the case when Josiah went mad, the servants
were nowhere to be found. There was speculation that
the juju people had a firm hold on those servants and
that they might have done away with Cannon and his
mistress as revenge for some of Cannon's shady dealings
with the swamp folk. But no one ever found the servants, and the cleavage was too clean to have been the
work of any sword or knife.

And so it was that Hankin House was closed again,
and more generations passsed as the silent old house
looked on. The original panic and talk of a juju hex had
caused some townspeople to cry out that the building be
razed to the ground. But since Cannon's will left the old
place to his local business syndicate, such talk was
quickly suppressed. Besides, by the time talk became

action everybody was convinced that the servants and the Bayou people had done the deed.

Hadn't they?

In 1898 the battleship *Maine* sank in Havana harbor, and America for the first time since the War of 1812 went to war a sovereign nation. One of the eager volunteers had been Robert Hornig, a youthful captain with the Fifty Calvary Brigade. He had fought in Cuba, was wounded, and then returned. He chose as his point of disembarkation both from the war and the military the port of New Orleans, for he was a man with no family save the army. Now that he no longer had even the army, he was a man without a direction—only a discharge and a limp.

When he stopped off on the river trail westward at Newtownards he was immediately struck by the charm and simplicity of the town. He was also fascinated by the old deserted house atop the hill, and this fascination grew when inquiries to the locals brought forth blood-curdling stories.

The house cost him a bit more than he actually had, as all important acquisitions do, but it was worth every penny to Captain Hornig. A lonely man, he loved the old place as a man would love his bride.

After a while, he was no longer alone. An orderly named Murray, who had also faced the test of battle in Cuba, passed through, as much a drifter as the captain had been. Here was the man, thought Hornig, who would at least temper the loneliness and who might also aid in financing the renovation of the house. Although the captain was a crusty sort, the young orderly liked both the man and the town, and assented.

They found Hornig at the bottom of the grand stairway, his body sprawled out on a rug in the entrance hall. Murray's body was in the dining room; he had been shot through the heart with a pistol, a pistol never found. The coroner's verdict of a murder-suicide did not fit all the facts, of course. But what alternatives were there? At least, this time, both victims still retained their heads.

Again the house was shut up and remained so until

1929, when Roger Meredith moved into the house with his wife and daughter. A heavy stock-market investor, he had selected Newtownards and the house carefully as a quiet and peaceful place in which to bring up his child and to escape the hustle and bustle of Wall Street, where his services were no longer required. He was quite a comfortable millionaire and originally a Louisiana boy as well, and so the townspeople offered little protest at his arrival.

When little Carol Meredith was observed—bloody and hysterical, crawling up Main Street not seven weeks after the family had moved in, her face full of buckshot —they said it was another murder-suicide, the last act of a man driven mad by the collapse of the stock market. As usual, the coroner's jury did not bother with details. How could a small man like Meredith ever throw his wife out of the west window? How did he, himself, inflict the merciless blow to the head the doctor stated had killed him? And what of the little girl, lying in the arms of storekeeper Tom Moore, life oozing out of her, who turned her face to his and, with a queer, maniacal smile, whispered as she died: "Daddy shot it!"

World War II came, and passed, and the house remained empty. No longer did fancy riverboats ply the Mississippi at the foot of the hill, but the town remained. Freight traffic had increased, and those ships still needed fuel.

Wars, hot and cold, passed, and generations came and went. The old house sat silently, as always, its mysterious demon undisturbed. Until one day...

August was a bad month for Newtownards. It was horribly hot and as humid as the air and the laws of physics would allow. Most people at midday would close their stores and stretch out for a nap while the intolerable heat of the day dissipated. But in the schoolyard, under the shade of a tall, old tree, there was activity.

"I am not yella!" the red-haired, stocky boy of about fourteen yelled to the tall, angular leader of the group of boys, "but nobody's stupid enough to commit suicide, Buzz Murdock!"

The tall, blond-haired teenager towered over the object of derision. "Ya must be, ya half Yankee!" Buzz Murdock replied haughtily, and not without a deliberate sneer. He was playing to his audience now, the group of young teenage boys who formed the Swamp Rats, a *very* exclusive little club.

Ricky Adherne, the redhead, bristled, his face becoming so red and contorted with anger and rage that his freckles almost faded to invisibility. The "half Yankee" tag had always stung him. Could he help it if his noaccount pa had been from New York?

"Lissen," said Murdock, "we don't allow no chickens in the Rats." The other boys made clucking sounds, like those of a chicken, in support of their leader. "If'n ya caint prove t'us that ya ain't no stupid chicken, ya bettah git along home riaot now!" continued the leader.

"Lissen yuhself!" Adherne snapped back. "I don't mind no test o' bravery, but jumpin' inna rivah with a sacka liam is a shoah way ta diah quick!"

Murdock put on his best sneer. "Hah! Weall wouldn't be so afeared. We's Swamp Rats and ya ain't ouah type. Git along home, kid, afore we beat on ya!"

Adherne saw his opening, and he dived in. "Hah! Big ol' Swamp Rats! If ya *really* wanted a test o' bravery—why, you'n me, Murdock, we'd go upta ol' Hankin House at midniat and sit 'til morn!"

Murdock was in a bind and he knew it. He'd have to go through with this or he would lose face before his followers—*that*, he was smart enough to figure out. But, damn it all, why'd this little punk have to pick Hankin House?

It was 11:22 P.M. when town policemen Charles "Scully" Wills and Johnny Schmidt got into their patrol car—actually a loaned state police car with a radio connection to the Hawkinston barracks in case of emergencies—to make the rounds for the first time that night. As they drove toward their last checkpoint, Hankin House,

Schmidt thought he spied a bluish gleam móving about in one of the old structure's upper windows. But when he blinked and looked again the light was gone. He mentioned his suspicions to his partner, but the older cop had seen nothing; and, when the light failed to reappear, Schmidt told himself he was just tired and seeing things in the night.

The two men made an extra check of the seals on the doors and windows of the old house, though, just to be on the safe side. Nothing human could get by those seals without breaking at least one of them, this they knew.

When all the seals proved to be intact, they left the old, dark place for town and coffee. They'd make their rounds again in about three hours. Both men settled back to another dull, routine night.

It would not be dull or routine.

There was a sound like a hoot-owl, and Ricky Adherne advanced on the little party of boys waiting in the gully near the roadside. Hankin House looked down, grim and foreboding, in the distance.

Murdock was scared, but he dared not show it. Adherne, too, was scared, the sight of the old house by moonlight being even more frightening to him than was his previous all-consuming fear that his mother would check his room and discover he wasn't there. Throughout the evening he had mentally cursed himself for suggesting this stupid expedition, and he'd convinced himself that the Swamp Rats weren't worth the risk. But he still had to go, he knew. His personal honor was at stake. Newtownards was an open town, and he had to live in it, and with himself as well.

The chirping of a cricket chorus and the incessant hum of june bugs flying to and fro in the hot night air were the only sounds as the small party of boys, Murdock and Adherne in the lead, walked up the road to the old manor house. Suddenly they saw headlights turn onto the road and barely jumped into the tall grass by the roadside in time to miss the gaze of Scully and Schmidt as they rode up to the old house. Minutes passed like hours, but no boy made a move. Finally, after an eternity, the car returned and sped back down the hill.

"Man! That was *real* close!" Adherne exclaimed in an excited whisper.

"Shaddup, punk!" called Murdock, who felt like running himself but who, also, had to live in Newtownards.

The old house sat dark and silent as the group reached the tall front steps.

"Now how d'we git in, smaht guy?" Murdock demanded, believing he had discovered a way out of this mess. But Adherne, now pressed on by Murdock's sarcasm and the will to get an unpleasant thing over and done with, was already up on the porch.

"If'n we kin jest git this here crossboahd off'n the doah, we kin git in thisaway," he whispered, not quite understanding why he spoke so low.

Together the frightened boys pried off the wooden crossbar whose nails had been rusted and weakened by weather for better than thirty years. After much tugging the board gave, and one Swamp Rat fell backward, board in hand, with a yelp.

A blue flickering light shone in an upstairs window. Suddenly it froze.

"It's open," one boy whispered huskily.

Murdock swallowed hard and drew up all the courage he could muster. He suddenly pushed ahead of the red-haired boy, who stood statuelike, peering into the black gloom. "Me first, punk," he snapped, but the tall leader wondered why his voice sounded so strange in his ears.

First Murdock, then Adherne, entered the blackness.

The blue light in the upstairs window, unseen by any of the waiting boys encamped below, moved away from the window. And the climax to a strange quest, spanning not one century but more than a score, was close at hand.

2

As the small scoutship lifted from the landing grid and rose into the sky above the peculiar red-green surface of the planet men called Conolt IV, a signal flashed in a larger, more formidable, and very alien vessel hiding in the darkness of space. As the tiny Terran scout pulled free of the planet's thick atmosphere, the alien ship's commander gave a crisp order and set out after his prey.

The scoutship pilot, a giant Irishman named Feeny, spotted the dark raider just after leaving radio range of Conolt IV's spaceport. He punched a button on the ship's instrument panel, where myriad dials and switches lay before him.

"Doctor, I'm afraid we've been had," he said, his voice calm and smooth. Intelligence men did not break under pressure and survive.

In the aft compartment, Alei Mofad, a cherubic, balding man in his late sixties who was known as *the* scientific genius of his age, jerked up with a start.

"How far, Feeny?" he asked in a level voice.

"About twelve thousand, Doctor, and closing fast. Too damned fast."

Mofad turned and examined the small cabinet which, aside from the bunk and his own person, was the only other thing in the compartment.

"Feeny, how much time have we got?"

"Ten, twelve minutes at the most. Sorry, Doc. Somebody made one *hell* of a slip here."

"Yes, yes, I know, but no use crying over bad security now. I shall require at least fifteen. Can you give that much to me?"

"I can try," the pilot replied, dryly, and he began to do more than try. As Mofad worked feverishly to connect his equipment to the ship's power supply, Feeny began trying every maneuver in the book.

The alien spacecraft swung around out of the planetary shadow and shot a tractor beam, its purple glow slicing through the icy darkness of space. Feeny saw the beam only a fraction of a second before it was upon him, and his split-second reflexes urged the tiny scoutship upward, evading the powerful magnetic beam by inches.

The enemy craft swung around again, and for the second time shot out a purple ray from its bow tubes. Again

Feeny dodged by inches, banking left and downward as he continued to fight the hopeless duel, playing as if the two ships were master fencers, with one swordsman now disarmed but yet agile enough and determined enough to avoid his deadly opponent's thrusts.

Feeny knew he could not keep up the game indefinitely, but he was determined to give his illustrious charge as much time as was required. He dodged, banked, dropped up and down, all the time playing for Mofad's precious, essential seconds, while at the same time sending out a distress signal to the cruiser that should have been waiting nearby to pick them up, but was actually a hulk of twisted metal, the loser of an earlier duel with the enemy craft. Twelve minutes passed ... thirteen ... fifteen ... and then the goal was passed.

Eighteen minutes after the game had begun, it ended, when Feeny's lightning reflexes were no longer quite quick enough, and he began to tire. A tractor beam lashed out, enveloping the scoutship in a purple glow, pulling the tiny craft slowly toward the greater ship in the grip of the magnetic field.

"Doctor, they've got us," Feeny called into the ship's intercom. "Are you ready?"

"Yes, Feeny, I'm leaving now," came the physicist's reply, a tinge of sadness in his voice as he thought of the fate to which the faithful pilot had to be abandoned. "Do you want me to do anything, Doc?" Feeny called back.

"You've done enough, but yet you must destroy this machine. You know the detonator." Then, more softly, "Good-bye, Feeny."

Alei Mofad reached up on top of the plasticine cabinet and removed a small box. He stepped into the cabinet then, and vanished.

The two ships collided with a *thunk* which reverberated down the corridor of the smaller ship. Feeny rose from his pilot's chair and began the walk back to the aft compartment, struggling under the excessive gravity taken on when the two ships had linked and begun to roll. But he was too slow. The midsection airlock blew open before him, separating him from the precious cargo in the aft compartment. He stopped and stood straight, erect. After all, one died with dignity.

A creature entered the ship, a weird giant thing that could never have been spawned on earth. Humanoid was the closest to Terran that you could get, descriptively, for it stood erect, towering a full seven feet, on two thick, stiff legs. But it wore a chitinous exoskeleton that, as natural body armor, was as strong as sheet metal, yet half-transparent, so that the viewer could get a glimpse of veins, muscle tissue, and even the creature's brain. The two very long arms differed from one another. The right one, which ended in a five-digit hand whose fingers were extremely long and triple-joined, bore a pistol, aimed at Feeny's head. The left arm, however, ended in a massive set of razor-sharp pincers—the Sirian ceremonial claw, used as a two-fingered hand or used in many Sirian rituals, including the mating ceremony of the species.

Colonel Rifixl Treeg, Hereditary Colonel of Empire Intelligence, fixed one of his stalklike eyes on Feeny, the other on the door to the aft compartment. There could be no outward expression intelligible to a Terran in that face that resembled the head of a lobster, nor any sound, for the Sirians communicated—it was believed—telepathically. The alien colonel motioned with his pistol for Feeny to move back into the pilot's cabin.

Feeny complied, staring in fascination at his first Sirian. Only a few Terrans, such as those in the original discovery expeditions like Mofad, had *ever* seen them. The Sirians ruled a great stellar empire of allied and vastly different races. They did not fight wars; they directed them.

Feeny decided on a desperate gamble. If he could surprise the Sirian, at least long enough to run to the far wall and throw the generator-feed switches, it was possible that he might be able to blow up the ship.

Treeg watched the Terran captive almost halfheartedly; this was not the prize he was after. As he stepped backward, another member of the Sirian crew entered, partially blocking the colonel's view of Feeny. Feeny saw his chance and dived for the switches. The Sirian who had just entered swung around and fired his pistol at the advancing Feeny. The Terran lurched back with a cry and was instantly consumed by the white-hot pistol fire. Only a burning heap on the control-room floor betrayed the fact that anyone named Feeny had ever existed.

Treeg was annoyed at the killing; he preferred his prisoners alive for interrogation, as his orders specified. There had been talk of late that the old colonel was getting too old for his duties, and this slip would not help his position with the High Command. Still, he was more than annoyed at what he found in the aft compartment—or, rather, what he did not find.

There was a bunk and a plasticine cabinet of dubious purpose. Nothing else. Alei Mofad was not on the ship. Treeg went over to the cabinet and examined it with both eyes. Apparently the only moving part was a small relay on the side which flipped up and down, up and down. Atop the cabinet were two small boxes, each without any writing—just thin little boxes with two buttons, one red and one green: purpose, also unknown.

The law of the survival of the fittest breeds certain characteristics common to all races who struggle to the top, and Treeg exercised one of those characteristics—he beat his fist in frustration against the compartment wall. He then turned and stormed out.

In every age there is a special one, a genius who can see beyond the horizon—Copernicus, Edison, Einstein, and the like being prime examples.

And Alei Mofad.

An explorer and trader in his youth, as he approached middle age, a wealthy and industrious man still full of life, he had built a great laboratory on the quiet Federation world of Conolt IV, and he had applied experience to experiment. His findings became the cornerstone in the later fight between his own people, the Trans-Terran Federation, and the other giant stellar empire he had aided in discovering, the Sirian League. The Terran-Sirian War of the Empires was a bitter, no-quarter clash between two equally ruthless and ambitious centers of power, born out of jealousy and greed and fed on misunderstanding and hate—too much alike in the way they thought to ever get along.

And in the midst of the conflict, Alei Mofad broke the fabric of time itself.

His original machine was still in his laboratory on Conolt IV, along with his notes and specifications. His newer, larger, model which Terran Command insisted be brought to Terra itself for its first public demonstration had been loaded secretly on a small scout. Then the doctor and one intelligence man had attempted to sneak off planet without arousing any curiosity, to link up with a cruiser off the sixth planet in the system. But Sirian allies could pass for Terrans, and their spies on Conolt had blocked the attempt. So Terran Control Center was left with just one clue, one hope of obtaining the crucial formulae that would make the Mofad computations on Conolt IV make sense. Mofad had that in his brain—but he had stated that, if he could escape, he would somehow place the location at the Terran test site, Code Louesse 155. They would use the original machine to retrieve it—and, hopefully, Mofad. But, the formulae were hidden in time itself. They knew where, but not *when*.

For the machines were still imperfect. The day would come when whole armies would be transported across space and time to the enemy's heartland in the remote past, then brought up to the present, an indetectable army of occupation.

Rifixl Treeg, too, had a time machine and the controls to make use of it. But he knew neither where nor when.

"The physics is quite beyond me," said the Empire's top physicist. "Mofad is someone centuries ahead of us all. However, the Terran pilot's failure to destroy the cabinet after Mofad escaped in it gives us more information than you might suspect, my dear Colonel."

"Terran intelligence knows what's happened, too, by now, and they have a head start," Treeg replied. "What can we do? You've already told me you can't duplicate the thing without Mofad's basic formula, and we can't get the formula without Mofad. It seems that he's beaten us."

"Pessimism simply will not do in an intelligence officer, Colonel Treeg. I merely told you that we could not duplicate the thing; I never said we could not *run* it."

"Ah!" exclaimed the colonel, and then he suddenly drooped again. "But we still don't know where or when. Terran intelligence at least knows *where*, although, as you tell me, the thing's too unpredictable for them to know *when*."

"Where is not a problem," replied the physicist. "Obviously the *where* requires a setting. Since Mofad wasn't there to unset it, the machine will transport you to the right place, never fear. Your own intelligence reports show the original test site to be in the northern and western hemisphere of Terra herself. Since I credit the doctor with foresight, that's where anyone using the machine will go. At this point we are even with Terran intelligence. But now we go ahead of them."

Treeg suddenly stood extremely erect, the equivalent of a start in a race that could not physically sit down.

"You see," the scientist continued, "Mofad also had the time *period* set. The machine will follow through there, as well, but not exactly."

Treeg slumped. "Why not exactly, if—"

"Because," the scientist went on in the manner of a professor lecturing a schoolboy, "the machine is imperfect. It will transmit within, roughly, two centuries, I'd say. The disguised control panel here," he said, pointing to a spot on the machine, "is elementary. We can regulate the time sequence much better than could old Mofad, who had to go blind into a two-century span. We could make short jumps in time, with our agent searching the immediate vicinity for traces of Mofad. Since an agent, friend or foe, could appear only minutes after Mofad—even if that agent left days later by our standards—he would have to hide the thing fast. Was there any sort of transcribing equipment missing from the scoutship?"

"Yes," replied Treeg, "a minirecorder. You mean—"

"Precisely. That recorder is somewhere very near the point of emergence, and it contains what we must have. Terran intelligence does not have our present dials, so it will have hundreds of centuries to search. We may yet beat them. Who will you send?"

Treeg was still smarting from the lashing given him by the High Command for allowing Mofad to escape. There had been thoughts all around of retirement.

"Me," he said.

The two Sirians stood by the machine. The physicist began: "The device is based on a geographic point of reference. Mofad in his haste left the two portable units behind, an inexcusable blunder, but one very fortunate from our viewpoint." He handed Treeg a small box that was surprisingly heavy for its three-by-five-inch size and that only contained the red and green buttons which had interested Treeg when he had discovered them.

"This is the portable triggering device. When you want to go, we set the machine, and you step inside. Then you press the green button all the way down, and the machine transforms you into some sort of energy form we don't yet understand and resolidifies you on a preset point determined by the cabinet setting. When you wish to return, you need only return to your exact point of emergence into the other time and place and press the red button down all the way. This will reverse the process. I don't pretend to understand it—this is what we need in the way of Mofad's formulae, that mathematics which will tell us the how of the thing. Let's say that the machine somehow rips the fabric of time and place, which are linked, and that the tear is mended when you reactivate the device, thereby restoring you to your point of origin.

"I advise you to mark your point of emergence on Terra carefully, though. You must return to it exactly or you will remain where and when you are. Are you ready?"

Treeg nodded, and with an effort squeezed his rigid

body into the upright cabinet. The scientist examined the control panel. "I have preset it—I think—for the earliest possible time. I will count down. When I say *Now!* you are to press the green button. All right. Five . . . four . . . three . . . two . . . one . . . *Now!*"

Treeg pressed the button.

The first thought he had was that there had been no sensation whatever. It bothered him; this tampering with time should not be so quiet nor so sudden. But—one moment he was squeezed uncomfortably in that cabinet on Sirius; the next moment he was atop a lonely hillside surrounded by lush, green swamp. Below the hill a large river, glittering in the sunset, flowed its way past the spot. The time was 1808, forty-one years before a man named Josiah Hankin would found a town on the flats below, a town he would name after the Belfast street on which he had been born—Newtownards.

Treeg was overcome by the wildness of the place and by the idea that he was the first of his race to travel in time. The air, he noted, was sweet and moist, and it was almost as hot here as his own native world. He stood there on he hilltop, a grotesque statue silhouetted in the setting sun, and thought. He had all the time in the world. . . .

He heard a rustling in the undergrowth.

Four men crept through the dense marsh grass, looking not at the hill and its weird occupant but out at the river. Two were old-time pirates who had fought with Laffite years before and had then changed occupations to become Bayou smugglers, finding the new line of work just as profitable but less risky.

The other two were renegade slaves, who joined the Bayou settlement as a sanctuary where they could relax, free from the fear of the law in a society where it was not race, but brains and muscle, that made a man a man. All four of them loved the art of smuggling, taking pride in it in the same way as a jeweler would pride himself in his skillful work.

Treeg had no ears with which to hear the men, and so, oblivious to the danger below, he began walking down the slope toward the base of the hill. He had decided that Mofad would surely have made traces in the virgin land if this was indeed the correct time, but he had a duty to perform, and all the time he would ever need. So he decided to check all the same. In the military caste society of his birth the first rule taught every youngling was "Never underestimate your enemy."

"Damn and double that stinkin' Joe Walsh," growled Ned Harrell as his eyes strained to catch a glimpse of a flatboat on the great expanse of the river. "If that pig's double-crossed me, I'll—Hey! Did you hear that?" A crash and crackle of underbrush sounded nearby.

Carl, a giant black with a fugitive's reflexes, had already jumped around. Then he screamed. They were looking at a giant demon out of hell come down from his high hill, a demon with the face of a monster and the look of the swamp.

Harrell instinctively grabbed his rifle and shot at the thing in one motion. The bullet struck the Sirian's midsection, a strong point in his body armor, and bounced harmlessly off; but the force of the blast knocked Treeg back, and he grabbed a long vine to keep from crashing to the ground. The initial surprise of the attack wore off almost immediately, and Treeg saw the situation for what it was—he was faced with a bunch of primitives, and scared ones at that. Treeg, a born killer trained in his art, charged. Three of the men drew back, but Carl stood his ground. Stopping a few feet away, the Sirian surveyed the Terran who was as big as he.

The big black man charged, and Treeg stepped aside, letting his adversary sail past. The Sirian had spotted Harrell furiously reloading his rifle and wanted to eliminate the threat. Drawing his pistol, Treeg fired. Harrell went up in smoke and flame. The two others ran off, the short black man known as Eliot shouting: *"Juju! Juju! Oh, God, we done raised a juju!"* as he stormed through the brush.

Carl had recovered from his missed lunge and, rising to his feet, charged at the back of the monster. He knew he was facing a demon, but he also knew that demons could be wrestled into submission—and Carl was the best wrestler of them all.

The Sirian went down, caught completely off guard. He had forgotten his initial and greatest threat while shooting at the others. Carl pounced on top of him and for a few seconds the two wrestled, the big black man not being able to do much damage to the hard-shelled creature, while Treeg found himself pinned in a viselike grip, not being able to free either claw or hand. They were stilled in a test of brute strength, a frozen tableau as Carl sat atop the giant creature and strained to keep those arms pinned.

Treeg was virtually helpless if downed, and he had to be able to roll over in order to bring up his claw. He heaved with all his might, at the same time marveling at the strength of this soft Terran ape, as he thought of all Earthmen.

Foam poured from the mouth of the frenzied Carl as he struggled against the giant creature's strength in that death grip. Finally, after a few seconds that seemed to both to pass like hours, Treeg felt a slight slackening as the man tired, and he kicked over to one side. Carl went sprawling over, and Treeg rolled to his right, at the stunned man, claw raised.

Rifixl Treeg had a terrible time bringing himself to his feet again. Rigid, unbending legs propped out, he used his long arms to lift his body semiupright, then grabbed an overhanging vine and pulled himself erect. He then looked down at the cut and bleeding body of Carl, a Terran. He had been more impressed with the courage and skill of this one creature than with any he had encountered before. The primitive should have run away with the rest of his group, yet he had chosen to stay and fight. He had been closer to winning than he knew, for Treeg had been tiring as well, and a mighty blow into the pulpy Sirian face would have penetrated into his brain, bringing instant death.

Treeg resolved not to underestimate these Terrans

again. He had often wondered why such seeming weaklings were any threat to the Empire. Then a saying one of his early tutors had drummed into him suddenly came back as he stood there: *Ignorance is not a synonym for stupidity, nor savagery for fear*.

Treeg cast one eye in each direction, looking for a sign of the return of the natives in force. He did not want to be caught off guard again. But he found no signs of any life save the crawling insects and flying birds; so, keeping a watchful eye, the Sirian decapitated the Negro, using the ceremonial claw, in the age-old gesture of respect for the dead of war. He then made his way around the hill, searching for the signs of a more civilized man's presence. He found none and, regretfully, walked back up the hill, back to where a stone marked his point of departure.

From back in the swampy glades, a group of cautious Bayou men and women, attracted by the sounds of a struggle, watched in awe and fear as a great demon stood atop the hill, visible as a fearsome specter in the last fleeting rays of the sun.

And suddenly vanished.

Treeg tumbled out of the time cabinet and onto the floor, unconscious. It was only a split second since he had vanished from the laboratory, but it was plain to the Sirian physicist that the colonel had been through an ordeal. The red blood almost completely covering the claw proved it, and Treeg was carried to the hospital, where Carl's blood was washed off and he was left alone to sleep off his exhaustion.

3

Less than two days later, Treeg was ready and able to try again. He had learned a lot about his enemy in his first try. This time, unhampered by the apprehension of transition, the passage to Terra was even easier to take. Yet this time, too, it held a surprise.

Treeg stood in a primitive dwelling made of wood.

The size of the room was very large, and it was lavishly furnished. A great, long table divided the room almost into two parts, with chairs stretching endlessly down each side. At the head of the table was a great, padded chair where the master of the house would sit. A long mirror hung on one wall and, overhead, suspended directly above the center of the table, was a massive iron chandelier.

Treeg's first thought was that there had been some sort of mistake. The jump was not more than forty years, he thought, and those primitives of the swamp were surely incapable of making such a dwelling as this. But, of course, forty years brings inevitable change, external as well. The dwelling and the small town below were products of outsiders, who had used the time to carve a slice of civilization from the swamp.

In that time that shrewd old trader Josiah Hankin had built a town and a mansion. He had also been warned not to build on the hill. An old juju woman had prattled about a demon, one her grandmother saw, who lived in the hill and could disappear at will. But Josiah was a hardheaded man, and he laughed.

It was almost midnight. The servants had retired, the slaves had been locked in their house. Josiah sat in his study studiously examining the previous month's account books. But as far as Treeg was concerned, the dark house was empty.

The Sirian took a small tube off his wide utility belt, the only clothing he wore. The tube snapped to life, its brilliant blue-white glow illuminating even the darkest corners of the large room. Treeg narrowed the beam after an initial visual scan of the place, and he began his search. Although not conscious of sound himself or capable of fully grasping what it was, he still moved softly and carefully, knowing that the Terrans possessed a certain sense that he did not.

Then, in the most comic of ways, Rifixl Treeg tripped on the edge of the lush Persian carpet at the doorway and hit the floor with a crash, the blue torch flying against a wall.

Josiah jumped at the sound. He had never been quite comfortable in the wilds and was always a little jittery after dark. Cautiously, the old man tiptoed out onto the landing above the grand stairway and looked down into the dark entrance hall. He heard the sound of movement as Treeg dizzily and with great effort hoisted himself back to his feet. Feeling certain that a burglar was in the house, Hankin went back and got out his old flintlock pistol.

In the meantime Treeg, oblivious of discovery, had started his methodical search of the dining-room area, looking for spaces likely to hide a small recorder. He felt certain that the recorder was hidden in an obvious place —a place somewhere in the house, and one where a Terran searcher would be likely to look, since, were it hidden too well, Mofad's own kind would miss the object of their search.

Josiah crept softly down the stairs, loaded gun in hand. The sounds of movement in the dining room continued. Raising his pistol, the old man stepped across the threshold of the room, now lit by a strange blue glow.

Treeg, very near the door, chose that moment to turn around. As he did so, his right arm swung around and hit Hankin hard, sending the old man reeling back into the hallway. The gun fired on contact, but the ball missed its mark and lodged instead in the far wall.

The Sirian walked toward the old man, who was just getting to his feet. The fellow looked up and into the pulpy, grotesque face, screamed, and ran for the front door. Treeg, being slower, did not give chase as the old man sped out the door and down toward the slaves' house, screaming hideously.

Treeg quickly resumed his search. He was certain that he was still too early in time, and so, with only a few more seconds to survey the downstairs layout—and with pursuit probably imminent—he stepped back to the point just behind the great chair that sat at the head of the long table and pressed the button.

Josiah Hankin, driven mad by the horror that had touched him and pursued him, saw monsters in place of bewildered slaves. He grabbed a heavy stick off the ground and started after one of the men, a field hand. The others finally subdued him.

Hankin would live out his life in a New Orleans sanitarium, always babbling a description of the truth that men of 1850 could only accept as the ravings of a maniac.

Private Fetters jumped nervously as Colonel Rackland entered the house. Rackland grinned. A tall, gaunt man with a now-famous blond goatee, he delighted in scaring his men. It kept them on their toes.

"Well, Private," he drawled, "have you seen any signs of those wicked old Yankees yet?"

Fetters relaxed "No, suh, but ah'm keepin' a shahp lookout, suh."

Rackland smiled again, and went over to the old padded chair that they had uncovered and put back where it rightfully belonged—at the head of the dining room table. The table was ideal for maps and conferences, and the east windows of the room gave an excellent view of the broad expanse of the Mississippi.

Two more men came in—the rest of the observation-post team, one of several Rackland had set up along the riverbank. Rackland walked over to the windows to confer with the new arrivals, and Fetters asked if he could be relieved. This granted, he walked over to the big chair. That saved his life.

Rifixl Treeg appeared between Fetters and the men at the windows, so close to the private that poor Fetters was knocked down. Treeg wanted no surprises and acted by reflex this time, drawing his pistol and firing pointblank at the men at the window.

The wide beam caught all three at once, and each man screamed once, then died from the intense heat. Fetters was only singed slightly, and he saw the creature in the room. One look was enough. Fetters managed to leap up and jump out one of the windows, then ran off, screaming and yelling for help as he raced down the hill toward the town below.

Treeg cursed himself for allowing one to get away, reflecting sourly that that seemed to be all he was doing of late. He made as quick a search as he could, but decided that if this place was being used by these men—seemingly soldiers—Mofad's presence would be marked in some way. Still, he made the rounds of the usual hiding places and then looked over the other downstairs rooms as well. His duty done, Treeg walked back over to the focal point just behind the great chair and pressed the red stud.

She took one look at the creature and fainted, something which puzzled Treeg, who was ever ready to kill but was unused to potential victims dropping unconscious without pain as a precipitant. He decided to kill her while she was out in order to save problems later. Then, despite the fact that head-taking was usually a ceremony of honor, he sliced off the woman's head simply because it seemed the easiest way of killing her.

For once, Treeg allowed himself every luxury of time. He had no reason to believe that anyone else was about, but he kept one eye on the main hall anyway. Lucky for him he did.

Phil Cannon bounced down the stairs, gun in hand. He had watched as the weird creature severed Mary's head cleanly with that claw, but the vision had not driven him mad. Cannon had lived too long and done too much to be scared of any monster that simply was more foul than he. He had accepted Treeg as a reality, probably some sort of unknown animal from the swamps, and he had reached for his .44.

He felt no emotion at Mary's passing. People were things to Phil Cannon; they could be replaced. What mattered was killing the thing in the dining room before it killed him.

Treeg saw movement out of the corner of his eye, drew his pistol, turned, and pulled the trigger. The shot was wide and on a thin beam as well, and it missed Cannon, who darted to cover behind the wall partition, completely. Cocking his pistol, Cannon dropped low to the floor, then darted out, firing a volley at Treeg. One shot struck, and though it did Treeg no harm, it had the force to make him drop his searpistol.

Treeg realized that he had no cover and no weapon, and decided immediately that he had to rush the man. He bounded across the dining room and reached out, but Cannon was too fast.

"Com'on, you brute," Phil Cannon whispered, "com'on out where I can get a clear shot with this thing."

Treeg decided to oblige, chancing that the Terran would aim for his midsection. It was a risk, but there was nothing else to do. He charged, and guessed correctly. Cannon fired into the Sirian's chest, to no effect; but Treeg, ready for the blow of the bullet, was able to keep up his charge. Hand and claw reached out for Cannon, picked him up and threw him into the dining room, where the con man landed with a *snap*.

Treeg made certain that the man was dead by severing his head, but as he started to move the body, part of which was on the focal point, he saw people running for the house, attracted by the shots. Treeg decided that this time period was without doubt still much too early for Mofad anyway, and he pressed the stud.

When he arrived back in the Sirian laboratory, he discovered that Phil Cannon's severed head had come along as well.

Cannon's servants, running in the front door in response to the shots, stopped short at the gruesome sight in the dining room. Crossing himself, the butler said: "We'd all bettah git out of heah fast. They's gonna think *we* done it."

So it was that the town investigating committee found two bodies, one head, and were able to place the blame on the servants.

Murray was in the dining room when Treeg appeared. Stunned for a moment by the creature's sudden appearance, he recovered before Treeg could effectively act and ran to a wall, on which a prized pistol sat, ever loaded, the captain's symbol of his life.

Treeg advanced on him, and Murray fired once, the bullet glancing off Treeg and putting yet another hole in the old house's wall.

The Sirian reached out and grabbed for the young ex-orderly, but missed and fell to the floor. Murray, in dodging, was thrown off balance and fell, too, but he retained a grip on his pistol.

Treeg saw the pistol and lashed out his hand, catching the man's arm in an iron grip. They struggled, rolling along the floor, each trying for possession of the pistol. The gun suddenly reversed under Treeg's mighty pressure, and fired. Murray jerked, then was still. Treeg had killed him by forcing the muzzle of his own gun to his side.

Rising, he went immediately to the dining-room doorway, not taking any chances on another Phil Cannon coming down the stairs.

The captain was standing at the head of the stairs. At the sound of the struggle he had painfully gotten up from his bed, where he had been for several days, fighting an old leg wound that had flared anew. At the sight of Treeg he drew back. His bad leg gave out from under him, and he fell headfirst down the grand stairway. When he hit bottom, he lay still, his neck broken in the fall.

Treeg looked down at the body, which was undeniably dead, a bit stunned at this death. It was, at least, the easiest of the lot, and Treeg was glad of that after his tussle with Murray.

This time the search was not interrupted, and Treeg explored the upstairs as well.

The little girl was playing with her doll in a corner of the dining room. She didn't see Treeg, who stood for a second pondering what to do. Younglings meant adults nearby.

Treeg was correct. Meredith walked down the stairs, spotted Treeg, and grabbed his shotgun, which was in the hall in preparation for a day of hunting. He stormed into the room and fired point-blank at Treeg before the slower-moving Sirian could react. The buckshot spread across the room, parts of the shot striking Treeg in the face; others, deflected, hit the little girl in the face as she watched in horror. Treeg blundered about in pain and in rage and lashed out in all directions. Roger Meredith froze as he caught sight of his daughter, bleeding and in shock, inching along the wall. He was thinking only of her when one of Treeg's blows smashed into his head, killing him instantly.

Mrs. Meredith came running in, and all but bumped into Treeg. He grabbed her and threw her hard away from him, doing so with such power that the unfortunate woman was thrown out of the west window to her death.

Treeg didn't see the child, could think only of getting back. The pain bit at him, driving him almost into a frenzy. This allowed little Carol Meredith to back out the dining-room door, out of the house, and to make it to town, where she would bleed to death in a merchant's arms.

Treeg stabbed at the button on the time-distorter unit, but nothing happened. Suddenly, drawing in great gasps of air, racked by nearly intolerable pain, he realized that he was not precisely over the focal point. With effort he stumbled to the place behind the big padded chair and pressed the stud again. Again nothing happened. He panicked. He pressed, and pressed, and pressed. Finally he pushed the red button instead of the green.

It took two weeks in a Sirian hospital to heal the wounds sufficiently for Treeg to continue. Command had all but ordered him to get another man, but Treeg knew that if he chose another in his place, he would be finished—a final failure. The finding of Mofad was no longer a mission with Rifixl Treeg, it was an obsession. To a born warrior retirement would be a living hell—he would commit suicide first.

This time he was very cautious. As soon as he emerged in the darkened house he drew his pistol, prepared to fire on sight. But the dining room was empty, the furniture piled in one corner. Everything was covered with white sheets, and a thick carpet of dust and cobwebs was everywhere. Treeg glanced around in relief. The house was unlived in at this time.

First he checked the traditional spots, and then the rest of the lower floor. For the first time he was completely uninterrupted, but he never let down his guard. Slight pains in his face reminded him to keep vigilant. His pale blue torch flickered as Treeg mounted the grand stairway with effort.

He found a body at the top of the stairs—a fresh one. Treeg, to whom all Terran apes looked alike, knew this one on sight, every feature from the tiny mustache to the potbelly burned indelibly into his brain.

Alei Mofad, in the initial stages of rigor mortis, lay on the landing, dead neither by murder or suicide, but from a weak heart deprived of its medicine.

Treeg felt a queer thrill run through him. This was it! Even on this mad planet, Terra, he felt, he was still in command of himself.

Mofad had been upstairs, obviously. But had he been going up, or coming down? Coming down, Treeg decided from the angle of the body. Treeg stepped over the body of the scientist, dead in a remote area, remote in time and space—dead many centuries before he would be born. He walked down the second-story corridor.

The master bedroom, in the same dusty condition as the dining room, nonetheless had the look of being used. A big old stuffed chair, the same one that had been in the dining room through many reupholsterings, stood in the middle of the room, a stool resting in front of it. Clearly Mofad had spent his time here, awaiting Terran security, fearful that he would be overlooked and stranded. As Treeg searched the darkened room, his eyes caught the glare of headlights outside.

The police car pulled up and two men stepped out. They checked the front and back doors, and then went back to their car, got in ... and drove off. Treeg waited a few seconds to make certain of their departure, then resumed his search. It would be midnight shortly, and the moon shone brightly in the window.

Suddenly Treeg glanced out the window again, nervously checking to see if the car would return. After a moment he made out a small group of figures creeping up on the house. Youngling Terrans, he decided. He watched as they moved closer, then up and out of sight underneath him.

Treeg crept out of the bedroom and back over to the stairwell. He watched the front door. After a while, it started to move. This time Rifixl Treeg would not be caught off guard! He switched off his light and melted into the shadows, still watching.

Two young Terrans entered cautiously, even fearfully, each one seeming to urge the other on. They stood for a moment in the hallway, then went into the dining room, where moonlight flooded the interior. They pulled two chairs off the heap, very carefully, and sat down, backs to the wall. In silence, their eyes wide, apprehensive, they gazed at the open door.

Treeg decided that, with the others outside who might run for help, he could wait them out. He relaxed a bit, and leaned against a wall to wait, one eye fixed on the front doorway and the other on the entranceway to the dining room. He wasn't about to run and give the prize away. It was too close!

Hours passed, and Treeg fumed with impatience to get on with his search. But it was evident that for some reason—perhaps religious—those boys, scared as they obviously were, were going to stay the night.

Johnny Schmidt and Scully Wills drove back up to Hankin House. They had gotten bored as usual and decided to give the route a fast, clean check before turning in.

As their headlights reflected against the dark shingle of the house, Schmidt caught sight of a small figure running around the side of the place—a figure he knew.

"Hold up there, Tommy Samuels!" he cried, and the boy, who was more scared of the night than of the police, stopped, turned, and obediently came back to the front. Slowly the other Swamp Rats appeared as well. The game was up, and Tommy was known to be a blabber-mouth anyway.

"Now, just what the *hell* are you kids doing up here at this time of night?" the irate officer demanded, and in confused snatches the entire story was told.

"Well," said Schmidt disgustedly to his partner, "we'll have to go in and get them. Let's get it over with." With that the two men mounted the steps and threw open the door.

At that instant a bored and impatient Treeg, curious as to the meaning of the flashes of light outside, chose to risk a peek from his hiding place. So his face was fully outlined in Schmidt's casually aimed flashlight beam.

"Oh, my God!" yelled the police officer, who dropped and drew his pistol. Treeg jerked back, but not without sound.

"Did you see what I saw?" Scully whispered huskily.

"I hope not," replied Schmidt, and then a thought struck him. *"The kids!"*

"Buzz Murdock! Ricky Adherne! You two get outa there fast, on the run, when I give the word," Scully shouted. "Then run like hell for town and tell 'em to bring help. We got *something* cornered upstairs."

The two boys ran out, joined their frightened compatriots, and ran down the hill as fast as their legs could carry them. None of them would give a warning! They hadn't seen anything.

"Scully, get out to the car and call the state troopers. Tell 'em we don't know what it is but to get some heavy stuff up here and *fast*!" Scully crept back out the door and ran for the car. There was noise on the second floor, as Treeg retreated to the master bedroom. He knew from the way they reacted that these men were armed professionals, and he wanted a good place both for a stand and for a view of the road.

He set the pistol charge to high intensity and aimed for the patrol car below at which the unfortunate Scully was standing, giving his call for aid to the state-trooper barracks. The beam lashed out from the upper window, exploding the car with a blinding glare and shock wave that was seen and heard in town. People awoke, looked out, and saw a burning heap in front of Hankin House.

Schmidt was knocked flat by the blast, but quickly picked himself up and stationed himself behind an overturned hall table near the stairs. Whatever was up there he was determined to *keep* up there until reinforcements arrived.

Treeg knew that with only one man downstairs he could get away, but he would return a failure, return to death. Better to make a stand here, he decided, and at least *find* the recorder, if only to destroy it. If the Sirian Empire didn't have it, then at least it would not be used against them.

A small group of villagers ran up the hill. Treeg saw them coming and aimed a shot that exploded the earth just in front of them. Men started screaming. Those unharmed ran back toward town.

Lights went on all over town, including those in the house of National Guard Major Robert Kelsoe, who had two advantages. He had a full view of the old mansion from his bedroom window, and he lived next door to the Guard armory.

Treeg fired a third shot, on wide beam, that cooked swamp grass and vegetation in a five-foot path down the hillside. He did not know where the other Terran man was lurking, but felt that he wouldn't charge without help. And the hilltop shots would discourage anyone coming to help. He continued his search.

Schmidt heard the thing moving furniture around upstairs. He tried to imagine what it was and what it was doing up there, failing on both counts. But he was Newtownards born and bred, and he knew the legends. He knew that he had just seen the demon of Hankin House and that no matter what it was, it was solid.

Major Kelsoe wasted no time in opening the armory. He didn't know what was going on, but he had seen the beams from the house and knew that some sort of power was loose up there. Three of his Guard unit were awaiting him at the armory, and they discussed what they had seen and heard as they broke out submachine guns.

It was eight and a half minutes since Scully had called the state police. Two cars roared into town, having done eighty along the narrow road. They matched Scully's incredible radio report, cut off in midsentence, with what the Guardsmen had seen. The state police corporal looked over at a far rack. "*Hey!*" he exclaimed, "Are those bazookas?"

A few minutes later a cautious group of men, three of them armed with bazookas, crept up the side of the hill to Hankin House.

When they reached the summit and were standing in front of the house, across from the crater left where the patrol car had exploded, Corporal James Watson found his voice and yelled: "*Wills! Schmidt!*"

Schmidt heard the yell and called back, "This is Schmidt in here! Wills was caught in the blast. This thing is unbelievable! It's upstairs moving stuff around at a fearful rate. Come in slowly, and watch it!"

As if on a commando raid, the men zigzagged across the road and up onto the porch, seconds apart.

"Thank God," Schmidt sighed when he saw them. He spotted the bazookas and said, "Get those things ready. The thing's sort of like a big crawfish, I think, and that body armor will be awfully thick on a baby this size. The thing's got to come down this way—maybe we can give it a bellyful."

Treeg was thoroughly frustrated. Not being able to hear anything at all, and not having seen the band of men creep up and into the house, he fancied himself still with only the problem of the lone sentinel below.

Mofad must have hidden the recorder downstairs after all, he thought disgustedly. He'd have to get rid of that pest down there and then have another look.

Quickly Treeg stepped out onto the landing, over Mofad's still body, and started down the stairs slowly, pistol in hand.

The bazooka shell, designed to penetrate the toughest

tank armor, sliced through his body like a hot knife through butter. The great, alien body toppled headfirst down the stairs and landed with a crash at the feet of the men below, almost exactly where Captain Hornig had lain after his fall.

Colonel Rifixl Treeg, Hereditary Colonel of Empire Intelligence, was dead.

The newsmen had left; the police and Guard had finished their examinations of the building, and the alien body, or what was left of it, had been carted off to Washington, where baffled biologists would almost be driven mad in their unsuccessful attempt to identify the thing. The physicists regretted that the bazooka shell had passed through the curious beltlike container the creature had worn, destroying forever the new science in the ray-pistol power pack and the portable time link.

The excitement was all over, and Hankin House was again boarded up. There was talk of finally tearing the old place down, but in the end the house gave the economy of the tiny town a much-needed boost. The only tourist attraction in the state that drew more year-round visitors was the Latin Quarter of New Orleans.

4

A man, Terran, materialized in the hallway, almost on the spot where Rifixl Treeg's body had fallen. He removed a sheet of paperlike material, upon which was written the location of the agreed-upon rendezvous Mofad had established before he had ever left Conolt IV. The slip stated: "LOUESSE 155—EMERGENCY LOCATION IN CASE OF ENEMY ACTION, POINT OF REFERENCE 221."

The agent mounted the stairway, turned at the landing where Mofad's body had lain—he who now was at rest as a John Doe in the potter's field—and went directly into the master bedroom.

The place was a shambles. Treeg had moved everything around, torn down cabinets, mantels, and other such hiding places.

"Now, where the devil would I hide a minirecorder in here if I wanted a place another Terran would probably find but a Sirian probably would not?" That was the problem.

Where?

After some exasperating searches the agent crossed his arms, stumped, and surveyed the room. Dammit, Point of Reference 221 in this house was the master bedroom!

The agent suddenly felt tired—he had had a day that spanned twelve centuries. He decided to sit down and think the problem out. Grabbing the overturned master's chair that had once sat at the head of the diningroom table and had, indeed, been Mofad's only comfort, he turned it over and sank down.

Click. "The frequency modulation of point seven two betas—"

The man jumped up out of the chair as if he had been shot. But then he smiled, and then he laughed. And then he couldn't stop laughing.

Where was a good place for a Terran to look but a Sirian to overlook? What might a tired Terran do when he reached here: chair and stool set up, inviting... but *when you're guarding against a race that was incapable of sitting down*! A simple matter for a genius like Mofad to rig the recorder. Treeg could have torn the chair apart without noticing the tiny minirecorder—but he would never have pressed hard on the seat!

Mofad's voice droned on, telling those precious formulae and figures that would win Terra the war. The Terran agent, still laughing, slit open the seat of the chair and dug into the wooden frame structure which Mofad had built as his recorder's final resting place. Only heavy pressure on the center of the seat would have made it begin playing.

The agent removed the recorder and shut it off. He then walked out of the bedroom, down the stairs, and into the main hallway. He took from his pocket a small control box, on which were two buttons. Pressing the red one, he disappeared.

And the last ghost of Hankin House vanished into time.

INTRODUCTION TO
"WHERE DO YOU GET THOSE CRAZY IDEAS?"

Writers seldom get together and discuss plots or ideas or stories in general. We discuss business, and publishing personalities, and the like, but rarely anything having to do with writing beyond "what word processor do you use?" and "what's your computer?" One favorite sport, however, is comparing clichés. Not the clichés that writers use, but the clichés the public uses when they try and deal with this profession. This is the only business where this sort of thing happens with regularity and happens to writer after writer almost without exception. The vaudevillian drum rolls are optional.

"What do you do for a living, Mr. Chalker?"

"I'm a writer."

"Oh? Have you sold anything?" *Barumph! Bump!*

"Thirty novels or so and some short stories. I make my living at it."

"Oh? What name do you write under?" *Barumph! Bump!*

"My own."

"I've never heard of you." *Barumph! Bump!*

"Well, I've never heard of you, either. What do you do for a living?"

64

"Oh, I'm the assistant manager of housewares at K mart."

And so it goes. A fiction writer has a pretty weird place in the scheme of things, one that is never quite fish nor fowl. Whether we like it or not, commercial writers are always in show business. We are in the entertainment as well as the information and art fields, and we don't quite fit in any of them. Going to an SF convention and having a hundred people line up for your autograph is a big deal; they also want to hear what you have to say (whether you have anything to say to them or not), and as for the publishing industry—all those folks who wouldn't let you in the door at their parties back before you sold anything are suddenly buying you dinner and hovering all around. Newspapers and magazines do spreads on you, call you when something major happens (like the *Challenger* tragedy or the death of someone with a movie connection like Frank Herbert), and bookstores set up fancy signings. The Star Treatment.

But we're print animals working in small and isolated personal offices in mostly out of the way places. Our faces aren't instantly recognized, our voices are not commonly heard beyond the printed page. Even Norman Mailer and Kurt Vonnegut can do their own shopping if they want, and their visages are far better known than most writers'. In effect, we're more like radio personalities in the way our celebrity status affects us and our lifestyle. Most of us don't look anything like writers or readers' mental images of specific writers. We rarely dress up, and we tend to be unglamorous. Stephen King once noted that most writers look like the fellow who sweeps up the bookstore before closing. Even the richest and most successful of us don't look like we could possibly be making any money. I am constantly searched by customs when crossing the U.S.–Canadian border in a car, for example, because I simply don't look like the sort of fellow who could be driving his own Mercedes bought with money honestly come by.

But even in situations where you are an instantly recognized and regarded celebrity, the clichés continue. This may be hard for some people to believe, but this is still the most asked question I get at any gathering:

"Oh, where do you get your ideas?"

The second most asked question, if you're interested, is "Now that you're a successful self-employed writer, when are you going to move to? (Fill in the blank with Florida, South-

ern California, etc.) This second question is easy to answer
—since I am self-employed and independent I don't have to
live in Florida or Southern California or whatever. I like it
where I am. I mean, I am physically allergic to the sun. I like
warm weather but I'm not addicted to it; climatological variety is nicer. Maryland has two basic seasons—sub-arctic and
equatorial. Spring and fall generally last a couple of days
each. Marylanders don't think that way. The two seasons
here are oyster season and crab season. I like 'em both. Any
place that you can't buy Old Bay Seasoning is simply a place
lacking in appreciation of the finer things in life.

The first question, however, is not so easily answered no
matter how many times it's asked, since it goes to the heart
of the creative process. Sure, I realize that most people who
ask the question are sincere because they want to write but
don't have the talent, but how do you explain or quantify
talent? Nobody asks a great painter questions like this because most people can't paint and know it, but almost everybody who reads can type and it looks like a simple matter.
Just get some ideas. Just about everyone can speak but only
a few are great orators or storytellers. "How do you get up
from a chair?" You just *do*, that's all. I cannot imagine not
being able to do this sort of thing. It's what I do.

I am a horror at auto mechanics. If the car breaks (or the
plumbing, or whatever) I have to call a mechanic or plumber
or whatever to fix it. I'm the one human being Heathkit let
fail. No matter what the pretentious say, this talent isn't any
different than other talents, it just pays a lot better if you
have it and use it to full advantage. The reason why industries allied with show business pay so much better is simple
economics: they can afford to. Think—it only cost three
bucks to get in to see *Star Wars*—once, anyway—so nobody's getting ripped off there, but a *hundred million* three
buck tickets were sold. The book business is simpler and
more direct so the splits are bigger even if sales don't approach a film's. You get a book that took months or years to
write and maybe a year to produce for, say, four bucks. Not
much, and if it's a literary equivalent of *Star Wars* you don't
have to pay to get in again—reasonable. And I average
maybe thirty-eight cents for each and every paperback book
sold, so it adds up. The publisher nets about a buck for each
one sold, which is why so many publishers are on the Forbes
rich list.

Of course, the publisher also has to eat the flops, too,

while I get to keep all the front money no matter what, so it's an even trade.

Similarly, the auto mechanic gets a cut for each hour spent fixing a car, but there are only so many cars he or she can work on, right?

Unlike auto repair or plumbing, however, writing is only partially a craft—that is, something you learn and something that can be taught. Sometimes you can take someone with the talent, the art, and make them better at it by teaching them craft and technique, but you can't teach talent and you can't put what isn't there in. The vast bulk of you have no talent for writing or storytelling, thank heavens, and so you pay for books like mine. If you haven't got it, I can't give it to you—nobody can. If you have, then I can teach you the craft, the skills, to write even better, and the business side so you can sell what you write. There are several successful writers—and artists—around now who are where they are because I helped them. But I couldn't make them talented writers or illustrators; they already were that.

Just as many people can learn the craft of painting but produce no works of art, so vast numbers can learn the craft of creative writing and produce nothing anyone else would want to read. I am constantly beseiged by would-be writers who have this "great idea" and they could be rich and famous if only I would write it for them. The ideas are usually lousy or highly derivitive, but even if they weren't it wouldn't matter. I am not a ghost writer, and the profession of noncreative fiction writing is called Hollywood Script Writers. They get between $20,000 and $40,000 to write scripts they're told to write based on "treatments" (outlines, basically) by somebody else who put into words what a producer wanted but which said producer, being illiterate, couldn't write down himself.

I get more money than that most of the time, and I get to write what I want. The Meredith Agency employs a number of financially strapped writers to do that sort of ghostwriting for set fees but with no guarantee of a sale. Why should *I* do it? Others show up to learn the Great Secret of Selling Professionally. There must be one—I'm a published author and they're as good as me, right?

The bottom line is, if you have the talent, persistence, and skill, you will write and eventually you will sell. If you don't, all the advice and help of a Shakespeare couldn't do a thing for you.

Which brings us back to ideas. Most of my ideas come from my background in studying and teaching history, of course, but they come from other places as well, often just by doing something different and going someplace new. In 1978, Judy-Lynn del Rey asked me to do an article on the origins of the Well World as a preface to the sequels; I complied, but then she decided not to use it. Not because she didn't like the piece but because, by then, *Midnight* had sold so well, she felt the sequels didn't need it. Since this is one of the few times when the complete creative process leading to one of my books can be traced and detailed ("Dance Band" being the only other clear case), and since it shows quite a bit about how my mind works, I thought it deserved inclusion here. It does not, however, tell you where Brazil and Ortega came from because I don't know. They were just there when I needed them, as many of my characters are.

Writing is not an easy or a secure way to make a living, and the *craft* of writing well is very hard work. But the creativity is something that just instinctively happens. It's there, or it isn't. Go to a piano, whether you know how to play or not, and try to play it like Horowitz. You can't? Then why expect to go to a typewriter keyboard and expect to write like a pro? Somebody taught Horowitz—and probably hundreds of others—to play the piano, but nobody plays it like he does. Millions can type, but only a few can create by typing. Sorry about that—the magic secret is a secret to me, too, and to everybody else who creates.

Oh, well, nothing's perfect.

A bibliographic note: the material I wrote at del Rey's prodding ends with "And it begins . . ." The balance is added on for the first time here, simply in the interest of completeness.

WHERE DO YOU GET THOSE CRAZY IDEAS?

YOU DECIDED TO GET AWAY FROM IT ALL, TO GO SOME-
place where you know no one and no one knows you and
just see what can be seen. It's been a tough year and, so
far, a nonproductive summer, and even though your
novel's out now and you're a Pro, you really haven't
given much thought to the persistent requests for something new from your publisher. Perhaps this trip will
clear the mind and give you some ideas. You pick Washington State because it's a state you haven't spent much
time in, but were impressed with when you passed
through on the way to Alaska a couple of years back,
and you know that the state has plenty of your passion
—ferryboats. You wonder how long it would take and
what sort of effort would be required to ride every ferry
line in Washington. Lots of driving, sure, but you think
best when driving long and hard anyway.

Just before you left, you re-watched *Forbidden Planet*
on television, and you can't get it out of your head. The
cast is better, the ending weaker, than you'd remembered, but it is still a stunning film full of interesting
ideas and vistas. Flying up to Seattle, you get to thinking
about it again, particularly the basic premise—the Krell,
gods through technological advancement, taking that

69

last, final step toward an existence without instrumentalities. Godhood. But in *Forbidden Planet* the Krell experiment failed; they had forgotten their evolutionary ladder, the primitive psyche below their sentient minds, and it had destroyed them. An interesting idea. What if the Krell had been beyond all that? What if the experiment had worked?

The Olympian splendor of Mount Rainier is in front of you as you drive south from the airport in your rented car. The gods of Olympus could not have had such a home—and what about them? Weren't they always meddling in the affairs of Greece out of sheer boredom, out of a need to find something to do?

Crisscrossing the western part of the state, riding the ferries through spectacular scenery, and staying for a time in the state's excellent national parks, you can't escape the sheer beauty and majesty of the places—and the lonely inspiration they engender. Out on the Olympic Peninsula, in Olympic National Park, they even have a mighty Mount Olympus of their own, isolated from man and civilization.

And, you think, after a short while of playing at gods and having all the fun they might have imagined when they, as mortals, had dreamed of this godhood, malaise would set in. It would be slow, insidious, inexplicable. Here was a race that developed to the highest possible point by seeking godhood; now they had attained all their goals. Boredom, stagnancy, a drift would certainly occur. Their very minds would be repelled by the sheer lack of anything more to discover, any higher plane to seek. And yet, they had it all. Had it all, and were unhappy, even miserable. And since they are now as complete and as perfect as they were capable of being, they have the uneasy feeling that something must have gone wrong someplace.

Some Buddhists equate the highest level of consciousness as true and irrevocable death—when you've been incarnated *ad infinitum* and you've reached the highest spiritual plane and are omnipresent and omnipotent, that's really it. There's no more purpose to hanging around since you can't go up and might only go down. Wasn't that sort of the theme of *A Jungle of Stars*? Well, not quite. That was "if you don't go up you can only go down," but it's close enough.

This race wouldn't see it that way. They would be firmly anchored in the technological, in the history and culture that had raised them to such a height. Some, of course, would indeed see that there was no reason to continue and destroy themselves, but these would be considered mad rather than pragmatic by the majority of the others. To cure the madness, to stop potential racial extinction, they would be desperate to find the flaw in their own ladder that had brought them to this point. You're sure of that. And after poking and probing and rejecting as sheer madness the truth, they would eventually decide that, somehow, they hadn't quite achieved what might be achieved. Something had gone wrong. Perhaps the only way to rectify this would be to start again.

But what would be the variables? Culture, physiology, geography—everything. They couldn't just go back and become again what they were, right? That way hadn't worked.

By this time you have ridden all the ferries and seen all the parks in the western part of the state, but you have noticed a single ferry line crossing Lake Roosevelt in the east part, a line most Washingtonians don't know about, and you head there over back roads and farm roads and you find it, then see Grand Coulee, and continue on back toward the west once again. Just before dark, and by sheer chance, you come upon the lumber town of Chelan, which has a few restaurants and a couple of motels and appears to be at the bottom end of a huge lake. You learn that the lake is fifty-five miles long and naturally carved by glaciers, not by dams as you had originally assumed. You can't drive up that lake, which points like an arrow into the heart of North Cascades National Park, but there's a boat, once a day. *The Lady of the Lake*. It's irresistible, even though you know you'll have only an hour at the other end either to find accommodation or to return.

Less than ten miles up-lake the roads stop, and soon after you lose any visible signs of human habitation. True, the boat occasionally comes close to shore, against the sheer cliffs, and some little old lady toddles over to the cliffside, looks far down at the boat, and yells, "Hiya, Charlie! Got any mail for me today?" but that's about it. It takes hours to get to the other end, and all you know about the other end is that there's a National Park lodge and visitor center there.

There is more than that. There is, in fact, a town, or what remains of a town. It's called Stehekin, which in the local Indian tongue means "the way through." It was originally an Indian camp, then a logging town, and now it's Park Headquarters but has some private getaway homes. The lodge is small but it can accommodate you; you watch the boat ease away from the landing, turn, and head back down-lake, and you suddenly feel more isolated than you ever did in Alaska or anywhere else. Radio and TV signals can not penetrate; there is no microwave link and so there are no telephones, either. The world could end, and Stehekin would be the last to know.

So you sit there, pad on your knee, looking out at the head of the lake and the majestic Cascades and Stehekin Pass, which is at over 14,000 feet up—some pass! There are very few people, and, as it darkens, the silence is deafening. Even the few insects seem to be wearing silencers.

To devolve, by choice. To voluntarily surrender a godhood that has become meaningless. To create an infinite variety of races and ecosystems and cultures out of your own selves and then wind them up and let them run. But these were a logical, scientific people, after all, not supernatural beings—although they might appear so to us. They wouldn't just do it—they'd test things first, particularly before surrendering their own lives and powers. They would make models and they would test them out.

A world. A world artificially created by the gods as a testing ground for later planetary colonization by their re-mortalized selves and their children. *The Well World*. The name comes to you, unbidden, on the soft chilly breezes off the lake, because it is right.

The next morning you are eating breakfast when the bull cook asks what you're doing and what you're writing, possibly suspecting that you're some sort of GSA evaluator come to check out the concessionaire undercover, or perhaps a travel reporter. You explain to him that you are writing a novel, and are grateful when he asks what you've written rather than ask if you've sold anything.

"Uh huh. And you're writing science fiction *here*?" he asks, incredulously.

You nod. "Why not?"

"Are you gonna put Stehekin in the book?"

It suddenly strikes you that you really have no idea what this experimental world would be like. "Could be," you respond, and finish up and walk out into the crisp morning air, and on the pad you write, "Aboard the Freighter *Stehekin*."

Yes, here, at the end of this lake, with the high mountains in back—it would be a nice module. Two deer pass close by as you ponder what sort of creatures would live in a place like this, and at what level. Certainly highly skilled, or they couldn't have gotten here. Certainly not high tech, considering what had to be done to feed electricity to the lodge and how isolated it was.

You walk up to Rainbow Falls, an impressive waterfall that's all the day-trippers ever get to see (other than five-dollar hamburgers from the only place in town or ten-dollar beef stew), and you watch the source of that lake fall down and the sunlight catch the droplets to form tiny rainbows as the water cascades into a pool as clear as water ever gets before it overfills the basin it's dug for itself and flows on down to the lake. And suddenly the scene from *Fantasia* arises in your mind, and you see the centauresses at their bath in the pool and under the falls.

Centaurs. That's who should live here. Folksy, back-
woods centaurs.

Well, okay, but that didn't solve the problem of what
the world would be like, only one tiny corner of it. So
you catch a Park Service shuttle to the trail head, and,
after some misgivings considering that even the Air
Force couldn't get you into condition, you walk in a
ways and up and around a bit—and you are in snow.

It's deep snow, but heavy now in summer, and the
trail has been cleared and then tramped down by persistent marchers. You know this trail leads all the way—
through the pass and then down several miles to the road
you'd come in on. You know you could never climb
mountains—that was why you had never gone to the
bottom of the Grand Canyon. Getting there was fine, but
getting out would be impossible (you're a Big Person and
the maximum weight for canyon mules is less than even
the insurance companies say you should weigh). But this
was a trail that climbed only a hundred feet or so, then
went down, through a vast and complex switchback system, through the wilderness and back to civilization
below. You turn back, find a ranger, arrange to have your
things transported back to Chelan on the boat, and decide to go for it.

The snow field is impressive in and of itself; the trees
are somewhat stunted, the vegetation sparse but persistent, and here and there you spook an animal or two,
mostly white like the snow for protection. And now
you're over the pass and going back down. One switchback, two—and the snow is magically gone. One final
turn and you have gone from subarctic to dense northern
forests. Farther down, *way* farther down, you can see a
rainstorm—but here the sun is shining on you.

The trees are different here, the vegetation is different, *everything* is different. You have changed slopes and
are going down in altitude. The vegetation, even the
greens are radically different here, and the animals seem
brown and not really related to the ones just a few
hundred feet farther up.

You look up at the sun, then down at the rainstorm,

and it hits you. *This is what the Well World would be like!*
Abrupt transitions, each module self-maintained, with
only water and air passing through.

By the time you are halfway down you have experienced at least two more radical changes in lifeforms and
where you've come from is deeply shrouded in clouds,
and the Well World's basic nature and how to describe it
in terms of the Stehekin Pass Trail is very clear in your
mind.

You bet Stehekin is going to be in this book!

You reach bottom and the road and get picked up by
the bus. Then you switch buses again and again, until,
after midnight, you finally make Chelan once more and
are able to awaken the motel keeper and collapse onto a
bed for an incredibly deep sleep. Most people dream
when they sleep, but you never remember your dreams
from sleep. Writers, however, dream equally well when
they are awake. There is a part of you that is almost
always dreaming. That is part of the creative personality.

You are sitting on the plane home, pad out on the tray
table in front of you, and you are making up names and
descriptions of key races. The names are easy—any exotic and meaningless combination of sounds will do. You
start with some anagrams—Dilia for the centaurs, for
example, a scramble of Iliad. What better name for cen-
taurland? Most, however, are meaningless but sound
pretty good. There's a publisher's rule that you can't use
any alien terms that would be unpronounceable to
humans. So be it.

The technology would have to be deliberately limited
to avoid spoiling the models. Non-technological, semi-
tech, and unlimited high tech seemed the most logical
choices, so these are assigned. And you think back once
more to Washington, and to the billboard put up a few
years before by the Boeing unions when the company
lost the SST contract and there were massive layoffs.

WILL THE LAST PERSON TO LEAVE SEATTLE PLEASE
TURN OFF THE LIGHTS?

Okay, so our godlike beings have made this world where they experiment and create and fine-tune their creations before doing it larger and for real in the universe, but eventually they would all have to become part of the experiment. That solved one big problem—the last hundred, or thousand, worldlets they invented in model would remain most likely as they had been created, giving the Well World its population and enough temporal distance between populations so even the inhabitants really wouldn't know how their world came to be or why. They wouldn't even have access to the machinery, the computers, the whole technology of the Well World—it would be too dangerous.

Somebody had to be left of the old gang. Somebody had to go down to that machinery and lock it from the inside, making sure nobody could get in and fiddle with it in the future. And this guardian would have to stay around to make sure the experiment went to its conclusion.

Who turned out the Well World's lights? And what was he doing now, the last of his race?

The legend of the Wandering Jew comes to mind and seems to logically fit with the Greco-Roman mythology and the rest. The mechanic who has to hang around to see that nothing breaks and everything's going well and, if drastically necessary, to push the "reset" button.

But why would he choose to masquerade as and live as a human instead of one of the thousands of other races? Of course, no matter which race this creature chose would provoke the same question, so the obvious response was, "Why not?" For reasons you can not say, this mysterious figure begins to take shape in your mind and says, "Hello, I'm Nathan Brazil." The reason for the name itself is pedestrian. Nathan because you'd always like their hot dogs and it was vaguely Jewish sounding but melodic; Brazil because there was a story in the paper about a football player named Brasil, and it seemed to go nicely with Nathan. *Guys and Dolls*, the obvious source, never entered into it, although so many later assumed that it had that you finally went out of your way to *see* the play and later titled a different book *And the Devil Will Drag You Under*.

The description of Brazil comes easily. Three days after you return home, you go to a meeting of the Washington Science Fiction Association, and among its members is a fellow you've known for a while named Dave Kogelman who looks just the way Nathan Brazil should look. And the "frame" is equally easy—we must have some innocents drop in so we can tour the place, and Brazil must be among them. He locked the Well World door, but nobody was left on each of the old worlds to lock the matter transmission gateways by which the super race migrated in stages back to this place.

The frame is *The Wizard of Oz*. It requires a high-tech but black-and-white future; a futuristic, technological Kansas. Listening at that same meeting to a small group of leftist radicals describe with enthusiasm their ideas of a future world, you realize that their utopia, fully realized, was exactly the kind of bleak cookie-cutter future you required. But what of the world itself?

Having already begun writing, you go up to New York for a party and discuss the problem casually with Ben Yalow, a New York SF fan. You want a regular shape, which would allow many travel options from any point, but each worldlet had to be small enough to journey through several in order to deliver on the premise. Ben suggests hexagons such as those used in Avalon Hill board games. We use the rounded-off circumference of the Earth, then lay the map for *The Battle of the Bulge* on top of it. Excellent. How many are there if we make the hexes roughly two hundred and forty or so miles across, point to point? Fifteen hundred and sixty. Okay, that was plenty of variety. But there is a problem—you can't cover a sphere with hexagons.

No sweat. You have to have someplace to get these large masses of resigning gods in, and a mechanism for distributing them in new forms. Why not the polar caps? And the Well would have to be accessible equally well from the bulk of the hexes. Why not the equator? That might also provide a real physical division of the hemispheres allowing for non carbon-based life, which would logically be required but which would poison the carbon-based life hexes and in turn be poisoned by "our" air and water. The equatorial barrier was logically consistent; the use of not one entrance and exit but two was also obviously convenient. Two polar caps. Two Zones.

You live near Avalon Hill and, in fact, knew the founder. It is easy to get blank hex maps and pads and draw in the parts of the world you need.

Now all that was required was the outside observer. We would be going to a lot of places, and for dramatic tension, the McGuffin had to be some sort of race to the Well. Without an outside observer to tie things together it would be very easy, perhaps inevitable, that the reader would get confused. And, of course, Brazil would have to be briefed from the start on the nature of what was on the other side or there would be no motivation for him to join the race. We had to have someone culturally accessible to the readers yet exotic in form to set up the rules. A vision of South Zone comes unbidden and complete into the mind, and a creature riding the outer belts to meet you. It is fully formed and comes from some dark recess of your mind with name and personality already attached.

"*I am Serge Ortega; welcome to the Well World,*" he says, and Kansas fades and Oz goes to Technicolor. And it begins...

From the name "Well World," your vision of the place flows naturally: you drop through its gates and find there, like precious waters, the core of the life and power and order of the universe. Now there remain only the details and mechanics of the story—and a title. "Well of Souls" comes easily to mind—it is both literal and exotic-sounding. But has it been used before? You check and find that it does not show up in any of your references. Fine. Now you have a poetic name and a poetic title to crown the book. (True, a certain film producer with whom you shared a publisher would later steal the name and devise intricate rationalizations involving "an-

cient theology" to prevent your suing him. The same
production company had offered you a job writing books
based on their successful blockbuster SF film which you
turned down, but what the hell. More people probably
bought *Midnight* thinking it had something to do with the
movie than it ever mattered to filmmakers.)

And now the book flows. The whole work is done;
only the typing remains, and you type really fast. You
are proofreading the manuscript at the 1976 World SF
Convention when your editor, Judy-Lynn del Rey,
comes up to you and asks when you are going to write
another book for her. The temptation is inevitable. The
manuscript isn't proofed, but you hand it to her then and
there. She buys it four days later.

After a few squabbles which you lose—a few coarse
words removed, the sex scenes toned down to PG, and
one small episode removed because it really does get in
the way of the climax—it's done. But the end, the very
end, still bothers you. Reading galleys, you come back to
that last page again and again, and suddenly strike
through the last few sentences and write a paraphrase of
a Mark Twain line, adding, "Still waiting. Still caring.
Still alone." A decade later readers will still tell you
about the force the ending had on them. How did it come
together at the last moment?

Somehow, it always does.

INTRODUCTION TO
"FORTY DAYS AND NIGHTS IN THE
WILDERNESS"

My first published novel of science fiction was *A Jungle of Stars* (Ballantine Books, 1976 and still going via Del Rey Books). I'm not really certain how far back the whole concept goes, but I had the basic character of Paul Carleton Savage in my mind, hook and all, in my middle teens and played around with ideas for him. He was always a private detective; he was also always a ghostbreaker, a detective who stumbled into or specialized in SF and supernatural (or supernatural-appearing) cases. Only one of those cases was ever actually written down, though—in 1959, I believe it was. The title was *Hello, Charlie*, and it was a really decent little tale of a highly unpleasant alien who crashes into a lake near a small town and, by parasitically manipulating the local ice cream man, begins to take over the children of the community.

I don't know why I never did anything with it; Charlie, who resembles a little purple haystack, was illustrated in my first fanzine, *Centaur*, back in 1960, and I find references to the story in other writings of the period, but I have no record or memory of ever attempting to submit the tale to any publisher, amateur or professional. Possibly my encounter with

Meredith's $100-a-shot rewrite department was more trau-
matic than I remember. I did submit it to the fiction contest
being run by the National Fantasy Fan Federation in 1960,
though; Fred Pohl was judge, and while he praised the writing, he rejected the story because he said it had a fatal flaw
—and it did. Charlie's power emanated at least partially
from his use of a new color that drove people mad; Fred was
impolitic enough to note that while the color might well
exist, it would be biophysically impossible for us to see it.

I put Charlie away and tried another, more grandiose Savage story, this one involving an interstellar war between
forces headed by two parasitical survivors of a once godlike
race reduced to hating each other and fighting for crumbs.
They were, more than metaphorically, God and the devil,
with the irony that the authoritarian villain was God and the
likable fighter of oppression and conformity was the devil
character. The story was called "Jungle," and it had all the
elements that later went into the novel—but all in 12,500
words. It was, in other words, a tad light on characterization
and very, very crowded. Still, it was published—in a fanzine,
Mirth and Irony, edited by Tom Haughey (pronounced
"Hoy") and illustrated by Joe Mayhew. It drew very kind
comments from a number of pros, including Don Wollheim, then editing Ace, who told me that if I ever wanted to
flesh it out and develop it as a novel, he would be very interested in it.

At that point, though, I tried a few times to develop the
thing and failed. *"Jungle"* became almost a parlor game
around the Washington Science Fiction Association with various members trying to develop their own plots or ideas, and
there was a subsidiary game on figuring out who was our
villain, The Bromgrev, and just how to kill the thing once we
figured what it was. I had trouble with it—I kept bogging
down in the middle when it refused to go where I thought it
would—and I finally abandoned the project. However, as
noted in my introduction to "No Hiding Place,'" I am cursed
to throw nothing away without a gun placed at my head, so
"Jungle" remained in my desk drawer. Haughey left (he's
now a radio preacher in Texas who writes Christian detective
novels on the side), *Mirth and Irony* vanished into obscurity,
and all was calm and serene. I went on to college, the Air
Force, teaching, and building up The Mirage Press, Ltd. But
I never really forgot old Paul or Charlie or the others.

In 1975, a bunch of things in my life all went bad at once.

I needed a nasty bit of surgery and then had a hairy time
waiting to see if the infection had penetrated my lymphatic
system and was going to kill me or not. My business partner
in Mirage, who typeset the books and whose family also put
up much of the capital, fell ill, had to completely withdraw
from all activity, and was hospitalized for several years while
his family seized all the business machines we owned to recover what money they could. I even had a long-standing
romance of many years collapse utterly and forever. I needed
money to keep Mirage afloat, and what little I had was eaten
away by my own medical bills, so I turned to my typewriter.
It was actually owned by Mirage as well, but those relatives
missed repossessing it, and I still have it. I still own Mirage
Press, too.

That typewriter is a baby blue Selectric, the first with a
correction key IBM sold in Maryland. I stared at the auto-
correct key and figured, what the hell? I always knew I was
going to write professionally someday—why not now? Since
I needed money and time was pressing (and I was still teaching), the natural one to do was "Jungle." To the Savage character I added a Vietnam background to give him some depth,
and to the basic fanzine outline I added "Hello, Charlie,"
this time without any crazy color but rather with a device
that accomplished the same purpose—otherwise the original
story is pretty well intact within the novel itself, which is why
it's not here. The title was broadened to *A Jungle of Stars*
simply because it sounded better (I didn't want anyone to
think I wrote a novel about the meat packing industry) and
because Norman Spinrad's *The Men in the Jungle* had just
been reprinted and I wanted to avoid confusion.

My big problem was that "Jungle" was, at its heart, a
traditional closed loop murder mystery and I had been unable to write it through. I sought advice from Wilson "Bob"
Tucker, an old friend who was proficient at writing both
mysteries and SF, and he suggested I write it like a mystery
—backward. "Do the finish first and don't violate it. It'll
keep you on the straight and narrow while roaming far afield
in your universe. And, if you have any slam-bang scenes
you're just dying to write, write them and put them away and
slip 'em in when you get there. Best get them out of your
system. You'll make a tighter book that way and they'll set
smaller target goals." I took his advice, and it all fell into
place. I wrote the entire book in less than three weeks, starting with the last chapter. Since that time, with only one ex-

ception, I have always written the last chapter first. It still works.

"Wrote in three weeks" is not really true, however, and I don't want to give the impression that these things are just cranked out. Remember that the two stories which formed its core were both done twelve to fifteen years earlier, that it had been discussed in depth for years, and had been in my head all that time. I *typed* it in three weeks. I *created* it over a span of fourteen years.

I had sold some Mirage Press titles on which I controlled subsidiary rights to Ballantine to raise more money for the Press, so Judy-Lynn del Rey was the obvious choice to send *Jungle* to. I did so, and heard nothing for a very long time. Finally, since we were also in negotiations on the rights to *A Guide to Middle-earth*, and because she, Lester, and I had known each other for a long, long time, she couldn't avoid me. She ultimately admitted she hadn't read it because she was afraid it would be dreadful and I'd take offense and blow the other deals and maybe our friendship. I assured her business was business, and she promised to read it. A week later, I got a phone call from her. "Jack! I read your book! It's fun! The contract's on the way!"

Just like that, I was a professional novelist. No long-term, anguished wait for rejection letters, no room to wallpaper with "Thanks for submitting . . ." forms, no try this or that editor. I wrote it, sent it to one person, and she bought it.

The fact was, putting the story back together again was fairly easy, and I had a lot of leftover ideas and materials. I always had the idea, even back in the fanzine days, that this would be the first in a series of Paul Savage novels, and I outlined a sequel in early spring and also wrote two sample chapters, one new, one adapted from an older but unpublished story. This time the results were not as good; Judy-Lynn didn't like the sequel's plot, and she didn't like the amount of ESP and mysticism it also entailed. She liked the sample chapters, though, and suggested I develop them into independent stories. It wasn't until late in the next year, though, that I decided to do that with one, "Forty Days and Nights in the Wilderness." I submitted it to Ben Bova at *Analog* because I thought it was his kind of tale, and I was right. Back came a contract and a check. The story was published, however, as "In the Wilderness," which kind of defeats the idea of the title, because, according to Ben, the full title just wouldn't fit on the bottom of an *Analog* page.

At any rate, this is the only other appearance of Paul Carleton Savage to date, in the same universe as *Jungle* and perhaps ten or twenty years later. It should be noted that our bad guys here were the bad guys of the proposed novel that never got written. Just exactly who and what they were and what they were all about was the focus of the proposed book. For now, and particularly for the integrity of this story, I think they're still more effective in the shadows.

Oh, yeah—what about the other story? Well, that's a story in itself, but since it was never published anywhere until now you'll have to wait and get the gory details later. It's "Moths and Candle," the last story in this collection.

FORTY DAYS AND NIGHTS IN THE WILDERNESS

IT IS NOT EVERY DAY THAT THE DEMON HORDES OF hell materialize in your backyard.

It took the Watch Officer a few seconds to comprehend his vision: great ships, huge and black against the darkness of the universe, yet sharp and clear to the watchman through his augmented senses.

They were Guara ships—thousands of them, perhaps their whole main fleet, winking in suddenly along almost two parsecs of sky, globules of metal framed by two enormous, stylized "wings" like those of a monstrous, frozen gull, curving around and almost, but not quite, touching the main body of the ship again at their tips.

The Watch Officer did not need to sound an alarm; he and several others were cybernetically linked to their control ships, and could communicate in real space at the speed of thought.

The little timer by the right hand of his comatose, helmeted body clicked and set in both modes. Within less than one minute the initial interceptor squadron was away; within two minutes nine squadrons totaling over five hundred ships were out in pursuit.

The Watch Officer felt control switch from his own

com to that of a flag officer; now he launched his own squadron.

No person on the intercept ships allowed himself the luxury of spurious thoughts; the cybernetic link provided pinpoint concentration on but the single objective of destroying the enemy.

And yet, deep down in that unreachable recess of every thinking person was a single thought: *At last! The Guara have decided to fight at last!* Even this was tempered by a realization that swept away the anticipation, for the main fleet was on leave and undermanned. Mobilization would be impossible in the subjective time of the battle.

The Guara outnumbered the defenders fifteen to one.

Both sides used different methods to power their ships, yet both types involved inducing negative half-spins in their tachyonic drives. In effect, real time was slowed, even reversed, although usually only for a few seconds under full power. Time negated distance, but it meant fighting on a multitude of different temporal levels separated by milliseconds. Fleets on the defender's side were controlled by crews cybernetically amplified and linked to their ships, and to each other.

Nobody knew how the Guara did it.

But when fleet-sized masses were moved, it was necessary to spread them out to avoid cancellation when the ships phased into objective time, and there was an inconstant braking factor. Fleets tended to come out scrambled up and spread all over creation, like the Guara had; in the precious few minutes of objective time it took them to regroup, they were vulnerable.

A star-shaped unit of nine ships, surrounding the controlling officer's com ship in its center, broke off and started after two isolated Guara vessels that had materialized nearby only moments before.

Bolts of searing energy, visible only to the people on the ships, lashed out at the two black gulls, and struck full amidships. The captains of the invaders applied full power, and both vanished.

Suddenly, it was over—just like that.

The first strike had told the Guara force where they were, and they hadn't even waited to see what was hitting them.

The entire Guara fleet had done a scatter run.

"No use chasin' them," the field officer commented, a trace of disappointment in his mental tone. "They have several seconds on us in lag and speed. Casualties?"

There were none. Not one of the Guara ships had defended itself. Faced with a challenge, they had run—as always.

"Energy trail!" reported the com from the one unit to get in a strike at the enemy. "We got one—maybe both!"

The field officer trained his sophisticated tracking devices in the area of the strike and saw it.

Almost anyone, even with the best sensors, could have missed it, *should* have missed it—but the unit com had *felt* the hit with the intuition that only a veteran combat pilot could have. He'd searched for it—and found it.

A tiny, thin wisp of a trail, as nebulous as a single strand of a spider's web, went off into the deep of space.

Instantly ordering most of the force back to station in case the black ships realized their folly and returned, the field officer took one squadron spearheaded by the strike unit and started to follow the already dissipating trail.

Several times in the lengthy track they lost it, but had enough regression time to recapture the wisp and proceed at flank to where it was stronger.

After a great distance, it became easier to track. Whatever had been hit had been hit bad. The pilot was good; he—or it—was holding the engines together with spit and prayer.

There was a sudden, localized energy burst, and the squadron emerged into normal space-time.

An aged red dwarf glowed dimly, far off. The nova, perhaps a million years before, must have been spectacular; the star's collapse had also torn its solar system apart. And yet, circling the eerily glowing center, were that system's remains: millions, perhaps billions of chunks of matter, from microscopic size to over a thousand kilometers in diameter, continued their vigilant orbits around their diminished but still supreme master.

The strike unit broke off, heading for the medium-sized chunk of matter about three hundred kilometers in irregular, jagged diameter.

The one with the spot that glowed on their sensor plates.

The nine ships edged ever closer, until they were only a few thousand kilometers from the planctoid.

Suddenly the tiny energy spark below flickered, changed hues, and reached out at them.

The nine ships vanished, and the energy arm that clutched and crushed them withdrew.

The field officer's fury was so strong that it almost, but not quite, broke the programmed controls. He wanted to bomb the son of a bitch into a nebulous mass.

Instead, he pulled back his forces to the minimum distance experience that his computers felt was safe, and ordered a photo probe.

A jagged, craggy landscape, reminding the observers of microscopic views of rust crystals, passed slowly before them. Eerie pinnacles, weird spires, and twisted shapes of deep red and dull gold forever in deep shadow showed the little world's ugly sterility.

"We're coming up on it in a moment," a deep voice commented in the darkness of the viewing room. "There! See?"

Suddenly there was a blinding flash that obscured all vision, yet it radiated from a sparkling, seemingly solid core of energy that was curiously shining and alive. Then, just as suddenly, it was gone, replaced with more of the reddish landscape.

The screen flickered, and the approach was repeated from just before the appearance of the brightness. This time it was frame-by-frame, very slow and methodical. The glare started, but didn't quite overtake the view. They blew it up, focused it, played with its spectrum and microdot composition, trying to clear it.

"Look how the terrain's torn up," a voice commented. "The ship came in hard and fast. It's incredible that he survived—I'm pretty sure none of us would have."

"He's still alive, all right, or a machine," the first voice responded. "And he's got teeth." The tone turned bitter. "Thirty-two lost."

The picture changed again, the computer playing now with the shot of the exact center of the energy burst, toning, warping, shielding and filtering the picture, focusing on the living brightness in the center of the mass.

A fuzzy shape, the best that could be done, emerged. It was a Guara ship, all right—flickering, indistinct, but unmistakable—one of its strange curved "wings" had been clipped off, the other twisted. Part of the bow seemed crumpled and distorted.

The second man sighed and flipped off the wall-sized picture. The lights flickered and winked on.

It was an odd assortment that sat in the room; a collection of three dozen different life forms with shapes ranging from centauroid to anthropomorphic. Many others, unable to share the biosphere the others mutually tolerated, watched on remotes.

This was the Board of Advisors, a collection of dominant races who were still struggling to pick up the pieces from the civil war less than a dozen years before.

"So one is down at last," came a voice from what looked like a huge, tentacled housefly, amplified and translated by devices hidden in the walls and transmitted to each member's hearing-piece. "Now what do we do?"

At the head of the table sat a Terran; his body was young and muscular, yet he had short-cropped white hair and a hook for a left hand.

And the oldest eyes of anyone in the room.

"I needn't tell you that the Guara is the greatest threat to reconstruction we have faced—and perhaps the greatest threat to us all in our history, not excepting the late war," he said gravely.

"Why not just let it be?" a creature that resembled a four-legged turnip asked. "It can't get off, and we can't get to it without losing people. Besides, doing nothing further to provoke it might show our peaceful intent and nature."

"Do *nothing*?" roared the Terran, emotionally upset. "*Provoke* it? What the *hell* do you mean by that—no, don't bother with the translation! How can you suggest such a course?"

"We have over eleven hundred worlds wrecked and ruined in the late war," the creature reminded him. "Our reconstruction will take centuries as it is."

Paul Carleton Savage, the Terran Chairman, stood up and faced them all. "And *I* have four dead planets," he snarled. "Dead. About thirty billion people gone. Two of them among the gentlest, most peaceful people this galaxy has ever produced. Killed. Wiped out in a single, concentrated attack—a few minutes, no more. A few more of those and we'll equal the casualty rate of the entire Civil War! And by who? A mysterious group who's never communicated with us, never given any motivation, never even shown its face. Only one word— one word from Grumiad as they were igniting its atmosphere. One scream from the victims we can't even translate—'Guara'!"

"But they are not totally destructive," a satyrlike creature noted. "Eleven other planets received sudden visits, too. Telikial—its dehydration miraculously reversed. Basiodl—the depleted ozone reinstated in moments, beyond our wildest technology. These people think the Guara are gods!"

A creature that resembled a great grizzly bear raised its head. Being telepathic, it needed no translator.

"One moment!" the bear called forcefully into the shouting match. "It seems that both of you are talking of the same things. What we have here is not a friend, not an enemy, but something alien. No matter how strange we are in form, no matter how wildly different our worlds and cultures, there is a basic commonality among us. We are the products of a consistent evolution that, when stripped of physical and cultural differences, reveals basic similarities in our deepest natures. That is how we can assemble here.

"But for the Guara we have none—their actions are apparently psychopathic, motiveless. Great power applied in what seems to be a random, capricious manner. And yet, races that build such ships as theirs and possess technological skills far in advance of any of ours, don't act randomly. What we are operating from is a lack of knowledge—of knowing who and what they are, where they're from, and why they're here doing what they are doing. We need *facts*, not guesses. I don't want my world to be the next one they decide to eliminate—nor yours, either. I want to *know*, now, while I can still do something."

Savage nodded. "That's really it. This is our first opportunity to learn something about them, to perhaps contact them, to begin to understand them."

"Perhaps if we hadn't attacked them we'd already know," the turnip chided. "Our first face-to-face meeting, and we fired on them!"

"Beside the point," the bear responded brusquely. "We *did* shoot, and the situation is as it is and that's that. Savage, how *do* you think this should be handled? After all, it zapped our ships."

"But not our photo probe," Savage pointed out. "Warships—no. But a small ship, a single passenger, a single landing. One to one. And wired, of course."

They were all silent for a few moments, digesting the idea, imagining themselves down there, on that jagged speck, alone with the unknown. Finally it was the pacifistic turnip that broke the silence.

"Where in the vast galaxy are you going to get someone dumb enough to volunteer for *that*?" it asked.

Following is the official edited transcript of Project Shepherd. The actual elapsed time was 37 hours, 22 minutes, 13 seconds to EOM. The mikes ran continuously for this period, and involve a great deal of technical and routine commentary as well as the expected random comments and long silences, and only those parts directly bearing on the subject Mandeus and the mission are included here. Tapes and complete tran-

scripts are available through the Exchange. All commentary is as recorded via relay at the Base Station, established in stationary orbit approximately sixty million kilometers from the target asteroid, this being about ten million kilometers beyond the minimum known safety range from Guara surface weapons. For annotations, and interpolations see Board minutes PS-345762397, 399, 412, and 436.

MANDEUS: . . . Forty thousand and closing. No sign of any actions toward me or the ship as yet . . . Thirty-five thousand. Looks like a tiny blood clot on the screens; still too far to see it without aid. Thirty thousand. God! That's a weird looking place! Twenty-five. Systems look green and no sign I'm noticed. Twenty. There go the brakes. Readout looks fine here. Fifteen thousand. Doesn't seem any slower but I know it must be. Yes, the dials are starting to become reasonable. Ten thousand. It really *is* a tiny speck—I guess I'll be on it before I see it without magnification. Sure this thing's there? . . . Seven thousand. Sure is dark out there—a dead place to die— no, hell, that doesn't make any sense, but what does? . . . Five thousand. The galaxy's asshole . . . Nothing there but the dark. *Whump!* Little bumpy here, I guess we must be gliding in. What a nightmarish place. The Guara sure can pick them. Wonder if they think this is a resort? . . . One thousand and I still can't see the damned thing. Oh, yes . . . wait a minute. Little nothing about like the head of a pin.

SAVAGE: How's my transmission to you? You're coming in beautifully here.

MANDEUS: Perfect. Wow! Just got a flash like somebody shined a light in the nose camera! That must be our baby.

SAVAGE: Our video signal's getting strong interference. I don't like it. Doesn't show up on audio, though.

MANDEUS: Cheerful thought. Maybe I'm expected. *Whups!* I've been talking too much. The thing's huge out there now, distance . . . let's see . . . *fifteen* kilometers! Looks even uglier up close, but the shadows and dim light make it even worse. Good setting for a ghost story.

Making the swing. How's the picture now? I'm trying to straighten it out.

SAVAGE: Real bad, but forget the adjustments now. I want to know what you're seeing. The energy field shouldn't cloud your direct sight.

MANDEUS: Coming up on it. Funny—it really *does* put out a golden glow. Just over the next range. Here we go—*ow! Ah!* The hell with your theories! It was just like looking directly into a star! Damn near burned my eyeballs out!

SAVAGE: It burned our cameras, anyway. Any permanent damage to you?

MANDEUS: No, no. Things are starting to come back in now, eyes readjusting. I see from the screens it's the same story. Burned out. Think the old boy did it deliberately?

SAVAGE: Remains to be seen. We're putting you down about fifteen hundred meters southeast of him, so that mountain range as you call it will be in the way. All sensors except vision are perfectly normal—interesting. Should have at least generated static or pulses. I'd have to guess he knows you're there and did it deliberately because he knows *I'm* here. You're the eyes of the project now, boy! Make it count!

MANDEUS: Here we go . . . Into the valley of death and all that. *Umph!* A rotten touchdown, damn near jarred my teeth out. Here, I'm going to undo the straps. Any visuals yet? How about the internal cameras? *They* should be working. See me?

SAVAGE: Negative. They're all out. Apparently the damage is to the antenna or replay amplifier. I don't like this. You'll have to be our eyes now. Just remember we're blind when you see something.

MANDEUS: (*sighs*). I'm not sure I like this, makes me feel even more alone than ever. I wonder what he doesn't want you to see?

SAVAGE: Just remember that *you* will see it! That may have sinister implications.

MANDEUS: I'll remember. Doesn't matter much, does it?

[*grimly*] You and I both know why I'm the one that's down here.

SAVAGE:: Now stop that! I want you back alive! If you dwell on that sort of thing you won't be any good to anybody. We've been over this ground before.

MANDEUS: All right, all right, mother. Let me straighten up the housekeeping here. A lot of stuff got banged up all over the place when we landed hard. *Humph!* No gravity to speak of—that's to be expected, of course. Speck like this wouldn't have much anyway. Just lightly tossed a pencil and at the rate it's going it'll hit the floor in about a day and a half. I'm going to have to be careful of quick motions.

SAVAGE: Just be careful, period. The fact that you're there is important—it means that he didn't want to zap you. He's almost certainly got our number and is listening in. If so, he knows you're unarmed, alone, and that we only want to talk.

MANDEUS: I'm sure he's a bright enough boy for you not to have to draw pictures. So now we wait, I guess. How long?

SAVAGE: Give him some time. Right now it looks like he's running the show. If we don't get anything from him in a day or so, you'll have to go calling on him.

MANDEUS: Well, it's been some time now. What's the old saying? Minutes creep like hours or something. I keep looking out at the dead landscape, and the more time I do the more I start dwelling on the dead. Funny. You'd think I could look back on it more dispassionately now, but I can't.

What did the last dodo bird think about?

Other dodo birds, of course...

Hell, I'm not an explorer, an adventurer. I'm a perfume salesman. How and why did I get here, doing this?...

...No change in that glow. Damn! Almost a full day now, and this little chunk is haunted with ghosts. There's five billion ghosts staring at that glow with me. I can feel them, feel their presence, feel them asking what I ask, pleading for the answer we crave.

Why?

Do any of you up there *really* know what it is to be lonely? Can you imagine yourself in a zoo, among nothing but alien life forms, seeing nothing familiar? Can you understand what it's like to know it'll always be that way? That your home's a burnt-out cinder, that not only your world and your civilization but your *kind* is gone?

Oh, we think similarly, most of us. If your race pulls itself up from the slime it shares a kinship with all others who do the same. Universal constants, I guess. 'Nobody's *really* alien,' those glib psychologists tell you. But that's even worse—a disembodied spirit, still roaming the worlds, witnessing happiness it cannot share, seeing love it cannot join, watching children that can never be his children . . .

. . . The glow has changed. I can't really describe it, but the color's different, and the intensity. I wonder if it really is the power pile? Maybe they're over there making repairs. Welding torches? Maybe they're building something . . .

. . . What universal constants do we share with them, I wonder? A body, certainly—they use ships. But—*inside*? What sort of thing could do what they did and have a reason? Is their whole race insane? I swear I can hear Jewell and the twins behind me. More ghosts . . . Sad ghosts? They seem to be pleading . . . Why? Why? . . .

Oh, my God! If they don't come soon I shall have to go ask them. I shall have to look them in the eye or whatever they have and scream it at them. Why? Why did you do such wonderful things for all those planets, some of whom are violent, nasty people? Why did you choose my people to murder? We who outgrew war, tamed our world, lived in happiness without hurting ourselves or others? What harm could we have done? Whom did we wrong? [*A crashing sound*]. Why? God damn you to all nine Hells, *why*? . . .

. . . I'm going out there. It's been almost forty standard hours, and if I don't get out there I'll kill myself.

Might as well go over and scream that they have to complete the set—they missed one who was off-planet. One without the guts to join his friends...I'm suiting up. Looks like a nice day for a walk...

... Pressure down to zero. Lock clear. All secure. I'm pressing the outer lock control now. There she goes! Lord! This crummy speck looks even worse in person!

... Grainy red dust all over. I'll have to walk through a mound of it kicked up by the landing. Seems to be about thirty centimeters deep. I'm in almost to my knee. This'll be tough going. Say, now! That's interesting. I haven't been as ignored as I thought! There are some tracks out here!

SAVAGE: What sort of tracks?

MANDEUS: Looks kind of like a three-runner sled. Long, continuous grooves, very thin and evenly spaced. they sunk all the way in but didn't churn up any dust. Almost like the thing was built for this little pisshole. Wonder why I didn't see them? Are the bastards invisible?

Well, I—what the hell? I've got a suit malfunction! Pressure's going down very slowly!

SAVAGE: Get back in the ship quickly! We're too close to end it like this. There's patching material and such to build a whole new suit in there if we need to.

MANDEUS: Funny...Checked everything. Well, I'm already back in. Door closed, pressure starting to go up. I'll match it to the suit and then remove the thing. Hmmm...Wonder if I'm not permitted to go out? What if I were to try a takeoff right now? How close are they?

... Looking out the window here, and I can't see the tracks. Guess the angle's wrong. If they were reddish and low to the ground they could be zipping all around and I wouldn't hear them. [*loud thump*].

My God! Something's at the airlock!

VOICE: Man! [*The voice is a deep baritone, but sounds strangely altered, as if dozens of identically voiced men were speaking at the same time. It is vocal, not telepathic—the microphone picked it up, and it records.*]

VOICE: [*again, same patient tone*]. Man!

MANDEUS [*nervously*]: I am here. Can you hear me? Are you the Guara?

VOICE: I am of the Guara. As such I answer to the need.

MANDEUS: You—you what to the who? I don't understand.

VOICE: You have an injury to the soul. I must minister to that need.

MANDEUS: You are a missionary?

VOICE: I am a physician.

[*Long pause, no sound except automated equipment*].

MANDEUS: A physician? How can this be? Did we then shoot down a hospital ship?

VOICE: We are all physicians. It is our purpose and our mission. It is our destiny. We minister to those in need.

MANDEUS [*bitterly*]: You kill.

VOICE: We save.

MANDEUS: Then why do you destroy whole worlds? Why?

VOICE: We must maintain the order and the balance. We are mandated to provide to those seekers who require, to cure those diseases which you might not even recognize as such.

MANDEUS: Do you cure by mass murder? Surely those you cure in such a manner are cured indeed!

VOICE: We cleanse. Pretenders must be removed lest their cancer spread and infect the whole of the social body. Only disease is excised, so the whole may grow. As physicians, we must ethically remove the disease.

MANDEUS [*highly emotional*]: But you have destroyed whole civilizations! Billions of innocents! My own... [*sobs*].

VOICE: Is a virus guilty? It seeks only to feed, to reproduce. Is there evil intent in the cell of the body that malfunctions and grows cancerously throughout the system? Are such terms as good and evil relevant in such a case? We do not presume to judge. We diagnose. As for your own people—I recall them not, yet there are so many, our operations so far-flung, that it is not impossible that I overlooked it. Still, I must confess, it puzzles me greatly, as I can detect no abnormality within your mind. You require service, not surgery. I confess to being too lowly for such decisions, yet you I must aid, for you are suffering. What is done may be undone. All that is done is yet to be done. I shall help—and, if possible, should I survive this ordeal, plead your greater cause, as what I can do on my own, with my damaged equipment, is unhappily limited.

MANDEUS [*incredulous*]:. You can—you can restore my people?

VOICE: As I say, my own powers are quite limited. Yet does not she whom you love live yet within you? Can I not restore at least what was yours alone to you?

MANDEUS: What? Wha—?

VOICE [*fading away*]: Will you be my prophet when I come? Will you bear witness to the others? Shall you give testimony that our cause is to the greater good? [*The voice is far away now, and fades. There are only echoes of its eerie tones*].

SAVAGE: Mandeus?

MANDEUS [*distantly*]: Yes?

SAVAGE: Was it there or some sort of projection?

MANDEUS: I can't tell. There was definitely something attached to the airlock. That's obviously how the voice came through.

SAVAGE: Check the windows, man! See what you can see! Quickly!

MANDEUS: Yes, of course, you're right—oh! My God!

SAVAGE [*anxiously*]: What is it? Can you see it?

MANDEUS: Savage! The scene's changed! Either I have been moved, or it has changed things! You—I can't believe it! I must be mad! I must be insane, or dead! My God!

SAVAGE: You're still where you were. What do you see? Damn this vision blackout!

MANDEUS: It's—it's like home, Savage! Rich, green foliage native to my own world, just as I remember it! Bright flowers of purple and gold, swaying in a soft breeze! And—a path! A path of rough stones! I cut and hauled those stones, Savage! It is my own land that I see! I must go out to it!

SAVAGE: Your suit's broken! Don't go out there! It's creating the illusion to get at you!

MANDEUS: The hell with you! If it's illusion, it's the way I want to die! It got our ships, anyway. It could get me easier in a thousand ways. As for my suit—I shall not need it. I'm going out. [*An alarm rings. Mandeus has pressed the inner lock switch without depressurization. A second alarm as he presses the outer lock switch. There is a humming sound as the door slides open.*]

SAVAGE: Mandeus!

MANDEUS: I'm here! There's air! It *is* my home, Savage! I'm going up that path! My house—my family—lies at the other end.

SAVAGE: Keep talking! Tell us what you see!

MANDEUS: There it is! The house! And—in the courtyard...[*voice breaks*]. The children! My precious Jewell! [*Shouts*] Jewell! My love! She turns joyfully! She—my God! What's wrong? That look on her face! The children, screaming, running away. No, no, don't! Come back! It is Mandeus! Jewell! Do not recoil! I—I ...What in God's name is wrong here? There's a noise behind me! The Guara! I—Oh, my God! I remember! *I know!* It's—

There was a sound like none of the listeners could ever imagine, a feeling of immense pain and sadness that went through them, though it had no substance. It reached out to them in its agony from that tiny little asteroid, reached out to their distances and rolled past, until it was lost to space.

Savage and the others sat stunned for a few moments. Suddenly the Terran said, "We're going down."

Slugodium, the science officer, shook its massive, elephantine body from its stupor. "Big energy flare-up, two locations," it reported. "Whatever was giving off those Guara radiations just exploded."

"Let's go!" Savage urged.

They approached cautiously, and all nine members of the monitor team breathed collective sighs of relief when they passed the point where the fighters had been blown apart. Quickly now they neared the dark planetoid.

A brief survey showed that the area of intense radiation was now just that—a bubbling, seething mass without form or substance. They held their breaths again as they slowly came over the jagged outcropping Mandeus called a mountain, and saw the area around the ship.

"Oh, by the gods!" someone swore.

The land, for two or three square kilometers around the ship, was as Mandeus had described. It was green, lush, even close in to the little survey ship whose shiny, rounded nose stuck out from the center of the growth. There was a shimmery bubble of atmosphere around the area which offered no resistance to their landing.

The atmosphere, although a bit rich in oxygen for what the oddest of them were used to, was pronounced fit to breathe, and there was no trace of airborne microorganisms.

They grabbed pistols and disembarked.

The air temperature was about 26°C, and somewhat humid.

Savage shook his head in awe and wonder. "This powerful!" he muttered over and over to himself. "My god! This powerful!"

Slugodium kept looking around. "Stable, too. Incredible. It outlasted its makers. Where does the light come from, I wonder? Phosphorous in the upper air bubble? But, then, where's the heat from?"

A young communications specialist who looked like a tiny, red-furred cross between a monkey and a fox, commented, "If this is what one could do with damaged equipment, no wonder the whole bunch can change a planet! They should be able to create one!"

Savage nodded grimly. "I think they can. Remember, this one said that Mandeus's world could be rebuilt."

"Over here!" Slugodium called urgently. "This burnt-out area! Look!"

They hurried over. The blast had been intense. There was little left of anything.

"Damn!" Slugodium muttered to himself. "Used too much tititherite."

"Can you get anything?" Savage asked.

"Oh, probably, with months of lab work," the science officer replied. "I had no idea that the two would be practically together when and if Mandeus blew himself up. I erred on the side of too much explosive—better, I thought, to overdo than underdo."

"Don't blame yourself," Savage consoled. "You were right. We never expected anything like this. Obviously when the wife-simulacrum saw Mandeus and recoiled in horror, the truth hit him and he turned and ran straight into the thing. With his dreams restored, then abruptly and absolutely snatched from him, it was the only thing left to do."

"Well," interjected Goreath, the psychologist, "at least we know a lot more about them now."

"Do we?" Savage retorted, eyebrows up in surprise, a humorless grin on his face. "Do we, really? Physicians? To what? For what? Why do they destroy those worlds? Do we truly understand anything?"

Goreath nodded grimly. "Of course. Imagine being able to do all this—and be able to die. It must be horrible, much more so than for us. They must live in constant terror. Imagine such godlike power—and mortality. I suspect it's behind everything they do.'"

Savage shrugged. "At least it explains why they never fight."

They continued on the path, and reached the house.

They stopped short. Fear crept through them, and Savage felt it most of all.

"Lord!" he breathed. "We forgot about that!"

Huddling behind a far wall of the courtyard, hunched down, protecting her two children and trembling violently, was Jewell, wife of Mandeus.

Slowly, Savage walked toward them. "Don't be afraid," he said gently. "You've had a lot of pain, but it's over now. It's all over. We won't let anyone hurt you again."

The woman trembled slightly, but summoned a reserve of courage and stood up, facing the strange man.

She looked like an incredibly beautiful Terran woman, small but lean and muscular, like a dancer. Auburn hair fell across her exposed breasts, her skin a golden brown, her eyes sparkling like jewels—and down her back two great, frail-looking faery-wings, transparent and folded like a butterfly's. She seemed to stand poised on tiptoe, like a ballet dancer, and looked with a mixture of puzzlement and caution on Paul Carleton Savage.

"You are like Mandeus," she said at last, her voice sounding like it was made of musical bells. "And yet you are not of our people."

"Yes, like Mandeus," Savage responded softly.

The little fox-monkey communications officer looked up at the giant Slugodium and whispered, "I joined this project as a last-minute replacement, but up until now I thought I understood things. Will someone please tell me what that's all about?"

"Time was of the essence," the science officer replied slowly. "Volunteers were hardly plentiful. So we took a Valiakean android and impressed some basic personality and emotive memory patterns on it. There never was a Mandeus, nor a world like this, nor a Jewell and twins, except in Paul Savage's vivid imagination.

"He made them all up about five days ago . . ."

INTRODUCTION TO
"DANCE BAND ON THE *TITANIC*"

1977 should have been a good year for me in many ways. I had rescued Mirage Press, albeit temporarily, begun a writing career with four novel sales under my belt, and there had been no sign of medical disaster from my earlier problems and the odds were getting better all the time.

Yet, for some reason, I was in a deep depression most of that year and it remains a dark time in my memory. I am subject to occasional deep, depressive moods in which all is extremely black, but this was the longest sustained one. Since an idle brain is the devil's playground, I decided, particularly after the end of teaching in June, to keep myself active and going places. Westercon that year was in Vancouver, B.C., a city I'd never visited, and one that I'd always intended to visit since it is a terminus for a number of ferryboats and headquarters for B.C. Ferries, the largest single ferry corporation in the world.

Now, I'm a real nut on ferryboats. I was born in Baltimore during the last days of Maryland steamboats and ferries. My state is one quarter water, the largest true bay in the U.S.—the Chesapeake—bisects it, and until 1952, the only way to cross it was by ferry. Much of my family hails from Norfolk, Virginia, and we were down there so much it was as if that city was home, too. If you drove down, you just about had to take ferryboats to get into and out of Norfolk; the alternative until 1963 was the car-carrying overnight steamboat down the Chesapeake, The Old Bay Line. I was on steamboats and ferryboats so much in my formative years that I knew those boats, their crews, their routines, even their rivets and boilers, like I knew my own house. There are still hundreds of ferries operating in the U.S. today, including four in Maryland, but none now cross the Bay, and I have to go far afield to recapture the same feelings I had growing up.

Some people like locomotives, some trolley cars, others fancy automobiles. Somewhere there must be somebody who loves Greyhound buses. There are enough steamboat buffs to form the Steamboat Society of America. I love steamboats and their cousins the ferryboats—working boats, each unique, each a real experience. When they let me ride in the locomotive, I might catch the steam train disease, but if you see one antique passenger car, you've seen 'em all. Not so with ferries, where you can often visit the wheelhouse, always talk to the crew as well as the passengers, and often roam bow to stern.

That year of the great depression, 1977, an old friend of mine who happened to be female had a much greater tragedy than I had ever experienced. Her husband had been cold-bloodedly murdered in their apartment and she had come home to find the body. Now she was back home in the Midwest, drinking constantly, and without any real direction or fun left. I offered, no strings, to take her out to Westercon. I was driving, of course—I have often driven cross-country (I once drove from Baltimore to San Francisco for a convention and then drove back via Tijuana and Calgary) and across other countries from Europe to Australia. There's nothing like teaching history and geography (or writing novels) to make any trip deductible. Nor did we go alone; I had a packed car of people willing to share gas and motel to get out west cheaply.

It was a good, enjoyable con, and I rode a bunch of ferries and took a lot of folks aboard with me, converting them to ferryboat fandom as well. On the way back, I made more of the small, obscure ferries, the river ferries that few but the locals know about, and I headed back toward home by the usual circuitous route, eventually bumping into Lake Michigan at Milwaukee, which at that time had a car ferry across to Luddington, Michigan. Since I had to drop the lady home in Michigan, that was the route—but we were early getting back.

Luddington is about three hours drive from the Detroit area, where I had to eventually drop her off, if you go direct, but we were early, and I love doing things the hard way. So I drove north, just the two of us now, to Sault Ste. Marie, stayed there a day or so, then drove east in Ontario for hours, then took a right at Goodman's motel and down a sixty-mile winding, unscenic little road with a one-lane car and railroad bridge for a mile right in the middle. We made our way down to South Beymouth, Ontario, to catch the *Chi Chiman* (Iroquois for *the big canoe*) across Lake Huron to Torbermary and then hours more of flat dullness and into Detroit from the east.

The trip cheered the lady a bit, but did absolutely nothing for me. If anything, I was in a deeper depression (except when riding those boats) than ever. The Huron ferry was the one that fixated me, though. It was far too huge, too grandiose, to be on that run. The ship in the following story is an accurate description of the *Chi Chiman*, taken from experience and from the ship's specs listed in its descriptive brochure.

This is not to say that the ship is unusual for major ferries —it's about the same size as the ones in B.C. or the CN ones to Prince Edward Island—but those are ocean-going ferries connecting provinces or major population centers. Here was one just as large just to connect two little towns that were hard to get to and not worth the bother. It doesn't even cross Lake Huron—just Georgian Bay at the narrowest part. The description of the towns and the ferry docks in the story is also accurate. I remember seeing that ship—it would be somehow wrong to call this one a boat even though by definition it is—round the point for the first time, gleaming white, and thinking, *That ship has no right to be here!*

And, even though it was indeed a Wednesday evening, it disgorged a full load of cars and trucks all apparently going to this nowhere little town miles from anywhere else, then loaded a nearly full load for the return trip, a load that had also somehow materialized from nowhere since we'd arrived. All for an hour-and-forty-minute local ferry run.

After dropping off the lady, I drove home, all the time thinking to myself about that boat. It fascinated me. It's still incredible that a ship the size of the big ones running from

Vancouver Island to Vancouver itself should be on a nowhere run like that, and more incredible that it does that kind of business. This combined in my head with my depressed mood and the sad lady I'd tried to cheer up, and when I got home and slept off the drive, I went immediately to the typewriter and wrote the next story in two relatively brief sessions broken only by sleep and social necessities. Not one word was rewritten—the story simply wrote itself. I wish others would write themselves like this one did, but it's the only one.

I sent "Dance Band" to George Scithers, then editing *Isaac Asimov's SF Magazine*, partly because we were old friends, partly because he'd been bugging me to send him a story, and mostly, I suspect, because George is as passionate about trolley cars as I am about ferryboats, and I knew he would understand. He did, although suggesting some changes most of which I rejected. He bought it anyway.

Don Wollheim and Art Saha picked the story for their annual *Year's Best SF 1978*, and my book club curse continued. That series has been a book club selection since it was initiated in 1968; only one volume in the entire series to date was not picked up by the clubs and had only a paperback run in this country. Guess which one. The story in *Best SF* is textually very slightly different, and I think superior, to the original magazine version, and is the one used here. It is word for word as I wrote it. Since then, the story has been anthologized elsewhere in the U.S. and in Europe. It is the story I tend to read whenever a convention asks me to do a reading, and it's remarkable—much of the audience who were reading SF in the late '70s remembers the story fondly, but to a one they never remembered, or bothered to note, that I wrote it. It remains, for me, my all-time personal favorite of all the things I have written, long or short, and is the only thing of mine I've ever reread that I didn't sit there cursing and wishing I could rewrite it or tried to mentally rewrite as I read it.

Immediately after I wrote and sent off "Dance Band," I turned to writing a novel. That one, too, turned out to be very downbeat and melancholy, although it remains something of a personal favorite of mine, called *Dancers in the Afterglow*. As with all my novels so far (and at this writing), it's still in print and available, although not one of my popular bestsellers. Don't read it while you have Harry Chapin tunes on the stereo, though, or you'll slit your wrists.

More significant, I think, is the level of hope in this story in the face of my depression. Maybe it was therapy; I don't know. I sent the lady in question a signed manuscript. I have no idea what she's doing now, but I have hope for her as well. If she's doing okay, I like to think that the sentiments in this story might have had something to do with that. In the end, it's what I was trying to tell her during that long trip and couldn't successfully do at that time.

I have often thought of going back to the *Orcas*, possibly making a novel out of it using "Dance Band" as a centerpiece and foundation. I may well do it, but I like the story enough that I am adamant that the larger work (or subsequent stories) be at least up to this one. So far I haven't found sufficient good material here to do that, although a hundred *schlock* stories come to mind. It's really quite a "little" story about two people interacting, but there are momentous and mysterious things going on in the background.

It would be interesting to know just what the Bluewater Corporation really is and just how much power it has, though, wouldn't it?

It is coincidence that the story's title is the same as the Harry Chapin song of the same year. The story was written before I'd heard or knew of the song. I think we both picked the title for the same reason.

Possibly because of my love affair with ships and boats, the *Titanic* story has always fascinated and still grips me, but one scene in particular always gets to me: the sight of the ship's band, there on the decks as the ship was sinking, not panicking, not running for their life, but doing their duty by sitting there and playing and giving strength and comfort to those who were about to die with them and the lucky few in the boats. I don't know if Mike Dalton plays an instrument, but if he had been back there on the *Titanic*, he'd have been right there with them, keeping time.

DANCE BAND ON THE *TITANIC*

THE GIRL WAS COMMITTING SUICIDE AGAIN ON THE lower afterdeck. They'd told me I'd get used to it, but after four times I could still only pretend to ignore it, pretend that I didn't hear the body go over, hear the splash, and the scream as she was sucked into the screws. It was all too brief and becoming all too familiar.

When the scream was cut short, as it always was, I continued walking forward, toward the bow. I would be needed there to guide the spotlight with which the Captain would have to spot the buoys to get us all safely into Southport harbor.

It was a clear night; once at the bow I could see the stars in all their glory, too numerous to count, or spot familiar constellations. It's a sight that's known and loved by all those who follow the sea, and it had a special meaning for we, who manned the *Orcas*, for the stars were immutable, the one unchanging part of our universe.

I checked the lines, the winch, and ties in the chained-off portion of the bow, then notified the Captain by walkie-talkie that all was ready. He gave me "Very well," and told me that we'd be on the mark in five minutes. This gave me a few moments to relax, adjust my vision to the darkness, and look around.

The bow is an eerie place at night for all its beauty; there is an unreality about a large ferryboat in the dark. Between where I stood on station and the bridge super- structure towering above me there was a broad area always crowded with people in warm weather. The bridge—dominating the aft field of vision, a ghostly, unlit gray-white monolith, reflecting the moonlight with an almost unreal cast and glow. A silent, spinning radar mast on top, and the funnel, end-on, in back of the bridge, with its wing supports and mast giving it a futur- istic cast, only made the scene more alien, more awe- some.

I glanced around at the people on the deck. Not as many as usual, but then it was very late, and there was a chill in the air. I saw a few familiar faces, and there was some lateral shift in focus on a number of them, indicat- ing that I was seeing at least three levels of reality that night.

Now, that last is kind of hard to explain. I'm not sure whether I understand it, either, but I well remember when I applied for this job, and the explanations I got then.

Working deck on a ferryboat is a funny place for a former English teacher, anyway. But, while I'd been, I like to think, a good teacher, I was in constant fights with the administration over their lax discipline, stuffed- shirt attitudes toward teaching and teachers, and their general incompetence. The educational system isn't made for mavericks; it's designed to make everyone conform to bureaucratic ideals which the teacher is sup- posed to exemplify. One argument too many, I guess, and there I was, an unemployed teacher in a time when there are too many teachers. So I drifted. I'd lost my parents years before and there were no other close rela- tives, so I had no responsibilities. I'd always loved ferry- boats—raised on them, loved them with the same passion some folks like trains and trolley cars and such —and when I discovered an unskilled job opening on the old Delaware ferry I took it. The fact that I was an ex- teacher actually helped; ferry companies like to hire people who relate well to the general public. After all, deck duty is hectic when the ferry's docking or docked, but for the rest of the time you just sort of stand there, and every tourist and traveler in the world wants to talk. If you aren't willing to talk back and enjoy it, forget ferryboats.

And I met Joanna. I'm not sure if we were in love— maybe *I* was, but I'm pretty sure Joanna wasn't capable of loving anyone. Like all the other men in her life, I was just convenient. For a while things went smoothly—I had a job I liked, and we shared the rent. She had a little daughter she doted on, father unknown, and little Harmony and I hit it off, too. We all gave each other what each needed.

It lasted a little more than a year.

In the space of three weeks my neat, comfortable, complacent world came apart. First she threw that damned party while I was working, and a cigarette or something was left, and the apartment burned. The fire department managed to get Joanna out—but little Harmony had been asleep in a far room and they never got to her through the smoke.

I tried to comfort her, tried to console her, but I guess I was too full of my own life, my own self-importance in her reality, that I just didn't see the signs. A couple of weeks after the fire she'd seemed to brighten up, act more like her normal self.

And, one evening, while I worked on the boat, she hanged herself.

Just a week later that damned bridge-tunnel put the ferry out of business, too. I'd known it was coming, of course, but I'd made few plans beyond the closing—I'd figured I could live off Joanna for a while and we'd make our decisions together.

Now here I was alone, friendless, jobless, and feeling guilty as hell. I seriously thought about ending it all myself about then, maybe going down to the old ferryboat and blowing it and me to hell in one symbolic act of togetherness. But, then, just when I'd sunk to such depths, I got this nice, official-looking envelope in the mail from something called the Bluewater Corporation, Southport, Maine. Just a funny logo, some blue water with an odd, misty-looking shape of a ship in it.

"Dear Mr. Dalton," the letter read. "We have just learned of the closing of the Delaware service, and we are in need of some experienced ferry people. After reviewing your qualifications, we believe that you might fit nicely into our operation, which, we guarantee, will not be put out of business by bridge or tunnel. If this prospect interests you, please come to Southport terminal at your earliest convenience for a final interview. Looking forward to seeing you soon, I remain, sincerely yours, Herbert V. Penobscot, Personnel Manager, Bluewater Corp."

I just stood there staring at the thing for I don't know how long. A ferry job! That alone should have excited me, yet I wondered about it, particularly that line about "reviewing my qualifications" and "final interview." Funny terms. I could see why they'd look for experienced people, and all ferry folk knew when a line was closed and would naturally look for their own replacements there, but—why me? I hadn't applied to them, hadn't even heard of them or their line—or, for that matter, of Southport, Maine, either. Obviously they had some way of preselecting their people—very odd for this kind of a business.

I scrounged up an old atlas and tried to find it. The letterhead said "Southport—St. Michael—The Island," but I could find nothing about any such place in the atlas or almanac. If the letterhead hadn't looked so convincing, I'd have sworn somebody was putting me on. As it was, I had nothing else to do, and it beat drinking myself to death, so I hitchhiked up.

It wasn't easy finding Southport, I'll tell you. Even people in nearby towns had never heard of it. The whole town was about a dozen houses, a seedy ten-unit motel, a hot dog stand, and a very small ferry terminal with a standard but surprisingly large ferry ramp and parking area.

I couldn't believe the place warranted a ferry when I

saw it; you had to go about sixty miles into the middle of nowhere on a road the highway department had deliberately engineered to miss some of the world's prettiest scenery, and had last paved sometime before World War II, just to get there.

There was a light on in the terminal, so I went in. A grayhaired man, about fifty, was in the ticket office, and I went over and introduced myself. He looked me over carefully, and I knew I didn't present a very good appearance.

"Sit down, Mr. Dalton," he offered in a tone that was friendly but businesslike. "My name's McNeil. I've been expecting you. This really won't take long, but the final interview includes a couple of strange questions. If you don't want to answer any of them, feel free, but I must ask them nonetheless. Will you go along with me?"

I nodded and he fired away. It was the damndest job interview I'd ever had. He barely touched on my knowledge of ferries except to ask whether it mattered to me that the *Orcas* was a single-bridge, twin-screw affair, not a double-ender like I'd been used to. It still loaded on one end and unloaded on the other, though, through a raisable bow, and a ferry was a ferry to me and I told him so.

Most of the questions were of a personal nature, my family and friends, my attitudes, and some were downright *too* personal.

"Have you ever contemplated or attempted suicide?" he asked me in the same tone he'd use to ask if you brushed your teeth in the morning.

I jumped. "What's *that* have to do with anything?" I snapped. After all this I was beginning to see why the job was still open.

"Just answer the question," he responded, sounding almost embarrassed. "I told you I had to ask them all."

Well, I couldn't figure out what this was all about, but I finally decided, what the hell, I had nothing to lose and it was a beautiful spot to work.

"Yes," I told him. "Thought about it, anyway." And I told him why. He just nodded thoughtfully, jotted something on a preprinted form, and continued. His next question was worse.

"Do you now believe in ghosts, devils, and/or demonic forces?" he asked in that same routine tone.

I couldn't suppress a chuckle. "You mean the ship's haunted?"

He didn't smile back. "Just answer the question, please."

"No," I responded. "I'm not very religious."

Now there was a wisp of a smile there. "And suppose, with your hard-nosed rationalism, you ran into one? Or a whole bunch of them?" He leaned forward, smile gone. "Even an entire shipload of them?"

It was impossible to take this seriously. "What kind of ghosts?" I asked him. "Chain rattlers? White sheets? Foul fiends spouting hateful gibberish?"

He shook his head negatively. "No, ordinary people, for the most part. Dressed a little odd, perhaps; talking a little odd, perhaps, but not really very odd at all. Nice folks, typical passengers."

Cars were coming in now, and I glanced out the window at them. Ordinary-looking cars, ordinary-looking people—campers, a couple of tractor-trailer rigs, like that. Lining up. A U.S. customs man came from the direction of the motel and started talking to some of them.

"They don't look like ghosts to me," I told McNeil.

He sighed. "Look, Mr. Dalton, I know you're an educated man. I have to go out and start selling fares now. She'll be in in about forty minutes, and we've only got a twenty-minute layover. When she's in and loading, go aboard. Look her over. You'll have free rein of the ship. Take the complete round trip, all stops. It's about four hours over, twenty minutes in, and a little slower back. Don't get off the ship, though. Keep an open mind. If you're the one for the *Orcas*, and I think you are, we'll finish our talk when you get back." He got up, took out a cash drawer and receipt load, and went to the door, then turned back to me. "I *hope* you're the one," he said wearily. "I've interviewed over three hundred people and I'm getting sick of it."

We shook hands on that cryptic remark and I wandered around while he manned his little booth and processed the cars, campers, and trucks. A young woman came over from one of the houses and handled the few people who didn't have cars, although how they ever got to Southport I was at a loss to know.

The amount of business was nothing short of incredible. St. Michael was in Nova Scotia, it seemed, and there were the big runs by CN from a couple of places and the Swedish one out of Portland to compete for any business. The fares were reasonable but not cheap enough to drive this far out of the way for—and to get to Southport you *had* to drive far out of your way.

I found a general marine atlas of the Fundy region in McNeil's office and looked at it. Southport made it, but just barely. No designation of it as a ferry terminal, though, and no funny broken line showing a route.

For the life of me I couldn't find a St. Michael, Nova Scotia—nor a St. Clement's Island, either—the midstop that the schedule said it made.

There were an *awful* lot of cars and trucks out there now—it looked like rush hour in Manhattan. Where *had* all those people come from?

And then there was the blast of a great air horn and I rushed out for my first view of the *Orcas*—and I was stunned.

That ship, I remembered thinking, *has no right to be here. Not here, not on this run.*

It was *huge*—all gleaming white, looking brand-new, more like a cruise ship than a ferryboat. I counted three upper decks, and, as I watched, a loud clanging bell sounded electrically on her and her enormous bow lifted, revealing a grooved raising ramp, something like the bow of an old LST. It docked with very little trouble, revealing space for well over a hundred cars and trucks, with small side ramps for a second level available if needed. I learned later that it was 396 feet long—longer than a football field by a third!—and could take over two hundred major vehicles and twelve hundred passengers.

It was close to sundown on a weekday, but they

loaded more than fifty vehicles, including a dozen campers, and eight big trucks. Where had they all come from, I wondered again. And why?

I walked on with the passengers, still in something of a daze, and went up top. The lounges were spacious and comfortable, the seats all padded and reclining. There was a large cafeteria, a newsstand, and a very nice bar at the stern of passenger deck 2. The next deck had another lounge section and a number of staterooms up front, while the top level had the bridge, crew's quarters, and a solarium.

It was fancy; and, after it backed out, lowered its bow, and started pouring it on after clearing the harbor lights, the fastest damned thing I could remember, too. Except for the slight swaying and the rhythmic thrumming of the twin diesels you hardly knew you were moving. It was obviously using enormous stabilizers.

The sun was setting and I walked through the ship, just looking and relaxing. As darkness fell and the shoreline receded into nothingness, I started noticing some very odd things, as I'd been warned.

First of all, there seemed to be a whole lot more people on board than I'd remembered loading, and there certainly hadn't been any number staying on from the last run. They all looked real and solid enough, and very ordinary, but there was something decidedly weird about them, too.

Many seemed to be totally unaware of each other's existence, for one thing. Some seemed to shimmer occasionally, others were a little blurred or indistinct to my eyes no matter how I rubbed them.

And, once in a while, they'd walk through each other.

Yes, I'm serious. One big fellow in a flowered aloha shirt and brown pants carrying a tray of soft drinks from the cafeteria to his wife and three kids in the lounge didn't seem to notice this woman in a white tee shirt and jeans walking right into him, nor did she seem aware of him, either.

And they met, and I braced for the collision and spilled drinks—and it didn't happen. They walked right *through* each other, just as if they didn't exist, and continued obliviously on. Not one drop of soda was spilled, not one spot of mustard was splotched.

There were other things, too. Most of the people were dressed normally for summer, but occasionally I'd see people in fairly heavy coats and jackets. Some of the fashions were different, too—some people were over-dressed in old-fashioned styles, others wildly under-dressed, a couple of the women frankly wearing nothing but the bottoms of string bikinis and a see-through short cape of some kind.

I know I couldn't take my eyes off them for a while, until I got the message that they knew they were being stared at and didn't particularly like it. But they were generally ignored by the others.

There were strange accents, too. Not just the expected Maine twang and Canadian accents, or even just the French Canadian accents—those were normal. But there were some really odd ones, ones where I picked out only a few words, which sounded like English, French, Spanish, and Nordic languages all intermixed and often with weird results.

And men with pigtails and long, braided hair, and women with shaved heads or, occasionally, beards.

It was weird.

Frankly, it scared me a little, and I found the purser and introduced myself.

The officer, a good-looking young man named Gifford Hanley, a Canadian from his speech, seemed delighted that I'd seen all this and not the least bit disturbed.

"Well, well, well!" he almost beamed. "Maybe we've found our new man at last, eh? Not bloody soon enough, either! We've been working short-handed for too long and it's getting to the others."

He took me up to the bridge—one of the most modern I'd ever seen—and introduced me to the captain and helmsman. They all asked me what I thought of the *Orcas* and how I liked the sea, and none of them would answer my questions on the unusual passengers.

Well, there *was* a St. Clement's Island. A big one,

too, from the looks of it, and a fair amount of traffic getting off and wanting on. Some of the vehicles that got on were odd, too; many of the cars looked unfamiliar in design, the trucks also odd, and there were even several horse-drawn wagons!

The island had that same quality as some of the passengers, too. It never seemed to be quite in focus just beyond the ferry terminal, and lights seemed to shift, so that where I thought there were houses or a motel suddenly they were somewhere else, of a different intensity. I was willing to swear that the motel had two stories; later it seemed over on the left, and four stories high, then further back, still later, with a single story.

Even the lighthouse as we sped out of the harbor changed; one time it looked very tall with a house at its base; then, suddenly, it was short and tubby, then an automated light that seemed to be out in the water with no sign of an island.

This continued for most of the trip. St. Michael looked like a carbon copy of Southport, the passengers and vehicles as bizarre—and numerous—and there seemed to be a lot of customs men in different uniforms dashing about, totally ignoring some vehicles while processing others.

The trip back was equally strange. The newsstand contained some books and magazines that were odd to say the least, and papers with strange names and stranger headlines.

This time there were even Indians aboard, speaking odd tongues. Some looked straight out of *The Last of the Mohicans*, complete with wild haircut, others dressed from little to heavy, despite the fact that it was July and very warm and humid.

And, just before we were to make the red and green channel markers and turn into Southport, I saw the girl die for the first time.

She was dressed in red tee shirt, yellow shorts, and sandals; she had long brown hair, was rather short and stocky, and wore oversized granny glasses.

I wasn't paying much attention, really, just watching

her looking over the side at the wake, when, before I could even cry out, she suddenly climbed up on the rail and plunged in, very near the stern.

I screamed, and heard her body hit the water and then heard her howl of terror as she dropped close enough so that the propwash caught her, sucked her under, and cut her to pieces.

Several people on the afterdeck looked at me quizzically, but only one or two seemed to realize that a woman had just died.

There was little I could do, but I ran back to Hanley, breathless.

He just nodded sadly.

"Take it easy, man," he said gently. "She's dead, and there's no use going back for the body. Believe me, we *know*. It won't be there."

I was shocked, badly upset. "How do you know that?" I snapped.

"Because we did it every time the last four times she killed herself and we never found the body then, either," he replied sadly.

I had my mouth open, ready to retort, to say *something*, but he got up, put on his officer's hat and coat, and said, "Excuse me. I have to supervise the unloading," and walked out.

As soon as I got off the ship it was like some sort of dreamy fog had lifted from me. Everything looked suddenly bright and clear, and the people and vehicles looked normal. I made my way to the small ferry terminal building.

When they'd loaded and the ship was gone again, I waited for McNeil to return to his office. It looked much the same really, but a few things seemed different. I couldn't quite put my finger on it, but there *was* something odd—like the paneling had been rosewood before, and was now walnut. Small things, but nagging ones.

McNeil came back after seeing the ship clear. It ran almost constantly, according to the schedule.

I glanced out the window as he approached and noticed uniformed customs men checking out the debarked vehicles. They seemed to have different uniforms than I'd remembered.

Then the ticket agent entered the office and I got another shock. He had a beard.

No, it was the same man, all right. No question about it. But the man I'd talked to less than nine hours before had been clean-shaven.

I turned to where the navigation atlas lay, just where I'd put it, still open to the Southport page.

It showed a ferry line from Southport to a rather substantial St. Clement's Island now. But nothing to Nova Scotia.

I turned to the bearded McNeil, who was watching me with mild amusement in his eyes.

"What the *hell* is going on here?" I demanded.

He went over and sat down in his swivel chair. "Want the job?" he asked. "It's yours if you do."

I couldn't believe his attitude. "I want an explanation, damn it!" I fumed.

He chuckled. "I told you I'd give you one if you wanted. Now, you'll have to bear with me, since I'm only repeating what the Company tells me, and I'm not sure I have it all clear myself."

I sat down in the other chair. "Go ahead," I told him.

He sighed. "Well, let's start off by saying that there's been a Bluewater corporation ferry on this run since the mid-1800s—steam packet at first, of course. The *Orcas* is the eleventh ship in the service, put on a year and a half ago."

He reached over, grabbed a cigarette, lit it, and continued.

"Well, anyway, it was a normal operation until about 1910 or so. That's when they started noticing that their counts were off, that there seemed to be more passengers than the manifests called for, different freight, and all that. As it continued, the crews started noticing more and more of the kind of stuff you saw, and things got crazy for them, too. Southport was a big fishing and lobstering town then—nobody does that any more, the whole economy's the ferry.

"Well, anyway, one time this crewman goes crazy, says the woman in his house isn't his wife. A few days later another comes home to find that he has four kids—and he was only married a week before. And so on."

I felt my skin starting to crawl slightly.

"So, they send some big shots up. The men are absolutely nuts, but *they* believe what they claim. Soon everybody who works the ship is spooked, and this can't be dismissed. The experts go for a ride and can't find anything wrong, but now two of the crewmen claim that it *is* their wife, or their kid, or somesuch. Got to be a pain, though, getting crewmen. We finally had to center on loners—people without family, friends, or close personal ties. It kept getting worse each trip. Had a hell of a time keeping men for a while, and that's why it's so hard to recruit new ones."

"You mean the trip drives them crazy?" I asked unbelievingly.

He chuckled. "Oh, no. *You're* sane. It's the rest of 'em. That's the problem. And it gets worse and worse each season. But the trip's *extremely* profitable. So we try to match the crew to the ship and hope they'll accept it. If they do it's one of the best damned ferry jobs there is."

"But what causes it?" I managed. "I mean—I saw people dressed outlandishly. I saw other people walk *through* each other! I even saw a girl commit suicide, and nobody seemed to notice!"

McNeil's face turned grim. "So that's happened again. Too bad. Maybe someday there'll be some chance to save her."

"Look," I said, exasperated. "There must be some explanation for all this. There *has* to be!"

The ticket agent shrugged and stubbed out his cigarette.

"Well, some of the company experts studied it. They say nobody can tell for sure, but the best explanation is that there are a lot of different worlds—different Earths, you might say—all existing one on top of the other, but you can't see any one except the one you're in. Don't ask me how that's possible or how they came up with it, it just *is*, that's all. Well, they say that in some worlds folks don't exist at all, and in others they are different places or doing different things—like getting married to somebody else or somesuch. In some, Canada's still British, in some she's a republic, in others she's a fragmented batch of countries, and in one or two she's part of the U.S. Each one of these places has a different history."

"And this one boat serves them all?" I responded, not accepting a word of that cazy story. "How is that possible?"

McNeil shrugged again. "Who knows? Hell, I don't even understand why that little light goes on in here when I flip the switch. Do most people? I just sell tickets and lower the ramp. I'll tell you the Company's version, that's all. They say that there's a crack—maybe one of many, maybe the only one. The ship's route just happens to parallel that crack, and this allows you to go between the worlds. Not one ship, of course—twenty or more, one for each world. But, as long as they keep the same schedule, they overlap—and can cross into one or more of the others. If you're on the ship in all those worlds, then you cross, too. Anyone coexisting with the ship in multiple words can see and hear not only the one he's in but the ones nearest him, too. People perception's a little harder the farther removed the world you're in is from theirs."

"And you believe this?" I asked him, still disbelieving.

"Who knows? Got to believe *something* or you'll go nuts," he replied pragmatically. "Look, did you get to St. Michael this trip?"

I nodded. "Yeah. Looked pretty much like this place."

He pointed to the navigation atlas. "Try and find it. You won't. Take a drive up through New Brunswick and around to the other side. It doesn't exist. In this world, the *Orcas* goes from here to St. Clement's Island and back again. I understand from some of the crew that sometimes Southport doesn't exist, sometimes the Island doesn't, and so forth. And there are so many countries involved I don't even count."

I shook my head, refusing to accept all this. And yet, it made a crazy kind of sense. These people didn't see each other because they were in different worlds. The girl committed suicide five times because she did it in five different worlds—or was it five different girls? It also explained the outlandish dress, the strange mixture of vehicles, people, accents.

"But how come the crew sees people from many worlds and the passengers don't?" I asked him.

McNeil sighed. "That's the other problem. We have to find people who would be up here, working on the *Orcas*, in every world we service. More people's lives parallel than you'd think. The passengers—well, they generally don't exist on a particular run except once. The very few who do still don't take the trip in every world we service. I guess once or twice it's happened that we've had a passenger cross over, but, if so, we've never heard of it."

"And how come I'm here in so many worlds?" I asked him.

McNeil smiled. "You were recruited, of course. The Corporation has a tremendous, intensive recruiting effort involving ferry lines and crewmembers. When they spot one, like you, in just the right circumstance in all worlds, they recruit you—all of you. An even worse job than you'd think, since every season one or two new Bluewater Corporations put identical ferries on this run, or shift routes and overlap with ours. Then we have to make sure the present crew can serve them, too, by recruiting your twin on those worlds."

Suddenly I reached over, grabbed his beard, and yanked.

"*Ouch!* Dammit!" he cried and shoved my hand away.

"I—I'm sorry—I—" I stammered.

He shook his head and grinned. "That's all right, son. You're about the seventh person to do that to me in the last five yers. I guess there are a lot of varieties of *me*, too."

I thought about all that traffic. "Do others know of this?" I asked him. "I mean, is there some sort of hidden commerce between the worlds on this ferry?"

He grinned. "I'm not supposed to answer that one," he said carefully. "But, what the hell. Yes, I think—no, I *know* there is. After all, the shift of people and ships is constant. You move one notch each trip if all of you take the voyage. Sometimes up, sometimes down. If that's true, and if they can recruit a crew that fits the requirements, why not truck drivers? A hell of a lot of truck traffic through here year 'round, you know. No reduced winter service. And some of the rigs are really kinda strange-looking." He sighed. "I only know this—in a couple of hours I'll start selling fares again, and I'll sell a half dozen or so to St. Michael—and *there is no St. Michael*. It isn't even listed on my schedule or maps. I doubt if the Corporation's actually the trader, more the middleman in the deal. But they sure as hell don't make their millions off fares alone."

It was odd the way I was accepting it. Somehow, it seemed to make sense, crazy as it was.

"What's to keep me from using this knowledge somehow?" I asked him. "Maybe bring my own team of experts up?"

"Feel free," McNeil answered. "Unless they overlap they'll get a nice, normal ferry ride. And if you can make a profit, go ahead, as long as it doesn't interfere with Bluewater's cash flow. The *Orcas* cost the company over twenty-four million *reals* and they want it back."

"Twenty-four million *what*?" I shot back.

"*Reals*," he replied, taking a bill from his wallet. I looked at it. It was printed in red, and had a picture of someone very ugly labeled "Prince Juan XVI" and an official seal from the "Bank of New Lisboa." I handed it back.

"What country are we in?" I asked uneasily

"Portugal," he replied casually. "Portuguese America, actually, although only nominally. So many of us Yankees have come in you don't even have to speak Portuguese any more. They even print the local bills in Anglish, now."

Yes, that's what he said. Anglish.

"It's the best ferryboat job in the world, though," McNeil continued. "For someone without ties, that is. You'll meet more different kinds of people from more cultures than you can ever imagine. Three runs on, three off—in as many as twenty-four different variations of these towns, all unique. And a month off in winter to see a little of a different world each time. Never mind whether you buy the explanation—you've seen the results, you know what I say is true. Want the job?"

"I'll give it a try," I told him, fascinated. I wasn't sure if I *did* buy the explanation, but I certainly had something strange and fascinating here.

"Okay, there's twenty *reals* advance," McNeil said, handing me a purple bill from the cash box. "Get some dinner if you didn't eat on the ship and get a good night's sleep at the motel—the Company owns it so there's no charge—and be ready to go aboard at four tomorrow afternoon."

I got up to leave.

"Oh, and Mr. Dalton," he added, and I turned to face him.

"Yes?"

"If, while on shore, you fall for a pretty lass, decide to settle down, then do it—*but don't go back on that ship again*! Quit. If you don't she's going to be greeted by a stranger, and you might never find her again."

"I'll remember," I assured him.

The job was everything McNeil promised and more. The scenery was spectacular, the people an ever-changing, fascinating group. Even the crew changed slightly— a little shorter sometimes, a little fatter or thinner, beards and mustaches came and went with astonishing rapidity, and accents varied enormously. It didn't matter; you soon adjusted to it as a matter of course, and all shipboard experiences were in common, anyway.

It was like a tight family after a while, really. And there were women in the crew, too, ranging from their twenties to the early fifties, not only in food and bar service but as deckhands and the like as well. Occasionally this was a little unsettling, since, in two or three cases out of 116, they were men in one world, women in another. You got used to even that. It was probably more unsettling for them; they were distinct people, and *they* didn't change sex. The personalities and personal histories tended to parallel, regardless, though, with only a few minor differences.

And the passengers! Some were really amazing. Even seasons were different for some of them, which explained the clothing variations. Certainly what constituted fashion and moral behavior was wildly different, as different as what they ate and the places they came from.

And yet, oddly, people were people. They laughed, and cried, and ate and drank and told jokes—some rather strange, I'll admit—and snapped pictures and all the other things people did. They came from places where the Vikings settled Nova Scotia (called Vinland, naturally), where Nova Scotia was French, or Spanish, or Portuguese, or very, very English. Even one in which Nova Scotia had been settled by Lord Baltimore and called Avalon.

Maine was as wild or wilder. There were two Indian nations running it, the U.S., Canada, Britain, France, Portugal, and lots of variations, some of which I never have gotten straight. There was also a temporal difference sometimes—some people were rather futuristic, with gadgets I couldn't even understand. One truck I loaded was powered by some sort of solar power and carried a cargo of food service robots. Some others were behind—still mainly horses, or oldtime cars and trucks. I am not certain even now if they were running at different speeds from us or whether some inventions had simply been made in some worlds and not in others.

And, McNeil was right. Every new summer season added at least one more. The boat was occasionally so crowded to our crew eyes that we had trouble making

our way from one end of the ship to the other. Watching
staterooms unload was also wild—it looked occasionally
like the circus clown act, where 50 clowns get out of a
Volkswagen.

And there *was* some sort of trade between the worlds.
It was quickly clear that Bluewater Corporation was behind most of it, and that this was what made the line so
profitable.

And, just once, there was a horrible, searing pain that
hit the entire crew, and a modern world we didn't meet
any more after that, and a particular variation of the
crew we never saw again. And the last newspapers from
that world had told of a coming war.

There was also a small crew turnover, of course.
Some went on vacation and never returned, some returned but would not reboard the ship. The Company
was understanding, and it usually meant some extra
work for a few weeks until they found someone new and
could arrange for them to come on.

The stars were fading a little now, and I shined the
spot over to the red marker for the Captain. He acknowledged seeing it, and made his turn in, the lights of Southport coming into view and masking the stars a bit.

I went through the motions mechanically, raising the
bow when the Captain hit the mark, letting go the bow
lines, checking the clearances, and the like. I was thinking about the girl.

We knew that people's lives in the main did parallel
from world to world. Seven times now she'd come
aboard, seven times she'd looked at the white wake, and
seven times she'd jumped to her death.

Maybe it was the temporal dislocation, maybe she
just reached the same point at different stages, but she
was always there and she always jumped.

I'd been working the *Orcas* three years, had some
strange experiences, and generally pleasurable ones. For
the first time I had a job I liked, a family of sorts in the
crew, and an ever-changing assortment of people and
places for a threepoint ferry run. In that time we'd lost

one world and gained by our figures three others. That was 26 variants.

Did that girl exist in all 26? I wondered. Would we be subjected to that sadness 19 more times? Or more, as we picked up new worlds?

Oh, I'd tried to find her before she jumped in the past, yes. But she hadn't been consistent, except for the place she chose. We did three runs a day, two crews, so it was six a day more or less. She did it at different seasons, in different years, dressed differently.

You couldn't cover them all.

Not even all the realities of the crew of all worlds, although I knew that we were essentially the same people on all of them and that I—the other me's—were also looking.

I don't even know why I was so fixated, except that I'd been to that point once myself, and I'd discovered that you *could* go on, living with emotional scars, and find a new life.

I didn't even know what I'd say and do if I *did* see her early. I only knew that, if I did, she damned well wasn't going to go over the stern that trip.

In the meantime, my search for her when I could paid other dividends. I prevented a couple of children from going over through childish play, as well as a drunk, and spotted several health problems as I surveyed the people. One turned out to be a woman in advanced labor, and the first mate and I delivered our first child—our first, but the *Orcas'* nineteenth. We helped a lot of people, really, with a lot of different matters.

They were all just spectres, of course; they got on the boat often without us seeing them, and they disembarked for all time the same way. There were some regulars, but they were few. And, for them, we were a ghost crew, there to help and to serve.

But, then, isn't that the way you think of anybody in a service occupation? Firemen are firemen, not individuals; so are waiters, cops, street sweepers, and all the rest. Categories, not people.

We sailed from Point A to Point C stopping at B, and it was our whole life.

And then, one day in July of last year, I spotted her.

She was just coming on board at St. Clement's—that's possibly why I hadn't noticed her before. We backed into St. Clement's, and I was on the bow lines. But we were short, having just lost a deckhand to a nice-looking fellow in the English colony of Annapolis Royal, and it was my turn to do some double duty. So, there I was, routing traffic on the ship when I saw this little rounded station wagon go by and saw *her* in it.

I still almost missed her; I hadn't expected her to be with another person, another woman, and we were loading the Vinland existence, so in July they were more accurately in a state of undress than anything else, but I spotted her all the same. Jackie Carliner, one of the barmaids and a pretty good artist, had sketched her from the one time she'd seen the girl and we'd made copies for everyone.

Even so, I had my loading duties to finish first—there was no one else. But, as soon as we were underway and I'd raised the stern ramp, I made my way topside and to the lower stern deck. I took my walkie-talkie off the belt clip and called the Captain.

"Sir, this is Dalton," I called. "I've seen our suicide girl."

"So what else is new?" grumbled the Captain. "You know policy on that by now."

"But, sir!" I protested. "I mean still alive. Still on board. It's barely sundown, and we're a good half hour from the point yet."

He saw what I meant. "Very well," he said crisply. "But you know we're short-handed. I'll put Caldwell on the bow station this time, but you better get some results or I'll give you so much detail you won't have time to meddle in other people's affairs."

I sighed. Running a ship like this one hardened most people. I wondered if the Captain, with twenty years on the run, ever understood why I cared enough to try and stop this girl I didn't know from going in.

Did *I* know, for that matter?

As I looked around at the people going by, I thought about it. I'd thought about it a great deal before.

Why *did* I care about these faceless people? People from so many different worlds and cultures that they might as well have been from another planet. People who cared not at all about me, who saw me as an object, a cipher, a service, like those robots I mentioned. They didn't care about me. If *I* were perched on that rail and a crowd was around most of them would probably yell "Jump!"

Most of the crew, too, cared only about each other, to a degree, and about the *Orcas*, our rock of sanity. I thought of that world gone in some atomic fire. What was the measure of an anonymous human being's worth?

I thought of Joanna and Harmony. With pity, yes, but I realized now that Joanna, at least, had been a vampire. She'd needed me, needed a rock to steady herself, to unburden herself to, to brag to. Someone steady and understanding, someone whose manner and character suggested that solidity. She'd never really even considered that I might have my own problems, that her promiscuity and lifestyle might be hurting me. Not that she was trying to hurt me—she just never *considered* me.

Like those people going by now. If they stub their toe, or have a question, or slip, or the boat sinks, they need me. Until then, I'm just a faceless automaton to them.

Ready to serve them, to care about them, if *they* needed somebody.

And that was why I was out here in the surprising chill, out on the stern with my neck stuck out a mile, trying to prevent a suicide I *knew* would happen, knew because I'd seen it three times before.

I was needed.

That was the measure of a human being's true worth, I felt sure. Not how many people ministered to *your* needs, but how many people *you* could help.

That girl—she had been brutalized, somehow, by society. Now I was to provide some counterbalance.

It was the surety of this duty that had kept me from

blowing myself up with the old Delaware ferry, or jumping off that stern rail myself.

I glanced uneasily around and looked ahead. There was Shipshead light, tall and proud this time in the darkness, the way I liked it. I thought I could almost make out the marker buoys already. I started to get nervous.

I was certain that she'd jump. It'd happened every time before that we'd known. Maybe, just maybe, I thought, in this existence she won't.

I had no more than gotten the thought through my head when she came around the corner of the deck housing and stood in the starboard corner, looking down.

She certainly looked different this time. Her long hair was blond, not dark, and braided in large pigtails that drooped almost to her waist. She wore only the string bikini and transparent cape the Vinlanders liked in summer, and she had several gold rings on each arm, welded loosely there, I knew, and a marriage ring around her neck.

That was interesting, I thought. She looked so young, so despairing, that I'd never once thought of her as married.

Her friend, as thin and underdeveloped as she was stout, was with her. The friend had darker hair and had it twisted high atop her head. She wore no marriage ring.

I eased slowly over, but not sneakily. Like I said, nobody notices the crewman of a vessel; he's just a part of it.

"Luok, are yo sooure yu don' vant to halve a drink or zumpin?" the friend asked in that curious accent the Vinlanders had developed through cultural pollution by the dominant English and French.

"Naye, I yust vant to smell da zee-zpray," the girl replied. "Go on. I vill be alonk before ze zhip iz docking."

The friend was hesitant; I could see it in her manner. But I could also see she would go, partly because she was chilly, partly because she felt she had to show some trust to her friend.

She walked off. I looked busy checking the stairway supports to the second deck, and she paid me no mind whatsoever.

There were a few others on deck, but most had gone forward to see us come in, and the couple dressed completely in black sitting there on the bench was invisible to the girl as she was to them. She peered down at the black water and started to edge more to the starboard side engine wake, then a little past, almost to the center. Her upper torso didn't move, but I saw a bare, dirty foot go up on the lower rail.

I walked casually over. She heard me, and turned slightly to see if it was anyone she needed to be bothered with.

I went up to her and stood beside her, looking out at the water.

"Don't do it," I said softly, not looking directly at her. "It's too damned selfish a way to go."

She gave a small gasp and turned to look at me in wonder.

"How—how didt yu—?" she managed.

"I'm an old hand at suicides," I told her, that was no lie. Joanna, then almost me, then this woman seven other times.

"I vouldn't really haff—" she began, but I cut her off.

"Yes, you would. You know it and I know it. The only thing you know and I don't is why."

We were inside Shipshead light now. If I could keep her talking just a few more minutes we'd clear the channel markers and slow for the turn and docking. The turn and the slowdown would make it impossible for her to be caught in the propwash, and, I felt, the cycle would be broken, at least for her.

"Vy du yu care?" she asked, turning again to look at the dark sea, only slightly illuminated by the rapidly receding light.

"Well, partly because it's my ship, and I don't like things like that to happen on my ship," I told her. "Partly because I've been there myself, and I know how brutal a suicide is."

She looked at me strangely. "Dat's a fonny t'ing tu zay," she responded. "Jost vun qvick jomp and *pszzt*! All ofer."

"You're wrong," I said. "Besides, why would anyone so young want to end it?"

She had a dreamy quality to her face and voice. She was starting to blur, and I was worried that I might some-how translate into a different world-level as we neared shore.

"My 'usbahnd," she responded. "Goldier vas hiss name." She fingered the marriage ring around her neck. "Zo yong, so 'andzum." She turned her head quickly and looked up at me. "Do yu know vat it iz to be fat and ugly und 'alf bloind and haff ze best uv all men zuddenly pay attenzion to yu, vant to *marry* yu?"

I admitted I didn't, but didn't mention my own experiences.

"What happened? He leave you?" I asked.

There were tears in her eyes. "Ya, in a vay, ya. Goldier he jomped out a tventy-story building, he did. Und itz my own fault, yu know. I shud haff been dere. Or, maybe I didn't giff him vat he needed. I dunno."

"Then you of all people know how brutal suicide really is," I retorted. "Look at what it did to you. You have friends, like your friend here. They care. It will hurt them as your husband's hurt you. This woman with you—she'll carry guilt for leaving you alone the whole rest of her life." She was shaking now, not really from the chill, and I put my arm around her. Where the hell were those marker lights?

"Do you see how cruel it is? What suicide does to others? It leaves a legacy of guilt, much of it false guilt but no less real for that. And you might be needed by somebody else, sometime, to help them. Somebody else might die because you weren't there."

She looked up at me, then seemed to dissolve, col-lapse into a crescendo of tears, and sat down on the deck. I looked up and saw the red and green markers astern, felt the engines slow, felt the *Orcas* turn.

"*Ghetta!*" The voice was a piercing scream in the night. I looked around and saw her friend running to us after coming down the stairway. Anxiety and concern were on her stricken face, and there were tears in her eyes. She bent down to the still sobbing girl. "I shuld neffer haff left yu!" she sobbed, and hugged the girl tightly.

I sighed. The *Orcas* was making its dock approach now, the ringing of bells said that Caldwell had managed to raise the bow without crashing us into the dock.

"My Gott!" the friend swore, then looked up at me. "Yu stopped her? How can I effer? . . ."

But they both already had that ethereal, unnatural double image about them, both fading into a world different from mine.

"Just remember that there's a million Ghettas out there," I told them both softly. "And you can make them or break them."

I turned and walked away as I heard the satisfying thump and felt the slight jerk of the ferry fitting into the slip. I stopped and glanced back at the stern but I could see no one. Nobody was there.

Who were the ghosts? I mused. Those women, or the crew of the *Orcas*? How many times did hundreds of people from different worlds coexist on this ship without ever knowing it?

How many times did people in the *same* world coexist without noticing each other, or caring about each other, for that matter?

"Mr. Dalton!" snapped a voice in my walkie-talkie.

"Sir?" I responded.

"Well?" the Captain asked expectantly.

"No screams this time, Captain," I told him, satisfaction in my voice. "One young woman will live."

There was a long pause and, for a moment, I thought he might actually be human. Then he snapped, "There's eighty-six assorted vehicles still waiting to be off-loaded, and might I remind you we're short-handed and on a strict schedule?''

I sighed and broke into a trot. Business was business, and I had a whole world to throw out of the car deck so I could run another one in.

INTRODUCTION TO
"STORMSONG RUNNER"

Before I got married, I used to travel quite a bit to vary my social life and contacts. Not the big trips—I still do those—but just routine travel. For many years I was a member of the New York SF Society (The Lunarians) and the Philadelphia SF Society as well as the Washington group I had started with and still belong to. It worked partly because I like to drive; it lets out my tensions and helps me think. I'm even a member of the Los Angeles SF Society and once drove from my Maryland home to one of their meetings.

In late 1977 everybody was bugging me for more short stories at the same time I was looking more and more at novels. Novels paid very well; they were my natural form and far more natural for me to write than short fiction. As I said earlier, I am someone who likes to paint on a broad canvas, not on the head of a pin. Too, I was just reaching that golden point where I could really become a professional writer rather than a profitable hobbyist—the point at which you can never get rejected because instead of selling everything you write you write only what you have already sold. I mean, I'd just been offered quite a good contract on the basis of a three-word synopsis—"Well World sequel"—and my agent was negotiating the final contract nuts and bolts before I got half the money. There was no such security in short stuff, very little money (comparatively), and few markets, none of which were certain.

And yet, there are some ideas that just come unbidden and won't go away until they're dealt with. It was on the New Jersey Turnpike; I was driving home alone from a Lunarians meeting in late March when I saw a flash of lightning. It was one of those things that's hardly newsworthy but not terribly common that time of year, but some little inner voice asked me as I sped toward home, "I wonder who's in charge of thunderstorms for the southern West Virginia district?" Since I was in New Jersey at the time there is absolutely no reason for the setting suggested, but that's what came out.

Initially I had a tongue-in-cheek reply in mind to that one, the kind of story H.L. Gold might have done in the early forties for *Unknown*, but when I started to write it, it turned out to be a far different story indeed—so different, in fact, that while I was happy with it when I finished it, I hadn't the slightest idea what to do with it. It didn't have the large fantastic element for the traditional SF markets, and it was just a bit too off the wall for most mainstream short fiction editors. The background and setting came from life; my nephew had just finished building a gigantic Lincoln-log style cabin on some land he'd bought on the poorest section of Appalachia and the people and the region kind of stuck in my mind.

Then Stuart David Schiff, publisher of the best amateur magazine of fantasy at that time, *Whispers*, told me that his first anthology of original stories for Doubleday with the same title as the magazine had gone well, and Doubleday had asked for another. Did I have a story, strictly fantasy, no SF elements, that might work for *Whispers II*?

Well, yeah, I did, and I sent it up to him. He bought it immediately, and it appeared in the anthology and got some very nice review comments, showing at least that people had read one of my shorts for a change, although the fantasy audience is far different than the SF one. The joy was short-lived; *Whispers II* had only a 5000-copy run and sold out almost immediately, yet it was not reprinted and did not have a paperback edition until 1988, a decade later. This story, then, remained relatively obscure and was one of my least obtainable until now.

And that's a major reason for this book in the first place.

STORMSONG RUNNER

I WONDER WHO'S IN CHARGE OF COLD WEATHER FOR this region. I'd like to talk to them. You see, I—no, I'm not crazy. Or maybe I am. It would simplify things enormously if I were.

Look, let me explain it to you. About three years ago, I graduated from college in Pittsburgh. There I was, twenty-two, fresh, eager, armed with a degree in elementary education. All scholarship, no problems. I sailed through.

And back then, as now, that degree and half a buck bought a large coffee to go.

So I drifted, bummed around, took any job I could get, while firing off applications to dozens of school districts. The baby boom's over, though—there were few openings, none that wouldn't make you cut your throat in a couple of years.

I was on the road to failing the most important course of all—life. I started drinking, blowing pot, and sniffing coke, and was in and out involved with a bunch of flaky girls more into that than I was.

What rescued me was, oddly enough, an accident. I was driving a girlfriend's old clunker when this fellow ran a light and hit me broadside. A couple of weeks in

137

the hospital, a lurking lawyer I'd known from high
school, and I suddenly had a good deal of the other guy's
insurance company's money.

I bought a place down in southern West Virginia, up
in the hills in the middle of nowhere, and tried to get my
head on straight. It was peaceful in those mountains, and
quiet; the little town about three miles away had the few
necessities of life available, and the people were friendly,
if a little curious about why such a rich city feller would
move down there. Grass is greener syndrome, I suppose.

As I wandered the trails of my first summer, I made
some acquaintance with the people who lived further
back, primitive, clannish, and isolated from even the tiny
corner of the twentieth century that permeated the little
town. I even got shot at when I discovered that they still
do indeed have stills back there—and got blind stinking
drunk when we straightened it out.

The grinding poverty of these people was matched
only by their lack of knowledge about how destitute they
really were. State social workers and welfare people
sometimes trekked up there, but they encountered hos-
tility mixed with pride. And, in a way, I admired the
mountain folk all the more for it, for in some things they
were richer than anyone in this uncertain world—their
sense of family, the closeness between people, the love
of nature and the placement of a person's worth above
all else—these were things my own culture had long ago
lost, called corny and hick.

Most of these people were illiterate, and so were their
kids. Most of the time the kids were kept hidden when
the state people came up—these folk were too poor to
afford shoes, pens and pencils, and all the other costly
paraphernalia of our "free" school system. They preferred to ignore the state laws on education as much as
they did the federal ones on making moonshine.

Well, I talked to some of the state people, who knew
of the problem but could do little about it, and convinced
someone in the welfare department that I could make a
contribution. They accepted my teaching certificate, and
I became a *per diem* teacher to the hill people on the

West Virginia State Department of Education. Not much, but it was a job, and I was needed here. The only way these people were ever going to break the bonds of poverty and isolation was through education, at least in the basics. I was determined that my students—perhaps a dozen at the start—would be able to read and write and do simple, practical sums before I was through—and that's more than most modern high school graduates in urban areas can do these days.

It was tough to get some of those parents to agree, but when the first snow fell in early October I had a group. We met in my house—a two-story actual log cabin, but with only two large rooms (one more than I needed). The kids were fun, and eager learners. I wound up with an ominous thirteen, but it was perfect—each one got individual attention from me, and I got to know them well. When they ran into trouble, I'd go up to their shacks, stomach lined as much as possible with yogurt or cream against the inevitable hospitality, and we'd have extra lessons. In this way I sneakily started teaching some of the parents as well.

Their ages ranged from nine to fourteen, but they all started off evenly—they were ignorant as hell. And I got help—the state was so pleased to make any kind of a dent in the region that they sent us everything from hot lunch supplies to pens, pencils, crayons, and even some simple books, obviously years old and discovered in some Charleston elementary school's basement but perfect for us.

Schooling was erratic and unconventional. The snow was extremely deep at times, the weather as fierce as the Canadian northwoods, and there were whole weeks when contact was impossible. Yet, as spring approached progress had been made; their world was a little wider. They were mostly on Dick and Jane, but they were *reading*, and they were already adding and subtracting on a basic level.

And they taught me, too. We spent time in those woodlands watching deer and coon, and, as spring arrived, they showed me the best spots for viewing the wonderful flowers and catching the biggest fish.

They were close to nature and were, in fact, a part of it. It sometimes made me hesitate in what I was doing. "Poor" is such a relative term.

Only one of the students was a real puzzle—a girl of ten or eleven (who knew for sure?) named Cindy Lou Whittler, the only child of a poor woman who made out as best she could while tending the grave of her husband just out back. She was fat and acne-ridden, and awkward as hell; the other kids would have made her the butt of their cruel jokes in normal circumstances, but they steered clear of her. She sat off by herself, talking only haltingly and only when prompted—and you could cut the tension with a knife.

They were scared to death of her.

Finally I could stand it no longer, and had a talk with Billy Bushman. He was the oldest of the group, the most worldly-wise, and was the natural class leader.

"Billy," I asked him one day, "you've got to tell me. Why are you and everybody else scared of Cindy Lou?"

He shuffled uneasily and glanced around. "'Cause she a witcher woman," he replied softly. "You do somthang she don' liak, she sing th' stormsong an' thas all fo you."

A little more prompting brought the rest of the story. They thought—knew—she was a witch, and they believed she could cause lightning and thunder.

I felt sorry for the girl. Superstition is rampant among the ignorant (and some not so ignorant, come to think of it) and an idea based on it, once formed, is almost impossible to dislodge. Seems a couple of years back she and a boy had had a fight, and she threatened him. A couple of days later, he was struck by lightning and killed.

Such are legends born.

Shortly after, contemplating her sullen loneliness in the corner, I called her aside after class and talked to her about it. Getting any response from her was like pulling teeth.

"Cindy Lou, I know the others think you're a witch," I told her, feeling genuinely sorry for her, "and I know how lonely you must be."

She smiled a little, and the hurt that was always in her eyes seemed to lessen.

"I heard the story about the boy," I told her, trying to tread cautiously but to open her up.

"Didn't kill nobody," she replied at last. "Couldn't."

"I know," I told her. "I understand."

Finally she couldn't hold it in any longer, and started crying. I tried to soothe and comfort her, glad the hurt was coming out. To cure a boil—even one in the soul—it must first be lanced so tears can flow.

"I jest make 'em liak ah'm told ta," she sobbed. "Ah caint tell 'em what to do."

This threw me for a loop. In my smug urban superiority it had never occurred to me that she might believe it, too.

"Who tells you?" I asked softly. "Who tells you to bring the thunderstorms?"

"Papa come sometimes," she replied, still sniffling. "He say ah got to make 'em. That everybody's got a reason for bein' heah an' mine's doin' this."

I understood now. I knew. An ugly, fat little girl *would* see her father, now two years dead, and she would rationalize her loneliness and ugliness somehow. This was in the character of these people so much a part of nature and the hills—she wasn't the ugly duckling, no, she was the most important person, most powerful person in the whole area.

She made the thunderstorms for southern West Virginia—and she was here for that purpose.

It made life livable.

The beginning of spring meant the onrush of thunderstorms as the warmer air now moving in struck the mountains; and as they increased in frequency, so did her loneliness, isolation—and pride. As the kids became more scared of her, she knew she had power—over them, over all.

She made the storms. She.

I tried to teach them a little basic meteorology, to sneakily dispel this fantasy for the rest of them, but they nodded, told me the answers I wanted to hear, and kept on believing that Cindy Lou made the storms. Outsiders couldn't understand. And this gave them some pride, too—for they were smugly confident that, for all my education, they knew for sure something that was beyond me.

It was the middle of May now, and my job had been among the most enjoyable and rewarding that I could imagine. I started to pick up other students as word got around, and began to travel as well, to teach some of the adults who managed to swallow just enough of that fierce pride to get me to help them.

One day I was coming back from one such student— he was seventy if he was a day, and I had him up to Dr. Seuss—when I passed near the Whittler house. I decided to stop by and see how Cindy Lou and her terribly suffering mother, the oldest thirty-six I had ever seen, were getting along. Classes were infrequent now; in spring these people planted and worked hard to eke out their subsistence.

As I approached the house, I thought I heard Cindy Lou's voice coming from inside, and I hesitated, as if a great hand were lain upon me. Frozen, her words drifted through the crude wooden shack to me.

"No, Papa!" she cried out fiercely. "Ah caint do this'n! You caint ask me! You know the wata's too high now. A big'n liak this'll flood the whole valley—maybe the town, too!"

And then there came the sound I'll never forget—the one that made the hairs on my neck stand up.

"You do liak yo' papa say!" came a deep, gravelly and oddly hollow man's voice. "Ah ain't got no choice in this mattah and neither do you. Leave them choices to them what knows bettah. You do it, now, heah? You know what happen if'n you don't!"

Suddenly the spell that seemed to hold me broke, and I stood for a moment, uneasily shivering. I considered not dropping in, just going on, but I finally decided it was my duty. I knew one thing for sure—somebody definitely *did* tell Cindy Lou to make the storms; she could never have made that voice outside a recording studio.

I had to know who was feeding her this. I knocked.

For a while there was no answer. Then, just as I was about to give up, the door creaked open and Cindy Lou peered out.

She'd been crying, I could see, but she was glad to see me and asked me in.

"Mama's gone ta town," she explained. "Cleanin' Mr. Summil's windas."

I walked into the one-room shack that I'd been in many times before. There was no back door, and only the most basic furnishings.

There was no one else in the shack but the two of us.

My stomach started turning a little, but I got a grip on myself.

"Cindy Lou?" I asked anxiously. "Where's the man who was just here? I heard voices."

She shrugged. "Papa dead, you know. Cain't hang around fo' long," she explained so matter-of-factly that it was more upsetting than the voice itself. I shifted subjects, the last refuge of the nervous.

"You've been crying," I noted.

She nodded seriously. "Papa want me t' do a big'n tonight. You been by the dam today?"

I nodded my head slowly. There was a small earthen dam used to trap water. Part of it was tapped for town use, and the small lake it backed up made the best fishing in the area. I had walked by there only a half hour or so earlier; the water was already to the top, ready to spill over, this mostly from the runoff of melting snow from the hard winter.

"If'n it rain big, that dam'll bust," she said flatly.

Again I nodded. It was true—I'd complained to the county about that dam, pleaded with them to shore it up, but it was low on the priority list—not many voters in these parts.

"Ah din't kill that boy," she continued, getting more anxious, "but if'n I do what Papa want, ah'll kill a lot of folk sure."

And that, too, was true—if the dam burst and nobody heeded any warnings. I tried to think of an answer that would comfort her. I was terribly afraid of what would happen to her if that dam *did* break in a storm. She paid a heavy price for assumed guilt by others; this one she'd blame on herself, and I was sure she couldn't handle that.

"What happens if you don't bring the storm?" I asked gently.

She was grim, face set, and her voice sounded almost as dead and hollow as that man's eerie tones had been.

"Terrible thangs" was all she could tell me.

I didn't want to leave her, but when I heard that the storm was set for before midnight, and that her mother probably wouldn't come home until the next day, I decided I had to act. Cindy Lou refused to come with me, and I had little choice. I was afraid that she might kill herself to keep from doing her terrible task, and I needed reinforcement. I made for town and Mrs. Whittler.

It took me over an hour to get there, and another half hour to find her. She seemed extremely alarmed, and it was the first time I'd heard her curse, but she and I rushed back to where no cars could go as quickly as possible.

Clouds obscured the sky, and no stars showed through that low ceiling as sundown caught us still on the rutted path to the shack. Ordinarily, no problem—it was usually cloudy on this side of the mountains—but that deepening blackness seemed somehow alive, threatening now as we neared the shack.

We burst in suddenly, and I quickly lit a kerosene lantern.

The shack was empty.

"My God! My God!" Mrs. Whittler moaned. "What has that rascal done to mah poor baby?"

"Think!" I urged her. "Where would she go?"

She shook her head sadly from side to side. "I dunno. Nowheres. Everywheres. Too dark to see her anyways if she din't wanta be seen."

It was true, but I didn't want to face it. Nothing is more terrible than knowing you are impotent in a crisis.

There was a noticeable lowering of the temperature.

The barometer was falling so fast that you could feel it sink. There was a mild rumble off in the distance.

"There must be *something* we can do!" I almost screamed in frustration.

She chewed on her lower lip a moment. Then, suddenly, her head came up, and there was fire in her eyes. "There's one thang!" she said firmly, and walked out of the shack. I followed numbly.

We walked around to the back in the almost complete darkness. Small flashes of lightning gave a sudden, intermittent illumination, like a few frames of a black and white movie.

She stood there at the grave of her husband, the little wooden cross the only sign that someone was buried there.

"Jared Whittler!" she screamed. "You cain't do this to our daughta! She's ours! Ours! *Please*, oh, God! You was always a good man, Jared! *In the name of God, she's all I've got!*"

It seemed then that the lightning picked up, and thunder roared and echoed among the darkened hills.

Now, suddenly, there was a cosmic fireworks display; sharp, piercing streaks of lightning seemed to flash all around us, thunder boomed, and the wind picked up to tremendous force.

It started to rain, a few hard drops at first, then faster and faster, until we were engulfed in a terrible torrent.

And yet we stood there transfixed, in front of that little cross, and we prayed, and we pleaded, oblivious to the weather.

Suddenly, through it all, we heard a roaring sound unlike any of the storm. I turned slowly, the terror of reality in my soul.

"Oh, my God!" I managed. "There goes the dam!"

There was a sound like a tidal wave moving closer to us, then passing us somewhere to our backs, and continuing on down into the valley below.

As suddenly as it came on, the rain stopped. Both of us still stood there, soaked to the skin, now ankle-deep in mud. Now the storm was just a set of dull flashes in the distance to the east, and a few muted rumbles of what it had been.

She turned to me then. Though I couldn't really see her, I knew that she was stoic as all hill folk were in disaster.

"You're soaked," she said quietly. "Come in and git dried off. There'll be work to do in the town tonight."

I was shocked, numb, and silently, without thought, I followed her into the shack where, by the light of the kerosene lantern, she fished out some ragged towels for me to use.

We said nothing to each other. There was nothing left to say.

Suddenly there was a noise outside, and slowly, hesitantly, the old door opened on creaking hinges.

"Cindy Lou!" her mother almost whispered, and then ran and hugged her, holding the child to her bosom. Cindy Lou cried and hugged her mother all the more.

After a time, Mrs. Whittler turned her loose and looked at her. "Lord! You a mess!" she exclaimed, and went over and threw the girl a towel.

I stood there dumbly, trying to think of something to say. She sensed it, and looked up at me.

"Ah went to the dam," she said softly. "If'n it was gonna go, ah wanted to be goin' with it. Papa come to me then, say, 'These things hav'ta happen sometimes.' He say you goes when th' time comes, but it wasn't mah time, that you an' Mama was heah, callin' fo' me."

"It had to happen—your papa's right about that. If it hadn't been this time, then a few days from now," I consoled.

She shrugged.

"Ah couldn't do it. Papa got the man in charge of eastern Kentucky to do it," she said. "Papa say he don't want me doin' this no mo'. He gon' try ta git me changed to handlin' warm days."

And that was it.

We spent days cleaning up the mess; my cabin was the highest ground near the town, so it became rescue headquarters and temporary shelter. It'll take months to dig that silt out of the town itself, but, miraculously, no lives had been lost.

The state says they'll do something real soon now. By that time I'll be dead of old age, of course—but, no, I'll die of helping everybody with the red tape first.

Cindy Lou? Well, she seems happier now, convinced that she's switched jobs to something potentially less lethal. I go up there often. The kids still aren't all that friendly, but I take Cindy Lou with me on my rounds; realistically, I know I'm the father figure she craves, and she is almost like a daughter to me, but, what the hell. You get to analyzing why you do something and you go nuts.

And my students? More each day seem to show up, ages five to eighty-five. No teacher can find more satisfaction in his work than I do.

Every time there's a thunderstorm, though, I get to thinking—and I'm not sure that's good, either.

The weather bureau had predicted that storm; the Charleston paper showed a front right where a front should have been, and I looked at back issues and that front had been moving across the country for three days. Anybody used to this mountain country could tell a storm was brewing that day.

And that man's voice? I don't know. I'm not sure whether Cindy Lou's voice can go that low or not, but . . . it must have, mustn't it? She hasn't seen Papa much these days, she tells me. He's mad at her, and she doesn't care at all.

And yet, creeping into my mind some lonely, storm-tossed nights, I can't help thinking; what if it's true? Is it truly a disturbing thought or is it, in some way, equally comforting, for if such things actually are it gives some meaning to practically everyone's usually dull life.

Does each of us have a specific purpose here on Earth? Are some of us teachers to those who need us, and others stormsong runners?

INTRODUCTION TO
"IN THE DOWAII CHAMBERS"

With the large demand for my novels and increasing success in that area, and with the lack of reaction to stories like "Dance Band," which I considered at least worthy of note by others in the field, I felt no impulse at all to do much more short fiction. Then George R.R. Martin wrote to bug me for another; he had been editing an anthology of new stories by writers nominated for the John W. Campbell Award for best new SF/fantasy writer, and I'd been nominated in 1977 and 1978 (losing the first year to C.J. Cherryh and in the second to Orson Scott Card). I had good company in the losers arena—Elizabeth Lynn, Stephen R. Donaldson, Carter Scholz, Bruce Sterling—so I, unlike my wife, didn't take the losses seriously or personally. Instead, I was somewhat intimidated at coming up with a good story for the book, considering the company. Most of the others who would be in there are short story people, and C.J. is one of those rare ones comfortable in both camps.

Initially, I sent a hastily reworked "Moths and Candle" to George, but he rejected it (see the introduction to that story for the gory details).

However, Judy-Lynn del Rey had bugged me for a story for *Stellar 4* a couple of years before, and I had come up with

148

this weird idea of a group of people physically trapped somehow inside a giant printed circuit board. I did some of the story and sent it up to her for comments and, if need be, encouragement, but instead she told me not to bother sending the whole thing to her—it just wasn't her kind of story. She suggested *F&SF*. I never did finish that version and that part of it that was done is now lost somewhere. I just don't have much incentive to write short fiction.

When my novel commitments permitted, I turned to that idea as a possible one for George, but I totally rejected my initial concept. Instead, I used the bare bones to come up with a very different and, I think, very effective SF piece. Even so, it went slowly; I kept going off to do other things and it looked like it would never get done. After all, all the other stories had been in, some for a year or more, and I was the fellow holding up the party and publication. I'm not sure what finally kicked me to do it—perhaps the anonymous letters from New Mexico threatening my family had something to do with my sudden motivation—but I decided I was ready to try. At any rate, once I really got started, the whole thing just fell into place and it really flowed.

I was pretty happy with the story, and so was George, but, again, I was not motivated to do more. Almost no one reviewed the book; almost no one that I met had even read the story. Those who had purchased or read the book and reviewed or commented on it seemed to have read only the Cherryh story; if the other stories in the book were mentioned at all, it was in a clear context of somebody who obviously hadn't read beyond the title page. Debbie Notkin, now an SF paperback editor but then a reviewer, wrote in *Locus* that it was "a typical Chalker adventure story," while Darrell Schweitzer said it was "serviceable old-style pulp fiction." One might or might not like this story, but I can not see how it can be called typical of my work, adventure, old-style, or pulp fiction, except that, for all its moodiness and the fact that it's a character play, it is in fact a traditional *Astounding/Analog* problem story, of people trapped in a technological nightmare who know they're trapped but appear to have no way out. With reactions like these, you can understand why I am not motivated to sit down and do a lot of short fiction.

As I've said before here, a short story is basically a concept. I never thought of this one in terms of a problem story, although it is; to me, the concept was everything.

Humanity is, in its present form, somewhere around a million years old. The Cro-Magnon brain was every bit as large and as well organized as ours and physically they weren't any more different from us than racial groups are from one another today. Human history, on the other hand, is just a bit over six thousand years old, history being the written record of human accomplishment and learning. Did we spend that million-plus years as hunter-gatherers in a primitive culture growing and learning very little, creating no civilizations, advancing no knowledge? I find that nearly impossible to believe. Short of a time machine or some astonishing discovery of ancient remains, however, that's the picture we're presented with and the one we're stuck with. Archaeologists have some good guesses going back almost twelve thousand years, but they are guesses based on often contradictory evidence and still represent only a fraction of time in the human experience. It's the Ozymandius Syndrome, only not even the plaque remains.

Maybe that period was filled with slow, primitive, and rather dull development, but one can't help wonder otherwise, and if science fiction is anything we can state in a sentence, it certainly involves wondering about the unknown.

What has time and nature cheated us out of? What great heritage must we forever be ignorant of because we have no means to discover it? If you asked that all too human question, and you had the means to discover it, wouldn't you?

IN THE DOWAII CHAMBERS

1

THE SUN ROSE HIGH OVER THE DESOLATE LANDSCAPE, burning away the ghosts and shadows of the night. Through the landscape only a single dirt track led into more and more of the burnt orange of the southwest desert, and on it, like some desperate alien beast being chased by the rising sun, a lone pickup truck roared through the lonely land, kicking up clouds of dust and small pebbles as it went, the only sign of life for, perhaps, fifty miles. For all that those in the truck could tell, they might have been invaders of another planet, a planet as stark and dead as the moon.

But the land was not dead, merely hard. Once the same harsh hills and dry, dusty plains had held great civilizations, many of whose cliff-dwelling cities and complex road patterns remained for the aerial surveyor, then the archaeologist, and finally the tourist to discover and explore. Even now this was Indian land, although not that of the descendants of the great ones who had thrived here so many centuries before. These Indians were newcomers, interlopers here on the land in this very spot less than six hundred years, but they were no less tied to it than the vanished old ones, nor did they love it any less.

The pickup reached rocky tableland now and took an almost invisible fork in the road to the right, up into the hills of pink and bronze whose colors changed constantly with the position of the sun. Up now, into the highlands, and through a gully that even four-wheel drive found a problem, until at last they came upon a small adobe dwelling, a single room set under a cleft in the rock and shaded by it. Nearby grazed some horses, getting what they could out of the weeds that grew even here, and, a bit farther down, some burros did likewise.

The pickup pulled up almost in front of the tiny dwelling and stopped, causing almost no stir among the animals idly grazing, and the driver's door opened and a young, athletic-looking man got out, then helped a young woman out as well.

Theresa Sanchez came out of the tiny building to greet the newcomers, then stopped in the doorway and looked them over critically. *They look like a designer jeans commercial*, she thought sourly.

A second man got out of the truck, stretching arms, legs, and neck to flex away some of the stiffness. He didn't seem to fit with the other two, his clothes older and more worn, his stocky build and crazy-quilt reddish beard doing little to disguise his pockmarked face.

Theresa Sanchez looked them all over and wondered again what the hell they were all doing here. The driver, Mr. America—blond, blue-eyed, muscular, a bit over six feet, in tailored denim work clothes, hundred-dollar cowboy boots, and a large, perfectly formed white Stetson—was George Singer, the ambitious originator of this project. He was, she knew, twenty-six and a doctoral candidate in American archaeology. The woman with him, in a tight-fitting matched denim outfit, cowboy hat, and boots, had to be Jennifer Golden, George's current housemate and an undergrad at the same university. That left the big, ugly brute as Harry Delaney, a geographer and, at twenty-nine, also a doctoral candidate.

Despite their tans, she couldn't help but think how very—*white*—they all seemed.

"Welcome to the ghetto," she couldn't resist calling out to them.

Only Delaney smiled, perhaps because he was the only one to understand the comment. He had never met Theresa Sanchez before, but he knew a bit about her from George, and he couldn't help but examine her in the same way that she had looked at all of them. The woman was surprisingly small and wiry, hardly more than five feet and probably under a hundred pounds. Her skin was a deep reddish brown, almost black, her deep black hair long and secured by an Indian headband, and her faded and patched jeans and plain white T-shirt made her look not only natural here but also somehow very, very young. He could imagine her, in more traditional Indian dress, as a young girl of these hills, living as her ancestors had.

But she, too, was a bit more than she seemed, he knew. Not the fourteen she seemed but twenty-five, her Spanish name not close to her true one but one given her in Catholic mission schools, her field so complex and esoteric that she'd either be the world authority in it one day or condemned to obscurity by its very oddness. She was a philologist, but not just any sort of expert on words. George had said that there wasn't a language known that she couldn't master in six weeks or less, nor one that she couldn't become literate in within a year. She was one of those born with the special talent for the word—anybody's word. But although she'd tackled many just for interest and amusement, her interest and her passion was the myriad languages and dialects of the Amerind, many of which no one not born to them could speak. She could speak them, though—a dozen or more, in hundreds of dialects. How important she became would depend on her own aims and ambitions; it was certainly a wide-open field.

Oddly, she was as much an alien here as the other three, although only she truly understood that. She was an Apache in Navajo lands, which made her as wrong for this place as a Filipino in Manchuria. Somewhere, far back, there was common ancestry, but that was about all the sameness there was.

George looked around. "Did you fix it with the old man, Terry?"

"And a good morning to you, too," the Indian woman responded sarcastically. "The soul of tact and discretion as always, I see."

The blond man looked at her a little sourly, but shrugged it off. He looked around. "Is he here?"

She nodded. "Still inside and praying a bit. He's still not too sure he wants to go through with this."

Singer looked slightly nervous. "You mean he might back out?"

She shrugged. "Who can say? I don't think so, though."

"What's he worrying about? That we're gonna disturb his gods?"

"He has only one god, in many forms," she told him. "No, he doesn't worry about that. He's a fatalist. He's worried about us."

"Us?" Delaney put in.

She nodded. "He believes we are to become ghosts, and his conscience is troubling him. To him it's a dilemma much like whether or not to give a loaded gun to one who you suspect of being suicidal. No, check that. More like giving a stick of dynamite to people ignorant of what explosives are and how they work."

Singer sighed. "Superstition. It's always the same."

"Are you sure, George?" she responded, not taunting but with an air of real wonder in her tone. "Are you so sure of yourself and your world? These people have been here a long time, you know."

Singer just shook his head in disgust, but Delaney felt something of a chill come over him, a shadow of uncertainty. For a moment he felt closer to this Indian woman than to his two companions, for he was not so certain of things. This was the modern, computerized world they all lived in; yet, here, even in the heart of the great cities, some still feared the darkness, some still wondered when the wind whistled, and many still knocked wood for luck. Great architects whose computers spewed three-dimensional models of grand skyscrapers and who worked in mathematics and industrial design still didn't put the thirteenth floor in their glass-and-steel edifices.

They had unloaded and set up a crude camp before they saw the old man for the first time. He emerged, looking almost other-worldly himself, a wizened, burnt, wrinkled old man with snowwhite hair stringing down below his shoulders, wearing hand-woven decorative Indian garments of buckskin tan, although decorated with colorful if faded Navajo designs. Only his boots—incongruous US Army–issue combat boots, well-worn but still serviceable—betrayed any hint that he was even aware of the twentieth century.

Whether he could speak or understand other languages, none of them knew, but it was certain that he would speak, and answer to, only the complex and intricate Navajo language.

Theresa Sanchez—Terry, she told them—not only knew the language but could quickly match the old man's dialect as well. Delaney, who'd almost washed out by his near inability to master German and French, felt slightly inadequate.

They ate some hot dogs and apples prepared over a portable Coleman, and the old man seemed to have no trouble with the modern ways of cooking or the typically American food. He wolfed it down with relish, and a can of beer from their cooler too. Finally finished, he sat back against a rock and rolled a cigarette—the three newcomers all thought it was a joint until they smelled the smoke—and seemed content.

Harry and Terry had helped Jenny with the cookout and now helped clean up. George let them do it.

Finally they got it squared away and went and sat by the ancient Indian. It was impossible to tell how old he was, but Harry, at least, thought that it was impossible to be that old and still move.

"*He's* going to guide *us*?" he said unbelievingly.

"Don't let his appearance fool you," Terry came back. "This is his land. He's strong as a bull—you oughta see him push around those burros—and healthier than you are."

"How long has he lived here?" Jenny asked in that thin, high voice of hers.

"I asked him that. He says he doesn't remember. It seems like forever. He complains a lot that he can never remember not being old and out here."

"Why's he stay, then? He could enjoy his last days in comfort if he came out of here and went down to a home," George noted.

Harry kept looking at the old man, who seemed half asleep, wondering if he understood any of this. If so, he gave no sign.

"I doubt if you'd understand the answer to that, George," Terry responded. "Lucky you decided to take up artifacts. People would confuse the hell out of you."

He smiled and looked at Jenny. "I do fairly well in that department." He sighed and turned back to Terry. "So okay. When do we go on our little trip?"

The old Indian's eyes came half open and he muttered something.

"He senses your impatience," Terry told him. "He says that's why he lives so long and you will die much quicker."

George chuckled. "If I had to live out here under these conditions to get that old, I think I'm the winner. But, as I asked before, when do we get going?"

She asked the old man and he responded.

"He says tomorrow, a little before dawn," she told him. "We'll travel until it gets too hot, then break, then take it up again in the cool of the evening."

"How far?"

She asked him. "He says many hours. Allowing for terrain and the animals, early evening the day after to-morrow."

"Ask him what it's like," Harry put in. "What're we going to see when we get there?"

She did. "He says there's nothing visible on the surface, nothing at all. He calls them chambers rather than caverns or caves, which indicates, to me at least, that they're man-made tunnels of some kind going deep into the rock."

"That squares with the old legends," George noted. "Still, I'll believe 'em when I see 'em. What kind of Indians could ever have lived here that could develop a rock-tunneling ability? Chipping houses out of hillsides, yes, and even moving stones great distances—but they have to be man-perfected natural tunnels. There are bunches of those, although not around here particularly."

She said something to the old man, possibly a rough translation of George's comments. The old man responded rather casually but at some length.

"He says that none were made by nature, as you will see, although he didn't claim they were man-made. Artificial is more correct."

"If not men, then who made 'em?"

"The Dowaii," she said. "You remember the legends."

It had begun the previous year, or perhaps much earlier, when an undergrad under Singer had stumbled onto some ancient Navajo legends and seemingly correlated them with a number of other legends from Mexican, Spanish, and pioneer sources. It was a brilliant piece of work, impossible without both luck and the computer, and when George saw it he knew that it might be something big. Naturally he took full credit for it—although the undergrad was noted for his hard work in assistance —and it had led to George's grant.

A number of ancient Indian legends from many tribes were involved, although the Navajo's was the most complete and gave the most information. Still, like Noah's flood, there were other accounts, distorted and fragmentary, that bore out at least the fact that *something* was there. That *something*, if it really was there, would not only give Singer his Ph.D. but put him immediately in the forefront of his field. It was the kind of once-in-a-lifetime chance you just *had* to take.

After God had created the world, the legend went, and made it a true paradise, He dwelt within it and loved it so much that parts of His aspect went into all things

which he loved, and they became spiritual echoes of
Himself. Echoes, but also independent; managers, one
might say, of the earth and its resources. Elemental
spirits who not merely controlled but *were* the air, the
sun, the trees, the grass, the animals, and all else of the
perfect world.

But a perfect world needs admirers, and these sprung
automatically from the spirits, or aspects, of the Great
Spirit. These were a race of perfect material creatures,
the Dowaii, who were, in and of themselves, the second
generation of the descendants of God.

The elemental spirits, being once removed from God,
were, of course, less than God, and the Dowaii, being
once removed from the spirits, were lesser still, although
great beyond imagining. Still, they were aware of their
imperfections, and some aspired to godhood themselves.
Out of their desires and their jealousy sprang the races of
man, another step removed from God yet still an aspect
of Him and descended from Him. God, however, was
angered by the Dowaii's jealous pride and cursed them
from the light of day, condemning them to the places
under the earth and giving the earth to men. Those men
who remained true to nature and the land, and loved it
and life, would never die, but their souls would be
brought to a true heaven that God Himself inhabited, a
world without spiritual intermediaries. Men, then, could
become at least as great as the Dowaii if their souls were
as great on earth. Most men did not and died the permanent death, to return to the earth and nourish the next
generation of life. But the First People, the true Human
Beings who were descended from the first of the Dowaii,
kept their covenant with God while the rest of mankind
did not, aided by the Dowaii, who, locked in the rocks
beneath the earth, cursing man and God alike, created
the hatred that became evil in the minds of men.

The legend was striking in that it was not really common to any of the Amerind religions except for an obvious common origin. Although Navajo, it was not known
to the majority of those proud people but only to a select
few—a cult, as it were. In a sense it was almost Judeo-

Christian, in that it in some ways echoed Eden, and the Fall, and the battle between Heaven and Hell, which were not very Indian concepts.

Judging from the fragments and distortions from other tribes, though, it had apparently once been widespread, crossing tribal and national boundaries as well as linguistic ones, but it had dead-ended, died out, like so many other cultist beliefs, except for a small handful out in the southwestern desert. These, like the old man, were the guardians, the watchers at the gates of Hell.

Because the gates of Hell were two days ride from the old adobe shack.

Those few who remained faithful didn't seem to be concerned that their faith had died out long ago. It didn't matter to them, as long as their people retained the *essential* values—worship of God, love and respect for the land. Nor did they believe they would totally die out. Their own beliefs said that they inherited the beliefs from the Old Ones whose civilization had risen and fallen here before their people had come, and that the Old Ones had gotten it from still more ancient peoples. Some would go on.

For the Dowaii could not defy God and emerge from the rocks. They could only come here, close to the surface in the place of their ancient great cities, and remember the greatness they had lost. And they were still great and powerful beings, more powerful than men, who could lure and tempt and use men who came too near, although the pure ones, the unsullied First People, could dare them and defy them if they were pure enough in their souls.

An ordinary cult legend, yes, but there was more that led George to believe that something else might be here.

Of their great city and civilization not one trace remained—on the surface, or so the legends went. But on that site, below ground, were the great chambers of the Dowaii, where their spirits were strong and their power great. The last of the Dowaii of the great city dwelt in the rocks there and spoke through the chambers, and a remnant of their past glory was kept there, great and ancient treasures and knowledge beyond men's dreams.

Many of the strong and pure of the First People had entered those chambers, some as tests of courage or manhood, some as seekers after knowledge and truth. A very few emerged to become the greatest of leaders, almost godlike themselves. The Old Ones' great civilization was built by such men, but could not be sustained when they passed on.

Many more who entered the chambers emerged mad, their humanity gone. Most who entered did not come out and were said to remain there, forever trapped in the chambers, doomed forever as spirits, their ghosts trodding the chambers, suffering the torments of the Dowaii and at the same time seeing the great treasures and knowledge that was there while being powerless to do anything about it. Doomed forever, their anguished cries could sometimes be heard in the still of the desert, which is why the Navajo cult called the place the Haunting Chambers.

If it had stopped there, that would have been it, but in modern times modern men, too, had fragmentary tales.

A patrol sent out to the place by Coronado, believing the chambers might be the hidden gates to the Seven Cities, had gone, and one had returned, the one who had not gone in but had waited with the horses. His report, dismissed even at the time, of a huffing and puffing mountain that swallowed the rest of his patrol and from which only one had emerged, frothing at the mouth and gibbering like some rabid animal, and whom the lookout had finally been forced to shoot to death, was consistent —if one knew the Dowaii legend. The Spanish story also related how the madman had emerged clutching a large shining chunk of what proved to be pure silver, although this was not discovered to be so until much later.

Other, similar stories, each tied to rich artifacts, were around almost up to the early part of the century—but also, it was said, whenever anyone returned to find the chambers, they never could locate them or vanished without a trace.

It was slim but interesting evidence to hang this little

expedition on, and even though Singer had academic blessings, his grant barely paid the gas. It was Delaney's grant, for a preliminary survey of the region, that provided what little real capital there was, all of it sunk into the mules, horses, and supplies.

The key, though, had been Singer's encounter with Terry Sanchez at a professional conference on southwestern Indian cultures in Phoenix. She'd been doing work on the legends of some of the Navajo people as part of an oral history project and she'd heard of the cult and the Dowaii story. More, she could talk to the right people. She didn't like George very much but was intrigued by his idea that the chambers actually represented a pre-Anasazi cave-dwelling civilization never before suspected.

It had taken two years to get this far, and it was no wonder that George Singer was impatient.

Most of the afternoon was spent unloading and checking supplies, and there was surprisingly little conversation. Except for George and Jenny, they were all virtual strangers.

It was pitch-dark in the canyon, the stars brilliant but giving little illumination and the moon not yet up. Only the reddish embers of a dying fire gave off any light, and it was precious little.

Harry Delaney had tried to sleep but couldn't yet manage it. It was the total dark, he knew, and the lack of noise of almost any sort except the occasional rustle of the animals or the sound of one of the others turning or twisting.

Those sounds, of course, were magnified all out of proportion, including, after a while, the unmistakable sounds of George and Jenny making out in the darkness. It stopped after a bit and the two seemed to lapse into sleep, but it only brought Harry more wide-awake, and eventually he got up, grabbed his cigarettes, and walked over to the other side of the fire.

He flicked his lighter to fire up his cigarette and took a few drags, then stopped still, as he saw in its flickering glow Terry Sanchez sitting against the shack, watching him. He frowned and slowly walked over near her.

"Couldn't sleep, huh?" she whispered. "Not with the, ah, sound effects?"

He chuckled. "Partly that, anyway. You?"

"I sleep more soundly out here—but less." She gestured in the dark. "You don't like our friend George very much." It wasn't a question but a statement.

"He's not very likeable," Harry replied. "I dunno. Even if he weren't an egomaniacal bastard I'd probably still hate him. Looks like a German god, doctoral candidate at twenty-six, and all the beautiful women fall all over him while all the men on the make follow in his wake. He's everything our society says a man should be. Naturally I hate his guts."

She found that amusing. "Then why are you here?"

"Oh, I follow his wake, too, I guess. It was irresistible. He needed the money to follow his little story to glory, and I had this little grant in the neighborhood. If he's right, I'll share a little of the glory. Oh, he'll have the best-seller and the talk shows, of course, but I'll have a secure little professorship with a reputation."

"And if he's wrong?"

"Then I'm no worse off for wasting a few days on this."

"Do you think he's wrong?"

He stared at her. "What do *you* think?"

"I think he's wrong, of course, but not in the way you think. I think there's something out there, all right. You only have to look at his evidence to suspect that, and in addition I've talked to these old hermits. They aren't spouting legend; they've been there."

He looked idly at the shack. "That bothers me, though. Why, if there *is* something, would they take us there? Why show us this sacred spot when the Sioux will never even tell outsiders what Crazy Horse looked like, let alone where he's buried, and your own Apaches guard the grave of Geronimo? Particularly for three whites and a native of a different tribe not exactly known as a friend of the Navajo?"

She chuckled. "That was my first thought and my first question after making friends with him. He's very opinionated about women in general, and Apache women with Spanish names in particular. The nearest I can explain it is that he and the others guard the Navajo from the Dowaii. Oddly, only if we had a Navajo here would there have been trouble. He considers the rest of us already corrupted beyond redemption and, therefore, already the Dowaii's property."

"So we're sacrificial lambs," he sighed. "I don't like the sound of that. A crazy cult out here in the middle of nowhere, leading us around on their turf. I wonder if—"

"If the disappearances are caused by them? I thought of that. I'm sure George has too. That's why we'll all be armed from sunup on, and why one of us will always stand watch after. Still, I don't fear an attack by geriatric fanatics. There's something out here, all right. Not what George expects or what you or I expect, either, but there's something. You can almost feel it."

He shivered slightly. "I think I see what you mean." He sighed. "It must be nice to be like George. I doubt if he fears much of anything."

She got up and started over to her bedroll. Abruptly she stopped and turned back to him. "That, perhaps, is why we, you and I, are more likely to survive than he."

He snuffed out his cigarette and went back to his own sleeping bag, but he didn't sleep right away. For brief, episodic moments he felt the urge to flee, to tell them in the morning that they could go with his money and without him.

Something out there . . . Feel it . . .

It was a hot, rough day's ride over nasty terrain. A lonely ride, too, as even the normally unflappable George seemed somehow grim, taciturn, even a bit nervous.

The dry, wilting heat didn't help matters any, with any of them, as long as you didn't count the old man. Nothing, but nothing, seemed to bother him, and even his breaks, long and short, seemed more for the benefit of the animals and his charges than himself.

Harry tried to renew hesitant contact with Terry, but she seemed as stoic and indifferent as the old man. At one of their shadeless rests, though, George took Harry aside, a bit from the rest.

"I saw you making a few moves toward Terry," he whispered very low. "Just a friendly hint to forget it."

Harry was annoyed. "What's it to you? You already *got* Jenny."

"You got me wrong, Harry. I'm just being friendly. She don't mean nothin' to me except the way out to the chambers. You just aren't her type, that's all."

"Oh, come off it, George," he grumbled.

"*Jenny's* her type, Harry. At least, that's the only one around here she'd be attracted to."

He started to open his mouth, then closed it again. Finally he said, "Damn you, George," and stalked back to the others.

He felt miserable now, although he knew that that hadn't been George's intent. George could only see other people's actions in the same way *he* saw those actions, and the warning was actually a friendly gesture. George would never understand, he knew. He was still back there, puzzling over why he was just cursed out for doing somebody a favor.

Hell, he'd never have gotten romantic with Terry Sanchez—not really. But George had robbed him of even the illusion, coldly bringing reality into this fantasyland where reality had no place being. George wouldn't ever understand that, never comprehend it in the least.

Damn it, George, I don't care who or what she really is, but I neither wanted to nor had to know.

It was a lonely night, with more aches and more sleep but no new conversation.

The next morning found the old man and Terry seeming anxious to push on, while the three others all felt every bone and muscle in their bodies, which all seemed bruised and misplaced. Groans, curses, and complaints became the order of the day now.

Jenny seemed to suffer the worst. This was different than riding some nicely trained horses on a ranch or bridle path, and she really wasn't cut out for this sort of thing—not that George, and particularly Harry, were, either.

At least, Harry decided, the agony took your mind off brooding.

The scenery had changed into a rocky, gray landscape with rolling hills. Far off in the distance were some peaks and even a hint of green, but they turned from that direction and went close to a red and gray hill not distinguishable from the rest of the desolate mess. Finding a sheltered spot beneath a rock cleft, the old Indian signaled them to a halt and dismounted.

Terry talked with him at length, then came back to the rest of them. "Well, we're here," she announced.

All three looked startled and glanced around. *"Here?"* Harry managed.

She nodded and pointed. "That ugly hill over there, in fact."

George looked around at the landscape, a part of the region that didn't even have the beauty and color of the rest. It was an ugly, unappetizing place, one of the worst spots any of them could remember. "No wonder nobody found this place before," he said. "It's a wonder that *anybody* did."

Jenny turned up her pretty nose. "Smells like shit too."

Harry and George both frowned. "Sulphur," Harry noted. "I'll be damned. Doesn't look like anything volcanic was ever around here, does it?"

George shook his head. "Nope. But I don't like it all the same. Terry, your old man didn't say anything about sulphur. We might need breathing equipment if we have to go into caves filled with the stuff, and that's one thing we ain't got."

"I don't remember anything about it," she told them. "I'll ask him, though." She went back, talked to the old man, then returned. "He says the Dowaii know we are here and why we are here and are cleaning house for us—at least, that's the closest I can get. He says they'll put on a show tonight, then call for us."

George looked upset. "Two days of hell and a dead end. I'm sure as hell not going into any damned cave filled with gas."

"He says the air inside will be as sweet as we wish it to be."

"So *he* says." He sighed. "Well, let's bed down, anyway. At least we can make some preliminary surveys and see if there's anything worth coming back for."

The sun set as they unpacked and prepared the evening meal. Harry sat facing the mountain, digging into his beef and beans, as the land got darker and darker. Something in the back of his mind signaled that something was not right, but he couldn't put his finger on it. Finally he settled back and looked up at the mountain and dropped his plate.

None of the others noticed, and he finally said, "George, we have a Geiger counter, don't we?"

George looked up, puzzled, and said, "Yeah. Sure. What—?" He turned to see where Harry was looking and froze too. The two women also turned and both gasped.

The mountain glowed. It wasn't a natural sort of glow, either, but an eerie, almost electronic image in faint, blue-white light, a matte 3-D ghost image of the mountain that seemed to become clearer as darkness became absolute.

"Well, I'll be damned!" George swore. "What the hell can cause something like that other than a Hollywood special-effects department?"

Harry had already retrieved the Geiger counter and, with the aid of a flashlight, tried to take readings.

"Anything?" George asked.

He shook his head. "Nothing but normal trace radiation. My watch gives off more juice than this stuff, whatever it is. I can't figure it out."

George studied it for a moment. "Let's go see." He

went and got a flashlight, joining Harry, then looked over at Terry and Jenny. "Want to come?"

The contrast on the two women's faces was startling, at least to Harry. Jenny was just plain scared and not being very successful in trying to hide it. Terry, on the other hand, seemed fascinated almost to the point of being in some sort of mystical trance.

"George, don't go. Not now," Jenny said pleadingly.

"We're just going to the edge of the thing," he explained patiently. "I'm not about to go mountain climbing in the dark."

Terry said nothing, just stood there staring, and the two men realized that she wasn't about to join them. They turned and both started walking toward the strange display.

Suddenly the old man cried out, "No!"

Both men froze and turned. It was the first intelligible word they'd heard him utter.

"Hold on, Pop, we'll be back," George told him, and they set out again over the rocks toward the oddly glowing site. No one tried to stop them or accompany them.

It was only about fifty rough yards to the start of the display, and they approached it cautiously but quickly. It looked different this close, though.

"It's not glowing," Harry noted. "It's very slightly *above* the rock. See?"

George peered at it in nervous curiosity. "I'll be damned. It's—it's like electricity."

"It *is* electricity," the other man noted. "It's an electrical web or grid of some sort that makes a kind of holographic picture of the mountain. Where's the energy come from? And how is it kept in this form?"

"I don't know. I never saw anything like it that wasn't faked," George responded. "What the *hell* have we discovered here?"

"I'm going to toss these wirecutters at it," Harry said tensely. "Let's see what happens." He removed them from his belt kit and lightly tossed them at the nearest part of the display.

The wirecutters hit the current and seemed to stop,

frozen there just above the ground, enveloped and trapped in the energy field. They remained suspended there, not quite striking the ground, and began to glow white.

"Let's get back," Harry suggested, and George didn't argue.

They'd barely returned to the clearing when there was a rumble as if from deep within the ground, and at the top of the hill a bright, glowing sparkle of golden light grew. It, too, was some sort of energy field, they knew, growing to a height of several feet and sparkling like the Fourth of July.

From other points on the mountain other fields rose, all the same shimmering sparkle, but one was blue, another red, another green—all the colors of the rainbow and more.

They all stood there watching it, even the old man, for some time, perhaps an hour or more.

"Well, at least we know how the earlier people found the place," George noted.

"George, this isn't what we bargained for at all," Harry noted. "Listen—feel it in the ground? A rumbling. Not like a volcano or an earthquake. More steady."

George nodded, unable to avert his eyes for long from the display. "Like—like some giant turbine or something. Like some great machine gearing up."

"That's it exactly. Don't you see, George? That's what it is. Some kind of machine. That turbine or whatever deep below us is producing the energy for that display."

"It can't be. The stories go back centuries. It'd be impossible for anybody earlier than the past twenty or thirty years to build such a machine, never mind why. Unless..."

"Unless the Dowaii were not of this earth," George finished.

The display, but not the glow, subsided after ninety minutes or so. Harry turned to Terry, who was still standing, staring at the place. "You okay?" he asked, concerned.

For a moment he was afraid she was beyond hearing him, but finally she took a deep breath, sighed, and turned to look at him. "Listen! Can't you hear them?'"

He stared in puzzlement, then tried to listen. Presently he heard what she meant. There was a sound, very faint, very distant, somewhere down deep from within that mountain. A sound that seemed to be a crowd of people, all talking at the same time.

"The machine's noise," George pronounced. "At least now we can see why the old man talked about ghosts there. It *does* almost sound like people. The easy part of the legend is solved, anyway. Just imagine primitive man coming across this—even as primitive as the last century. It'd make a believer out of you in an instant. Maybe drive you nuts. The force field, or whatever it is, might well account for the disappearances."

Harry sniffed the air. "Smell it? Ozone."

"Beats the hell out of sulphur," George, the pragmatist forever, responded. "Well, now we know how legends are made. Unfortunately, we don't know who or what made 'em. One thing's for sure, though: We got the find not just of the century but maybe the greatest find of all times."

"Huh?"

"It's pretty clear that, centuries ago—maybe a lot longer than that—somebody who was pretty damned smart stuck a machine here that was so well made and so well suppplied with power sources, probably geothermal, that it's still working. That means an infinitely self-repairing device too." He frowned. "I wonder what the hell it does?"

"It's the extension of that *I* don't like," Harry responded. "Not just self-repairing. It knows we're here, George. It *knows*."

"Aw, c'mon. Don't shit in your pants at the unknown."

"I'm a little scared, I admit that, but that's not what I mean. If it did this every night, it'd have been spotted a long time ago. This place has been photographed to death. The whole damned world has, through satellites, day and night, and in the infrared, X-ray, you name it. And if they'd spotted anything, they'd have been here a long time before *us*. Uh-uh. The old man's right. This baby turned itself on just for us. It knows we're here, George. It *knows*."

George didn't like that. "Maybe, then, it's defending itself."

2

Nobody got much sleep that night, but there was a limit to how long you could watch even such an eerie phenomenon without discovering that your basic needs hadn't changed. The old man, of course, slept just fine; he'd been through this before.

Still, with the sun barely above the horizon and the sky only a dull, pale blue, there was movement. Harry felt himself being pushed and awoke almost at once. He was barely asleep, anyway. It was George, and Harry's expression turned from sleepiness to concern when he saw the other man's face.

"What's the matter?"

"It's Jenny—she's gone!"

"Jenny?" Harry was up in a moment. "Any sign of where she went?"

"Yeah. No horses or burros missing. Even if she was panicked out of her gourd, she'd take a horse. And there are a few tracks."

Harry turned toward the mountain, which looked as ugly and undistinguished as it had at first sight. "There? Hell, she'd never—"

"I know, I know. But she did. Either that or some of the old boy's buddies came along and got her."

"Let's get Terry," Harry suggested, but it was needless. The Indian woman had heard their not-so-whispered conversation and was already up and approaching them. The old man seemed to be sleeping through it.

"What's the matter?" she asked, and they told her quickly. She looked over at the mountain with a mixture of fear and concern, yet she didn't seem surprised.

"I've felt its pull myself since last night," she told them. "Haven't you? All night I lay there and I swore I could hear voices in many languages, all calling my name—my Apache name as well. There was a tremendous pull and I had trouble resisting it."

George shook his head wonderingly. "Damn! That's all right for you and your mysticism, but—hell, Jenny? Not a brain in her head and scared to death of her own shadow. *You* saw her last night. She wouldn't go near that thing for a million bucks and a lifetime Hollywood contract."

Terry looked at the tracks. "Nevertheless, that's what she appears to have done. It couldn't have been too long ago; I don't think I slept more than a few minutes, and all of that in the last hour."

Both men nodded. "Looks like we're gonna find out a bit more than we bargained for last night," George grumbled, sounding slightly nervous. "I hope that thing's inactive in the daylight."

They grabbed a canteen and a couple of Danish from the supplies, and checked their guns. They wasted no time.

"Ready?" George asked, and they nodded. "Hey, what about the old boy?"

Terry looked back at the sleeping form. "He'll know," she said mysteriously. "Don't worry. Let's see if we can get her."

The rocky ground wasn't good for tracks, but it was clear that she had gone to the mountain. Any lingering doubts ended at the point where the glow had begun the night before. George looked down and again shook his head in wonder. "Jenny's boots—and socks too," he muttered. "What the hell? Barefoot on this shit?"

Harry stared at the footwear, not sitting as if removed but tossed, as if discarded, and felt a queer feeling in his stomach and the hairs on his neck tickle. *Don't go,* something inside him pleaded. *Chicken out! Go back and*

wait for them! He looked up at the usually impassive
Terry Sanchez and saw, unmistakably, some of the same
feelings inside her. She gave him a glance that told him it
was true, and in that glance was also the knowledge they
both shared that they would ignore those feelings in spite
of themselves.

George bent down and picked up something, handing
it to Harry. He looked at it critically. It was his wirecutters, looking none the worse for wear. He sniffed them,
but there was no odd smell or sign of burn marks or
anything else, either.

There was a small sound and a few tiny rocks moved.
They all jumped and looked up, and George, at least,
relaxed. "Lizard," he told them, sounding very relieved.
"Well, if *he* can live in a place like this, *we* shouldn't be
electrocuted." With that he set foot on the mountain and
began walking up.

It wasn't really a tall hill—no more than eight
hundred feet or so—and while this side wasn't exactly
smooth, it was mostly sandstone and gave easy foot-
holds.

The other two followed. "Where are you heading?"
Harry called to him.

"Just up here a bit," George responded. "When I saw
the lizard I spotted something else." He was at the spot
in a minute or two and stopped again, looking down.
They caught up and saw what he'd seen.

"Jesus! Her jeans!" George breathed. "Has she gone
out of her mind?"

Terry looked up at him and scowled. "That *would* be
the explanation running through your mind."

"Got a better one?"

"Maybe. Let's go on with it."

He looked around. "Which way?"

"Up," she replied. "The easiest way."

It wasn't a hard trail to follow. A bit more than halfway up they discovered all her clothing. Unless she'd
changed, there was no doubt that Jenny Golden was now
somewhere on or in the mountain stark naked.

George kicked at Jenny's bra. "This would be the last of it. So now where do we go?"

"I think I know," Harry managed, his voice sounding as frail as his stomach felt. "Remember our display last night? The fountains of sparkles?"

They nodded.

"Well, unless I miss my guess, the opening for the blue one should be only a little over and maybe ten feet farther." He stared at the barren landscape. "Yup. There it is."

They went up to it with little difficulty and stood around it, looking at it. It was by no stretch of the imagination a cave, but rather an opening in the rock layers barely large enough for one person to enter. Harry removed his pack and set it down, removing lantern-style flashlights and mining caps with small headlamps. The others did the same, and quickly they had what they needed—what they thought they might need—to explore a subterranean remain. They quickly donned the gear, including gloves, and Harry looked at the other two. "Well? Who's the hero?"

George stared nervously back at him, and Harry caught the expression.

Put up or shut up, Big George, he thought a little smugly. *The time for big talk is past.*

"Okay," the blond man said at last, resigned to it. "I'll go in first. If everything's okay, Terry, you should be second, with Harry bringing up the rear."

Harry saw Terry's impulse to let George off the hook and prayed she wouldn't do it. She didn't.

George fixed the rope to his harness and looked nervously at the coil. "How much we got?"

"A hundred feet. Don't worry about it," Harry told him. "If you need more than that, then she's dead and beyond saving. If you need it much at all, in fact."

That sobered them.

George spent a little time checking and rechecking everything, although it was pretty much show, a bid for time to get up his nerve. Finally, though, he swallowed hard, went to the hole, and examined it. "No odors, sul-

phur or anything else," he noted. "Looks natural." He
sat down and cautiously put himself into the hole, feet
first. He kicked a bit. "Seems like a sloping ramp. Feels
smooth, so keep a grip on that rope."

"Don't worry," Harry assured him.

Cautiously George slid into the hole in the hillside.
Terry stood at the mouth, listening, as Harry played out
the rope.

"Smooth rock and a gentle slope," George called
back. "Funny—looks more like limestone, although the
surrounding rock is sandstone for sure. Considering how
it spouts, probably something akin to geyserite. Stuff
from deep down. Wonder how far?"

"Any sign of Jenny?" Terry called to him.

"Nope. Funny, though. Should be getting cooler, I'd
think, but it's not. The rock's warm, but not hot."

That concerned them all. The geyserite implied vol-
canism beneath, and also intermittent steam eruptions,
which might have been what they had seen the night before. Some form of them, anyway.

George was about twenty-five feet in now and called
up, "I'll be damned!"

"What did you find?" Terry called back.

"Handholds! This thing starts down and there's handholds of some kind of metal. No rust or anything. They
look machined. It's wider down here now. Let me turn
. . . Yep! It's a long tube going down at about a sixty-de-
gree angle, and it's got both handholds and metal steps.
Damn! Those steps look like they're naturally imbedded
in the sandstone. That's ridiculous, of course."

"Wait there!" Terry called. "I'm coming down!" She
turned to Harry. "Secure the rope and I'll just use it as a
guide. Whatever we're going into, somebody built it."

He nodded. "When you get down, send George down
the hole and wait for me. I'll rig the rope so I can free it
and pull it after. We might need it, and there's no way
we're going to get packs in there."

She nodded and was soon into the hole and out of
sight. Harry fixed the rope, then waited for her call.

When it came, he started in himself, barely fitting through the opening.

George was both right and wrong on the geyserite, he decided. If it were really the product of the steam eruptions, it would cover all sides of the cave, but it didn't—only the floor. The substance was similar, but he doubted it was there from natural causes.

Once alongside Terry, Harry freed the rope and reeled it in as she descended.

He waited in silence and near-darkness as her light quickly vanished below. Soon there was no sound at all, and when he shouted down, only his echoes returned. Again the feeling of panic seized him. What if things weren't all right down there? What if whatever had seized hold of Jenny had also now gotten *them*?

He shined his light on the ladder. It was an impossibility and he knew it, as if someone millions of years before had positioned the metal steps and then waited for the sedimentary rock—which, of course, was only laid underwater—to compact over them, leaving the perfect staircase.

Sighing, he descended into the dark.

It was easy—almost as easy as climbing down a fire escape. He found that George hadn't exaggerated the heat, though. If anything, it was hotter inside than out, but incredibly it also was terribly, terribly humid.

He descended until he felt he would just keep going down forever, but finally he reached bottom.

The cavern—no, *tube*—in which he found himself was oval-shaped but quite large, perhaps twelve feet across by eight feet high, and seemed perfectly manufactured out of the same smooth rock as the floor above. More interesting, it glowed with some sort of greenish internal light. Not enough to make the place bright, but enough to see by, that was for sure. He kept his miner's cap on but switched off his flashlight, then looked around. There was no sign of the other two.

Again the fear gripped him, along with the eerie silence, and this time he turned toward the stairway that led back.

The stairway wasn't there. The hole wasn't there. In back and in front of him was only the same green-glowing chamber.

He felt a stab of sheer panic and looked around for the rope and other gear—and did not see it. *It's got me! My God! It's got me!*

He felt like throwing up but did not. Instead he looked in both directions, decided on the one he'd been facing, and started walking.

What were these eerie chambers? He couldn't help wondering. Were they the exhausts of some millennia-lost spaceship? Or, perhaps, corridors within that ship, or some ancient extraterrestrial colony? If the latter, what would they be like, who made their tunnels like this in shape and texture?

He walked through the sameness of the chambers, and he finally ceased to fear or wonder or analyze. All those things seemed to flow out of him, leaving him almost empty, a shell, a lonely wanderer of subterranean alien corridors conscious only of the need to move, to walk forward. That and of the heat.

Faintly he struggled, but his resistance grew weaker and weaker as he walked. And as he walked he became aware of others, too, walking with him, under a heat that no longer came from within but from above, from a warm sun in a cloudless sky, one that he could not yet see or comprehend.

He was born.

His parents called him Little Wolf because he was born with so much hair on his head, and he grew up a curious and intelligent child in the world of the People. Unlike the subhumans who roamed the plains, the People lived in semipermanence beside the shore of a great lake on the edge of a beautiful forest. The men hunted and fished, while the women bore and reared the children, maintained the village, and in season, when the priest said all the signs were right, planted and tended some crops, mostly maize but occasionally nice vegetables as well.

In his thirteenth year manhood came upon him, quite
unlike what Little Wolf expected it to be but that which
he'd anticipated and prayed for all the same, and thus,
the following spring, he entered the teaching circles of
the warriors and learned the basics of survival—the use
of the bow, the science of the spear, the patience needed
to capture deer and birds and other creatures, and also
some of the arts of war. Of the codes of war he needed
no instruction: Those were a part of the culture of the
People from the time of his birth and were as much taken
for granted as the air, trees, and water.

By late spring he was accompanying the men into the
forests on hunts, and out on the lake in canoes to use the
coarse skin and bark nets made by the women to catch
the silvery fish. He was neither the best nor the worst of
the candidates for manhood, and, finally, he brought
down a young doe with his bow and handmade flint
arrows, and passed the final preliminary. The ceremonies
of manhood were solemn and took several days, but in
the end he was anointed, his head was shaved, and he
was branded painfully on the face and chest and hands
by the priest with the signs of manhood of his people and
did not flinch or hold back and was, therefore, proclaimed a man.

He enjoyed his new status and took particularly well
to the hunt, showing an ability to go for days without
food far from home in search of community meat. Because of this he chose his man's name as approved by
the elders of his tribe, that of Runs-Far-Needs-Nothing,
a name he was very proud of.

In the fall the elders met with all the new men and
brought forth the new women, those whom the gods had
shown by the sign of blood were now women. Runs-Far-
Needs-Nothing took then one whom he'd known from
childhood, a small, lithe, attractive woman who accepted
him as well and whom he gave the woman's name
Shines-Like-the-Sun, a name approved by her parents
and the elders and by she herself.

His early years had been remarkably peaceful, with
little commerce and no major conflicts with the subhu-

mans, although an occasional one of these strange ones
would come to bargain for food or passage rights, and
there would be occasional contests between the men,
which the People usually won—which was good, since
losing such a contest to a subhuman would bring such
shame that suicide would usually be called for.

It wasn't until his seventeenth fall, however, that any
real trouble appeared. The spring rains had not come in
their usual numbers, and the snows of the previous
winter had been light, insufficient to fill many of the
smaller creeks that fed the lake. Through some irrigation
a substandard crop had been raised, even with the lake
many hands below its normal level, and the People knew
they would survive the drought with what they had and
the ministrations of the high priest. After all, game was
plentiful, as the dryness drove more and more animals
closer to the lake's precious water, but they had little to
spare.

Shines-Like-the-Sun, meanwhile, was again with
child, having already borne a son and a daughter to him,
and they were content.

One day, though, still in the heat of early fall, a subhuman arrived looking grimmer than usual. The game
had fled the northern plains, he told them, where in some
places the land was scorched as by fire and baked harder
than the hardest rock, while rivers that had always run
pure and clean and deep as long as his people could remember were hard-caked mud. Without the game and
waters of the lake, his people could not hope to survive
to the spring, and he wished permission for his people to
establish their own camp on the far side of the lake.

This was much debated by the elders, who finally
consulted all the adults of the People, and what they
concluded was grim news indeed. Such a large group as
the subhumans would tremendously deplete the game
around the lake, and as those others knew none of the
skills of net-fishing and looked down upon farming as
inferior work, the burden on the wild edible vegetables
and fruits and the game would be tremendous, possibly
too great for the lake to stand. Worse, as nomads, the

subhumans had no sense of conservation, worrying not a bit about whether such a place as this land would still bring what was needed a year or more hence. They would trade game and hides for fish and grain, of course, but in this case it would be the People's own game and hides. In effect the subhumans would be taking half the limited wealth of the People, then trading it for some of the remaining wealth while making the land poor. While charity would be a virtue, it would only lead to such insults as that, with the People becoming poorer and weaker by far. Therefore, they recommended that permission to settle the nomads be denied.

This, of course, would leave the subhumans with no choice. Rather than move another week or more to the south, only to face the same situation or worse, they would fight, and they were a barbarous lot, without honor or mercy.

The People were as one to fight nonetheless, and the men went to prepare for battle. The subhuman emissary was notified and took the news well, as if he expected it—which he probably did. When he departed, several warriors discreetly shadowed him back to his people's encampment and set up a watch.

At dawn two days later the subhumans moved—not on the People's village, but to the place opposite on the lake where they had originally wished to go. Clearly they had realized that they could not launch a surprise attack on the village and had chosen instead to establish their own camp and dare the People to evict them.

The subhumans were a rough warrior race, but their idea of war was pretty basic and without real tactics. They expected to hold crude earthworks built in a single day to shield their tents, and they expected hand-to-hand overland attack or perhaps a seige. They had left their backs open to the water.

The People *would* attack, from both sides, but in a coordinated manner. The added factor would be a waterborne attack after the dual attack overland drained the enemy's manpower away from the rear. Almost two dozen canoes filled with the best would attack then.

Runs-Far-Needs-Nothing was one of those who would attack overland. He and most of the others felt no real fear or concern for the battle. After all, were these not subhuman barbarians? Besides, tales and legends of battles were a part of his growing up, and they were romantic adventures. He and his fellows welcomed the chance to show their superiority, their skills and cunning, and perhaps add to the legends.

The subhumans *were* caught somewhat off-guard, because they expected a dawn attack and it was well past midday when the People launched their drive. There was good reason for this: The sun was across the lake, causing near-blinding reflections and therefore masking the lakeside attackers and their canoes, a trick remembered from one of those legendary battle tales.

At first it went gloriously, with bowmen shooting hails of arrows into the subhuman encampment from both sides, then spearmen moving forward under arrows' cover. The battle was fierce, and the subhumans were brave and skilled fighters, but they were clearly outnumbered.

Still, the young warriors of the People learned that war was not romantic. Blood flowed, innards were spilled, and close friends of a lifetime lay lifeless around them. Still they pressed on, knowing they were winning and that the canoes would soon land to finish off the rest who were even now falling back.

But inexperience was costly, and the People paid dearly for it as the woods erupted on all sides with almost as many of the enemy as they had faced. It placed the People's warriors between an enemy sandwich and both confused and demoralized them. Caught in crossfire, they fell in great numbers, while the added warriors of the enemy allowed those in the village to split off and defend the beach against the incoming canoes. Most of the brave warriors of the People died without ever realizing that they had been tricked very simply by an old, tough, experienced foe who *knew* his emissary would be followed back to camp and a count made of his men. A foe who had shown less than half his true numbers to those scouts while the others were already moving to positions across the lake.

Runs-Far-Needs-Nothing understood none of this, but he knew now that his people had lost, and he felt fear both for himself and for his wife and children, a fear that turned to a fierce hatred of this enemy. He never even saw the one who killed him, an experienced man of eighteen...

Harry awoke slowly in the corridor and for a moment didn't know who or where he was. Two languages ran in his brain, two cultures, two totally different sets of references, and he could not come to terms with where he was or what he was. It came back, almost with a rush, but it seemed almost unreal and so very long ago. Even as he recounted his identity to himself over and over, and knew as he became more and more himself once again that he had had some sort of chamber-induced hallucination, he still marveled at his white skin and hairy body, a body that seemed wrong for him.

It was some time before he was suddenly aware that he was not alone. A small sound, a movement in the greenish-tinged oval cave, caused him to whirl and come face-to-face with Jenny Golden.

For a moment they just stared at each other, saying nothing. She looked as if in shock, somewhat vacant and, somehow, *older* than he remembered her. The eyes, he decided. It was the eyes. He wondered idly if he looked much the same.

After a few moments of looking at one another, he grew somehow alarmed that she was not aware of him, or at least of who he was. She seemed to sense this apprehension.

"How did you die?" she asked in a hollow, vacant tone.

"In a battle," he responded, his voice sounding thick and strange in his ears. He was conscious of a slight difficulty in shaping the words, as one ancient language coexisted with a modern one. The same effect was noticeable in her voice. "I'm not too clear on the particulars."

"I died in childbirth," she told him, that tone still there and still somewhat frightening. "Giving birth to my ninth child."

3

He had been sleeping. How long he didn't know, but it was a deep, dreamless sleep, and when he awoke he knew immediately who and where he was with an almost astonishing clarity of mind. Abruptly he remembered Jenny and for a moment was afraid that she'd be gone again like some will-o'-the-wisp, leaving him alone and confused. He was relieved to see that she was still there and looking a bit calmer and saner than she'd seemed the first time. Still, when she turned to look at him, she seemed much older, somehow, than he'd remembered, and her eyes still seemed to reflect some inner pain.

He sat up, stretched, and nodded to her. "How long was I asleep?"

She shrugged. "A long time. Who can say in here?"

"I'm sorry for passing out on you so abruptly."

Again a shrug. "I did the same thing. You come back kinda dizzy and not really knowing who you are, then you conk out, and when you wake up—well, I don't know."

He nodded sympathetically. "You've changed, Jenny. You've—well, I'm not sure how to put it. Grown up."

"Aged, you mean. Or maybe you're right. Anyway, I know who I am now and all that, but I also have the memories of that other life, just as real, but I'm in control, if you know what I mean."

"Yeah. The same way. Any sign of the others?"

"Not yet. I really was beginning to think that I'd never see any of you again, when you popped up." Her voice seemed to soften, then crack, and tears formed in her eyes. "Thank God you showed up."

He went over to her and just took her hand, squeezing

it lightly to reassure her and tell her he understood.

And when she'd cried it out, she wanted to talk about it. He let her take her own time.

"You know, I always us'ta have these fantasies," she said. "I dunno—we're all supposed to be liberated, you know? And I like the freedom and all, but I'd still fantasize. Submission. Bondage. You know, like I was a slave girl in some sultan's empire. Like that, you know. I mean, I never really *wanted* that; it was just a fun thing, for masturbating, that sort of shit."

"You mean this thing gave you your fantasy?"

"Sort of. It was way far back, I'm pretty sure. An Oriental tribe, somewhere in Asia. Nobody was too clear on geography, you understand."

He nodded. "I've only an educated guess as to where I was too."

"Well, anyway, it was a nomad tribe, picking up and moving from valley to valley and across big mountains and deserts. They were a rough, tough group, too, and they didn't think much of women. They treated us like *slaves*, like *property*. Some of 'em got so mad when they got daughters they killed them. Just little babies. We cooked, we cleaned, we took down and put up the tents and fucked whenever the men got in the mood, and we got beat when we did it wrong or too slow or even if the man had problems. And we bore babies. God! Did we have babies!"

She fell silent, and he waited for a while to make sure she was finished. Finally he said, "Well, I wasn't nearly as bad off, even though I was just about as primitive." He described his life and realized with some surprise that he was almost nostalgic about it and them. "The big trouble was how naive they were," he told her, and, in so doing, told himself. "They were too peaceful and too inexperienced for what they faced—a group much like your tribe. Somewhere there I think there's a lesson in both our—other lives—but I can't put my finger on it yet if it *is* there. I got, I think, a clue, though, as to what we were put through and why." He sighed. "If only we could link up with the others! If their experiences bear out the idea, maybe I can get a handle on what we're facing in here."

"Well, I'm not going looking for them," she responded. "Look, I was sleeping at the camp when suddenly I kinda half woke up and knew I was walking someplace. I thought I was dreaming. It was just like some kinda magnet, you know, pulling me into the mountain. I *do* remember crawling along a dark tube, then going down some stairs, then along this tunnel— and that's it."

He nodded. "We followed you when we discovered you were missing and wound up doing the same thing. I was the last in. Until I got to this tunnel area, though, I had a clear head, and I was on the watch, but it got me anyway."

"But—why me? Why did it call *me*?"

"There could be a number of reasons," he told her, preferring not to contrast her intellect with the others', "but I suspect it's some kind of hypnotic process."

"You mean I got hypnotized when I was watching the colored lights?"

He nodded. "That's about it. Some people are more hypnotizable than others. It hooked you then and used that hook to draw you to it, giving you some kind of subliminal instructions."

She looked around and seemed to shiver slightly. "But who? Why?"

"I'm not sure it's a *who*. I doubt it. I'm pretty sure it's just a machine. An incredible, impossible, near-magical machine, but a machine all the same. It's nothing I know, but I just sort of feel it."

"A machine? But who built it? And why?"

"I'm not sure yet. I need more information."

"Harry?"

"Yes?"

"Are we—did we—live lives of people it trapped in here? Will we just go through all of 'em until we die of starvation or something?"

He thought about it. "I doubt it. First of all, neither you nor I were ever near this place in our other lives.

Second, I doubt if any people like you describe—physically, anyway—were ever anywhere near New Mexico. No, my people might have been: there was something very Amerind about them. But not yours. As for dying of starvation, do you feel hungry?"

She thought about it, a curious expression on her face, as if she'd never thought about it before. "No. Not at all."

"Neither do I. And my hair and beard are about the same length as they were, and your shaved legs are still smooth, so we probably haven't *really* been here long at all. Either that, or time has no meaning for us here in the literal sense. I'm not sure. I *was* hungry when I came in, and you should have been too." He considered that further. "Look, you've been here, subjectively, a long time. Have you had to take a crap? Or even a piss?"

"No, come to think of it."

"Then we're in some sort of stasis—limbo, whatever. The machine is taking care of us. I'm not sure we're exactly in time at all."

"Huh? What do you mean?"

"There were machined metal steps imbedded in the stone. Now, that's impossible. It took millions of years to lay that sediment, one grain at a time, so laying them as the rock was formed is impossible. But that's exactly the way they looked."

"So how's that possible?"

"It isn't. The only way I can figure it was that this whole gadget was sort of slowly phased into our existence so it became possible."

"But you just said that'd be real slow."

"Smart girl. But not if you're thinking the unthinkable, as I am. I think this thing was sent back in time."

"But that's ridiculous!"

"It sure is. But so is this machine and what it did to us."

She shook her head in wonder and disbelief. "But who sent it, then? And why?"

"Somebody in the far future, that's for sure. Some civilization that knows a lot more than we do. No, check that. Think about this, maybe: a future civilization that knows more science than anybody ever dreamed. A civilization that can build a machine like this and make it do what it does."

"But what kind of creatures are they?"

"People. Like us, maybe. Or close enough to us for— Hey! That's it! At least, it'll do until a better explanation comes along."

"What?"

"Okay, now suppose there's a war or something. The big one. The whole world gets wiped, but somehow some people survive. Build it up again, bigger and better than it was, maybe. Explore all the mysteries we would have if we hadn't been zapped. They know everything— except their own history and culture, all traces of which have been wiped out. So they have this project. They send back this machine and maybe a lot of remote machines connected to it. Put 'em all over. Start as far back as they can date any human remains and start there. Let the machines randomly record people's lives and cultures. A scientific sample, so to speak."

"But if they can travel in time, why not just come back and see for themselves?"

"Maybe they can't. I keep thinking of those steps in the stone. If you have to take millions of years just to phase in something—millions here, not to them—it might not work with people. Besides, if these people were from the year 20,000 or something, you realize the time involved? You'll never have enough time to look at, analyze, and know a million years of human history, particularly if you know so little to begin with. No, this would be the logical way."

"But look at the lives we had!" she protested. "They weren't important. Not really. No great people, great civilizations, nothing like that."

"No, and the odds would be against them ever really coming up with a great person, although I'm sure they've recorded many of the civilizations through the lives of people who lived in them. Ordinary people. Like us. The kind of information that tells you the important stuff—

what people and culture were really like in different places at different periods in human history. Yeah, that's *got* to be it. We've gotten ourselves trapped in somebody's grand anthropology experiment."

He ran down after that, feeling slightly exhausted but also somehow excited. He refused to consider that he'd made wild stretches of logic and imagination based on few hard facts, but, still, he was certain he'd gotten it right. He wondered idly if he hadn't picked at least the basics from the machine itself to which he and Jenny were so obviously tied.

She, too, was silent for a bit, and he realized that his own ideas were a bit too much for her to swallow or accept all at once. He sympathized with her. She didn't really belong here, he thought idly. Maybe as a *subject* for the machine, but not here, trapped inside of it. His own reaction was curiously different. Understanding it, as he thought he did, made all the difference. To lose yourself in time, to live the lives of others through the ages while never aging yourself...

"Harry?"

"Yes?"

"Why *us*? Why suck us into it?"

He thought a moment. "Well, if I'm right and it's sent back by people—our descendants—and it's just a dumb machine, the world's grandest tape recorder, it might just figure we're part of the folks who built the thing. It struck a chord somewhere in you and drew you to it, probably just to make sure you knew it was there. Who knows? People and cultures change a lot. Who knows how those future people think? Or what their lives are like? Anyway, it thinks we're the ones who it's working for, and it's playing the recordings for us."

She looked stricken by the thought. "My God! That means it'll keep playing the things for us. Hundreds of lives. Thousands. And we don't know how to switch it off or even tell it what to do!"

He saw her horror at the prospect he found so inviting and sat back, trying to think of some way to console her. Finally he found it.

"Look, remember the stories and legends about the chambers? Some never did come back, true—but *some did*! Some became great leaders and wise men."

"And some—most—went crazy," she noted.

He sighed. "Yeah," he acknowledged under his breath. "But think about it. Those who got out *got out*, if you see what I mean. They—smart, wise, or crazy—figured out the way out. And all of 'em were more ignorant, more primitive, than we. Cowboys and miners, Indians of the old culture, people like that. People who could never have understood what they were in. If *they* could figure it out, maybe we can too. It's got to be something simple, something basic. I wish we knew more about the ones that made it. Some common factor."

She looked at him strangely but with something akin to hope in her haunted eyes. "You know, I think maybe *you* can figure it out if anybody can." It was a statement tinged with admiration, and he felt slightly embarrassed by it.

"I wish we could find the others," he said, trying to change the subject. "The more heads the better." He got up and looked both ways in the oval cavern. "Now, which way did we come in?"

"From there," she told him, pointing behind him. "But you're not thinking of going on! It'll happen again!" There was an undertone of terror, almost hysteria, in her voice at that prospect.

"We've got to," he told her. "It's the only natural thing to do. Otherwise we'll just sit here forever."

"Harry—don't leave me!" It was a plea.

"Come with me. We'll do it together."

She got up hesitantly and looked nervously down the long, seemingly endless corridor. "Harry, I'm afraid. I—I can't. I just can't!"

"Jenny, I think the ones that just sat stayed. Either stayed or went nuts from just sitting endlessly."

She went up to him, trembling slightly. On impulse he reached out to her, drew her to him, and just hugged her close for a while. The act, one of compassion, nonetheless turned him on, a fact he could scarcely conceal from her.

She didn't mind. She needed it, needed *somebody*, a fact he soon recognized, and allowed it to happen. With an inner shock and surprise he realized that he needed it too.

It went with a degree of passion and intensity neither had ever really felt before, and it bonded them, at least for that moment, closer to one another than either had ever been to another sexual partner before.

And when it was finished they just lay there, caressing, saying nothing for quite a long time. Finally she said, "I think I'm ready now, Harry. I think I can go on."

He got up slowly, then helped her to her feet. "Let's take a walk," he said gently, and they began walking, his hand in hers, down the corridor.

They were approaching another time chamber, but even as they were aware of the fact, it became impossible to break free of it. They were sucked in and enveloped by it before they could even think of backing out.

He was born, the fourth son of a fisherman, and, as such, grew up in his father's trade. There was no question of where or when he was or what he was this time. He took his religion and religious training seriously, and was proud at his bar mitzvah, proud of his Jewish heritage and sincere in his belief that he was of God's Chosen People. Did not David, the greatest of Hebrew kings, rule in Jerusalem, and was not Israel growing under his leadership into one of the great civilizations of the world? Never was life, or destiny, or God's will, more certain to a man and his people than in that time.

And he prospered, having his own boat and making his own living by his seventeenth birthday. Although his marriage was properly arranged, there had never been any real question as to whom it would be. The beautiful Naomi, daughter of the fisherman Joshua, the son of Benjamin; he had known and loved her all his life. It was a natural marriage and a happy one, and she bore him three sons and two daughters, whom they raised and loved.

Things were hardly perfect. There always seemed to be wars and threats of wars, but somehow they never directly came to the village and the fishers. They grieved at news of Israel's losses and rejoiced and celebrated at news of ultimate victories, but it seemed, for the most part, far away and not quite connected to their lives. Some of the young men went off to wars, it was true, and some did not return, and there were occasional large masses of soldiers in and around, but they were always on their way from here to there. And Amnon, son of Jesse, lived seventy-three years and then died, and his wife of most of those years followed shortly after.

And when they had slept awhile in the corridors, they awoke once more.

"You don't look as frightened this time," Harry noted.

She smiled. "It was better this time. Much better. Civilized."

"Me, too," he responded. "Kind of dull, but interesting. And even though I lived a long time and died of old age in bed, making my life as Amnon longer by far than Harry Delaney's, I can handle it better."

"*What!*"

"I said I can handle it better."

"No, no! Who were you?"

"Amnon. A Galilean fisherman in the time of King David."

She almost leaped at him excitedly. "But I was Naomi! *Your* Naomi!"

His jaw dropped. "Well, I'll be damned!"

She grabbed him and kissed him. "This is great! We had one together!"

He hugged her, then sat back down again. "Well, I'll be damned," he repeated. So they took more than one sample in a given place. At least one male and one female. Did they, in fact, take an entire group sample? The whole tribe in the earlier case, or the whole village in the last one?

"That's *much* better!" she continued to enthuse, life coming back into her spirit. "It means we don't have to be alone anymore!"

"Perhaps. Perhaps not," he responded cautiously. "We'll have to see." But he had to agree that it was a satisfying possibility.

She hesitated a moment at his comment. "Please, Harry. Don't spoil it. Not when I have hope."

He smiled and squeezed her hand. "Okay, I won't. In fact, it seems something important was learned, but I cannot put my finger on it yet. Another piece of the puzzle." He looked at her. "You know, your moves, your gestures, even your speech, is more Naomi than Jenny."

"And yours," she responded. "So, you see, you are stuck with me. I have been your wife and the mother of your children. You know what that—" She broke off suddenly with a gasp.

"What's the matter?"

"Turn around."

He turned and was suddenly frozen. Facing them now was a very dazed-looking Theresa Sanchez. She took a couple of hesitant steps toward them, mouth open, then collapsed.

They rushed to her, but she was out cold. "It's like you the first time," Jenny told him. "We'll just have to wait for her to wake up."

He nodded and went over and sat back down. "Well, at least now there's only George to find."

4

Terry was as happy to see them as they were to find her. "I thought we were separated forever," she said to them.

"Well, at least we know it's not a maze to get lost in," Harry noted.

Terry looked puzzled. "Look, I'm a linguist, but you'll have to speak English or Spanish, I think. Anything but that."

Harry and Jenny looked at each other. He concentrated, realizing suddenly that he had been neither speaking nor thinking totally in English since coming back for the second time. It was an easy transition to make, but not one he'd have realized on his own.

"Sorry. Didn't realize what we were doing. What did it sound like to you?" he asked Terry.

"Some form of Hebrew," she told him, coming and sitting facing the other two. "I heard you two talking as I was waking up. Funny kind of unintelligible accents laced with English words here and there. You still have something of an accent."

"A fine thing for a Delaney," he noted humorously.

"Well, I was Jewish to begin with," Jenny noted, "so it's not so radical. Still, I never knew much Hebrew or anything else before. I guess we just carried it over."

"Carried it over?"

Harry nodded and explained the connected past lives of the two of them. In the course of it he also told Terry of his suspicions as to the nature and purpose of the machine.

She nodded and took it all in. "You went further than me, but that was pretty much my line of thinking too. How many lives have you two lived so far?"

"Two each, one together," Jenny told her.

Terry sat back looking at them. "That fits. Same here. I guess it's one life per chamber." She chuckled. "Looking and listening to you two made me wonder what George would think. Things have sure changed."

"Yeah," Harry responded, for the first time wondering about George in other than compatriotic terms. He was beginning to like this bond he had with Jenny, and, thinking of George's attitudes and Jenny's past attachment to him, he felt a twinge of insecurity at the thought of the big man returning now. He tried to put it from his mind. "Tell us of your lives—if you want to."

Terry nodded. "Sure. The more information the merrier, I suppose, if we're ever to figure a way out of here." The attitude she had and the way she said it carried a subtle hint to Harry, at least, that Terry didn't really want to leave. It made him reflect that he'd thought the same thing at one point, but now he wasn't so sure. In a place that never changed, suspended in time, personal changes seemed incredibly accelerated.

Terry's own experiences had followed the pattern. The first time she'd been born into a southeastern African matriarchy, a tribal society organized around a cult of priestesses, although in many ways the mirror was the same as with most primitive groups. The men hunted and soldiered; the women made the political and social decisions as well as supervised and worked the farms. Their world view had been strictly limited, without knowledge of any save their own dark race and little understanding of the world beyond their villages. The religion was animist and marked by many dances, festivals, and animal sacrifices, but it was, on the whole, quite civilized in its limited way. In many ways it reminded her of her own native Amerindian cultures of the Southwest. She'd been a priestess of the lower ranks, a somebody but not a big somebody, in charge of allocating the communal food supply, and she'd felt content. The only wrinkle in the whole thing was the severe lack of medical care and understanding, which caused many, if not most, of the tribe to be afflicted early with various diseases, and she had died in what she guessed to be her twenties, of infection, in a land where very few lived much beyond that.

She had awakened in the tunnel, finally analyzed her situation as much as she could, and then decided, like they had, to press on in hopes of finding the key to the place. In her second life she'd been born in a small village in the Alps in the tenth century A.D. and had become a Catholic nun in an order forever sequestered in the convent from the outside world. She described little of the routine of her very long life there, but indicated that it was terribly uncomfortable by modern standards and yet, somehow, happy and fulfilling to her.

When she'd finished, Harry considered the additional information carefully. In all three cases, he realized, the first life had been primitive, tribal, prehistoric, and yet somehow keyed to all three of them. He realized, perhaps for the first time, that the peaceful, romantic primitivism of his own first life had been through his late teen years, anyway, a romantic vision he himself had had. A deep concern for nature and the land, living in harmony and balance with it—the Rousseauan model. And if the reality hadn't quite matched the dream, well, that was the way with dreams.

Jenny had been given her sexual fantasy, and in this case the dream and reality had clashed with a vengeance, but that was always the way with dreams. Terry, an Indian, which set her apart—particularly in the white society of the modern Southwest—on her own, too brilliant to accept or live long in the reservation's primitiveness, yet unable to be fully accepted outside of it. Apart, too, from her native culture in particular, by her alleged lesbianism, which made her an outsider in modern culture and an object of hatred and scorn in her traditional one. Her first life had been a primitive matriarchy—again, not the dream, but it fit the facts.

And their second lives. Jenny and he together in a civilized pastoral setting; Terry a nun in a convent. Again it fit. And it made the leap he needed to understand the machine's strange system.

"Look, I'm analyzing all this," he told them, "and whether you like it or not, we got what our subconscious wanted at the time. It picked the stored life record to fit the individual. And that means it's not random at all." Quickly he explained to Terry his theories about how the machine recognized them as its possible builders. She nodded and listened seriously, although it was clear she didn't really like the idea that her two past lives had come from her own wishes.

"You see?" he continued. "It's not random. If it were, we'd all have had primitive, prehistoric lives the second time. History is only six thousand years old, while man is more than a million years old. The odds say that a random sample would put us ninety-nine percent of the time in prehistory. Don't you see the implications?"

Jenny just stared at him, but Terry nodded thoughtfully. "We *are* working the machine, then," she said, not really liking some of the implications of that. "It's waiting for instructions on what we want to study. Since we didn't give it any orders, it probed our minds and gave us what it *thought* we wanted."

"That's about it," he agreed. "And that means *we* could control the next life by conscious direction—within the limits of those pasts the machine's got stored and from what times and places."

Terry whistled. "It would be an interesting experiment. *Conscious* direction of the machine. We ought to try it. If we can do that, we might be able to figure it out completely."

Jenny groaned. "You mean *another* life?"

"Perhaps several," Terry agreed. "Don't you see that Harry's right? Even some of the primitive people of the past figured a way out. We are possibly the first people here who can take it a step further—who understand what kind of machine we are dealing with and can actually gain control of it!"

"But what sort of life would we choose?" Jenny pressed them. "Is there enough here to handle all three of us—together?"

"I dunno," Harry responded, thinking hard. "We know that it takes at least two readings from each era. It might take an entire tribe, or village, or whatever. There's really only one way to know."

"But we must agree as totally as possible on what we want," Terry cautioned. "We must all wish for the same things."

Harry sighed. "Okay, so let's see. We want the three of us to be together, at least in the same place at the same time. I, for one, want some civilization as well."

"And one where women have some freedom and mobility," Terry put in. "No offense, but I don't want to be a harem girl."

He nodded thoughtfully in agreement. "The big trouble is we don't know how comprehensive all this is. Are the gaps centuries apart, or do they take random samples from a specific age and place? Now, if *I* were putting together a project like this, I'd want random samples from as many cultures as possible at the same period in history, then advance the time frame for the new sample. That may mean dozens, perhaps hundreds, of different people and cultures for every given time. And the gaps, at least until the modern area of the Industrial Revolution, still wouldn't be more than a few centuries apart, to measure changes."

"So we need something fitting our requirements that existed for several hundred years culturally," Terry noted. "And one that fits our requirements."

He looked at both the women. "Any ideas?"

Jenny just shook her head, but Terry mulled it over and had an answer. "How about Alexandrian Egypt?" she suggested. "Sometime in the first couple of centuries A.D."

He stared at her. "Women weren't much thought of then," he noted.

She nodded. "I know. But I'm willing to take the risk just to see it."

He thought it over. "I'm willing if Jenny is. But let's be more specific if we use it. Let's assume that the machine catalogs a large sample from a specific place. If so, it might be possible to tell it not only where and when you want to be but *who*—in a rough sense."

Terry frowned. "Who?"

"Yeah. We want to be freeborns, not slaves. We want to be literate. If we're going, I'd love to get a crack at that great library."

Jenny looked at both of them quizzically. "I don't have the slightest idea what you're talking about."

"It was a great civilization," Terry told her, "mostly devoted to accumulating knowledge, which they kept in this huge library. The great minds of a great age were all there. They discovered the steam engine, and that the earth was round, and geometry, and lots more."

"How long ago did you say this was?"

"In the first centuries A.D.," she told her.

"Well, if they were so smart, how come it took us so long?"

"There was finally a revolution," Harry told her sadly. "They burned the library and destroyed the civilization.

Only a fraction of the books survived, those that were copied by hand and sent elsewhere, to Greece and to Timbuktu. But it was a great, lively civilization while it lasted."

Jenny looked at the two of them. "And we'll be together?"

"If we can pull it off," Harry replied. "And remember, another big if is that the civilization's in this machine's memory banks. We don't know."

"Then it's a risk."

He nodded. "But one we have to take. Will you try it with us?"

She looked first at one, then at the other. Finally she said, "You're going anyway, aren't you?"

He squeezed her hand. "We have to."

"Then what choice have I got?"

They went in together, consistent in their wishes, but they emerged again on the far side of the next chamber in staggered form. Harry was first, then Terry, with Jenny a bit behind.

And when they awoke after their deep sleeps, they found George waiting for them.

5

The shock of seeing George almost overcame their desire to share their experiences. They had all changed —grown older and more experienced—and it showed in their faces and manner and gestures. George, though, seemed to have changed very little from the last time they'd seen him so very, very long ago.

"Well, one big happy family again." He beamed, his voice betraying the curious accents of his own lives as theirs now did. "I'm really glad to see you."

He took Harry's hand and shook it vigorously and then tried to kiss Jenny, but she shied away from him and looked at him as if he were a total stranger. It clearly bothered him.

But first things came first. Harry looked at Terry with

some concern, because while she joined in, she seemed somehow hesitant, badly shaken. It was time to compare notes, then add George's data.

"Terry, you made it to Alexandria?"

She nodded. "I was—Hypatia."

Both Harry and Jenny gasped. "Hypatia!" he breathed. "I'll be damned. So they have some great ones in this memory bank."

She nodded. "It was a tremendous mind and will. It was an incredible honor to relive her life. She fought with all she had to save the library from the mobs, although she failed."

Both understood why she was so shaken. Hypatia, beautiful and proud, the last director of the Alexandria Library, had been cornered by a Christian mob and flayed alive. She looked at the others, knew they understood, and simply said, "You?"

"We met a few times. I was Claudius Arillius, aide to the governor-general."

She nodded. "I remember him. Intelligent but officious. Jenny?"

"I—I was Portia, your secretary at the library. I killed myself shortly after the mob overran the library."

Terry reached out and hugged Jenny. "You did what you could." She stopped suddenly. "What are we *saying*? We weren't those people. We merely relived their lives."

Harry nodded. "You find yourself getting used to it, too, huh? It becomes easier and easier to take and come out of, I think. Not that the experiences are any less intense, but somehow I have a clearer idea of my real self—old Harry here—than I did. It's Harry reliving a life rather than Harry living a new life."

They all nodded and turned to George, who seemed a little miffed that he'd been excluded up to now.

They sat down in a small circle and talked.

"I get the idea from what you folks were saying that you all wound up in the same place at the same time," George noted curiously.

Harry nodded. "And deliberately, George. We ordered it. We called it up and it was delivered."

George's mouth dropped. "Well, I'll be damned! You figured out how to work the thing! That's great! Hell, the potential for this place is limitless! It's the ultimate Disneyland and research center put together. You know, the Navajos are scared shitless of this place anyway, and it's near public land. With some finagling and a lot of politics, I bet we could own or control this thing. It's worth millions!"

They all stared at him in wonder. Finally Terry said, "George, is that all this means to you? A new money-making deal?"

"Well, ah, no, of course not. But somebody's gonna control this sooner or later and make a bundle. It might as well be us."

"First we have to figure out how to get out of here," Harry noted.

George's enthusiasm waned slightly. "Well, yeah, there's that. But hell, now that we know how to work it, it's inevitable we'll find the way out."

"*We* know," Jenny muttered sourly. "Already it's 'we.' "

George gave her an icy stare but decided not to respond. Instead he changed back to his favorite subject—himself. Which was just what Harry, at least, wanted to hear.

George followed the pattern and provided ultimate confirmation. In his first life he was in a prehistoric setting in the steppes of Russia north of the Fertile Crescent, a warrior race that sacked and looted other tribal groups throughout a wide area. He was one of those warriors, with seven wives captured in raids to serve him.

A distilled, basic George Singer fantasy.

He was in somewhat the same position in a far different time and place in the second, with the first ancient invasion of Korea by Japan. He got great delight out of telling the tales of that invasion, in which he was a samurai with the Japanese invasion forces.

In this last one he'd been a Moslem politician in Jerusalem during the siege of the Third Crusade.

All three were pretty consistent with what they knew of his mind, although Harry, for one, couldn't imagine George actually fighting or risking himself for honor or religion. Still, it hadn't been George but somebody else, somebody long dead who lived only here, in the memory banks of the Dowaii Chambers.

During the hours that passed, a great deal of data was exchanged, a great deal of speculation was made, and they searched for the key to the exit. There were also quiet periods, though, and those were the most trouble. It was plain that George was upset at Jenny's closeness to Harry. It was a combination of pride and egotism, not love or even lust. Women just didn't walk out on George. *He* walked out on *them*. And for an ugly brute like Harry Delaney, yet. In the end he resorted to making several overtures to Jenny, all of which were rebuffed, and even a few outright passes, which were put down even more strongly. This outraged him, and at one point he grabbed her angrily, only to have Harry coldly intervene. This startled George even more: Harry showing such bravery and threatening *him*? Still, the last thing he wanted was a fight over a mere girl, and he backed off, pride and ego wounded all the more.

At one point they roughly measured the distance between chambers as about a hundred and fifty meters. A long distance, and one that they could use as a sort of safety zone. After the showdown over Jenny, Harry and she kept well back in the tunnel, separating themselves from George unless it was time for a business talk.

Terry, whose contempt for George had been evident from the start, was nonetheless glad to be out of this argument. Her life as the brilliant Hypatia had affected her more than she was willing to admit, and she needed periods alone, just to think and get herself together. At one such time she was at the other end of the tunnel from Harry and Jenny—and away from George, who was sulking—just sitting and reflecting on her own feelings at this point. She loved the idea of this place now, of experiencing the lives and ages of mankind in a way no known social scientist ever could, but she realized George was right in a sense. The Dowaii Chambers needed the full range of modern science and the best minds in history, archaeology, anthropology, and related fields. Disneyland or a tool of research, George had said, and again he was right in ways he didn't really mean or understand.

If she bent to her impulses and remained inside, perhaps spending an eternity living those great and not-so-great lives stored here, then the Dowaii Chambers would be Disneyland—*her* Disneyland. Or, in a sense, her opium. Hooked forever in vicarious experience but contributing nothing.

They *had* to get out, she knew. Get out and bring the others back. The chambers were the greatest find in the history of mankind, and deserved to be used and shared —as, perhaps, its builders had intended.

Who were they? she wondered. Some future people like Harry imagined, or, perhaps, people from some long-dead civilization or even from the stars who left this great machine either as a recording mechanism for themselves or someday to show mankind the secrets it had lost.

What if that was true? What if our very creators had placed this here, not for mankind but as some sort of evaluative tool? Was this, perhaps, God's record of mankind? Was this the record that would be read out on Judgment Day?

The spiritual questions haunted her most, for she'd been raised a devout Catholic and truly believed, and those patrons of the early Church, led by Cyril—one day to be a saint—had flayed *her* alive and stormed and burned the greatest of scientific knowledge and culture. Anti-intellectual cretins running amok with power and torturing and murdering all those who would not totally agree and support their beliefs, all in the name of God and the holy Catholic Church.

Holy Mary, Mother of God . . .

"Hello."

She looked up and saw George standing there. He squatted down beside her. "You look lonely," he said.

"Not in the way *you* mean," she responded sourly.

"No, no. I really want to help," he said sincerely. "What's the problem? If a bunch of old Indians and conquistadores can get out of here, we sure can."

"I have never doubted it," she told him. "Just go away. You wouldn't understand."

"Try me. I'm not as dense as you think."

She looked at him seriously. "You have only lost your girl friend. I have lost my god."

He stared at her a moment in amazement, and then he started to laugh. It was a laugh of true amusement, not loud or overwhelming or cruel in tone, but it was terribly cruel to her.

"Don't you laugh at me, Singer," she spat. "Get out. Just get the hell away and leave me alone!"

His face grew suddenly grim and serious. "You know what your problem really is? You need somebody to fuck your brains out. I can cure you, Terry."

He grabbed her, and she stood with him and screamed, "Get your filthy hands off me, Singer!"

"C'mon. Try it. I got the cure to both our problems." He started to force her down onto the tunnel floor, but her knee came up and caught him in the groin. He let go and almost doubled over in pain, but the respite was short-lived. It had not been a serious blow and his anger masked his pain.

She tried to get around him, to get back to reinforcements, but he blocked her, a madness in his expression now not so much from the lust he felt but from his anger at being both scorned and kicked.

"I'll show you, you bitch!"

"*Harry*!" she screamed. "*Jenny!*"

He lunged at her and she moved back, toward the chamber not so very far away. Without any kind of measurement tools they were only approximating where the effects of the chamber might begin, and George ran after and caught her somewhere in the nebulous zone.

"Damn you, Singer!" she screamed. "I wish *you* could be on the receiving end of this! I wish *you* could know what I'm feeling!"

His grip on her, so tight that it was blocking circula-
tion, seemed to loosen, then go slack, as the chambers
caught him in their grip.

Grappling with him, Terry vaguely heard the calls
from Jenny and Harry in the distance, but they, and even
George, seemed to fade away into nothingness . . .

Terry Sanchez was born in southeastern Arizona in
the shadows of the hills of her ancestors. She had a
brother slightly older than she, but her mother died in
bringing forth a third, stillborn, daughter. In a modern
city, in white culture, it would have been easy to see that
the woman bore tremendous marks and bruises that certainly contributed to her death, but here, with one doctor
for several thousand square miles and him a very busy
one not overly concerned with Indians or Mexicans, it
went unnoticed. Terry was only four at the time, and her
memories of her mother were quite dim, mostly a haunting vision of a gentle, suffering face full of pain.

The source of that pain was a father who, in other
circumstances, might not have been a bad man at all.
Ill-educated, raised on the legends of his grandfathers,
with never a steady job or income, he had become hardened, bitter, and tremendously frustrated. He was an in-
ward-looking, brooding sort of man who took to drink
whenever depression hit him, which was often. He had
some hopes for his son, who was intelligent and ambitious, but when Terry was only ten her brother, playing,
fell into an abandoned and not very well-sealed septic
tank and died before anyone could get him out.

Her father had no feeling that women could amount to
anything more than sexual partners and baby-makers, so
the death of his beloved son increased his bitterness and
his drinking and he took it out on Terry, both in beatings
when she did anything he perceived as wrong and, occasionally, sexually. This brutalization came to the attention of an aunt, her mother's sister, who lived far away
but made regular trips through to see all her relatives,
and the aunt knew immediately what the situation was.
She pulled a number of strings with the government

agents, some of whom were idealistic young people who were shocked at some of the conditions they found, and also found an ally in the Catholic priest who served the entire desert area.

Although all expected her father to react violently, he was ashamed of himself—at least, he was ashamed that it had all come out—and did nothing to block the authorities from removing Terry and placing her in a Catholic home for young Indians, mostly orphans, near Wilcox. The nuns instilled in her a sense of something and someplace better, opened up the world to her, and encouraged and developed her talent for picking up other languages. They had hopes that she would become a missionary nun, of course, and she took the first steps toward entering the order when she became eligible for some state minority scholarships to the University of Arizona. Despite protestations that one didn't exclude the other, she put off joining the order and taking final vows and went off to university life.

It was still not easy. The conservative, mostly white university staff and student body had their own prejudices, but she was willing to face them. More important were some of the younger, more radical although small organizations on campus. She found herself very good at the women's center, counseling on rape, battered women, and other such subjects, and soon found herself the darling of the minority white, upper-middle-class "radical liberals" as they were called. The anthropology department, too, found her fascinating and useful, with her gift for languages nobody else could fully master, particularly southwestern Indian tongues totally unrelated to anything in her own background. Several different life objectives emerged from this, including an eventual major project to record and preserve the oral history of the hundreds of Indian tribes of the Southwest.

It was also during this period that she discovered, or at least admitted to herself, that she preferred the company of other women to that of men. Intellectually she knew that, unlike many other women who felt that way, at least obviously, her own childhood was mostly responsible, but she accepted it with little real guilt. Men just seemed too brutish, not gentle enough, and that was that. But it added another cross to bear in ultraconservative Arizona, and she found herself pulled between more tolerant San Francisco and the place where her life's work was. The only guilt she felt was that she knew she did not have the strength to become a nun; she needed the intimacy of sex or to have it available.

So she kept herself very unobtrusive, gave up most of her radical and liberal associations—many of whose politics caused too great a conflict with her Catholicism— and contented herself with one intimate roommate, her work, and constant field trips for the great project. A project that eventually brought her to George's own project and the Dowaii Chambers.

Thus did Terry Sanchez again enter the strange mountain, and again live three other lives, and again stand in the tunnel, fending off George's advances. And thus did George know Terry Sanchez more intimately than any had ever known another, for he had lived her life through the chambers . . .

George Singer had been born to money, but he'd been an only child, spoiled rotten by parents who would give the kid a twenty every time he just wanted a hug, and whose childhood and early teens were very lonely times, only partly due to the fact that he was tremendously fat and highly unattractive. He learned early on that girls said they wanted a friend but always went to bed with the macho types, and that the only reliable women were those you bought. It was a cynical, unhappy early time for the boy who had everything.

Finally he got sick and tired of it. He entered a series of classes to build his muscles while going on a stringent diet, a program that frustration had led him to. It took him three years, until he was twenty, to get where he wanted, but the physical change in him was enormous. Out of the ugly, flabby mass he'd always been emerged a handsome, muscular man. But it was the same man inside.

He had no trouble with women now, but he knew them for the shams they were. As he had watched them going for the muscles and the phony lines before, he knew that he'd spent all that time remaking himself into that image he'd always seen succeed—and it did.

Money was freedom and the only thing that mattered. He was lazy about scholarship, although by no means dumb, but he always found a way to buy a paper or a research project that would do, and his ability to bullshit his way convincingly through exams by giving the professors exactly what fed their pet ideas made his college career an astounding success. He spent his sports time in weight lifting and wrestling, not popular sports but ones that continued to give him the physique that everybody admired and women drooled over.

His gifted cynicism made him a top-notch con man in academia, and he exploited everything and everybody that came along. He felt no guilt, no remorse: Those were the same people who had turned their backs on him when *he* had needed *them*. He knew full well that the world ran on how you were perceived by those who counted, and money and fame greased the wheels.

He wanted the Ph.D. because *Dr.* before your name impressed the hell out of people, and he chose the social sciences because it was the easiest group of real academics to con. When his assistant put him on to the Dowaii Chambers, he knew at once that it meant not only a doctorate but tremendous fame within and, if spectacular enough, even *outside* the field. If it was really spectacular enough . . . The George Singer National Monument. Not bad, not bad . . . And if Carl Sagan could parlay something like astronomy into big-bucks show biz, it was time somebody did it with anthropology. *The Dowaii* by George Singer, Ph.D.—a Book-of-the-Month Club Special Dividend.

He had dreams and ambitions, did George Singer. And he'd put it all together, like the producer of a play, not even using his own field for the grants but that twerp

Delaney's; so Delaney would get his little project done, and Singer would get Dowaii, alone, exclusively. The dyke with the missionary spirit would be easy to handle.

And so, again, to the chambers, and so, again, into the mountain, and so, again, through three lives that confirmed his own view of the world and how it worked, people and power, and women.

But this time Terry Sanchez had lived it all with him.

Harry examined the two sleeping forms with some concern. Jenny just watched, shaking her head, a disgusted expression on her face. Finally she said, "Harry, what kind of thing would the machine *do* to them? I mean, my God, they went into the chamber during a *rape!*"

He got up and shrugged. "I don't know. We'll have to wait and see. If you'll help me, I think we ought to pick up Terry and put her over there a bit, so they don't wake up side by side, if you know what I mean."

"Getcha," Jenny agreed, and they moved her about ten feet along the tunnel, then positioned themselves between the two sleeping forms.

They waited a fairly long time, not talking much, anxiously wondering which of the two would wake up first, and were startled when both seemed to come around at the same time.

"Hmmm . . . *That's* never happened before," Harry noted. "You take Terry and, God help me, I'll take George."

But their concerns were needless. George awoke looking puzzled and somewhat upset, but without any signs of violence or rancor. Terry looked around, then over at George, and had the most extreme look of pity on her face Jenny had ever seen. George saw her and had a little of that same look, although it was more puzzlement than anything else.

Finally Jenny couldn't stand it any longer. "What happened?" she asked Terry.

"We—I lived his life!," she managed, her voice sounding a little dry and raspy. *"I was George!"*

Harry looked at George. "You too?"

George nodded and looked over at Terry. "I—I didn't *know.* Please—you got to forgive me. At least that."

Terry looked back at him. "You know I will," she responded gently. "Maybe—just maybe—something good came out of these chambers."

Harry and Jenny looked at the two of them, and Harry shook his head slowly. "Maybe it did at that. Certainly we've all changed. You two learned a little about life and maybe grew up a bit. Passive, insecure little Jenny here has enough self-confidence and fight now to go out and conquer the world."

Jenny smiled and stared at him a bit. "But you haven't, Harry. Not really."

He chuckled slightly. "Oh, yes I have, but in a different way. Somewhere back there in the chambers I lost my self-pity. Envy died, too, back there someplace. It's a little complicated, but take my word for it." He looked around at the other three. "But now I think it's time to get the hell out of the Dowaii Chambers."

Terry and George both started and stared at him. Finally George said, "You know how?"

He nodded. "As we thought, it's damned simple. Jenny and I came here, to where you emerged, *without undergoing another life.* It was simple, really. When we heard Terry yell we came running, but I saw it getting you and stopped her and myself. You know, it was the first time I could see the process in action, and it was fascinating."

"The two of you just started shimmering, then glowing," Jenny put in. "You turned all sparkly and golden, then seemed to vanish—but the chamber was lit up for the first time."

"It's a relatively small cavity," Harry went on. "It took the two glowing forms and seemed to suspend you there, in the middle. Tiny little sparkles, rivulets of energy, coursed all around you two. I realized that, somehow, you were both totally connected to the core memory of the machine at that point and that it would set you down when finished on the other side. My only concern was the amount of time it might take, but it took only a few minutes at most. The thing cut off, you were transported to the other side, and the chamber's light died as you stood there."

"Now we had the problem of getting to you," Jenny continued. "And Harry decided we'd take an extra chance."

He nodded. "I reasoned that if we were in direct connection to the machine at that point, it was a two-way communication. It was reading what we wanted and giving it to us. So, after briefing Jenny, we stepped into the chamber with the absolute instruction that we were simply following the two 'researchers' and did not wish any more data input at this time."

"The effect was amazing," Jenny added. "We started to feel woozy, you know, like we always do, but we just kept telling it to do nothing but let us pass. And it did! We got a little dizzy as it took us up, floated us through the chamber, and deposited us on this side—but that was all!"

"So you mean we just tell it we want to go to the exit?" Terry said unbelievingly.

"Well, not quite as simple as that," Harry replied. "I suspect that those earlier escapees had an advantage over us in that they thought they were in the grips of some supernatural phenomenon. The Indians, remember, sometimes used this as a test of leadership, if we can believe the old man. They entered *expecting* a mystical experience— and they got it. And when they were finished, they said, basically, 'Thank you, spirits. I've learned what I came to learn,' and they were shown the exit. The conquistador, too, would have some kind of religious experience. Most likely he got what his forces were looking for—a life in an ancient culture, possibly the Anasazi, which would pass for Cibola in his mind. At any rate he, too, thanked his god for showing him the true way to the pagan riches, and that was good enough."

"You forget the prospector, though. He came out crazy —and with a chunk of silver," George reminded him.

Harry nodded. "I can't explain the silver. Not yet.

But it's what the old boy came to get, and he got it. But I think timing is crucial. It isn't enough to want to get out, either, or we'd all have been booted a long time ago. The machine was built to serve and please, not just to exist. You've got to be in direct contact with it—in one of the chambers—when you make your wish, and you have to make it in terms the machine understands. *You have to tell it you got the information you were looking for*."

George's mouth was open. Terry, however, seemed a little nervous. "It seems to me you're making a lot of guesses on mighty little information. Remember, there were lots of people who never came out."

"You're right on both counts," he agreed. "But I've been right so far, and our experience in getting over here confirms much of it. But it's not so amazing when you start from the viewpoint that this is, in fact, a machine, and machines are built by people—or somebody—to do things for the builders. And one of those things is provide a way to leave the machine. It sucked us in because it wanted to serve us. If it thinks it has, it'll show us the exit. I'm willing to bet my own body on it."

The other three looked at him nervously. "So who goes first and proves or disproves the theory?" George finally asked.

Harry chuckled. "It doesn't matter. Sure, I'll go first, but you'll never know, will you?"

"If you get dropped on the other side a few minutes later we'll know," George retorted. "Okay, hero. Give it a try. And if you vanish, maybe we'll get up the nerve."

They walked to the perceived safety point in the tunnel. Harry peered into the nebulous greenish glow ahead a bit nervously. "I wonder how many chambers there are?" he mused. "And why they built so many?" He turned back to the others. "Okay, the thing to remember when you go in is to tell it that you have learned all you came to learn or completed your research—anything like that—and that you are now ready to leave. Do it before it really grabs hold, but don't get so nervous you muff it. Clear?"

They nodded.

He took in a deep breath, let it out slowly, turned to face the chamber, and said "Here goes" under his breath. He walked forward, slowly but confidently, until he felt the machine making contact, taking hold of him.

"I have completed my research at this time and learned what I wanted to know," he said aloud, almost forcing the words as the effect really took hold. "I wish to leave now, and thank you very much."

The other three watched as the chamber came alive, glowing and pulsating, and saw Harry's form change into that sparkling energy they'd described. The machine took the glowing, sparkling form and floated it out to the center of the chamber, but, instead of suspending it there, bathed it in a deep orange glow; then, abruptly, there was a flash, and the form that was Harry was gone. The chamber quickly lowered its volume and tone, faded, and became again just an apparent part of the green-glowing tunnel.

They stared at it for several minutes, dumbstruck. Finally Jenny said, "Well, he didn't come out the other side."

"He didn't come out at all," George said nervously. "It was as if the thing fried him—just vaporized him in some sort of laser."

"Well, there's only one way to find out," Jenny told them. "I don't really care anymore. Anything's better than spending an eternity in this place."

"No!" George almost shouted. "You'll be killed—like him!"

"So what?" she snapped, and stepped into the chamber.

6

"There's Terry!" Jenny shouted excitedly.

"Thank God!" Harry sighed. "I was beginning to give up hope."

Terry looked around, shielding her eyes against the

bright sunlight, then heard them call and came down. She was carrying a bundle—her clothes, they knew, which, like Harry's, had been scattered along the entry tunnel.

She saw them and came over to them, hugging and kissing them both.

"Hmmm . . . Harry's got his pants back on, but not you, Jen!" She laughed.

Jenny returned the laugh a little nervously. "Mine were spread all over the outside of the mountain, remember? So far I've found a bra and one boot. I don't know *where* Harry threw the rest of them. But I have some spares in camp—if it's still there."

Harry looked down the mountainside. "You know it is. You can see it from here. Looks like the old man's cooking something."

Terry put on her clothes, sitting on a rocky outcrop. "Feels funny to be wearing them. I wonder how long we were actually in there? I'm dying to ask the old man."

"Well, I hope he's not easily shocked," Jenny laughed. "I'm going to go strolling down there any minute now."

"Let him eat his heart out," Terry laughed.

Harry grew suddenly serious. "Where's George?"

Terry froze for a moment, then said, "I don't think he's coming. He tried to stop me; that's what took me so long. He thinks we all got atomized in there—that we're all dead."

"You of all people know him better than anybody," Harry responded. "You really think he won't be coming out?"

She shook her head slowly. "He's scared to death, Harry. The fear of death, of ending his rise and dreams of glory, is tremendous in him, and he has no faith to sustain him, nothing within or without himself. The whole world revolved around George—to George, that is."

"But he went in," Harry pointed out. "He's got *some* guts."

"That's true," she acknowledged, "but remember, he

was very literal in his view of the world back then. He was in control. And as long as he was in control, he'd climb a mountain or go into a cave. But here he's not in control. He's in a place where there's no way to guarantee the risk. No equipment to test. No strength. Nobody to pay or con. All alone, with nothing whatsoever to support him, he just won't be able to do it. Face it, Harry, he's trapped himself in there forever. Unless you or Jenny want to go back and get him."

The other two looked at each other. Finally Jenny said, "Poor George. Well, Harry, you said time didn't matter in there. For the first time I feel absolutely starved."

"Me, too," Harry agreed. "And perhaps you're right. I *do* plan to go back in there someday soon, now that I know exactly how to work it. Back with all sorts of sophisticated backup. I suspect, though, that we'll not be permitted anything inside except our bodies. The clothing was forcibly removed, remember; maybe it fouls up the chambers' fancy electronic systems. There's a matter-to-energy-to-matter conversion involved each trip. But I don't think I'm up to it again right now. I'd have to go through at least one more life to complete the programming of the machine and get out again."

"He trapped himself," Jenny pointed out.

"Don't we all," Terry responded.

They had been gone less than two hours, it turned out.

They waited for George for three days and nights, until, one night, the mountain vented again, putting on another of its dazzling displays.

"It's cleaning itself," Jenny said enigmatically. "Good-bye, Georgie."

The old man assured them that he would arrange for a watch in the area by him and some of his comrades. If George emerged, they would make sure he got back. They left a small cache of supplies, a note to that effect, and a flare pistol, and departed after that.

There was a sense of unreality to the world, they

found. They had lived more subjective time in other times, other lands, other bodies, than in this one, and they would carry those others with them, inside them, as part of them, as long as they lived.

Harry slid behind the wheel of the pickup and started it up.

"Harry?"

"Yeah, Jenny?"

"How do we know *this* is real? I mean, if Terry and George could live each other's lives, how do we know *this* isn't a new project of the machine?"

He laughed. "We don't. And we won't—until the day after we die. Let's put it this way, though: If it's all coming out of our minds, then all three of us are gonna have tremendous lives, aren't we?"

They all laughed as he backed up the pickup, turned it around, and headed back out across the haunted desert.

The old Indian watched them go, watched the dust cloud until they and all signs of them were out of sight. He turned, tended first to the burros, then the extra supplies, and, only when satisfied, went into his small adobe hut.

It was a simple one-room enclosure, primitive in the extreme, but across the far wall was hung a stunning Navajo blanket. Slowly, lovingly, he took it down to reveal only the bare walls, and carefully folded it and put it on his humble cot.

He turned again to the wall and began to speak in a language none had heard—none would hear—not for more than a thousand years.

The wall glowed a familiar greenish alabaster.

"The imprints for the latter half of the century numbered twenty by current history have been taken," he reported in that strange, alien-sounding tongue. "Three subjects emerged and were allowed to proceed. A fourth remained inside the Recorder and has been integrated into the memory banks with his fourth translation. He will serve as a control on the other three, who are now linked to the Recorder. Through them I will select the samples for this recording. I am taking samples at a more rapid rate now, as we are so close to the Holocaust. I have cut the intervals now to just twenty years and may adjust things further as the Holocaust draws nearer. When it appears imminent, I will attempt to coordinate with my counterparts a single full-phase world recording for analysis. Current subjects have the potential to live up to the critical period. Report completed."

The wall faded back to its adobe self, and he carefully rehung the Navajo blanket.

It had been a long task, this project, and there were longer times still. And he and his brothers, who manned the Recorders and remotes all over the world, as they had for the last million years, would continue to do their duty and wait. After all that time, what was another mere thousand years?

He wished the three well. He liked them and admired particularly their ability to solve the riddle of the machine rationally, the first he had encountered who were able to understand and appreciate it. They would never see him again, of course. He had arranged that during the translation back out. They would return, of course, and hunt and puzzle, but they would never again find this particular spot—which could be moved or concealed at will—and the machine itself would arrange for slight differences to keep them from ever finding it again. A simple energy-matter conversion, and a subtle one.

He wished the task completed, of course, and understood its importance fully. But he was content to wait, wait until those who had sent him came once again to their glory, and would read his reports.

He and his brother guardians were not programmed to feel loneliness.

Introduction to
"Adrift among the Ghosts"

You are eligible for the John W. Campbell Award twice—
once in the year following the publication of your first story
or novel and again the next year. After that, you can never
win it. I was nominated again along with Steve Donaldson,
Orson Scott Card, and others. I thought I might have a shot
at it, although I really thought that Donaldson's sales on the
Thomas Covenant books had been so high that he had developed more of a cult following than *Midnight* had and might
well win. When the results were announced in Phoenix, however, the winner was Orson Scott Card. So it goes.

Being nominated a second time did give me yet one more
slot in George Martin's *New Voices/The John W. Campbell
Awards* anthology, though, which was already many years
behind. There was hardly a rush; Berkley had dropped the
series and it was a while before someone picked it up, that
someone being Jim Frenkel's Blue Jay books. By the time
the one with "Dowaii Chambers" came out, none of us in it
were really new writers any more and the series title changed
to reflect this: *The John W. Campbell Awards*. By 1986
Cherryh, Card, Sterling, and I were almost edging into
the category of old farts of the field.

I have already chronicled the less than thrilling critical reception the "Dowaii Chambers" story received, and so I was even less motivated to do another story for the next one. By this time I was absolutely convinced that any short fiction I did was doomed unless I somehow weaved a novel out of it (*And the Devil Will Drag You Under,* for example, is really a short story collection with a common theme and a frame). My comments on the other stories here and their fates speak for themselves. I like my short fiction a lot; most people who read it seem to like it, too. But the stories die and fade away far too quickly, the pay is lousy, and lately the folks reviewing books and magazines weren't even bothering to read my stories while the readers read and liked them but never seemed to remember who wrote them.

I had the idea for "Adrift Among the Ghosts" a number of years ago—that is, the concept involved. It's actually a stock enough gimmick to have become an SF cliché, but I had a far different theory on the results than anyone else in SF seems to have had, as you'll see. Making a story out of it was much harder, and took a lot of work, and the only reason this came out at all was because of threats, pleading, and bribes on the part of editor George Martin and publisher Jim Frenkel. Ironically, Blue Jay ceased doing business the month this story was supposed to appear and it will not appear there. Oddly enough, although I was paid for it, this is the story's first appearance anywhere, since I elected to put it in this collection rather than leave it out and sell it elsewhere.

I am a techno-freak of the first order. Back in the heyday of the sixties, I was a part-time engineer for outdoor rock concerts, for example, with a mixer board that defied all logic and human reach, and my business partners and I had a good sideline in the computer typesetting business in the antique days of paper tape input and built-in repairmen. Even today, my stereo system in my office is so complex that no one but me has ever been able to simply turn it on, let alone play something on it. Thanks to *The Faces of Science Fiction* many people know I have a satellite dish in the backyard (although it must be pointed out that the house in that picture is my neighbor's, not mine—the photographer could either get my dish or my house but not both—and I don't live there any more anyway but I still have a dish), and while this is only a three-person household it contains four working

TVs, three VCRs, a nightmarish wiring network, four computers, and even my main computer, upon which this is being written, has two CRT screens so I can either do two things on it simultaneously or run various kinds of operating systems. I think I may have the only dedicated word processor capable of concurrently taking over NORAD. (A CompuPro 816C, by the way, if you're curious; my word processing program of choice is called FinalWord II and I print on an Apple Laserwriter Plus. See what I mean about techno-freak?)

My son roars through the house singing "Transformers—more than meets the eye" although he has a natural affinity as well for Chuck Jones's Looney Tunes and thus shows some taste (but why does he like the old reruns of *My Three Sons* and *Donna Reed*?).

In other words, this is a high-tech house with a lot of mass media coming in (although in its defense it also contains about five thousand books and we all read quite a lot) and there's always the question as to whether or not television actually is rotting my son's mind, particularly when, via the dish, he can get cartoons almost twenty-four hours a day including the raw feeds to the local stations. Some people will be shocked that I allow him to watch so much, but he's also a very active and creative kid as those who have met him at conventions will attest, and he was reading before he entered first grade.

I've had a TV around since I was five years old—the first one was one of those round-tubed Bendix models my father brought with an unexpected bonus—so I'm actually one of the first TV generation. My wife Eva was born much later than I, and TV was far more sophisticated and omnipresent in her growing up than even in mine. Maybe it's a comment that in the United States of America you can tell the poor families because they have fewer and less fancy TVs. We both grew up as avid, even voracious, readers anyway, and my life and my careers have all been bound up in the printed word, so I'm really not very worried that my son David will be warped or brain-damaged beyond repair by the TVs here. We are both convinced that kids whose parents read a lot grow up to be avid readers themselves and it's proving out so far. You can count the books in the homes of parents who berate us for letting David watch so much TV on the fingers of one hand. Want to bet which kid is going to be a life-long pleasure reader and which kid isn't?

I mean, his TV-generation parents turned out all right, right?

Right?

We did, didn't we?

Tell me that we did . . .

ADRIFT AMONG THE GHOSTS

"*I*T'S THE JACK BENNY PROGRAM, WITH JACK'S VERY *special guest Lucille Ball . . .*"

I flip on the autolock mechanism while the computer scans to see if this is one on my quota.

Oh, Donnn . . .

Alas for me, it is not, and the scan is automatically resumed. I tell the command module to shift to the next available signal, which might be the next thing in line or something completely different.

The lock light goes on, and I instruct my systems management computer to stick it on for evaluation. I'm getting worried about the manager. It shouldn't have locked on to the Lucille Ball guesting on Benny's program at all; even though she was a guest several times on the program, the voiceprints should have locked this one out. If it is defective . . . No! I just can not afford to have to go through all that random stuff again and again to find a new and previously unrecorded piece. Gods of Archus, please don't let the edit system break down now!

This new one is *Action in the Afternoon*, a live western serial done in Philadelphia, of all places. I know the country well, and I know the absurdity of a western coming from that city at all in any time and context. I don't need this one, but I instruct the manager to stay on it anyway. We are on NBC at the right period and I've had a number of malfunctions in riding the beam at this time. I am missing at least four *Atom Squad* episodes and countless *Howdy Doody*s, and it is worth the chance. Why not? There's not much else to do out here anyway.

That, and the fact that almost all of this project can be automated, is the second greatest problem with this assignment—this *sentence*, if truth be told. None of us who ride the beams are really anything more, or less, than politically connected criminals, although there's nothing on our records back home; we're considered "employees" and technically paid a wage. The money is hardly a consideration—lower civil service pay, only a token to make it look all nice and proper, as if we could spend it, anyway—but the deal is one that is difficult for someone in my position to turn down. I did, after all, kill four people. I should have been vaporized; the trial lasted barely ten minutes, and the evidence was not in dispute considering that they had the club so well monitored, they had recordings of the very act. How I wish I had known that, even guessed that they were so close on my heels! The four could have been eliminated one by one under perfect conditions. It just seemed so much more *efficient* to take them all out at once, as they were plotting my own demise.

Death. What did I know of death, or even crime? I sit and I watch these ancient recordings—how can I help but watch?—and I see experts. I listen to their newscasts and watch their documentary histories, and I wonder how such an incredibly gentle society as ours could have bred even such a rank amateur as myself—and those even ranker people in the club.

Computers do a lot for us, of course. It is a computer that maneuvers this ship with a precision no person could hope to match, and it's a computer that prepares my meals, records these ramblings, keeps me healthy. It was a computer that maintained the surveillance on the club, a computer that tried me, another which prosecuted me, yet another that defended me, and still another that sentenced me. And, but for one thing, this whole operation could be done by computer.

I suppose it might be boiled down to taste, although that's not quite the right word. I am the supervisor. I oversee the operations, check on what is going on, act as something of a repairman or even reprogrammer when the systems inevitably fail, and I separate the relevant from the irrelevant in terms of beam content. We want everything, of course, eventually—this sort of opportunity was only discovered by the merest of chances and might never come again to us or to any other civilization out here among the stars—but the beams keep going on, forcing us to pick and choose.

We may be the only other civilization to arise in this galaxy, although probably not. We will almost certainly be the only ones using reception devices that can translate this particular series of signals broadcast so long ago and from so far away, and probably the only ones who can see and hear the transmissions much the same as those who made these broadcasts did.

We are not at all like them, of course, or so we tell ourselves, and so even they would have believed. Certainly not physically. That took a lot of getting adjusted to at the start; they seemed like some strange, surreal creatures more suited to art or animation than the sort of beings you can think of as being live and real and sentient and even technologically proficient. Once, in a biology course at university, I was assured by a professor who was the greatest expert on everything that it was impossible for a bipedal lifeform to develop a complex technology, and that the fine manipulation of complex tools required a minimum of eighteen tentacles. I often wonder what that fellow is saying now, as these transmissions are brought back and analyzed. It pleases me to think of those pompous asses who seemed so powerful and self-assured to us helpless students to now be suddenly and irrevocably placed in the same position as some ancient was ten thousand years ago when it was proved that the world was indeed round and not flat.

And yet, as strange as their shape is, and how bizarre their architecture, one quickly comes to accept and even understand these alien creatures on the screen. It is far more fascinating to me to discover just how similar we are if you ignore the physical differences. We both see optically and hear acoustically. We both have two sexes —don't I know *that!*—and much of what we share in social structures and behavior seems to grow right out of that. We invented totally different machines, some in totally different ways, to do exactly the same things.

Our social structures are somewhat different, but we still have state education of the young, mass entertainment, vehicles for both individual and mass locomotion, and we both squandered a great deal of natural resources in our growth and fouled up our own planets with our wastes.

In a sense, they seem very much like us, although speeded up. The social forces that seemed to constantly rip and tear at them are vastly slowed in our own history, although, alas, violence seems to be necessary to shake things up and prevent stagnancy. They did in a thousand years what it took us ten thousand to accomplish, but they did it at the expense of developing technologically at a rate so accelerated that they were still socially and emotionally closer to their ancient ancestors when they developed the means of total annihilation.

I have no trouble with their dramas; I am, however, less comfortable with their jokes and humor. The sophisticated humor is no problem, and I now understand them well enough that their domestic situations correlate with those with which I am familiar even though it is not, of course, the same at all. I cannot, however, understand why slipping on a floor and sprawling is humorous to them, or why some of their undergarments seem filled with hilarity. This should not bother me; they are in many ways nothing like us, but still, it does. I cannot quite understand why it does, but it matters very much.

When you're out here, alone, riding the beam and adrift with the ghosts, they're the only real company you have. You get to know them, even love them, because they are at once so alien and remote and at the same time so similar. They are my family. For almost twenty years they have been the only companionship I have had.

It's not easy to ride the beams, even at the speeds we can travel. It is true that the old television signals traveled in a straight line into infinity—although they have become incredibly weak at this point, and it's often been theorized that our own signals might be intercepted some day in the same way—but it's not really a straight line. Planets rotate and they also revolve; suns move in their own orbits around the galactic center. Perhaps a quarter to a third of all they broadcast is lost because they were on the wrong side of their sun, or there was something else in the way of the beam. More is simply impossible to recover for other technical reasons, for the signals are not immune to the great forces of the universe, and the signal strengths we are talking about are on the equivalent of hearing a single speck of dust fall to a floor from the next solar system. Worse, they did not have a single standard. To get the British and affiliate nations' signals one must adjust for PAL; for French and Italian and many others it's SECAM, and others like the Soviet Union and Australia use hybrids. We missed a lot, too, because of directed uplinks, limited transmissions that did not escape, and cable.

But that's why I'm here, of course, with my quota. Eight hundred perfect hours of transmission. It sounded so simple, particularly when you think that the computer can just ride the beam and then match its swing and let the stuff flow in. It's not that easy. An entire program is a rarity. It often takes many passes, possible only because the same signals were sent many times and have arrived here by many different routes simply because of those forces that can bend light and split stellar images in two. Even then, we jump in and out of null-space with regularity, trying to keep ahead of them while still maintaining enough power to get the ship and the transmissions home.

Eight hundred hours of new programming. It sounded

like the easiest thing in the world, even considering all that. Compared to being vaporized, it was a wonderful offer; compared to life at hard labor it was even more so.

I didn't know about the traps, though. All the little traps, and the big one they don't tell you about because it's still classified top secret. One is that word *new*, of course. I have picked up tens of thousands of hours, but we are rarely updated on what the others have also sent in until we break for transmission and reception. And I have fragments of a great many programs I am still trying to track down, which is why I'm riding this particular beam now, and why I am so afraid that the computer is not remembering what it already has in its files. If I have to reprogram it, I will lose its knowledge to date—not the programs, of course, but the tagged records—and have to wait a very long time until it is restored to its previous selectivity. I sometimes suspect that they have deliberately built bugs into this program to cause this and keep me out here. I find it frightening, at least in part because I am not skilled enough to actually rewrite the master program, simply to repair and restore it.

I wonder about malice. Six billion people on my own world alone, one of many we inhabit, and the year I committed my crime there were but a hundred and three premeditated murders. We are a gentler sort. Perhaps we react in less gentle ways. I sit and watch *their* programs and there seem to be four premeditated murders an hour just in their entertainment, and dozens in a single big city newscast. Some of these murderers are executed, most are imprisoned, and a great many walk out of those prisons after a while for crimes far greater and with far less justification than my own. I can't see the worst of their societies offering a living trip to Hell as an alternative, but mine is a gentler race, and a more vindictive one.

And so you sit, and you make the jumps, and sit some more, and you watch and you come to love those people. I know who did it in every Perry Mason, and I've followed Superman in all his incarnations. I've suffered with them their long-ago agonies of war and terrorism

and disease and other tragedies, and I have rejoiced with
them their victories, discoveries, and conquests. I have
come to like and even appreciate their extremely bizarre
music and art forms; the personalities I see are like old
friends, where in the beginning they all looked alike to
me.

Kings and queens and presidents and dictators—they
are as much a part of me as my own history, my local
counsellor and legates. They are more than that; they are
all there is of me and my universe outside of the confines
of this lousy little ship. They are what is real to me. I
cannot find a frame of reference that is not of their reality rather than my own. It troubles me. When one lives,
eats, sleeps, breathes an alien reality with no contact or
reference to one's own, it becomes difficult to differen-
tiate the real from the unreal, the alien from the familiar.

I was always a collector with eclectic tastes, and
that's why they chose me for the beams. A collector,
yes; not a quivering, smelly thing locked inside a soulless
cage on a ride through Hell with ghosts for companions.
The ghosts are truly that and don't mind at all while I
must ride and watch and forbear and somehow *survive*.
But they will not break me; no, they will not do that. My
ghosts protect me, too, and are my salvation. Yet, when
we shift, when there's no beam to ride and we're in
search mode, there is no one here, no one but me and my
memories. The ghosts then are inside my head, and I
find them curiously intermingled, as if the alien ghosts of
ancient fantasy are more real than the actuality of the
world I was forced to leave behind so very long ago.

What was it like to actually breathe free-flowing natural air, to let wind and water bear on the sensory nodes,
to know *openness* first hand, and not through some
monitor's sterile window looking in on a landscape that
was not my own, that I had never known or experienced
or even imagined? To sit upon my own estate whose rolling blue moss-covered hills were carefully arranged with
crimson *byuap* topiary by master artisans!

Oh, yes, I had an estate. Only the leader classes go to
Hell alive; the *krowl* and *duber* and *nimbiat*, being of

lesser gene pools, are allowed to be vaporized. We *Madur* are supposed to be better than that, or so the geneticists claim. Bred to be the elite. When one of us goes awry it threatens the whole system. Examples must be made.

How many times have I thought of it all, gone over every second in my mind? How difficult, now, living these twenty years among alien ghosts, to separate the two, as fact and fancy blend effortlessly if incongruously in my mind. I have gone mad in order to remain sane.

I was in my spa being bathed with honey water and watching a recently retrieved episode of *The A Team* when he arrived. None below our class and few within it were permitted to see such things; I, however, as a ranking physician, had gained the first private access on the excuse of seeing if exposure to such alien thought and vision might be detrimental to one's mind. Idiotic, of course.

I was expecting him, but not this soon. He was a *duber*, a service-class individual, bred to be superb in a specific talent or occupation, but he had much impudence and no right to interrupt me. He should have waited, but impudence was also an essential part of his makeup. He stopped and stared in horror at the screen where two trucks and three jeeps blew up as they ran over some cleverly planted mines. He shuddered and averted his eyes. It took little in the way of experimentation to understand that no *duber* was strong enough to tolerate even short-term exposure. The masses were far too gentle and passive to understand it. The newcomer did not look back again or refer to the scenes on the screen, and seemed relieved when I muted the sound. He got straight to the point.

"She's going to leave you, sir, that's for sure," said *Richard Diamond, Private Eye. "She's a bit frightened of you, and somewhat intimidated, but she's making arrangements with a disreputable bunch to hide her and spirit her away."*

I was furious at this, even though I suspected it all and had hired the *duber* only to see how she thought she was going to manage it. "How do they intend to do it while remaining beyond my reach?"

"*A club in the city. The owner there will do almost anything for a price, and he's pretty good at it. Stick her in a safe house in a low neighborhood for a few days, then to Grand Central Station with phony ID, maybe disguised as a worker. Hop a spaceship and get off when it looks promising. Pardon me, but a girl that looks like she does won't have any trouble in a strange place for long.*"

"I'm well aware of that. It's why I can not allow it, even if it was not also degrading to her class."

"*But why fight it? She's only doing this with small amounts that aren't even petty cash to you. You don't love her. Why not just let her go?*"

I raised myself up on all my tentacles and almost grabbed the man. "Because I am a *collector*, something you would not understand. I collect, I do not give away any part of my collection. I want the names of these persons involved in this and the address of the club. I shall attend to this personally."

"*But, sir—someone in your position—you can't go there yourself! Alone, unprotected—it simply isn't done!*" Holmes objected.

I came out of the spa and headed for the main house. "In affairs of business and politics this is true, but this is a personal matter, and I can not allow others to be involved beyond you. Give me the information and you are discharged." *Sooner or later, everybody goes to Rick's . . .*

It was both not as bad and worse than I had imagined. The place itself looked respectable and catered to the middle classes, and inside it even had the proper moss pits and sweetly scented atmosphere of *albis* root, but the patrons did not wear their class outwardly nor have much inwardly, either.

Peter Lorre was at the bar, fetching drinks for a table seating Wallace Beery, Preston Foster, and Mr. T. The rest of the mob was more common, character actors, mostly, although here and there were potentially great enemies like Charles Middleton and Roy Barcroft. I was not in fear. In a sense, I had them cold, since they could not run, could not hide, from my power and influence should they attempt violence against me and I live—and if I died they would be automatically hunted down by the Special Police.

I could tell they were all a bit awed and unnerved that someone born with the golden headplate would even enter their miserable club, but they were a tough lot whose business was getting around the likes of me and the rule of law and society which I represented.

"*Yes, sir, yes, sir, what'll it be?*" asked Barton Mac-Laine *from behind the bar.*

"I doubt you would serve anything of the quality I require in this establishment," I responded icily. I was aware of a female edging near, and I rotated an eye socket on her.

"*Any kind of quality you want is available at the Long Branch,*" Miss Kitty assured me. "*We serve all classes here and fill their needs no matter what they might be.*"

I'll bet, I thought but didn't say. Drugs, drink, perversion—that was their stock in trade. I knew this place now, and also understood that I was not the first golden headplate to enter but only the latest. That was how they got hold of you, their evil then perverting and subverting the system. I loathed them all. They were less than people, lower than *nimbiats* at their worst, and yet difficult to assail, for they held no higher opinion of themselves than I held of them.

"*You* are the owner of this establishment, Madam?"

"*I'm the manager, and I ain't no madam. I can take care of anything you might want.*"

"I wish to see the owner. I have personal business to discuss with that individual alone."

She looked around uncertainly, and Lorre glanced up from his cards and gave her a nod and a head nudge. "Okay, buddy, follow me. Just so happens the owner's in back now . . ."

I could see the crowd stiffen, although the tension

wasn't so much aimed at preventing me from doing anything as the instinctual obligation of even these low-lifes
to protect their boss. I followed her back to a private
room. The owner looked up and offered me a place. It
was clear that he had overheard everything and knew
just who I was and why I was there, even though he
remained impassive.

*"Come, come, sir. No need to be surly here with your
lessers. It is beneath you,"* Sidney Greenstreet oozed in
dangerous mock friendliness. He wore a helmet over his
plate making his class impossible to distinguish, but
there would be only one reason for doing so: under that
idiotic cover the coloration had to be golden. Even his
dialect was proper *Madur*, although with a roughened
edge. From offworld, certainly, but also certainly one of
us gone bad.

"I see no reason to be more than minimally civil," I
responded. "You are plotting to take something from me
that belongs to me. I am here to see that it doesn't happen."

*"Come, come, sir! I haven't the faintest idea what
you are talking about."*

"I will not play games. No matter what she has paid
you, I will triple it in untraceable precious metals and
gems if you take her money and then deliver her back to
me. Don't deny that you are going to do it, or that you
do not know what I am talking about. You have over-
stepped your fertilizer pits this time. I will have this
place surrounded and everyone here, including you, subjected to Thought Probes. I doubt if any of you will walk
freely away after that."

*J.R. gave that evil chuckle of his. "You have that
power, I admit," he drawled with some amusement in
his voice, "but you have not invoked it as yet, and by the
time you can do so, this place will be a tabernacle for
retired nuns. You think I never expected a visit from you?
I spotted that tinhorn, upper-crust private eye from a
mile away. I won't stop it because I've already done it.
She's gone. Out of your life, off this planet, and buried
so deep you'll never find her." And he laughed.*

I rose on all eight tentacles, my blood pressure rising so high, my entire exoskeleton glowed green. Off the planet before I had even *begun*? "Who *dares* such impudency with a pod of the Imperial Regency?" I demanded. "I am physician to the Center!"

"I know who and what you are," responded the one-armed man. "But it means nothing to me, nor does your money. Seven times I have gone to the auction pits at Quimera in lust after some unique work of beauty and genius, and seven times you have bested me not with mere money but with influence and outright fraud. The chance to humiliate you, to take from you something that is uniquely yours, was literally thrown in my path, begging to be stolen and with no law to prevent it. Discovering she was impregnated by you only added fine sauce. I have cost you your wife and children, Doctor, and I am proud of it! Seven times I have lost to you, but you—you have never lost at all. Not until now. I wanted you to know how it feels to lose."

I stared at him. "Gomesh! You are Gomesh, Imperator Comptroller of the Litidal! I know you now!" It was worse than that. He was of equal rank and position and senior in age. I could shut down his foul club, which was obviously used in his collecting, but I could not touch him—legally or through my influence. To even press such a case against him would only subject me to embarrassment and humiliation.

And yet, he was correct. Up until that time I had never lost, and I could not accept it now. He saw my tentacles curl and uncurl and one of my eyes focus on a wooden ornament; a heavy, wooden ornament.

"Don't be ridiculous," snarled Don Corleone. "My men are everywhere and you are not in your element here, nor is this some alien horror chamber like the room in which you watch those intercepted grotesqueries. You are in an untenable position, and I intend to enjoy it."

Nobody talks that way to Charles Bronson!

I don't even remember the next minute or so very well, just a roaring blur, but something snapped inside me that I did not even suspect could ever go out of control. Tentacles snapped out, taking him completely by surprise, flipping him over with a strength I had never had before or since, while other tentacles reached for things in his compartment—bottles, pieces of furniture; a piece of rope that supported his privacy curtain became a whip in my grasp.

Naturally, this brought his bodyguard of thugs on the run. Gomesh was larger and heavier than I, yet somehow I managed to pick him up and actually throw him right over my head and into the bodyguards. Swiveling, one of the guards dropped an illegal stun gun. I spotted it with one eye and reached it before they could even move. I had never fired such a weapon before, but at that range a blind person could have committed a massacre, and this I did. I know that I did so. Later they showed me the recordings.

When it was over, Gomesh and three of his henchmen were dead, and all of a sudden, my rage simply fled me and I just remained there staring at the carnage. I offered no resistance when the Special Police arrived and led me away.

The trial was conducted very quickly with me alone in my cell. The defense computer discussed my options, which were few, and then the evidence was shown and the State made its verdict demands.

"Insanity," I said to my attorney. Even I was sickened and stunned watching the recording of the killings. We are too gentle a race for such things; the recording and most of the evidence itself was sealed to protect the public. It had to be. I was *Madur*. If the masses were ever to learn that one of my class was capable of such a thing, it would bring down the entire social structure, the whole of our civilization. "They have seen it and taken my mind print. They must know that this was no rational act."

"I'm afraid you wouldn't be allowed to plead insanity," my attorney replied. *"You see, you are technically above the law in your class, and the justification for that status and indeed the justification for Madur rule is that*

you are genetically perfect. Madur *are by definition incapable of such acts.* Madur *are, by definition, always sane and rational. Therefore, your crime is by definition premeditated."*

"But it was not! You and they both know that!"

He sighed. "Sir, it is beside the point what actually occurred. What matters is that it could not have occurred. Interestingly, because of the necessity of your sanity and the evidence of the deceased's bad moral character and provocations against you, I probably could have gotten you off with a sentence of exile to some remote little planet somewhere. But Gomesh is not the issue. You did not simply kill Gomesh, you killed three other people."

"Who would have killed me or done me grave injury saving their employer! It was self-defense!"

"You miss the point. These men were duber. *They were born and bred to be bodyguards and henchmen just as you were to be Imperial Physician. As such, they were acting as they had to act, genetically, mentally, socially, and morally, while your action was against all things that* Madur *stand for. They had a right to injure or kill you. You had no right to prevent them, just as it is your own responsibility for placing them in a position where they were forced to take such action against you."* Perry Mason sighed. *"I'm sorry, but even I had to lose one sooner or later."*

I was dumbstruck by the implications of what he was saying, and the rightness of it. I *was* responsible for their attempt on me, and as a result I did not have any right to stop it. My crime was not that I murdered four people; four people who I still thought deserved it. My crime was in not killing Gomesh, thus avenging my honor, and then allowing his bodyguards to kill me. This was no petty crime, not even murder; this was a crime against civilization as we knew it. If the lower classes ever even *suspected* a *Madur* was capable of even *thinking* emotionally, of losing control even in privacy and without harm, let alone insanity, no matter how temporary, no one could feel safe or secure again.

"In sentencing you I am faced with a dilemma for which the codes have no guidance," Judge Wapner told me sternly. *"As a result, I must break new ground. I could have you vaporized for the murder of Gomesh, of course, but that would not preserve the symmetry necessary here. There is another, perhaps more appropriate way, than that. It is clear that you yourself are not defective, but that exposure to these alien signals has somehow conflicted with your primary intellectual imperatives. That places us in a quandary but also makes you uniquely qualified to aid your people. We need to continue collecting those signals, those programs. Yet, how can we risk prolonged exposure by others to them? What we need is an experienced expert on the subject who can make the proper selections.*

"The collection may be automatic," Judge Roy Bean continued, *"but that is the trouble with it. Automatic. Someone must eventually go through it all and make decisions on what is worthy and what is not, what is redundant and what is new. It is a vital project—the only contact ever with another sentient race even if the contact is only one way—and there is much to learn. Computers can do some of it, but in the end it is a highly subjective process. It requires someone with a collector's sense and a high analytical and appreciatory background. It requires a* Madur. *We realize that your tortured soul craves vaporizing, but would you consider committing yourself to this project, which will help your race, instead? We would outfit a special ship and send you out as collector—and critic. It is too much to ask of some here, considering the mental price we might pay, but you have already paid it."*

The last thing my soul craved then was vaporization no matter what I should have felt. If my soul went that way, I would have let them kill me and given everyone but myself and Gomesh a happy ending. I was very stupid then. I leapt at the chance.

"I live to serve my people," I spouted nobly.

I did not understand what they were doing then, either. I was no mere murderer, no mere abuser of trust, for which simple vaporizing would have been a quick and easy answer. I had committed an impossible act, an act which threatened everything. Damn those machines!

Make the punishment fit the crime ...

The beam sensor alarm sounded, and I moved to check the monitoring station. I flicked on the recorders and attached the visual translators and it started to roll. Immediately I knew where we'd drifted, and immediately I tried to stop it, but the damned computer refused and flashed NEW MATERIAL—PICKUP REQUIRED. Damn that thing! Not new, not new at all! How many times had I seen it? How many times had I been forced to watch it when that mechanical mind of Hell insisted?

"This is the emergency broadcast system. This is not —repeat, not—a test." He was sweating and nervous, even though he was the best-known newscaster of his day delivering the biggest story of his or any career.

"No, no! Not my people! Not my family! Not my beautiful, beautiful ghosts!"

"... tactical nuclear exchange involved the elimination of almost forty percent of the Soviet Army, resulting in ..."

"Lucy! Desi! Uncle Miltie! Come! Tell us it was all just a joke! Tell me when to laugh!"

"... six hundred multiple warhead missiles. Washington, New York, San Diego, Norfolk, Los Angeles, San Francisco, and Seattle have already been obliterated by submarine-based ..."

"We are a gentle race!" I screamed, my exoskeleton glowing green as always. "Were you all mad? Were you all seized by a fit of insanity? You can not do this to me!"

"... midwestern cities such as here in Chicago in seven minutes or less. If you have a shelter, get to it immediately. Do not hesitate. If you have a storm cellar or basement, go to it. Sewer tunnels, subways. Do not let yourself be exposed to direct blast. Do not venture outside again for at least two to four weeks. Take what provisions you can ..."

"Not even a crime against civilization can deserve *this*! Computer, get me control. Tell them to blow this ship. Jettison life support! I will take anything, anything except this! How many times must I watch? How many times must I *know*?

"Please! Central Computer! In the name of all that's holy, *you can not make me watch them all die again!*"

INTRODUCTION TO
"MOTHS AND CANDLE"

Back in 1968, for some reason, I started playing around with short stories again. Perhaps part of it was that I was doing editorial and rewrite work in order to pay for my master's degree and I just got into the writing grove. It's also possible I was driven a bit by the success of my friend and near neighbor at the time, Roger Zelazny. The two stories from that year are very different, and the only thing other than the time period that they have in common is that both started out with titles I later used on other work.

The first of the two, "The Dowaii Chambers" (absolutely no relation to the story of almost the same name in this book), is a bad story nicely written. I showed it to Roger, I remember, who is one of the nicest men in the business and never says bad things about anything or anybody, and he sort of nervously cleared his throat and that was that. I never submitted that story to anyone, and although I am a packrat, it is highly unlikely that the story survives today. I remember it all too well, however, and have no desire to resurrect it. There may be a market out there for things even the author doesn't want shown—August Derleth did a number of Lovecraft books with stuff Lovecraft would have burned if he ever thought anybody might do that—but I always adhere to the secret of being a Great Professional Photographer.

Take a thousand shots and pick and show only the one that worked.

The second story of that year, however, was called "Or The Devil Will Drag You Under." My regular readers will immediately note that this title was later used as a novel title, corrected so that the leading word is consistent with the line in the song. I am never one to let a title go to waste if it's a good one. This story is quite different, having no other connection with the book of that name, and I like it a lot. I have no memory of showing it to Roger, but I did show it to some members of the Baltimore SF Society to more or less lukewarm reviews.

Since I had already had the *Jungle* universe pretty well worked out and so had a more familiar background, I set it there, in the time period *after* the events in the novel. In other words, this is a sequel to a book that wouldn't be fully written for another seven years.

Because I *did* like it, I became emboldened, and sent it off to the great and legendary John W. Campbell, Jr., for consideration in *Analog*. I knew John fairly well because of the many parties and conventions we attended over the decade of the sixties, and that meant I also knew that knowing him would have absolutely no bearing whatsoever on how unmerciful he might be. The original stand-alone story was good, as good as I thought, but the motivation behind the action was quite weak and not very logical, something that really hadn't occurred to me. It certainly occurred to Campbell, who wrote me one of those classic Campbell rejection letters dissecting the whole story—but also implying (if you knew Campbell) that if I could solve the problems, I might have something publishable here.

WARNING! If you don't want much of the story spoiled for you, stop reading this commentary *now* and skip directly to the story and read it. That's all right—I'll wait.

Back now? Read the story? Well, here's what Campbell said about the original version in his own words:

July 24, 1968

Dear Mr. Chalker:

   You've got a lot of highly interesting and original ideas here—but the story isn't coherent enough to stand as is.

The essential problem is motivation; that's what makes a reader identify with a story character. Here, you have—in essence—only mechanisms.

There's no understanding of the motivations of the Terrans—or what the galactic situation is. And a man's actions are either good or bad not in terms of what he does, but the circumstances in which he does them. Even the motivations are less important than the circumstance! A man, for some petty, personal, half-mad reason of his own might have assassinated Hitler in 1938—an act of evil motivation—which, in the circumstances, would have been a great benefit to Mankind.

Why are the Terrans disrupting the culture of the planet?

"For Wealth" is a damn poor answer; unthinking people may think slaves mean huge profits. They did —once. In the days before technology! When living organisms were the only available machines—they were as Plato said, "my animate agricultural instruments." But can you allow rebellious slaves to work on multimillion-dollar refinery plants, where a single act of sabotage can cost $50,000,000? Particularly when a microminiaturized computer chip can watch the controls more closely than a conscious mind?

Raw materials, metals? In a high-order technology that can mine asteroids in space, instead of going to the bother of stripping useless rock and dirt on a planet?

For organic products, food and fibers? Huh, where have you been?! You wear Orlon socks, a perma-press suit and shirt, and can enjoy *only* the products of the four billion years of local evolution—which you evolved with, and so are very specially designed to utilize successfully. And even among our own evolution's products, a lot of us have serious troubles, called allergies. Want to try the products of a 4-gigayear-alien development?

Labors? At what? Digging ditches, which slaves can be used for? When a power ditching machine can walk along as fast as a man can trot, making a 6-foot-deep, 18-inch-wide ditch, installing pipe or conduit, and filling the earth in behind? Watch the telephone company's cable laying equipment, with four huge tractors hauling a special plow that cuts a four-foot-deep furrow, lays in a cable, and neatly replaces the dirt, while hauling the trailer with the huge rolls of cable behind it.

There are things men want—but they never know until afterward. The fine-chemical type organics—the hitherto-undreamnt-of medicinals, for instance. Ideas and philosophies. Works of art. New and totally different viewpoints on life.

And for *this* hunger, a static culture is useless—as a static culture is, equally, useless to itself. In the truest sense, a static culture is meaningless—it's simply a repetition of the same message, like saying all clouds are white all clouds are white all clouds are white all clouds are . . . indefinitely. It can be shown mathematically, even, that such a redundant system carries no information or meaning. Do the inhabitants of that cracked record a favor—nudge the needle into a new groove! It may start getting somewhere.

Sure, it means misery for the generation that gets the nudges! It usually takes war and violence to shake 'em loose.

And yes, you could save them more misery by showing 'em which way to go next. Of course, it would be *your* way, but it goes down a well understood, already-smoothed pathway.

But that (A) defeats your purpose of getting completely new ideas and approaches and (B) prevents them ever developing their *own* potentials.

But enslaving a planet for metals and slaves and meat—man, you can't validate any one of those as economically practical in an advanced technology.

It won't take too much rewriting to switch the situation—and it'd make a hell of a sight stronger (also somewhat longer and remunerative!) story.

Basically, you need to explain the situation in the *galaxy*, and the *motivation of the Terrans*. The motivation of the aliens for the tricks they did is simple. They got stuck there, couldn't return, and were horribly lonely for something approaching a human environment. So they magicked one up!

Sincerely, John W. Campbell

Re: ". . . Or The Devil Will Drag You Under,"
    by Jack L. Chalker

Now, the story Campbell is commenting on is not *exactly* the one we have here, as is obvious if you did what I told you and read the story first. The original motivations of our exploiter team were far more basic and crass than the motives here, and one of Campbell's major objections was their motives.

I realize that most would-be writers, even having a letter like this, would have immediately worked like mad to answer all of Campbell's objections to the story and get it back in— you only got letters like this when Campbell really thought you had something. At least it was motivation to work like mad on another and send it up. I did neither, instead putting the story aside for quite a while. It wasn't ego; it simply wasn't a high priority item with me. In retrospect I think I probably should have; I feel certain I could have sold to Campbell (I have managed to sell to every editor I wanted to since) with a little work, and that would have been a nice start, but I didn't. Even so, the letter gives a feeling of what it was like to work with Campbell and how he taught you to look at your stories. It might give you a hint of why he's considered even today one of the great editors (not just of SF) to have worked in this century.

When preparing the *Jungle* sequel proposal, discussed in my remarks on "Forty Days and Nights in the Wilderness," I took this back out and looked at it and was surprised to find that my psyche had been playing tricks on me. Here was Koldon, for example, from *A Jungle of Stars*, even though Koldon was not a character in the old, pre-novel "Jungle," and I had thought I'd created him in 1975. Here, too, were *Jungle*'s Valiakeans, although that lineage was more direct and deliberate. It was always intended to be set in the *Jungle* universe that already existed, and the Valiakeans had been there from the original fanzine version back in 1962. They seemed handy here, since they are to the body alteration business in *Jungle* what Frank Herbert's navigators were to space travel in *Dune*.

I still thought the story was pretty good, so when, a few years later, I had the time to look over my old stuff, I rewrote it, trying to answer as many of Campbell's criticisms as I could without blowing the story (although JWC was long dead by this point) and incorporating it into the *Jungle* sequel with the Guara again as the bad guys (not, it must be emphasized, The Shaper, but using the Guara as the motivation behind Koldon and Company being on that world). As was said before, the *Jungle* sequel did not see the light of day (I only write 'em if I sell 'em, and since Ballantine had *Jungle* it seemed pointless to market it elsewhere when I had so many other good ideas), and the story went back into the drawer.

In 1978, pressed by George Scithers for another story after he bought "Dance Band," I took it out and reworked it again, eliminating the Guara (who were peripheral players anyway) so that it would stand alone while still answering Campbell's criticisms, and sent it in. George said he might like to see the novel it was from but that he still didn't think it could stand by itself.

In 1980, I was far behind on my novel work but George R.R. Martin was pressing for a new story for the Campbell Awards volume. Thinking of what I could send without spending real time doing extra work for low pay, I took this story and sent it off to him. After all, this work alone among my writings had a direct Campbell connection and was almost an ordered rewrite. Martin, however, said that it was old, old-fashioned, and not at all the sort of story he was looking for. He wanted new, original works, not trunk stories. Besides, he was morally appalled by the ending.

I put it back once more in the drawer and finally sat down to craft a story deliberately to George R.R. Martin's tastes. The result was "In The Dowaii Chambers" which is elsewhere in this volume. There is a touch of humor in that, since when "Moths" was bounced, I took the title of the other 1968 story, the lousy one, and used it on the one I finally sold to Martin.

Martin was perfectly correct in calling it a trunk story. That's trade jargon for a story that was written long ago, did not ever sell, and which the author has been trying to unload someplace ever since because he still likes it. Well, for better or worse it's found a home here because I *still* kind of like it, even though it's nothing weighty or great or earth-shaking.

It is also the first story of mine in which someone is transformed, unless you count the early and peripheral appearance of the Valiakeans in the fanzine version of *Jungle*, something that sort of became my trademark, and thus became in many ways a direct ancestor of the *Well of Souls* books. It also stands as an early but representative piece of my writing. The version here is the one submitted to Scithers and later to Martin, which overall stands best on its own of the three versions I have around. None are preferable stylistically or otherwise, and all tell the same story, so there's no mysterious lost variations or whatever. In fact, the story was not actually rewritten in the total sense since Campbell first saw it; a few pages here and there were excised, a few lines of dialogue or a paragraph to stick in the Guara or get rid of them here and there, or to remove the old motive and insert a better one, is all the difference there is between all three versions.

Interestingly, through all the hands it passed, Martin was the first and only one to be appalled at the conclusion on moral grounds, but the ending is deliberate and dead-straight logical considering the premise. The gods of this poor world are not humans, never have been, and share neither our history, moral sense, or way of looking at things. The gods of Olympus made such decisions with casual abandon; these are not much different. The problem the story presents at the end is a logical one; the alternatives are certainly discussed. One wonders what choice we might make under similar circumstances.

Indeed, it's because this is a very complex story involving complex problems not given to pleasant solutions, yet in the guise of a traditional Campbell-style problem story with romantic lead and all the trappings of older, more simplistic SF, that I like it.

So, here it is, under new title (to avoid driving nuts countless bibliographers—the present title was used for all post-Campbell submissions anyway), for the first time in public or print. Maybe I'm wrong. Maybe Campbell and Scithers and Martin were correct and this should never have seen the light of day. It is the *only* "trunk" story I have that survives and did not see publication elsewhere. You make your own decision.

MOTHS AND CANDLE

A BRISK WIND HAD CAUGHT THE GREAT SAIL OF THE ship; oars were laid to, the drum mallet that beat the cadence was stilled, and the great quiet on the waters was broken only by the splashing of the ship cutting through the chop the wind created on the ocean, and the sound of the spray coming up over the bow and misting gently onto the deck.

It was a good wind, but there were no signs of storm. It was near sunset, and the brilliance of magenta and crimson on the horizon, unblocked by any land or structures, painted the wispy clouds differently from moment to moment, creating an unreal, almost magical effect. Koldon stood there watching it with appreciation, although knowing he would pay a price for dalliance. Not that *she* would deign to come up on deck or make any move to see what his delay might be. No, that would be beneath her dignity. Better to yell and scream and fume and take her anger out on him than actually *do* something. Royalty didn't *do* things; people did things for royalty.

Even if she had decided to come up on deck, it wouldn't have mattered. She was not the type to ever find beauty in a sunset—hell, she was color blind anyway like the rest of them—or majesty in the quiet sounds of wind and wave. Beauty, for her, was found only in a mirror.

It had seemed such a simple, easy job. Her parents were the monarchs of Anrijou to the south; a vast feudal breadbasket land with good soil, ample rains, and the best drink on the planet. With preservation of natural foods next to impossible and an army of little critters that couldn't be kept out of any such stores, they made their ample surplus into various kinds of whiskey and other forms of liquor and traded that for the manufactured and artistic goods they desired or needed. They had little metal down there; even basic blacksmithing required the import of iron and bronze. Yet they were a rich, self-sufficient nation and would have been almost an idyllic place had they not also attracted, for that very reason, the worst bandits and marauding tribes known. That forced them to spend a tremendous amount of their gross national product on an army, and mercenaries, and sufficient weaponry, walls, and castles to protect what they could, and that was the reason for all this.

Three days to the north, across this vast sea, lay Tourkeman, a smaller, leaner kingdom whose major product was war and defense. Everybody was in the army and much of its vital fighting forces were rented out to kingdoms like Anrijou who needed them. Anrijou had been paying through the nose for a Tourkemanian standing army of almost three thousand which had the bandit problem under control but cost just about as much as the bandits had stolen over the years including the cost of repairs. King Lugai of Anrijou had been desperately looking for a way to compromise on this and restore good profits to his land. He was by nature a benevolent monarch who really wanted to give his people the highest standard of living this bronze-age culture could provide, but could not so long as he had to pay and indulge the whims of the mercenaries, one of whom might, without that protection, get the idea to be king himself.

Koldon's employers thought this was a good idea as well. They had great plans for Anrijou based very much on the careful introduction of certain specific genetic techniques that would allow the southern kingdom's produce to travel well and resist the creatures and spores that now made that next to impossible in quantity. The bandit gangs had nasty habits, like burning whole fields of grain and otherwise disrupting the kingdom such that agricultural innovation was extremely difficult to pursue openly. A merger of the kingdom of arms and the kingdom of plenty was clearly called for, at least as much of a merger as geography permitted. When King Mindor of Tourkeman had tripped on a carelessly stored chain and fallen over the battlement of his castle to the ground far below, it had brought his son Shom prematurely to the throne, and Shom had not yet wed.

Koldon wasn't sure whether the old boy had tripped so conveniently because of Providence, an overeager heir, or perhaps his own people, but it didn't really matter. What mattered was that the king of Anrijou had a beautiful daughter of marriageable age, and Shom needed quickly to provide stability to his throne, being the last of his line, lest some other nobles get their own ambitions and arrange another unfortunate accident. It was probably a marriage made in Heaven—or at least in orbit, where the Exploiter Team command ship with its senior staff and computers lay trying to solve the puzzle this world presented and at the same time form a useful pattern. Koldon had been down here the better part of two years, living among the natives undetected and carrying out assignments while learning what he could, Valiakean biological wizardry having made him appear as one of them. The world and its people seemed so simple and basic, yet they remained mostly a mystery to him.

For one things, they had no history to speak of. Records went back at most five generations, and the oldest structures were no more than four hundred standard years, give or take a few. There were no references, not even legends, taking them one year beyond that, and the artifacts that did exist showed a culture, society, and level of knowledge not much different then than now. There weren't any artifacts dating back more than a few centuries, nor, in fact, any ancient remains that could be discovered showing how these people came to be. His own ancestors on his own world had clearly evolved from fierce, hairy, taloned carnivores with a clear history that went back tens of thousands of years. Common ancestors still existed on his home world. Not here, though. It was as if some powerful god had simply looked upon this world, snapped His giant fingers, and brought it all into being pretty much as it was.

They were humanoid; closer to the Earth-type humanoid than he was in his natural form, or so at least they seemed to him. Their bodies were covered with very short, coarse hair except on the palms and soles of their feet and a few other places, although it flared out into a heavy head of hair on top, and their eyes were big, brown, somewhat bulging; excellent for seeing detail, shapes, and movements but color blind. The males also had short, stubby horns coming out of their head, demonlike, just at the top of their brows, while only the females had long, bushy tails looking like second sets of hair extending from the base of their spinal columns.

Well, maybe they didn't look all *that* Earth-human, but they looked closer to Earth-humans than to anything else on this planet.

Maybe it was the fact that, like most life bigger than a fist on this world, they were vegetarians, and he was from a proud if somewhat gory race of carnivores. At least there *had* been a lot of big carnivores on this world in the past, but they'd been mostly hunted to extinction by these people.

Their language was pretty, even a little elegant, but also very practical, with little range or subtlety. It was a unitary language with only mild dialect differences between the kingdoms, which was also significant. They had basic math but no written language as Koldon would regard it, or, it appeared, much desire for one. But if you had a talent for memorization you could go far around this place.

They were not a very imaginative lot, it was true. In fact, for a civilization this well organized, they really weren't all that bright. Even their religion was dull—a pantheon of five gods who were immortal and all-powerful but walked the world in the shape of men and were mostly seen as unwelcome meddlers. Their music was monotonous, their art was basically blocky and crude and, of course, colorless, their legends rather pedestrian, even their foods were pretty bland. Yet they were true craftsmen; this ship had been built at least twenty years ago, entirely by hand, yet it was tight as a drum, efficient, fast, and kept in almost new condition by its crew as were almost all things of consequence on this world.

The current theory was that these were all the descendants of some colony, or perhaps some wrecked ship never meant for this planet, whose members lost most everything and quickly descended into savagery before some bright ones with just a little ancient knowledge managed to get things stable. That theory was the most important reason why Koldon and his employers were wasting so much time and resources here. These people were unlike any known; if there was another spacefaring civilization out there not already co-opted into the Exchange, it was a potential threat and competitor until and unless it was discovered and enfolded into the system. Besides, if there were any clues to be had here that might lead to these people's ancestors and relatives, the first Company to find them got exclusive rights on all those nice ideas every alien civilization develops that are useful but which nobody else ever thought of. That was the profit. Just one new thing could repay a Company a hundred times over and make every Exploiter proportionately wealthy. Koldon, for example, had a half a percent on any valid patent from this operation.

It sure wasn't going to come from *this* hole, though, he thought morosely. He often wondered if the alien ship that had spawned them was carrying their retarded to a nice, safe world of their own.

Grupher the Sailmaker slid over to him as he stared at the steadily darkening sea. "Couldn't take too much more of her wailin', eh? Don't blame you. My ears hurt just to think of her."

Koldon grinned. "Just part of the job. Bad ears, lots of patience, and a hard head. She's aimed one too many jars and plates at it already."

"It's 'cause she's a virgin," the old man noted sagely. "Once she gets settled in she'll be okay. Uh—she *is* a virgin, isn't she?"

"Sure. It's her job, old man. Her role in life. Princesses are brought up as pampered, spoiled brats and taught only what they'll need to do the job, but the payoff is that they'll get to be queens someplace. If the captain needs a sailmaker, he looks for someone with long experience and high skills in sewing canvas, right?"

"Yeah, sure."

"So, a condition of the job for her is that she be a virgin. Nobody has her but the king. Then her job's to make babies, and the more the merrier, to keep the line going. She doesn't even have to raise them or teach them—they have people who do that, even wet nurses if needed. In exchange for making babies she gets fine jewels, the best perfumes, the best food all fixed for her by the best cooks, fancy beds and elegant stuff, a nice castle with all the servants she ever would need and where everybody has to bow to her and call her 'your highness' and cater to whatever her mood may be. If she's smarter than her husband the king, she'll wind up running things through him. If not, she stays a spoiled child forever. It's a fair deal."

"Umph. Maybe. Me, I like the sea and movin' around and seein' the world a bit and meetin' all them different folks. Maybe I ain't got no royal blood or nothin' special, but give me somebody with a good, solid skill ain't too many others can do."

"A fair idea," Koldon replied agreeably. "You got a wife or kids someplace, Grupher?"

"Yeah, sure. Several. Wives, that is. Dunno 'bout the kids, but I pretty well bet on it. Gettin' so I got to pick my ships and routes real careful or one of 'em's gonna catch up to me."

Koldon chuckled, then sighed, steeled himself, and went below and made his way aft along the narrow corridor to the captain's area. He paused at a door, took a deep breath, and knocked.

"Yes?" came her voice from inside, sharp and imperious.

"It's Koldon, your Highness. Just checking in."

"Enter!"

He opened the door to the spacious cabin and walked in. She was lounging on a silken divan idly going through samples of exotic material. For a race that had fur and insulating layers beneath it, the nobility's focus on fashion was an odd quirk. The common folk, both male and female, tended to dress for protection against grime and wear—work pants and boots, sometimes a pullover apron if need be, not much more. He himself was wearing worn, black, lined boots, a pair of traveling shorts with drawstring, and a matching cape that marked him as an official or agent of a king. She, on the other hand, wore a rather elaborate outfit designed to cover much of her, with bloused, satiny pants, a top of the same material, fancy jeweled belt on her hips, and enough jewelry to ransom a king—all for staying in her cabin and being bored. Upper-class women's fashions fascinated him because all women had those enormous tails—hers was "up" and as coiffeured as her almost-matching hair— that had to be accommodated, and all design was based on geometric patterns. However, to one who was *not* color blind, the combinations a color blind society blithely used were often hilarious—although they probably looked great in gray scale.

"You took your time up there," she said accusingly. "I called for you a number of times."

He sighed. "I regret that there was no way to bring along personal servants, your highness, but I am not a servant," he said for perhaps the ten thousandth time. "You know we must do this as secretly as possible. There are many in the royal house of Tourkeman who do not wish this union and might stop at nothing to see that it doesn't come off."

"I don't *care* if it doesn't come off," she pouted. "I am being hauled away from my own lands against my will to be married off to some lout I've never met in a desolate place where the national occupation is fighting. For this I'm forced to stay cooped up in this hole, half sick from all the rolling about, and when I *can* eat it's horrid food, terrible wine, and *incredible* boredom. There's no staff, not even to make the bed or clean the place, and I will not have this room violated by those—those *creatures* that sail this rotten hulk."

"They're just good, common seamen doing their jobs. They're pretty crude and they're not very sensitive to higher tastes, but they're people all the same, and without their kind this world would fall apart."

"They're vulgar *dests*," she retorted. She had never gotten used to being contradicted when she made a statement of opinion. The *dest* was this world's beast of the field—the source of milk and dairy products, the beast of burden, even the source of the leather for boots and belts and the like. They were big, lumbering, incredibly ugly animals but they made civilization possible. The entire economy and way of life of the world was dependent on them, but, of course, they were not exactly animals of respect and to call people *dests* was insulting—and just about the way royalty around here thought of the common folks. "I would not have one of them touch me," she added.

"Well, we'll be in port tomorrow. That's when it'll be most dangerous—we still will be three days' ride from Tourkeman."

"I don't see why they just couldn't send a military escort," she said, shaking her head. "They're the soldiers, and I'm to be their queen, aren't I?"

"Yes, Highness, but I'm afraid that it's the soldiers we have to be most cautious of. If something should happen to the king, then each of the barons would have about equal claim to the throne, and the barons each control a division of the army. Most are loyal, but we can't know which might not be. Some guesses, yes, but there would be no way of knowing whose troops were meeting us or who they were loyal to. Once in the capital and safely in the castle you'll be secure. The King's Own Division is loyal to the death."

"Then why couldn't they send *them* for me instead of making me skulk around in the shadows and sneak into my new kingdom like some common thief?"

"Because it's difficult to keep secrets in a royal court, as you should well know, and anybody can get some proper uniforms and swords and claim to be the King's Own. No, better to get you there this way than risk plots."

She snorted an imperial *Hmph!* "What's so hot about *you* that you can do it alone?"

He wasn't about to tell her that. Nor was he about to tell her that no one could really surprise him on this or many other worlds. Koldon's race needed no speech nor sound signals except as specific supplements to their thoughts. At will he could read the conscious, surface thoughts of anyone he wished. He would, of course, instantly know friend from foe, but mere knowledge wasn't useful if you were outnumbered twenty to one. This ability made him and his race perfect for this sort of job. No state secret was really safe from him, nor could foe ever be foisted off as friend to later betray him. He could not reach down to the deepest thoughts and plumb the very depths of others' psyches, but what he had was damned effective, if a little bit depressing. He'd read the minds of a hundred races, including some so incomprehensible in their thought patterns that he couldn't make them out anyway, but this was the first race where, it seemed, that what you saw was what you got. With others you always got disjointed fragments, some processes going on in the background while their foreground thoughts were on you, sort of like being at a party and having a friendly conversation with someone while your mind thought, *What a bore. I wish this party was over*.

Not here, with these people. What you saw and heard was what you got. It was one reason why the barons tried to stay away from the king and the king tried to have constant contact with the barons. Every damned one of these people was a lousy liar and hypocrisy was almost always easily revealed. The real danger lay in these transition times; clearly the barons as a group didn't like being under this young and inexperienced whelp whom they had no reason to fear or respect, and at this point, and until he earned that trust, it was nearly impossible to discern who simply disliked the king but believed in the continuity of the royal house and the royal line from those who figured their genes were better and to hell with tradition. Baron Rodir's loyalties, for example, were in question. He had little use for his nation's mercenary role; armies were to be used best in the service of their own king. Although loyal to young King Shom, Rodir was not above arranging things to his own ends and leading the boy down his own paths. A failure to deliver the princess would be a very nice pretext for turning a mercenary army in Anrijou's employ into an instant army of occupation.

Koldon was confident, however, of his ability to get her there. His people were keeping close watch on all the players and forces in Tourkeman that might intervene; other agents using technology undreamed of by these simple people would be waiting the moment they hit the dock to insure that the cordon of protection was not as obvious as an army escort but more dependable and far more resourceful. It was slow work building up a culture and creating a true civilization, but no matter what, it was worth it. A hundred political foundations would pay a fortune just for the right to shepherd these people into their own ideas of the millennium.

"Just get some sleep," he told her. "The ship's on time and should be getting in a little past midday tomorrow. Before we come in to the harbor we'll get off in the small boat and row to shore. It'll be only a short walk to a safe house that's been prepared for us. Just try and act a little less like a future queen if we meet anybody or you might as well announce it to the world. It's your neck as well as mine if they find out."

Not that they'd been able to keep such knowledge from the ship's crew. She was just too imperious and too spoiled not to blow their cover. He knew that the crew would keep quiet about it for a while, though—a fat bonus awaited everyone aboard ship if nothing leaked out until they were safely away, and he wouldn't give a fingernail for the health and long life of any man who blew that for the rest of them.

He bowed and left, going to his own small cabin next door. Tomorrow was going to be a very long day.

Koldon was awakened by the sounds of feet pounding the deck above him. He yawned and stretched, knowing it was by no means late enough to get up, but this much activity bore investigation. He pulled on boots, pants, and cape and splashed a little water from a pitcher on his face to wake himself up, then went out. He stopped briefly by the princess's door and heard her stirring. There were shouts now from up top, and he could feel the ship coming about, and he didn't like it at all.

It was just after dawn, but most of the crew was on deck, and Koldon saw as he went topside that the off-duty men had been issued bows and swords. That wasn't good at all.

"Can you make her sail mark now?" the captain called to the lookout.

"No, sir," came the reply. "The sail appears totally black, without any symbol on her."

Koldon peered out into the just lightening sky and finally spotted it. A ship, all right, smaller and faster than this one. More like somebody's private yacht than any merchant vessel. It was still hard to make out since it seemed to be painted completely black, including the large sail, which boded very ill indeed. All ships were registered by the symbol of their owners painted large on the sail as well as elsewhere on the ship so they could be instantly identified. An "X" on a black field might well have meant pirates, but this was all black, something that just wasn't done.

He stopped a crewman he knew. "You think it's pirates?"

The man shrugged. "Hard to say. Captain ain't takin' no chances, though. Ain't nobody paints all black unless they don't want'a be seen, though. She's a fast little craft, too. Be on us in half an hour tops. We ain't gonna outrun her, that's for sure."

Koldon turned and went below, rapping hard on the princess's door.

"What is it?" she snapped.

"Maybe trouble, Highness," he replied. He didn't wait for the invitation but opened the door. She was up and just starting to put on some royal-looking clothing. "Uh uh! No, Highness, now's the time for stealth. There's a ship coming in, no identification, closing fast. It might be pirates, in which case the last thing we want is for them to know that someone of importance is aboard. You wouldn't like being their captive. They have no respect at all for royalty except ransom, but by the time you were ransomed you would have been through hell."

That unnerved her a little. Pirates were nothing more than seafaring bandits, and she had seen bandits in chains before their execution and could imagine being entirely in the hands of animals like that. "What should I do?" she asked him.

"Put on the plain skirt, wrap, and sandals," he told her. "Stay below and keep out of sight. If they force you up, keep quiet, hold your temper, and stick to the cover story. If it *is* pirates, that might help somewhat. If your enemies have outguessed me and decided that this was the most vulnerable point—well, I'll fight hard and you'd better, too. They will have come to kill you anyway."

He went back to his own room and took out his small case, opening it with a security combination system beyond the ability of anyone here. He hadn't really figured on something like this—none of them had. They had joined the ship off the Anrijou coast after it sailed, using a small skiff, and he had been certain that it had been done in complete secrecy. None but the captain had known in advance about them coming aboard at all, and even he hadn't known who his passengers would be. Because there were so many Tourkemanian troops around

Anrijou, no one, not even the Queen Mother, had known when they would go or when they had, nor how the trip was to be accomplished. Even then Koldon had paid six ships' masters going to six different destinations the same amount and given them the same instructions, so that there had been little chance of anyone knowing which ship or port he would use.

After two days at sea, it was clear that those measures had worked. Any leak would have to come from the Anrijou side, and they would have been intercepted long before this. This ship was coming from the direction of their destination, yet it was bearing down on them with all deliberateness. There was no mass communications here and they'd made good time. This *couldn't* have anything to do with the princess. It was just rotten bad luck.

He reached into the lining of the case and removed a needler, then got a cartridge and snapped it into place, watching the little indicator as it rose and registered a full charge. He didn't want to use such weapons if he could avoid them, but, damn it, if they *were* pirates, then they might well be ready to kill the crew and take the ship as prize—and, to them, he'd be crew as well. Only the princess would survive, and he wasn't minimizing her fate if that was the case. They would have their sport with her before they ransomed her, and that would not only destroy her value, it would break her and brutalize her as well. Well, it was known that his company employed great magicians. It might be necessary to show a little deadly magic here.

He clipped the needler to the inside of his belt in the small of his back, so that the cape would conceal it. His eyes went to the communicator, but he decided not to use it. It was only for local service, really, and wouldn't likely be in range of anybody yet. The panic alarm was there, of course, but it wasn't time for that yet. Besides, he wasn't certain whether it would bring help or instant oblivion to protect the other secrets of the case.

He closed and sealed it again and went back topside. The atmosphere was tense as the black ship continued to close, its fearsome shape now quite visible in the bright light of morning, its distance no more than a kilometer now.

Grupher the old sailmaker stared at the stranger. "I seen a ship like that once," he muttered.

Koldon heard him. "Huh? What is it? None of the others seem to know it."

"Not too many seem 'em and live to tell. It ain't no natural ship. See—you can make it out right good now. See anybody on the lookout or in the riggin'? See any lights?"

It was still a bit far for that to be conclusive, but the captain had slowed his own ship, understanding that he couldn't outrun the smaller black one. Still, the old boy was right. The thing was sailing along very nicely, but it didn't seem to have a single human being on board.

"God ship. Ghost ship," the old sailmaker muttered. "Nothin' good ever came outa one o' those."

Koldon stared a moment at the old man, then turned back to the black newcomer. A god ship. A supernatural vessel for one of their five god figures who roamed the world as men but were not. He'd heard legends of such things, not only ships but coaches and the rest, but he'd dismissed them. Now, though—he turned and looked at their own sail and checked the wind. Yes, it was true— there was very little wind but what there was was coming from the east. The black ship was sailing against that wind, its sail blown inward, inverted, as if to emphasize the point, and there were no signs of oarsmen. If he hadn't known better he'd have sworn that the black ship had an engine in it.

It was quite close now, so close you could see the deck, and Grupher was proved correct. There seemed to be nobody aboard the damned thing. No—wait. One figure, extremely tall and covered entirely by a black hood and robe, stood on the wheel deck, not doing anything but just staring forward. It was impossible to see a face inside that hood, but it was clearly alive.

The captain was as unnerved as the crew by all this, but he was still all business. "Hello! You aboard the dark ship! What is your name and what do you wish with us?" he called out.

For a moment the dark one was unmoved, but then it raised its arms and they could hear a strong, clear voice state, "I command you to halt! I have some business aboard your ship. If I am not interfered with you shall not be harmed and will be able to continue on your way in a short time. If you interfere, you shall suffer. I am the Shaper."

That last sent a chill through all of them, and even Koldon felt it. This was something entirely new, entirely different, and outside the experience of any of his people on this world. Who and what *was* this guy, anyway? He wished he had a good analyzer aboard to scout out that ship and its occupant.

The wind died abruptly, and there descended on the freighter an unnatural calm. Even the sea became smooth as glass, and there wasn't a sound from ship or water. Koldon looked around and saw that they'd all dropped their weapons and were just staring, frightened and awe-struck, at this—whatever it was. Looking out, he saw the choppy sea all around them except in a circular patch that encompassed both ships. *Now how the hell is he doing that?* Koldon wondered. Illusion? No, it sure didn't *feel* like an illusion. The ship was steady as a rock.

However he was doing it, the Shaper had an impressive act. In a dead calm, the two ships sat motionless, parallel to one another and perhaps twenty meters apart. The Shaper turned and walked to the rail on his vessel, removed a segment, then stepped out into open air a good dozen meters above the level of the ocean. He then walked over the twenty meters between the two ships as if the air supported some kind of invisible bridge or gangplank. It wasn't levitation—the guy was definitely walking on air.

Koldon began to think that he would have preferred pirates.

He reached out with his mind to scan the mysterious godlike creature and got nothing. Either he was extremely well shielded or his mental frequencies were outside the common range entirely. Both weren't all that uncommon in the galaxy, but not *here*, not on this backwater world. Then a rather simple idea hit him.

A holographic illusion, he decided. *It's got to be.* Such a thing would be easy for the Company to pull off, if they had preparation. But how could anybody have prepared *this*, out here, right now?

By the gods I wish they'd let me bring a recorder! Koldon thought in frustration. *Nobody is going to believe this*. Still, he was less impressed with the act and the gimmickry than with the fact that it was being done at all. This wasn't any Company trick; somebody was illegally muscling in on their territory.

They had scanned this whole world backward and forward, inside and out, without a trace of machinery, stored or transmitted energy, you name it. Hell, they'd even considered using the gimmick of the five gods themselves on occasion if they really needed authority to do something. The only explanation that made sense here was that somebody else had decided to do it first. But why? Why for this simple little world? Hell, if they didn't have the five-year grant from that sociological foundation they wouldn't have bothered with this place.

The Shaper was not a slow walker and quickly reached the rail only a few meters from where Koldon stood watching. The black figure paused, then jumped down to the deck with a noticeable *thud* and the expected vibration. Either this illusion was being carried to extremes or this guy was real! But nobody could actually walk across thin air! That was impossible!

The Shaper stood there a moment, scanning the faces of the crew who stood there silent as death, then turned toward Koldon. The dark figure was very tall—Koldon was over a hundred and ninety centimeters himself, and this stranger was at least a head taller. The hands were covered with thin leather gloves that extended well up the sleeves of the loose-fitting robe, and while there was an opening in the hood it was darkness inside, with no exposed skin, no mask, no features of any kind. It was next to impossible to tell if the Shaper was even in the form of a native. One hand held a long, thick rod of dull silver that seemed to have a dull reddish tip. Koldon couldn't help thinking, *And now he waves his magic wand and we all disappear*. He casually shifted back, one hand going back toward the small of his back in a natural-looking motion.

The Shaper reached out and grabbed his arm and brought it forward with such strength that it caught the agent completely off guard. More than that—that hand was as solid and real as his own!

A robot? An android?

"Keep whatever weapon you were going for where it resides, mercenary," the Shaper said calmly. "You are just doing your job but you are out of your class here. Now, where is the girl?"

"My Lord, I am no mercenary. I carry diplomatic and trade credentials and am posted with my wife to Garmond City-State as trade consul for his Majesty King Lugai of Anrijou. What could you—?"

"I said you had done your job!" the Shaper snapped. "I do not wish this to be any more of an inconvenience to others than it has to be, but I am not a patient man. Summon her! From the top deck, please."

Koldon sighed and shrugged, then walked over to the stairway door and opened it. "Come on up, my darling wife," he called, prompting as best he could. "It's not pirates so you have nothing to fear." He wasn't sure if she'd come up or not, but there was no percentage in not seeing this out first. He had to wonder, though, why the Shaper seemed in such a big hurry. Was he just being imperious like all the top people around here or was he somehow vulnerable while away from his ship? If so, the question became what was he vulnerable to? Or who?

She *did* come, after a suitable wait, and she was dressed the way he'd instructed her to dress, but there was no mistaking the royal manicure and trim of both hair and tail, or her aloof manner. Still, she was scared enough to give the cover story a try. "Koldon, what?..." She stopped, seeing the Shaper there, and breathed, "Oh..."

"Come over here, girl, and let me get a look at you," the Shaper ordered.

His tone infuriated her. "Who are you to speak to me like that?" she snapped, and Koldon thought, *Oh, boy!*

"I am the Shaper," the dark one responded matter-of-factly. "I outrank you, my dear. You see, I am a god."

She hadn't seen his impressive show, just a very tall man in a lot of black, and she was not terribly impressed. "You are no god of mine," she responded. "You're just a big man hiding in a bigger robe."

Koldon was afraid that such a lack of respect would infuriate the man or whatever it was, and said, "My Lord, you have no right—"

The dark one laughed. "I have every right, my friend. It was I who created you all, after all. This would be terribly amusing if I could waste more time." His tone turned suddenly very menacing. *"I said to come here! Now!"*

The princess approached, slowly, hesitantly, stopping no more than an arm's length from him. Koldon was proud of her; she was scared to death, but she was holding her own pretty good. He felt helpless, though, and frustrated as well. If the thing was some sort of machine, as was likely, then the needler would have no effect other than to reveal that he was part of the Exploiter Team and not just a locally hired pro.

"You are quite beautiful," the Shaper noted, not lustfully but as if appreciating a work of art. "You would have made that young king a perfect queen and had him around your little finger. Unfortunately, that is something I can not permit."

Koldon frowned. "Why not, my Lord?" he asked. "What can such petty matters of state be to you?"

The Shaper was not put off by the comment. "You are not meant to understand the motives of your gods," he responded. "You, or the ones who hired you, are to be complimented, actually. Had you not been so thorough and professional I would not have had to personally intervene, something I very much dislike doing. She would simply have been kidnapped by bandits or vanished into the slave markets of Garmond. Because you are so professional, because you think of everything in a depth beyond your people's norm, I can not trust the old ways to work, and I do not kill my creations. Nor do I wish you harmed, mercenary. You show a level of intelligence, planning, and initiative far beyond anything I would have expected from your people. I should hate to have to prevent you from passing on such superiority to new generations."

This guy sounds really sincere about that, Koldon thought. *It's a hell of an act—or he's nuts and really believes it.* Still, he said he didn't kill, so he must be planning to take her off with him. When the big one made that move, Koldon would try the needler anyway.

The Shaper sighed. "Such a pity, but there must be no marriage. There must be an obvious default. Tourkeman must expand and Anrijou must fall, and I have been here too long already." He raised his wand and suddenly it began to pulse with a strong inner light. The light seemed to collect, then solidify, and rush into the crimson tip. The wand went all the way up over the Shaper's head, tip tilted a bit toward the princess.

An opaque energy field sprang from it; old and impenetrable. It struck and enveloped the form of the princess before anyone including she could react. It was so sudden and so spectacular that Koldon was as frozen as the crew, uncertain as to what was going on and what if anything he could do.

The energy field was not truly black. There were many colors in there; deep blues and purples swirled around in the nothingness like living things, colors and shapes only Koldon, of all aboard, could really see.

Now the field grew, taking on the ghostly outline of an object much larger and far different than the princess, but one that seemed very familiar...

It seemed like an eternity but it was really over in no more than thirty or forty seconds. The field solidified, then seemed to fade away as the shape it had made became solid reality. The wand was suddenly cold, dull, and lifeless once again, but nobody noticed.

Where a minute before the princess had stood, there now stood a creature with a tough, metallic blue-black skin, with two bony plates extending from its shoulders back to its long, thick tail from the end of which grew a single sharp, long, bone spike. The legs were thick and muscular, set off to the side of the body, each ending in an enormous hoof; the head was on a short but very flexible neck, with two big brown eyes looking out over a broad but blunt snout behind which two large ears twitched this way and that, independent of one another. It was definitely a female; between those powerful rear legs was an enormous gray udder.

It was actually quite attractive—if you liked *dests*.

"There!" the Shaper said, sounding satisfied. "Let's see you marry young Shom off to *her*!"

Koldon was an old hand at high-tech parlor tricks; his mind went out, trying to locate the real princess in a pretty impressive now-you-see-it illusion, and found her.

Why is everyone staring at me so? I feel so—strange.

The agent's heart sank. Damn it, he'd swear the *dest* was thinking that!

The Shaper turned. "She is a purebred and she's yours, my boy," he told Koldon. "She's fully functional and will breed quite well. Smart, too, although I'm afraid the *dest* brain is not as fully developed as yours, so conscious thought and memory will soon fade, and she'll become just an animal over time. She is better off that way—not knowing. Besides, look at it this way. Now for the rest of her life she'll actually perform useful work."

He was already back up on the rail, and with a touch of his wand to his hood, he turned and walked back on the air to his own ship.

Everybody else still seemed frozen stiff, but Koldon rushed to the rail and wide scanned the ship even as the Shaper reached it. Nothing. No conscious band thoughts at all, not from that direction.

The *dest* opened her mouth but all that came out was the usual *dest* gruntlike roar. In his mind, however, came her thoughts.

Koldon? What has happened? Why do I feel so strange?

He whirled around and came into immediate eye contact with the *dest*. Damn it! It *couldn't* be! He'd been the right shape and size to begin with and the Valiakeans, the greatest masters of biology known, had taken *weeks* to change him completely into this form! Nobody but the Valiakeans knew how to do even that much. Oh, you could genetically build what you wanted, but *change* something pre-existing to this degree? In thirty seconds? With a magic wand?

"Princess?" he asked softly, looking unbelievably at the *dest*. "Is that really you? Don't speak—just nod your head."

The *dest* looked at him and nodded.

"Oh, boy!" he sighed aloud. "I—I don't know how to tell you this, but the Shaper, well . . . Twist around as best you can and look at yourself."

The massive head was able to twist around on that neck and see backward pretty well, at least with one eye.

The *dest* roared as if struck by a spear in its side, and its tail thrashed about, but Koldon, who could see into the mind that was still there, at least for now, could hear a young girl's screams.

He spent most of the day with her up on deck. The crew gave them a wide berth and seemed both nervous and frightened, as well they might be, but not frightened enough that at some point a couple of them didn't ask if the bonus for keeping quiet was still in effect. The question amused him.

"No bonuses now," he told them. "Talk all you want to about this. Who's going to believe you, anyway? Would *you* believe it if somebody off a ship told it to you?"

He still wasn't sure he believed it himself. As a telepath, there was no question that what had been the princess was now the young female *dest* before him. As one from a technological society so much more advanced than this that most of what he took for granted seemed the blackest of magic to even the most knowledgeable kings and advisors of this world, he knew full well that what he had seen was, while obviously not impossible, as beyond the science of his people as his technology was beyond the princess's. This was no competitor, no illegal Exploiter Team working an angle they'd overlooked. The sheer energy alone required for something like this was staggering, yet this Shaper had done it with a simple magic wand. Even if it somehow received energy from a remote source and reformed or redirected it, which seemed likely, why hadn't that power source shown up on their own monitors and instruments?

It was very much like real magic, and he didn't believe in real magic. At least the Shaper himself kept things firmly grounded in reality. He was no supernatural force, even if he had access to powers Koldon's people did not. The Shaper had been worried about something. He tried to conceal it but even with all his trickery, he couldn't hide from a trained observer like Koldon. It was less a specific fear than a general one, as if by leaving wherever he usually lived he had exposed himself to some potential danger, a danger that was not from the likes of the natives or elements or even Koldon. The obvious conclusion was that the man had enemies of at least equal power.

And that begged the question of just why somebody like the Shaper would care if Tourkeman turned rogue instead of expanding its influence by careful nonmilitary means. If he was exposing himself to real danger by directly intervening, the matter had to be of great import to him—but why?

The Shaper had also figured out Koldon's strategy and closed on the princess at the most vulnerable point, yet he was not omnipotent. He clearly had no idea of Koldon's origins and true nature, nor even any suspicion of it, although the Exploiter Team had been around for several years and had been quite active and occasionally impressive in its own "magic." The only possible conclusion to be drawn from that was that, up until now, the two sides' interests had simply not conflicted, or possibly even intersected. They would conflict now, though. It was a whole new game from this moment on. Neither Koldon nor, he suspected, his bosses would even care any more about Anrijou and Tourkeman; all resources would shift to this new element. Just the little trick the Shaper pulled would break the Valiakean monopoly on biological changes and be worth untold sums, and it was just the tip of the iceberg.

But first he had to get into a position to tell somebody about it.

He sat down in front of the *dest*. "How are you feeling, princess?" he asked casually.

She just looked at him with those mournful eyes but her mind said, *"Hungry."*

"Well, there's not much we can do beyond the little bit I've brought you," he responded as if she'd spoken aloud to him. "Once we dock we'll get to someplace where you can eat and relax."

The head went up like a shot. *"Koldon—you can hear me? You understand me?"*

He nodded. "I can hear you, princess. Only me. I can hear what you think. I can hear what *anybody* thinks— except that wizard or god or whatever he was."

If *dests* could cry in the human sense she would have. She was miserable, and the sense of degradation and isolation had been tremendous.

"Koldon—what happened to me? How could it happen?"

"What do you remember?"

"I was standing there, angry at him for his arrogance. Nobody had ever spoken to me like that before! Then that rod went up, and there was a burst of light and a feeling—well, it was like a tingling, inside and out. I got very dizzy, I dropped on my hands and knees on the deck, and then it was over. I felt—confused. Strange. Everybody staring at me. I feel—degraded. Defiled. It's not fair!"

"No, it's not, princess, but for now we'll have to try to accept it. Unless we can find this Shaper and learn how to do this trick, there's no way to bring you back."

There was no purpose to going through any charades; the only way you could unload a *dest* was through the port facilities at Garmond. Not that it mattered any more; he seriously doubted if even the most powerful enemies of either king wanted or even cared about the princess now.

"Princess, we're going to have to compromise on this from now on," he told her. "I want to get down to the marketplace before it closes for the night. Remember, no matter what you think of yourself, or me, to everybody else you're just a *dest*. Do you think you could stand me riding you? We'll make better time, and time is of the essence here."

He was already mindful of that ticking clock, even though he had little hope for her in any event. It was necessary to keep her hopes alive so she'd fight it. She had been a *dest* for only twelve hours and there were already changes in her. He hadn't noticed it right off, but the fact was she wasn't thinking on more than an ele- mentary level when he wasn't directly talking to her. Everybody had thoughts all the time, but whenever she wasn't being forced to think she just sort of blanked out. While it made her easier to handle, he remembered what the Shaper had said about the *dest* brain simply not hav- ing the equipment to handle complex thought. They were pretty bright as cattle went, but that only meant they were easy to train and could carry out a simple series of commands.

The *dest* saddle sat just beyond the shoulder blades between the bony ridges. It was not a comfortable ride, but one got used to it, and at least the saddle was well padded. She resisted the bridle but was eventually talked into accepting it, much to the incredulous stares of long-time merchants who thought that this stranger was really crazy talking to a *dest* as if she were human. Koldon even had a couple of offers for her from *dest* merchants; apparently she had all the markings of a top line pure-bred. They were stared at and snorted at, and he politely declined.

It was too late to go anywhere tonight, and she

needed massive quantities of food to do any real traveling, so he found an inn with stables. She was so starved
that she didn't even object to being put in for the night
and began eating voraciously of the bales of grain there.

Koldon needed to get in touch with somebody and
fast, and headed to a small out-of-the-way shop in the
dock area. It was closed, of course, but not to those who
knew its secrets, including the small room below that
could be opened only by electronic combination. The
communications center was also shut down right now,
but it was easily activated.

The signal went up to a specially placed satellite and
then to the mother ship.

"Cornig here," came a voice. "Who's calling."

"Koldon. I've got a real situation here. Turn on the
data report recorders and hold on to whatever you can
because you're not going to believe this." Quickly but
thoroughly he sketched in the events of the day. Cornig
said nothing until he was through.

"If I didn't know you better, I'd ask you what native
drug you were on," the project manager responded when
the report was done. "As it is, I think we have to move
on this fast. I'm going to send this as is back to the Company. You're in far too civilized an area now to do any
good, and it'll take a couple of days to get everybody we
need assembled anyway. The important thing is to keep
her reasonably active. Talk to her often and make her
respond. We want her as whole as possible." He gave
coordinates for a rendezvous well out in the middle of
nowhere perhaps two days ride from the city—and away
from Tourkeman.

The princess had eaten and drank enough for two
dests and then had fallen into a very deep sleep. She
seemed happy to see him but was far more docile. The
anger, rage, even the fear seemed to have gone out of
her. She seemed almost eager to accept the bridle and
saddle. They headed out and away from the city-state as
quickly as possible.

"You seem to have slept well," he noted.

"Very well. I—something is funny in my head, Kol-

*don. Everything is all mixed up. A lot of words don't
make sense."*

"Just don't worry about it. Just keep thinking, keep
talking to me as we go." That, of course, was the trouble
with Cornig's orders. She never did have much depth or
experience, and what interests she had were princess
type stuff—fashions, jewelry, decor, that sort of thing,
all of which was irrelevant to her now and not very relevant for him.

She was certainly having no problems adapting to the
body, that was for sure. Riding *dests* developed a long,
loping stride that didn't seem to be quick but really covered ground, and she got the hang of it very easily under
his urging. Still, a trend was developing that he could do
nothing about. Her entire ego was undergoing a rapid
shift from self to him. She was rapidly losing her own
sense of identity and acting in every way simply to
please him. It *was* true that he was all she had, her only
contact with anything other than the animal kingdom,
but it was more than dependence, more like how a pet
regarded its master.

They made very good time, and were well away from
civilization by nightfall. Most of the countryside was
open range, and there were quite a number of *dests*
roaming about. The *dest* was essentially a herd animal
but often roamed far afield in its grazing. In the old days
of the large carnivores it had been a much stronger
group, but they seemed to have developed a sense that
the world wasn't all that dangerous any more.

He realized uneasily that he wasn't going to be able to
keep her tied up when he made camp. She needed to
graze for a long period in order to keep her strength up,
and he didn't have the means to carry along commercial
feed. "Stay close to me," he warned her. "If you get lost
out here I might never find you, and then it's all over. If
you run into any problem, call as strongly as you can
with your mind and keep calling until I come."

She promised him emphatically that she would not get
out of sight of him. He had at least kept to his own task.
She was a *dest*, it was true, but she had once been a

human princess and she believed still she might be again. Koldon would do it. Koldon would not fail. Koldon could do anything.

Still, the grass near the road wasn't very good or very plentiful and she did stray well away from him. She couldn't see very well at night, but her sense of smell was acute as to where the tasty clumps of grass and bushes were. It did not occur to her that others of her kind could smell them, too. She was no longer thinking very much, and certainly not very straight.

She caught the scent long before she could make out any shapes in the dark. It was a strange, compelling scent that she took in more and more. It was heady, intoxicating, making parts of her tingle in strangely pleasurable ways. She didn't understand it, but she felt drawn, even compelled, to follow it. Her tail went up and then forward, until it was resting on her back, countless tiny tendrils or hairs on its underside which she hadn't even been aware of before now tingled with tense anticipation.

The wild bull *dest* also caught *her* scent and, within a few meters, it roared its challenge to all others to stay clear. Hearing no answer, it proceeded to her, first nuzzling her, then going on through the instinctive rite that could end in only one way.

Koldon had slept pretty well through the night considering the events and the worries he'd undergone. He usually slept light, a corner of his brain always receptive to indications of danger or menace, and it had been pretty reliable over the years, catching many a thief or would-be assassin.

It was just past dawn; there were many *dests* about, mostly still sleeping standing up, a few grazing here and there, but, frankly, it was almost impossible to tell one of them from the other. He normally avoided broadcast telepathy while in the field, since one never knew who or what could pick it up, but there was no getting around it.

Princess?

There was no response, and he began to worry, fearing not so much that she wouldn't respond as that she had wandered too far, perhaps out of range. His telepathy was essentially line of sight and it was pretty bumpy in these parts. He had been nervous letting her run free but what could he do? He couldn't feed her and she needed bulk to travel.

Princess! This is Koldon! Answer me! Aloud he yelled, "Princess! Come here! Now! Come to me!"

And there was a response this time. *"Koldon—I do not wish to come. I should stay here."* The response was shaky, nervous, scared.

He tried to localize the thoughts, and got a fix not too far away. He began walking toward it, knowing he had to keep her talking in order to find her.

What's the matter? What's wrong with you?

"I—Koldon...Last night...There was a...bull...It took me...Violated me..."

Damn! That was something that just hadn't entered his mind. Changing her into an animal was one thing, but it just hadn't occurred to him that it was that complete a change.

"I—I didn't resist. I sought it. I couldn't help myself. I wanted it! Even now I still want it. I am a dest now, truly. It's getting harder to think. It's like I was always a dest, one who dreamed of being a princess. It has not been very long, Koldon, but I cannot remember what it was like. Walking on hind legs, I mean, or having hands. I remember it all, just as it was, but always in my mind I am as I am now. I am an animal. I am truly a dest now."

He had her now, and even while he felt sorry for her he felt relieved as well. He walked up and patted her gently. "Well, if you're a *dest*, then you are my *dest*," he told her. "Come. We have a long way to go."

It was quite an assembly, a small tent city in the midst of a desolate plain. Most of the ship's scientists and company had come down, and they'd brought all the best analytical equipment with links to the great computers aboard ship. They poked her and probed her and took many samples over several days. They gave her brain scans and body analysis and all the rest, although there was some problems in adapting the equipment to *dest* scale. When they had done all that they could do, and run the results and tests a hundred times and come up with all they could, they held a meeting.

Chief Biologist Surowak shook her head in wonder. "Koldon, if you weren't telepathic, and if you hadn't been checked out and analyzed yourself, and if she didn't still have that mental *persona*, I would say you were stark raving mad."

"I had considered the possibility," the agent responded sourly, "but unfortunately reality would not let me get off that easily."

"As you know," Surowak said, "the process by which many of us appear to be natives is biologically complex but still only a disguise. The Valiakeans can adapt our exteriors to look and behave convincingly if they have genetic samples from the target race, and even change our insides to tolerate the food, drink, and atmosphere where needed. It's effective, but still superficial. We can be easily reversed to our normal forms since deep down we are still genetically ourselves. Subject us to the kind of analysis we just did to her and our true colors would be easily revealed. That—animal—out there is different. It's a *dest*, inside and out, as genetically perfect and normal and natural as if it had been born that way. Her genetic code says she is and should be as we see her. She *is* a super-intelligent *dest*. Nothing more, nothing less. So perfect, in fact, that she is now a couple of weeks pregnant—with a *dest*."

Koldon was startled. "That one time with the bull was enough?"

The biologist nodded. "It happens, and *dests* are abnormally fertile anyway. Even if we took her to Valiakea and had them have a go at her, which would be expensive and cause panic on their part, it wouldn't matter. We couldn't regrow the parts of her brain that would restore her without destroying her mind anyway—and what's the purpose in that? The *dest* is a highly intelligent beast, but it has a rudimentary forebrain. This must have been a fairly rough world once, and the *dest* evolved in a far less peaceful atmosphere than now. Nature generally chooses the easiest route for survival—prolific breeding first, then strength, then size. Only if all those fail does a creature develop real intelligence or die out. These creatures breed prolifically, which is why they are the backbone and mainstay of this economy. They are strong and tough enough that ancient predators had to prey on the young, the weak, the diseased, and the infirm for their food. They are large so they win the competition for food and water when they need it. And, for animals, they are relatively smart, but not truly intelligent. There is less instinct, with survival skills basically taught by the mother. But this was enough. They don't have any real reasoning abilities. She is as intelligent as she is because she is drawing on Koldon for support, but she doesn't really have the equipment to sustain it. Her reasoning ability and vocabulary are already fading fast. She no longer has the ego to even fight for what's left."

Koldon nodded sadly. Little of the once proud and beautiful princess remained now, as the Shaper had predicted.

Cornig, the project manager, changed the subject. "We are less concerned with her at this point than with the one who managed to do this. Just wave a magic wand and *poof*! Damn it, I never believed in gods or magic and I'm not about to start now. Magic's just something somebody can do that we haven't figured out how to do yet. The fact remains that we've got someone on this planet who is possibly as advanced from us as we are from the natives."

"No," responded Wakut, the political officer. "Not that advanced. There are certainly no more than a few. Probably the five of the legends—all legends start with a kernel of truth somewhere inside them. Now, when you have access to that kind of power you need a really huge team, but it's clear they've been here a while. I was interested in Koldon's perception, which we share from reading the recordings from his mind, that this Shaper was nervous the whole time he was aboard the ship. Why? What was he scared of—or who? His fellow

aliens? Certainly not anything else, with that kind of
power at his fingertips. Consider—five people from a
highly advanced species, dropped on this world with access to that power and knowledge. Why? Research? It
doesn't hold up. Experimentation? Perhaps—but this
would imply that somewhere along the line the experiment went wrong. Who knows? And until we catch one,
if we can catch one, and ask him, we won't know. What
we *do* know is that somebody else is working the same
kind of game here as we are, and that's a violation of our
free market rights. We bought the rights to this hole fair
and square. Before these characters are anything else,
we must consider them illicit competition."

Cornig shifted in his seat. "Well, we're flying blind
and that's no help. If we're wrong and this is an active
experiment or active advance party, then any attempt to
dig them out without a naval fleet might result in some
pretty ugly experiences for us. A wave of a wand and
you turn a battle crusader into an aquarium. If they're on
their own, then we have the numbers and strength, at
least, with the equipment we've got. I, for one, have no
desire to be turned into a *dest*, but flushing them out will
be risky. We don't know what we're dealing with. We
don't know the limits."

"And that," Wakut said, "is the question. Do we flush
them out now or do we wait and get reinforcements?"

"A chance at the exclusive rights to this scale of technology—if we call in the Exchange with all its authority
and military force it won't be our show any more," Cornig noted. "The Valiakeans alone would halt all adapta-
tions, shutting us down, unless they had exclusivity to
this new process. This kind of technology would draw in
the powerful, and the rules would be out the window. I'd
say we have to make a stab at doing it on our own."

"I agree," replied Wakut. "Surowak is just salivating
with the idea of getting her hands on the computers and
energy sources that could do this kind of job, as are the
others. We stand to be in a commanding position with
incredible power so long as we maintain exclusivity, and

such gains are never taken without great risk. So—we flush them out. But how? Yes, Koldon?"

"They've been nothing but superstition to us the past two years," the agent noted. "Hidden, out of sight. And clearly, from the comments of the Shaper, they don't know that we exist, only that we're developing extra smarts and rocking their boat. I think it's pretty clear that this was precipitated by our attempt to forge an alliance between Tourkeman and Anrijou. For some reason, we stepped on this fellow's *own* plans by doing so. He wants a military takeover. He wants Tourkeman to break its neutrality and become a conquering power. I would say that the odds were quite good that the old king's trip and fall over the battlements wasn't a fortuitous accident after all. Put the young king up under Rodir's influence, and you have the makings of a military and militant power. The marriage would have had the effect of nullifying that. Clearly they prefer working behind the scenes, but this Shaper wants a strong and militant Tourkeman. If just a marriage could drive him to the surface, then something infinitely worse might just flush him out in desperation."

They all looked interested.

"The story of the princess has to be getting around by now—that ship's crew couldn't keep it in," Koldon noted. "So, we use it. Tourkeman and the black arts. Tourkeman the conqueror, with power and magic on its side. It'd be enough to give a king nightmares, wouldn't it?"

"All right," Cornig said, nodding. "So we whip up enough paranoid kings to form a considerable army. Half of Tourkeman's army is off serving in remote places like Anrijou, but the half they have remaining is pretty good. I'm sure we could convince enough leaders to muster an army, but will they be willing to go against a military state with an active god for a protector?"

"They would," replied Koldon, "if *they* had powerful magic, too."

* * *

The Grand Palace of Tourkeman was bathed in darkness except for the lines of torches lit around the guard posts and wall towers. Sentries patrolled the outer wall, although not with any real apprehension or anticipation of battle. Tourkeman was a military state; even its women and children could outfight ten of any foe, should anyone ever be insane enough to attack.

Young King Shom had been up late, listening to arguments from all sides on Baron Rodir's proposal to create something new, something which demanded a new word not now in their vocabulary, a word that represented *empire*. That Tourkeman had enemies the king did not doubt, and the proof was in the failure to deliver his bride from Anrijou. He did not credit tales of her being somehow cursed or bewitched and made some creature, but that she was dead or dishonored in some slave mart was easy to accept. He did not blame Anrijou for it, though; instead, he suspected the hand of the old baron himself. What was it Rodir had said? That her disappearance was the *ideal pretext* for breaking the covenant and centuries of tradition while seeming only to avenge the king's honor.

Shom, however, had a different concept of honor. As personal honor, he might well have sought retribution if he could determine the guilty parties, but he was no longer in a position to allow such personal things. He was the king, the state, and, as such, he represented the honor of the nation—a nation that had always prided itself on its strict neutrality and professionalism. Rodir's faction would have him place personal honor above the state's, and it was certainly tempting, but he could not see his way to do it. He was not, however, as foolish as his father. He did not believe he was immortal, nor did he trust the guard in an exposed position. A king was very vulnerable to treason, particularly when it could so easily be made to look accidental. Shom was an only son with no heirs; if he met with an accident, Rodir would have as much royal blood claim to the throne as countless other relatives.

How childish, how foolish, he'd been to imagine

being the all-powerful and absolute ruler! Some choices
they were offering him, couched as they were in specula-
tive and respectful forms. Choose—the honor of the
state or your life, and if you choose honor we will simply
have your replacement violate it. These were not the
sorts of choices one was prepared for in training. He had
gone to bed but had found it difficult to sleep, and was
even now only fitfully dozing.

Outside, overhead, bathed in darkness and hidden
from the eyes of guards, men did the impossible. They
floated there, silently, establishing their positions, wearing special glasses that gave them the power to see in the
darkness as well as headsets with little microphones that
came down and dangled just before their lips.

"Spotter One positioned and ready," said one softly.

"Spotter Two positioned and ready," came another
whispered voice in the night.

A third man rose and peered in the windows of the
towers. Finally he settled on one and judged distance
and difficulty and reported, "This is Sneak. The baron's
in there sleeping like a baby."

"All troops are positioned," the voice of Control responded. "Take a time reading. Operations commence in
two minutes from my mark. Stand by . . . *Mark!*"

On the parapet, two guards met and one looked up
and around nervously.

"Trouble?" the other asked.

"I don't know. I just got the funny feelin' I'm bein'
watched is all. I dunno. Maybe I been doin' this night
shift too long." He shrugged. "Even feels like the temperature's droppin'. Ain't never seen it so still, like some
big storm was comin'."

The other man nodded. "I feel it, too. Storm comin'
up, maybe. I . . . you hear anything out there?"

The clouds thickened and swirled above them, and
there was the sound of thunder and the almost crackling
power of a storm about to break, but within the cloud
were only occasional glows of lightning giving the whole
atmosphere an eerie, almost supernatural cast.

They both turned and looked out into the night and

listened. Through the gloom and above the noises of the gathering storm they *could* hear things—it sounded like the movement of a tremendous number of men in full battle gear trying to keep quiet.

"I don't like this," said the first guard. "Get the Sergeant of the Guard on the double!"

The other hesitated. "I don't know. It might be the storm, or the wind. If it's a false alarm, we'll pull this duty until our death day."

"And if I'm right, then *this* may be our death day. Get him!"

Hovering in the shadows above, Spotter Two decided that it was a little early for an alarm and aimed a small weapon that shone a beam invisible except through its spotter scope. The beam sat first on the head of the nervous guard and then a trigger was pulled. The guard jerked, but by the time he fell to the floor of the parapet, the beam was on the other man. He, too, fell before he could sound an alarm.

"I have the baron. Repeat, I have the baron," Sneak reported. *"Candy from a baby. I'm rigging him now. Tech crew to the window. Go in three minutes, repeat, three minutes. Mark!"*

Young King Shom slept uneasily in his bed. He was a very light sleeper out of necessity—when you led a kingdom that was basically a military autocracy, your power was always subject to a violent veto. The noise that broke out, awakening him suddenly and tensely, was not a subtle one but rather the sound of men shouting and running in such numbers as to wake his dead father.

"Guard! What is going on?" he shouted at his barred door, but there was no reply. Wary, he reached by his bedside and picked up his broadsword, then went to the window. It was well up along a sheer wall and he did not fear any attack from that quarter, but it provided a very good view of the west wall below.

It is no palace coup! he realized almost at once. *We are under attack!* The very thought of it was difficult to grasp. Tourkeman invaded others, but was never invaded itself. It had the most powerful army in all the world behind the most invulnerable castle and works!

He grabbed a speaking tube and yelled, "Baron! This is the king! We are under attack! I wish briefing at once!"

To his horror, the voice that responded from the tube was not only not the baron's, it sounded barely human at all.

"It is a briefing you wish, eh? Then look again at the west wall, *Majesty*." The tone was mocking, insolent, and the last word was spit out, but ended with a terrible cackling.

He went again to the window, and below, on the very wall itself, he could see the large, chunky form of Baron Rodir walking there, even as the torches and sounds of a mighty army were obvious just beyond. Yet there was nobody else on the wall! No soldiers there to repel what would surely be a mass scaling of the battlements! What treachery was this?

Rodir stopped, turned, then looked up at the king even though it was clearly impossible to see a figure in the window from that distance. Shom frowned, then watched, stunned, as the Baron's figure rose magically into the air until it was almost level with his window!

"We are undone, my King, by magic most dark," said the baron, floating impossibly there. "Yield to them or you, too, will suffer as I have suffered!" And, with that, Baron Rodir reached up and calmly removed his head from his shoulders, then threw it right at the window!

Shom screamed and stepped back, but the aim was a bit off, and the head struck the sill, boucing off and back down into the courtyard below.

"Son of a bitch! I'm getting too old for this!" Sneak swore into his headset. *"Five years ago I'd'a made it right in the window!"*

It made no difference. The sight of it terrified the defending troops who watched it as had the king, but before they could recover from their stunned gazes the first wave of invading troops was up and over the wall, and a squad was already freeing the bolts from the west gate.

Still, the sight of the invader shocked the Tourkemanese back into some semblance of normality. *This* they could understand. *These* were invaders, made of flesh and blood, inside the very royal compound!

The battle was joined in the outer courtyard and along the battlements, and, once into the real fight, the soldiers of Tourkeman were not to be taken lightly. They fought with a frenzy beyond even their normal high levels; it shut out the magic and the horror, and the reality of battle, the very acts of killing and dying, feeling momentary triumph and bitter pain, made their world and themselves real again.

Swords, maces, battle axes, and all manner of weaponry clanged and flew in a scene of prolonged carnage. Within minutes, the courtyard resembled less a battlefield than a butcher shop, and there seemed no end in sight as the dawn lit the sky.

Suddenly a terrible shout, like nothing any had ever heard, inhuman and cold and overpowering, commanding attention through the roar, sounded. *"Stop! I command you to stop! All of you! This is against the rules!"*

They heard it, but neither side was about to stop now.

Koldon, in one of the small gravity cars, knew that voice and quickly searched the castle's upper battlements. He had just spotted a dark shape on the portico above the main hall and was about to go in to investigate when that figure raised its cloaked arms and extended a wand.

Koldon suddenly stopped. "Watch it! All our men clear until he's done! All Teams out of there, then key on me!"

"I will stop you, then!" sounded that terrible, commanding voice again, and from his wand came that terrible purple and gold light, spreading out like a living thing over the entire battle scene, freezing the armies below in a tableau of violence—but not for long.

Everything still living within the battle scene was suddenly reduced, incorporeal, and those energy sparks were everywhere . . .

"I could pick him off from here easily," said Spotter Two.

"No!" Koldon shot back. "We want him alive! Just get this all recorded!"

And then the terrible light receded, and Koldon heard Surowak's voice whisper, more to himself than anyone else, "I don't believe it!"

The entire courtyard was now filled with milling, very confused *dests*—hundreds and hundreds of them, along with the broken and bloody remains of a *dest* slaughter-house. Nothing remotely human or humanoid remained.

"Well, at least he's got a one-track mind," Cornig said laconically.

Koldon had his needler drawn, set to high stun, and circled around and in back of the Shaper. They really hadn't had a plan for this; they had expected to draw the mysterious sorcerer, not confront him.

Something—a sound, a reflection, who knew what?—caused the Shaper to suddenly turn and see Koldon coming at him. Koldon got off a quick shot that missed, and the black-clad creature turned and quickly vanished inside the castle.

With no guards, armies, or anything else to worry about, the other team members entered where they could as Koldon jumped out and ran after the mysterious godlike man.

He spotted the Shaper apparently attempting to trig-ger some kind of hidden stairway entrance and fired again. The sorcerer whirled, then made for the wide grand staircase down to the ballroom, Koldon in hot pursuit.

The Shaper made it two-thirds of the way down when he suddenly stopped, faced with Cornig and Surowak below, having entered from different sides, now waiting for him to walk into their hands.

The sorcerer seemed less panicked than confused, as if this sort of thing simply could not happen. Then he reached inside his long sleeve and began to pull out the wand.

Koldon nailed him with a full beam in the back and the black figure stiffened, cried out, then crumpled and rolled down the stairs.

"All right, now let's see what we're dealing with here," Cornig said with a sense of satisfaction. He went to the crumpled figure and pulled down the hood, then removed the black mask from the face.

The thing revealed there was like nothing on *this* world. It was hairless, with a drawn, eerie face that looked more like a tree trunk with bulging, knotlike unblinking eyes, two long slits for a nose, and a narrow, lipless mouth. The skin was tough; wrinkled and barklike, and a mottled yellow. Strapped around that strange head was a device that looked very different than their headsets but that obviously served the same function.

"Ever see anything like that before?" Cornig asked the other two.

Koldon shook his head negatively, and Surowak grunted. "There are certain aspects in common with a number of races," Koldon said, "but I don't remember ever seeing any like this before. No, it's new, and certainly not of *this* world. I expected it, though, when I couldn't read his surface thoughts on the ship. Either they're racially specific telepaths or they use different wavelengths than the norm we're accustomed to."

"Watch it! He's coming to!" Koldon cautioned, and they stepped back, guns at the ready. "That kind of jolt would'a knocked any of us out for hours."

The Shaper groaned, rolled, and then sat up and looked at them. The orifice in its face vibrated rapidly, and a fraction of a second later that deep, rich baritone came out of the device. "Who are you?" it asked. "What manner of things are you? Who made you and how, and whom do you represent?"

"Still the arrogant one," Koldon noted sourly. "I don't think you're in a position to ask questions before you answer some yourself. Still, I will, just to get things started."

The Shaper's strange eyes fixed on him. "You. You were the agent with the princess!"

"Yes. I am Koldon, a Field Agent for the Exchange. This is Cornig, the project manager, and that is Surowak, the chief biologist. In spite of our looks we are no more

native to this world than you are. We used a—less efficient—process to conform our appearance to the norm
here and operate unsuspected."

The Shaper stood up, an enormous effort for one
who'd received such a shock as he had. "You—you are
not from the others? You are not part of the Game?"

"You mean the other four like yourself?" Koldon responded. "No, we've never even met them. We're a
small party here, preparing for bigger things. Our support ship is in orbit right now with the bulk of our team.
In fact, until I met you and saw you in action, we
thought you all were just legends."

"Ship? Orbit? But there are no habitable planets in
this solar system save this one."

"We come from far away, much farther than that,"
Cornig put in. "In fact, as our normal forms, the three of
us are alien beings to one another. None of us is of the
same race or planet."

"But—that would take thousands of years! The distances!..."

Koldon shrugged. "We found a short cut."

"Oh my! The kind of power that represents—the energy. Limitless. We must... have a Gathering. A truce.
The Game is over! And, like all the best games, there is
no loser."

"If you didn't get here in a spaceship, then how the
hell..." Koldon muttered, but there was plenty of time
now for answers.

"Our world is isolated," the Shaper told them. "It is
over three hundred light-years to the nearest star, much
farther for anything useful. It was frustrating. We knew
so much, yet the speed of light held us captive. Then, by
accident, when experimenting with a new and radical
power source for our dwindling resources, we discovered that you could move in a direction not at all like the
ones that imprisoned us as far as we could see. Another
universe. Another world. Gravitational forces kept such
planets paired up, and we sent robots, automatic probes,
and they returned with pictures and data on an entirely

new and uninhabited world. It was exciting. There was much competition for the first exploratory expedition. Eight of us originally, representing the best of our various disciplines. We were so—caught up in it, that we took short cuts, made miscalculations. Small probes with animals had gone through. We felt certain we could, too —and we did.

"For a while, all was wonderful. The world was virginal in a sense, unspoiled by sentience but teeming with life. The *dest* was everywhere, preyed upon by some vicious carnivores the likes of which none of us had ever seen or imagined. We lost two of our own number to the carnivores before we learned how to stop them, instead. But, before we could return with all that we had learned and build upon it, something happened. The energy field supporting us collapsed and try as they might they could not reestablish it. Too much mass for so long a time. We had sufficient energy to use our own devices, but not enough to even send messages back."

He sighed. "They tried. They really tried over there, again and again, for many years, as we did what we had to do here and continued our work, secure in the certainty that our technology would find a way. After better than fifty of our years, though, it became clear that they were not going to solve the problem, and, indeed, had stopped trying long before. We were dead to them, and this project with us." He sighed. "It was terrible. We had spent some of the time working on the project from this end and we knew where the mistake was—and had we sufficient energy, we could have punched back through from this side. But we could not tell them that, and they, too, must have seen that only from this side was a return possible. We were marooned in the flower of our youth —six males with not a female among us. Doomed not even to colonize, just to exist. Six in the whole world— and no one else. Nothing else. Eventually we got on each other's nerves to the point where murder was a possibility, madness a certainty. We would be here forever. Alone. That was how the Project came about, and, after, the Game."

They set about becoming the gods of their world. They had much knowledge and ample power to do what they wanted—with the exception of what they wanted most. The Shaper, the geneticist, was the key to the plan. A manufactured disease, harmless to them and most others, that wiped out the carnivores in two generations. They divided up the world then, and each took his equipment, his specialty, with him. They had created a sort of paradise—but it was even lonelier than before.

They were not immortal, but they aged very slowly here, as if their bodies were still tied to some different, far slower time frame, while their minds adjusted quickly to the pace of the new universe and world. And, over the next century, using their field labs and what remaining power they had, they had developed a new project.

"We designed them based upon the carnivores we had destroyed," the Shaper told them, "because we knew that the design worked. At first it was simply a matter of restoring balance—we had destroyed the predators and so the rest were overbreeding, tearing apart this world, starving. It was exciting to create a new race, even a primitive one. It made us feel like—well, the gods of this place. Once the design was completed, we used basic matter-to-energy-to-matter matrices to modify the brightest of the species in the most trouble into those who would rule over that species. They are maintained in this strange form by a planetary field that their own cells are attuned to."

"I don't understand how you do it, but I comprehend the mechanism in a basic way," Cornig responded. "That's why we didn't detect your power source. Since it is a stable planetary field it registered on our instruments as a normal characteristic of this planet, and we ignored it."

"Then it was careful breeding of the results until we created whole tribes," the Shaper continued. "The only thing we did not foresee was how incredibly intelligent the gentle herbivores we used actually were. We taught them how to walk upright, how to hunt, how to organize, and when they began to develop on their own various sounds we realized that they were capable of language and taught them a simple one."

"The *dests*," Koldon said through clenched teeth. "You're talking about the *dests*."

"Yes, the *dests*. Our term, really. You look at them and you see big, lumbering herbivores drifting about and you make certain—assumptions. Even after, most of us believed that they were simply short-changed by evolution. Without hands or anything else with which to build, and without vocal equipment to create the necessary variety of complex sounds, we felt they had dead-ended. It is entirely possible that they did not. Primitive, yes, but I have often wondered if such extreme intelligence would be warranted for this sort of equilibrium. It is possible that they might be far more complex than we believe, thinking and acting in a way alien to those like any of us."

"Or maybe it just developed as a defense against those carnivores," Surowak noted. "But—you made classical humanoids out of the *dests*, and they became something of a civilization."

"Our civilization. They have . . . limits. They are herd creatures—they go mad in isolation. They are very bright, but not all that bright. You can teach them things, such as how to build, how to herd, how to cultivate fields, even how to fight, and they understand and do it, but in six centuries we have never seen anything, not one idea, basic concept, or discovery, that they initiated. No great philosophers, thinkers, scientists—nothing. All that you see *we* created. We created it from our own history, from romantic legends, and from our own imaginations based on the requirements of the people."

"That explains why there are no artifacts or direct ancestral remains," Koldon said, nodding. "And why building designs, ship designs, everything, is so uniform even among the most distant kingdoms."

"And why the racial I.Q. is between seventy and eighty and why they are often victims of their own emotions," Surowak added. "Like children. Like a race of not very bright children."

"Exactly!" the Shaper responded. "And that is how the Game evolved. Out of this project, and out of boredom. We could take them so far and no farther, but the impulse to experiment with what we had proved irresistible. We all had our own ideas for the sort of societies to build and maintain, the best ways of management. We divided the world into zones roughly equal in land and sea and we became the gods of our lands. And, of course, we occasionally meddled in each other's affairs as well. Pretty soon it became a contest to see which of us could do the best job and, therefore, take lands and people away from the other. Elaborate rules were developed, and scores kept. Wagers were made, favors traded and bet. None of us were military men—those two had been killed by the carnivores in the early days—so we played the Game. It fed our egos, and kept us from going completely mad."

Cornig perched on the corner of a table and looked thoughtful. "You have a lot that you could teach us. About your energy fields, your transformation method, the means by which only seven of you transformed the world. Uh—that brings up a point. I thought there were only five of you."

"Now there are. One of us became overly brave a few centuries ago, and gambled directing his own conquests. There was only one way to stop him, and we did. He was the best of the lot at the Game, but he underestimated the resolve of his opponents. That is why I was taking such a risk intercepting the ship off Anrijou. My domain ends just out of sight of shore on this side, and I was directly intervening—and exposed."

"Can we talk to the others? Can we get you together?" Cornig prompted, seeing the profits from such an alien technology.

Koldon, for his part, kept silent, knowing it would do no good to speak at this point. The evolution of these "gods" was different, and their technology had taken far different turns, but for all that they were about the most petty and familiar alien beings he'd encountered. The memory of the slaughter outside, the frenzy of these people's battles, made him slightly sick. Playing gods, destroying an ecosystem because a couple of the more arrogant were careless, creating a new race so they could be marched to slaughter like wind-up toy soldiers . . .

These guys, he thought sourly, *will feel right at home with us.*

The Shaper was proving it, too. "We are always in communication, if we wish to be. They will think me mad at first, but I will open my mind to them. Yes, you are correct, I suppose. We do know things that you do not, and you know and have things that we do not, but you could not take that knowledge from us. Remove us and you remove the machines' power. We are in mental attunement with the devices, and they will shut down when the last of us dies. And, I assure you. we will all be of a mind to destroy this world rather than oe invaded or coerced."

Cornig, now the businessman and trader, smiled pleasantly. "Now, I don't think we have to do anything so . . . ugly. We want an exchange, not a new set of enemies. Your civilization is closed to us. We can't get there, because we don't know how and never knew it existed. Perhaps we can never have an eternal opening for people to pass freely through, or perhaps we can find a way, but whatever it is we can certainly trade information of a high order. At the start, when you first came to and learned what we were and how we got here, you said something about power. Several times you've talked about insufficient power sources. That's one thing we have in great abundance—power. If you have a way to go up and get it, or bring it down here. In exchange for valuable new discoveries, new technology, I think we can provide that power you need. Just—what's it worth to you to be able to go home?"

Koldon knew it was coming and could no longer remain silent. "No! Damn it, this world is full of *people*! I don't care how they were made or how bright or artistic or scientific they are, they are *sentient beings*. Millions of them now. You heard what he said—they leave and the machines stop. This field collapses. That's all he did to turn our princess into a *dest*! How he turned two whole fighting armies into *dests*. He created a local field that canceled out the larger field; that removed whatever they added to make these people look like they do! Genetically they're *dests*, artificially maintained in a form where they can do greater things. I *know* these people! I've lived among them! they are basically a good, gentle folk, and *they are people*! I saw what it did to the princess. Damn it, to do that is *genocide*. It is against all our law and custom!"

The Shaper stared at him. "We created them. All that they have we gave them. We did not give them what sentience, what intelligence, they have—we merely gave them a form and the benefits of a higher civilization to use and develop them. We have been marooned here for more than seven centuries. We grow older, and lonelier, and perhaps a bit insane. Your employer, here, understands. You would condemn us to the rest of our lives, our very long lives, here to preserve this culture for... what? Another five or six centuries at best? Until the last of us dies? Until your scientists can somehow duplicate our machines and attain equilibrium? For what? No, you ask too much of us. It is very easy to stand the moral ground when it is not you who have been here so long nor is it you who would have to remain."

"Progress always has its price, as does profit," Cornig noted, sounding businesslike. "The laws involve the destruction of indigenous sentient beings. Those are the *dests*, not the others. Perhaps our friends here can help the Valiakeans create a new carnivore to restore the ecological balance."

"You can't do this!" Koldon thundered. "I will take it to the Courts of the Exchange myself!"

Cornig looked at Koldon as he would look at a naive child. "Of course we can do it, son. It's our job."

Koldon almost cried, knowing that it was true, that it was all going to happen. "Somewhere there must be such a thing as justice," he muttered sourly.

"Not if you have good enough lawyers," Cornig replied.

"History will never forgive us."

"History," Cornig said quietly, "is always written by the victors, not the victims."

The walls of the castle were deserted now, the towns as well. Only the countryside was alive with millions upon millions of great, lumbering beasts. It was a lonely, desolate place now for all its beauty, and, looking away from the artifacts that remained for a time and off into the green hills, Koldon could almost imagine what it must have been like here, when they had come, when they had found themselves alone and trapped.

He rode the *dest* out a ways, trying to think, trying to sort it out in his own mind. A young calf, the progeny of the *dest* he rode, trailed loyally behind its mother.

On all the planets, in all the cultures he'd seen and walked among, there were always certain basics. The gods created the race. The gods had power, both good and evil, over the race both collectively and individually, and those people prayed for the good and against the evil. They worshiped the gods and they cursed the gods, but they remained in their own minds the playthings, the property, of those same gods. Not all, but most, had an eventual reckoning as well, when the gods would tire of their sport and would fight the final battle for supremacy and the world would end. Most, too, had gods fashioned roughly in their own petty, conniving image.

Just like here.

Did a god who made the rules have to abide by them? Was that the definition of a god? That the rules did not apply? How would the gods see their creation compared to themselves? And if it came to a final choice between a god and its creations, what god of any race or world would not unhesitatingly choose itself?

And if the gods were five lonely and isolated men who never considered their creations more than an adult's plaything...

He wondered, idly, what the priests and shamans and holy ones of those other, "respected" religions, would say if it were suggested that *their* gods regarded them much the same almost by definition?

Koldon no longer believed in gods. He believed in greed, in avarice, in self-justification and moral ambiguity, and the basest instincts of sentience. The gods became gods because they were smarter, tougher, meaner, and colder than the rest. How many sentient races had developed their world to the point where most of the animals were extinct, the waters and air fouled, and where the people still went down to worship and pray for forgiveness of their sins even as they went back out and committed more?

He stopped, dismounted, then undid the bridle and cinch and removed all the paraphernalia of civilization from the *dest*.

"I'm sorry, Princess," he said to her, "but your gods have deserted you. You have to make it on your own now."

She looked at him, not really comprehending anymore, but not understanding the finality of his dismissal, either.

He looked at her, and her calf, and hoped, just hoped, that the old Shaper was right, that these were a different form of intelligence and not the animals they seemed. He hoped, but he didn't really believe it.

"Go ahead, Princess! You're free now! Join the herd!" And he gave her a big slap on the rump.

She started, then began to move forward, picking up speed, the calf having a little trouble keeping up with her, but when she reached the edge of the nearest *dest* herd she suddenly stopped, turned, and looked back at him, questioningly.

Koldon felt a wrench in his stomach, turned, and began to walk slowly back toward the city where he would soon be picked up by the team. About twenty steps back he stopped, turned, and looked at where she'd been, but there was only a vast, rolling landscape of *dests*, each apparently no different from the other, just idly grazing. He sighed, then turned and started slowly walking back toward the deserted city.

AFTERWORD:
ON TRANSFORMATIONS AND OTHER LAST WORDS

I AM CONSTANTLY ASKED WHY I AM SO FASCINATED with transformations. I am reluctant to answer that question because I find the very fact that it was asked rather strange. I wonder if anybody ever asked Doc E.E. Smith why he wrote space stories all the time, or Phil Dick why he wrote "what is reality?" stories all the time, or asked Agatha Christie why she always wrote whodunits. On reflection, though, I think they *were* asked, time and again. I know that Dick was often asked why he was so hung up on the question of what is the meaning of reality, and that Harlan Ellison is constantly asked why all his stories seem to have strong elements of paranoia, so maybe I should talk about this.

People are always saying "Oh, another Chalker transformation story," as if it's the same story, and often asking "When are you going to write stories that don't have transformations in them?" Never mind the fact that I have written such stories: *The Devil's Voyage, A War of Shadows*, or even the entire *G.O.D., Inc.* series, to name but a few.

One reason is that I'm good at this kind of story, better than others who have tried it—you know it and so do I—just as Dick was best at his kind of story and Ellison at his. And you know it because you tend to buy far more of that sort of book than of my novels that don't have that element even as you carp about "another Chalker transformation story."

I don't want to give the impression, though, that I'm pandering to the marketplace (if I were that type you'd be reading *Well World #316*), but one good reason I write what I do is the same reason for writing fantasy and science fiction in the first place—the freedom it gives. The hardest novel I ever wrote was my World War II novel—I couldn't rearrange the events to fit the conveniences of my plot or to make my points. I was stuck with a very inconvenient and immobile historical record. Transformation allows an even greater element of freedom and flexibility since you aren't stuck with anything inconvenient. So if my most popular device is also the one that affords me the most freedom, I'd be a fool not to use it if the story called for it, wouldn't I?

There is also exaggeration for effect. I know what research is being done now, and what has been done in the past. I know how the mind can be changed, attitudes altered, and its grave potential for very evil and unpleasant ends. With the development of new technology growing exponentially every ten years, the tremendous discoveries in gene manipulation, and the very nature of personality and memory, we face problems far more insidious than the nuclear bomb. We have never really learned to live with nuclear energy in any form, and it scares all sane men and women that at any moment either of two world leaders can destroy all life on Earth by merely giving an order, and that lesser leaders can eliminate whole cities and even nations with just a few of these things. We were not prepared for the nuclear bomb, and we're certainly not prepared for the next equivalent development; and the next time, the technology won't blow up obviously in your face. It'll creep in, hardly noticed at first . . .

All science fiction and fantasy stories are at their very

hearts tales of transformation. History, which was my chosen field, is the study of transformation. A future setting requires extrapolating the transformations of history into a future landscape with future technology. I can not ignore the assumption that current research will be completed to do quickly what past authorities have done slowly without violating my own inner logical sense. Let's start with the basics...

You don't need science fiction to watch uneasy transformation in action. It isn't like turning into a centaur or a monster; it's far more scary. The women in Iran, fairly liberated under the old and repressive regime of the Shah, surrendered all rights, put the veil back on, and once again became fourteenth-century chattel. They will fight and die for the right to be submissive property. No fancy new technology was involved, and the process was quick.

Well, yes, but it can't happen here...

Germany was once the soul of the Renaissance and Enlightenment in Europe, the producer of philosophers and composers and great literary masters, of scientific genius and political radicalism. In just three years in our modern twentieth century, one man imposed on that nation one of the most brutal dictatorships in history and sent millions off to camps and gas chambers while the rest put on brown uniforms and raised their arms in praise and salute to him.

Well, yes, but that was the Germans, not us. Besides, it couldn't even happen in Germany again...

Within my own lifetime, in the Land of the Free and the Home of the Brave, a black man couldn't use the same *toilet* that I could, and ministers of God justified it from the pulpit. And in the year I was born, one of America's most revered liberal presidents, Franklin Roosevelt, was quite content to leave tens of thousands of native-born Americans who happened to be of Japanese ancestry where he had shoved them, by executive order and apparently with a clear conscience, into concentration camps not in Germany or Poland but in California and Arizona and Utah, while their lands and wealth were expropriated to the cheers of the populace, many of whom had names like Schultz and Rosenberg and Karanski and O'Flynn.

Just a few years ago, a native-born American of Chinese ancestry was set upon and brutally beaten to death in Detroit by laid-off auto workers who decided he was a Jap and deserved to be killed because the Japanese auto makers had put so many American auto workers out of work. Apparently they well represented "liberal" Michigan; no matter that their victim was an *American*, or that the Chinese are no more related to the Japanese than the French are to the Poles. The real shock is not the crime itself—ignorant idiots are found in every nation and in every epoch of history—but liberal Michigan's legal system's response to that act.

Honest mistake, boys. Probation, and next time check to see it's a real Jap, huh? That's my America. That's in the eighties.

Young people are sucked into cults and come out smiling and glassy-eyed, devoid of any thought except what they are told—our own sons and daughters, the products of our own culture—and they fight any attempt to bring them back.

And if, tomorrow, the drug trade brought out a drug that was instantly and totally addicting and turned users into happy, mindless slaves, a substantial portion of Americans—and all other nationalities as well—would flock to stuff it into themselves, believing they could handle it. We've seen the start of this with PCP and rock cocaine, but they are as the crossbow is to the hydrogen bomb compared with what modern science can and will concoct. Just recently one of the leading researchers in brain chemistry noted that our knowledge of brain chemistry was increasing at such a rate that within a mere generation we would have a "designer" drug problem that would make our current problems seem so slight that the eighties would be looked upon with nostalgia. Sure—they're doing this research to see if they can retard aging and maybe save people from the horrible fates of Alzheimer's and Huntington's disease, and they might. The price: drugs that can and will turn just about anybody into just about anything, mentally and emotionally, the chemist chooses—and that are instantly addicting.

That isn't science fiction talking—that's scientists, and they're talking about stuff they are beginning to create in their research labs even as I write this in mid-1987. That's what books like *The Identity Matrix* and some graphic (but very understated) scenes in *Lords of the Middle Dark* were really about. I have never *really* written about the far distant future, nor do most SF writers; if you can't grasp that, you are inevitably going to be a victim if you're not already. " 'Twas technology killed the beast," and those who wielded it and understood it best.

Liberal to conservative, pro to con, we swing back and forth from year to year and decade to decade changing our beliefs and our morals as if they were fashions.

Chemically, in the essential genes that make all humanity one, there's no real difference between an Iranian woman, a Hitler brownshirt, a black person in 1953, and you and me. The biological similarities between those Detroiters and their victim far outweigh the negligible differences between them. Not in intelligence, not even in ignorance or lack of it—not enough to matter. We are in constant, one might say stunning, transformation.

It won't be very long before science can change the body as easily as clever leaders can change the mind. Just because Hitler lost the war, don't think the heirs of those brilliant mad scientists who experimented on and carved up people in the name of research and breeding of better humans aren't still around and still hard at work with newer and better tools. The bulk of humanity lives, as it always has, under dictatorships and tyrannies well able to fund such work and to pervert medical research done in democratic countries under the light of public scrutiny.

In the Soviet Union, fervent opposition to the system is *prima facia* evidence of commitable mental illness that is to be treated with any and all means (and Pavlovian conditioning is still big there) until the patient is "cured." This is not merely a dictatorial device, it's a belief that's built into the ideology. Orwell emphasized it; I use it often.

I am a historian by training and education; I am fascinated with transformation, partly because you are not. But you should be, because it's already here and those who would manipulate the masses are getting better and better at it—and *they* don't just include the kindly saints and benefactors of humankind.

Complacency equals submission equals victimization. That kindly coach—is he really that nice or is he setting up your daughter? That fellow over there—is he trying to figure how to kidnap your kid? That politican there— is he the one who'll willingly push the button? Or will he merely vote against things of real importance and mortgage your kids' future and condemn us to a different, slower, and more agonizing form of oblivion?

I don't want you to take anything for granted. Not princesses nor haunted houses nor ferryboats. I don't want you to think, "The government'll take care of it," or "Sure it's safe," or "What's the use of worrying about it, anyway?" Particularly, I don't want you ever to think that it can't happen here, that it can't happen to you, or your children, that it was some flaw in someone else's character when it should be understood as a flaw in the *human* character. I've written more than one book in which I created a model, comfortably out there in the realm of science fiction, and took today's radical thinkers at their word and showed just what they were advocating. Most people didn't find them all that pleasant, although once I actually received mail from European radicals congratulating me on my grasp of radical theory.

"Yeah, but I'm different, I can always recognize it."

If you could, then I could go on to other themes.

Again, in the United States of 1987, a leading candidate of the Democratic party has a wife whose sole crusade the past few years has been to ban books that were unpleasant to her. An exhibit of books banned somewhere or other in the U.S. filled a large convention hall recently, and included *The Wizard of Oz*, *Huckleberry Finn*, some of Shakespeare, and many other classics. The liberals want to ban "fascistic" books and to prohibit "sexism" and "racism." The conservatives want to ban "perverting" political views, "godless" books, and pornography, which would, under their definition, include much of what I write. Everybody wants to ban something, and nobody seems to realize that one person's porn is another person's art, and even if it has no apparent redeeming social value it's very hard to ban it and find where the ultimate line of censorship will be drawn. The price of freedom is having to put up with tons of rubbish. If you are not willing to pay that price, then you do not truly believe in freedom and individual liberty, and sometime, maybe soon, you'll find that your own likes and causes are on somebody else's blacklist.

Is it liberal to ban any book, no matter how pure the motive? When you consider what has already been banned for the best of intentions, I fail to see any difference between censorship for *any* motive and the censorship of Nazi Germany. You are known as much by the company you keep as by your own protestations.

"Should we then stop where we are?"

You can't. Nor would I *want* you to be reactionary, terrified of change, of the shadows, of the boogeymen, because that change is going to come whether you're scared of it or not and whether you want it to come or not. If not here, then somewhere else. We must learn to live with change and, most important, to *deal* with it—to deal with a world transforming itself at a fantastic speed. The Sahara was once grasslands until humans cut down the trees on the Atlas and Antiatlas Mountains, thus causing enormous erosion. The Sahara's still growing today. In just the last fifty years we've seen mutations and deformations in the orange groves of southern California from pollution by automobiles. Ask a Canadian about acid rain sometime. In the midwestern U.S., the great underground aquifers that have irrigated the world's breadbasket are running dry. Think about that one.

America's heavy industry is collapsing; much of western Europe's has already effectively collapsed. Our entire economic base is changing. The son of a steelworker will probably not go into the mills because there won't be any mills to go into. The romanticism and mysticism of farming is vanishing in the cold reality of modern agricultural economics. Rather than face, adjust, and deal with social transformation, some farmers are putting guns in their mouths and pulling the trigger, often taking their wives and children with them.

And he seemed like such a nice *man...*

Complacency, egocentrism, rot...Drugs are the largest growth industry in the U.S. today and in many other parts of the world. Alcohol and marijuana, the old standards, are no longer enough, even though they've already screwed up so many millions of lives. Uh uh. Can't throw a party without a bowl of white powder. Got to take more white powder to keep the high on. Uh uh. It's not habit forming. Well, yeah, I know what it's done to some weak people but *I* can handle it...While some of our young hand their minds over to the cults, their contemporaries and their elders fall over each other trying to stuff chemical substances into themselves with a goal of permanent impairment.

The bottom line is that all those drugs are just effective examples of biochemistry; they work as advertised. They work so well, you don't want or need anything else. Of course this turns things like real creativity, achievement, and critical thinking down to the carrot level, but by God they're *happy* carrots. Is that what human beings should be striving for, to become happy mental vegetables?

Excerpt from a letter sent to me: *"I'd kill myself if they tried brainwashing me or turning me into a fluxgirl ...I wouldn't live a slave's life."*

Wanna bet? Addicts die all the time of their bad habits, but while most, when pushed, agree their life's a living hell, they rarely get off the drugs voluntarily, rarely stay off, and rarely commit suicide. I'm a cigarette smoker. I started when I was a teen because everybody else did it. I know what an addiction is, and how hard it is to break. It's why I neither drink nor do drugs stronger than NyQuil.

Indeed, that reader's comment misses the most salient points about the fluxgirl thing. Why does heroin have such a hold? Because it works. Heroin and a whole family of addictive drugs directly stimulate the brain's pleasure centers to a higher degree than can be achieved by real activity—satisfaction in work well done, sex, you name it. It delivers. The fluxgirl spell delivers. It makes the plainest Jane into a super-glamorous sex bomb whose body is attuned to maximum stimulation of the pleasure centers. It is so pleasurable and so ego-gratifying that those so changed will suffer any degredation to keep being that way. You didn't think of that? Well, you should have, because the future of biochemistry is pointing at attaining just that sort of potential, no flux required.

And, like the heroin addict, people will shoot their own mother (rather than themselves) to keep it coming even if they hate what they have to do to maintain the state. If a new designer drug came out that turned any woman who took it into the kind of creature I showed in the *Soul Rider* books, we'd be up to our armpits in fluxgirls. Not everybody, of course, but one hell of a number, with teens leading the way. You think not? Consider . . .

"You can never be too rich or too thin."

Yep. Ask Karen Carpenter, millionaire singer, dead at thirty-two of complications from *anorexia nervosa*, conditioned by a society where looks are everything and thin is in (and never mind the mounting medical evidence that obesity to a large extent is genetic in origin—that's not ideologically correct). Commercials and TV programs set the standards so that not only Karen Carpenter but hundreds of thousands of young girls who have no weight problem at all starve themselves to death, and millions of others follow nutritionally ridiculous fad diets that often harm the body in their desperate search to look like Buffy and Skip or maybe the Stepford Wives. And if we inflict our own bodies with this sort of crap, imagine what happens to our ideas and ideals.

Around the world and throughout history people trade freedom for security every time. That's how feudalism began. Most often, political revolutions are fought over who will be the masters and who will be the slaves without more than lip service to real freedom. There is a reason why large numbers of people go for religious cultism and radical politics. With drugs now appearing in grammar schools and some new substances producing nearly instant addiction at a low price, I don't have to reach very far to see a time when Americans would not only accept a dictatorship but plead for it. Such a solution would cure the problem but produce new and more terrible problems in return—because we won't deal with these situations now, we will pay horrible prices later.

Every day we, our friends, neighbors, co-workers, and kids, are faced with transformations more subtle but no less extreme than the ones I use in my own novels and stories: changes in jobs, economies, whole ways of life; drugs, cults, robots and computers, mass communications, and much more. We are living in a period of radical changes proceeding at a more blinding pace than anyone, including me, can fully comprehend. In general, the fund of knowledge in *every field of human endeavor* is doubling every ten years. Ain't it awful? But we're also living longer and at a level of comfort that even our grandparents couldn't have dreamed of because of these changes, and even the lowliest subsistence-level peasant in the worst nation on Earth is better off as well.

Consider: thanks to revolutionary advances in agriculture, nations like India and China are self-sufficient in food, barring rare disasters. More food is produced in the world today than all of us can consume. There is not a single documented case of mass starvation in the world that is not politically, rather than naturally, caused and sustained. The great African famine of the mid-eighties was a natural event, but a vast amount of food was transshipped to all the stricken nations, more than enough to feed the starving, and in time for most. In a few nations, thousands of people starved to death anyway because it suited the rulers of those nations to allow it. In some of those countries the governments were so corrupt they resold the food or let it rot because the bribes weren't high enough. In others, rebel generals shot down the relief planes.

There were a lot of African countries trapped in that famine, but only in a handful was there mass starvation. The ones with better, more caring governments, who had no need of food as a political weapon, got the food where it was needed in record time and their people survived.

If you see my themes as simplistic, that says more about you than about me.

Now, there are several ways people can deal with change. They can become Luddites, reactionaries who want to turn back the clock to an earlier day and freeze it there (and labor unions and other "liberal" political organizations are actually the most reactionary in this regard); they can adhere to Calvinistic churches and voluntarily surrender their minds not to the government but to the ministers or gurus; or they can head for the hills and build their fortresses. You can run or you can desperately try to fight, but short of a nuclear holocaust there is one thing any competent historian will tell you: You can't stop this constant, radical change, or even measurably slow it down, without also destroying yourselves.

You can refuse it, or ignore it, or run from it, but it won't go away. Think about all the folks who have the quick and easy answers, the simplistic homilies. *Ban the bomb!* for all their sentiment, there is simply no way to uninvent the atomic bomb. It's here. Grad students at Princeton can build one for a class project. If all the governments of the Earth scrapped their nuclear weapons, there is almost universal agreement that, before long, we'd be in a world war far more devastating than the last one, since the price wouldn't be quite as high and the temptation on all sides would be more alluring and eventually irresistible.

And then, of course, only the radicals and two-bit Third-World dictators with delusions of grandeur would have the bombs with which to blackmail everybody else. Press any arms negotiator or top politician, American or Russian, and they'll sweat a lot and finally admit this. In fact in 1986, when it appeared that the U.S. was offering to ban all short and intermediate range nuclear weapons from Europe, the Europeans (the same ones who condemn our nuclear policies and our troops being stationed there) got into a panic and *demanded* that we keep those same nuclear weapons around as their only protection against attack (and against the inevitable staggering cost of building up their own conventional forces). It was fascinating to see leaders of even Britain's Labour Party telling their own people they supported the idea while going on the air in the U.S. to denounce it as "horribly flawed." Whole economies and standards of living depend on the *retention* of the nuclear arms race. And you wonder why I'm cynical? Sure, they had to go along with an arms treaty or be dragged from office, but not until they'd fought the whole idea every step of the way.

Pandora's box can't be closed once it's open, and it's open in every field of human knowledge. The pace is irresistible and we aren't going to stop it, but human nature is the same as it's always been (though even that may change). We either learn to deal with transformation or we die by it. We must take nothing for granted. We must always be asking, *"What if..."* and preparing for the answer. I wish my transformation metaphors were simple entertainments, but they are not. Too much of history shows too many people taking everything they hold dear and important for granted and trying very hard to be sheep or blades of grass or carrots. That's why history is so filled with victims.

I have several reccurring themes and they are very basic. Take nothing for granted, consider the implications of what you wish for—you might get it—and, in general, oppose the forces in human society that insist on ideological correctness (for *their* ideological side) and that attack or attempt to suppress anyone doing something counter to their own standards. I detest the extremes of right and left because, in the end, the only difference between them is their individual goals and prejudices; they agree on all the basics—censoring unpopular points of view, protecting the masses from bad influences, controlling thought and ideas. Any other differences between dedicated leftists and Nazi rightists are irrelevant. If a bullet kills my child, I will not care about the motivations behind the shot.

Ban the bomb, and then what? I just told you. Or should we invent some mind-altering device and force the world through it so we forget the bomb and how to make it and erase any interest in it? And you say *I* write science fiction?

When all of Western civilization becomes fundamentalist Christian, we will have heaven on Earth.

The last time anything approximated that, the Europe of the middle ages, there were a thousand years of rigid oligarchy and technological darkness. It was 1835 before it was no longer a mortal sin, according to church doctrine, for the average Roman Catholic to *read* Copernicus. In 1986 the Vatican announced it was reopening the heresy trial of Galileo to see if an error was made. Galileo, by the way, wasn't hounded by the church for his discoveries but rather for his insistence that the people had a right to know them. This same church, the majority of whose adherents are in the world's poorest countries, has been trying to fight all attempts at contraception and population control. But let's not just pick on the Roman Catholics.

Recently in the U.S., a bunch of Christian fundamentalists sued a school district on the grounds that many of the school books taught religious *toleration* and thus had to be eliminated because they were offensive—and they won! Books they want banned include *The Diary of Anne Frank* and *The Wizard of Oz*. One serious fellow named Satan as a defendant in a recent suit in federal court in an attempt to ban Halloween. A lawyer who described himself as a "devil's advocate" got the case thrown out on the grounds that the plaintiff couldn't prove in court that Satan did business in Arkansas, but it still took three weeks for the judge to make a decision on this! A free society is based upon toleration of all views, which includes the absolute right to make an asshole out of yourself. The argument, whether Catholic or Protestant or Hasidic or Shi'ite or anything else, that people have a right to be protected from unpopular ideas is the antithesis of democracy and pluralism. Theocracy is intellectual death. Ask Galileo.

There is little basic difference in attitudes between the religious right in the West and the religious right of Iranian fundamentalists. Tell me again about how nice a theocracy would be.

When we eliminate private property we will eliminate evil.

Anyplace in the world where incentive has been eliminated, food exporters have suddenly become food importers and technological development has slowed to a crawl, dependent on the free market countries for breakthroughs they can steal. The radicals can kid themselves that their ideas are different, that there's never been true communism or [fill in the blank here], but the fact is they wish me and my children and countless innocents in generations to come to be the guinea pigs in their pie-in-the-sky experiments when all of the historical evidence is against them. When everybody else's ideas on this have inevitably caused untold human misery, I just don't trust those folks. I have witnessed too many one-time sincere and idealistic revolutionaries eating lobster and caviar while their people were reduced to starving slaves. And where revolution produces a system that works, albeit limply, it is at the cost of great self-delusion.

Diagramed out, there is very little difference between the way Russia is *administered* today than it was under the czars; almost all increases in the standard of living have come as a result of technological growth and expanding of knowledge and not from their system. Without their black market "garden plots," they couldn't feed themselves; their worker efficiency is, by their own admission, among the lowest in the industrialized world, while their infant mortality rate is on a par with Third World countries. Before ideology supplanted pragmatism, Russia was an exporter of food. Free and universal socialized medicine is a joke; the Party mandates that doctors see seven patients an hour! The only way to get decent medical care is to be a member of the Party elite not subject to the rules—or to somehow pay a doctor privately on the side. This is progress?

Nations like Cuba followed an even odder course. Cuba is not capable of being an economically independent nation in any real way (just like about half the nations in the UN). It basically has to be someone's colonial possession. It had the U.S. as a patron for sixty years and it was a mess, so the revolution transfered it to being a Russian colonial possession instead. No matter how proud and nationalistic (some communist ideal!) Castro is, he has been forced to do just what the Soviets order. If he doesn't, he goes bankrupt, his people starve, and worse. Just eliminate the fake sugar subsidy the Soviets pay for one year and Cuba would look like another Ethiopia. (And what do the Soviets do with that sugar, anyway? There's been a world glut for decades; the Russians don't like cane sugar and are awash in their favorite beet sugar. Is there a two-mile-deep lake somewhere in Siberia filled with Cuban sugar just waiting for a fourteen-ton tea bag?)

Far from fighting over ideals, most Third World revolutionaries are fighting over whose colony they want to be, and most disputes between the U.S. and USSR are over which colonies the other finds permissible, and where.

The world should be Libertarian with no government.

Social Darwinism—the survival of the fattest. The western U.S. between the Civil War and about 1890 was as close as possible to a libertarian society. Result: the fellow who could hire the most ruthless killers established local dictatorships, while Rockefeller, Morgan, Gould, and a few others gathered all the essential industries into monopolies creating de facto fascism called "trusts." If economic incentive alone is a panacea, why do we get such lousy service in restaurants from waiters and waitresses who are dependent on tips? If we now live in a service economy in this country, why is service so lousy? And anybody who thinks we'd have a single national park, wilderness area, pollution free zone, or any measure of personal freedom under such a system is no different from a fascist, a communist, or a good Baptist—all such systems require an act of pure faith unsupported by any facts.

A good libertarian would get rid of government aid to the poor. Without such aid, neither I nor my wife would have been able to go to college. That's why libertarianism tends to be an upper middle-class and rich guy's disease, with movements headed or financed by guys who made their money the old-fashioned way (they inherited it).

What are the libertarians really saying? A great many of you have experienced libertarian driving—in any mall or shopping center parking lot. And, of course, a good libertarian has to fight for the right to drive drunk at any speed. Think not? Then you haven't thought libertarianism through.

Let's unilaterally disarm and save the human race.

Save it for what? We found out in 1934–45 what happens to good Jews. What? You're not Jewish? Well, don't worry. First they came for the Jews, then the communists, then the trade unionists, then the Catholics, then... Eventually they'll come for you, unless you are either a perfect slave or one of the masters.

Universal socialism is the answer!

So far, every attempt to create a socialist utopia, even by sincere and well-meaning radical thinkers, has devolved rather quickly into a form of fascism with two classes—the party and the masses. Considering how many times this has happened, and how it happens every time without fail even though each revolutionary truly thinks it'll be different this time, how can anyone with an

ounce of brains still want to try this? Oh, there'll be pie
in the sky by and by...

I'm sorry, but after thousands of attempts at mixing
certain chemicals and each time having the mixture blow
up and kill thousands more people, I'd think it was time
to admit that maybe the experiment is impossible.

And why is it that all the most radical people who
want to destroy the tyranny of the bourgeoisie are bourgeois? Marx, Engels, Lenin, Stalin, Trotsky, Mao, Castro, Ortega... Check out the origins of members of
radical underground groups in Japan, Germany, France,
the U.S.A., and others. Where the hell's the proletariat?
Getting suppressed by General Jeruzalski or Russian
tanks or, in western democracies, working long and hard
to reverse progress and turn back the clock.

You see, both my wife and I actually *came* from the
proletariat—poor families, sometimes union, in low paying jobs. I inherited nothing; I never had anything in the
bank. I had to work at menial jobs to buy what most
parents buy their kids because my family didn't have the
money. I admit to being something of a con man. Everything I did when I was younger I did by conning somebody with money into bankrolling it. Amazingly (even to
me) they never lost money. I worked my way through
college and became the first in my direct line to ever
graduate (and go on to higher degrees, too). My wife and
I are both highly educated, but we can never forget
where we came from. So I get pretty sick and tired of
upper middle-class radicals who bleed for the poor un-
washed proletarian masses. Cynical? You bet.

At Versailles there is a perfect reproduction of a peasant village built by order of Marie Antoinette. She and
her courtiers would dress up in (clean) peasant garb, go
back there, and pretend to be peasants so they could get
a real feel for what it was like to be a commoner. Of
course, it was self-delusion; a rich kid's summer camp
and that's that. People can live among the proletariat,
but so long as they have the option of tapping family
wealth or influence, so long as they are hungry by

choice, they have as much chance of understanding the masses as Marie did.

Revolution—true revolution—is far different than the simplistic dreams of revolutionaries. I have found no evidence, for example, that "women's liberation" movements accomplished anything except the nebulous Yuppie phrase "raising consciousness." Yes, women have undergone a real social revolution, but what were its actual causes? The invention of the birth control pill is certainly foremost—a technological achievement. And economic factors which quite literally forced a change in society because, to achieve a high level of materialistic comfort (and in some cases even a minimal level) requires two incomes these days. And once women are in the workplace, being as intelligent as men, they want to have the same advancement, perks, and power as men have.

In fact, one of the most important (and largely ignored) stages in the "liberation" of women came during World War II, although they were somewhat liberated before that (or do you think the American west or Siberia was populated by men alone on dramatic expeditions in wagon trains?) If all the young men were off fighting the war, who do you think built those Liberty ships and vast number of airplanes and all the rest? Rosie the Riveter did, that's who, and she did one damned good job—otherwise those guys doing the fighting would have quickly run out of things to fight with. It was only after fourteen million young men were suddenly dumped back into the workforce at the war's end that our society developed this very restrictive and sexist *Father Knows Best* mentality and all the mythology that went with it. Just look at the movies, which often reflect a society's attitudes. Women were far more liberated in the thirties than in the fifties.

But the government and union-sponsored counterrevolution failed. The box was open; it couldn't be closed again for long. Now the challenges are different. If both parents work, then the State raises the kids. If women want business advancement and equality, they may have to forgo kids—and the birth rate reflects this. But then who pays the bills for when all of us get old? Social Security and pensions were predicated on the young paying the bills for the old. Even Marxism is totally predicated on a steady or rising birth rate. The Russians are really panicked at this discovery, and Marxist economists are having an even worse time dealing with this than non-Marxist economists, and they're in bad enough shape as it is.

And if you think only communist nations liberate their women, count how many women have been in cabinets, Politburos, and the like in the histories of all the communist nations on Earth, then compare it to European and American governments over that same period. Sure, the bulk of doctors in the Soviet Union are women—and about half the stevedores, too. When a country loses fourteen million young men in wars in a single thirty year period they'd *better* have women doing all that—although the women are still expected to make dinner and clean the house when they get home. Ask any Russian woman who's married (and then check out the Soviet divorce rate). And doctors in the Soviet Union are among the poorest paid professionals. Ah, ain't socialist liberation wonderful? . . .

The usual way an ideologue addresses a revolutionary situation is in terms of narrow moral judgments based on the least common denominator. The argument is always over absolutes. They argue for the elimination of all Euromissiles, or for their retention; they maintain that women should be equal in the workplace or they argue that the trend must be fought as a violation of God or biology or whatever.

But, as we saw, those Euromissiles made possible a strong and generally prosperous Europe that hasn't had to undergo a major war since 1945 in spite of major external threats. And while the Poles and Czechs, for example, aren't too keen about the heavy Russian hand on them, I bet an honest survey would show that their current situation is far preferable to their people than being the battlefields, bleeding grounds, and doormats of European militarism—a situation brought by Euromissiles.

In the case of women in the workplace, any argument over *whether* and *if* is irrelevant. The situation exists, and, thanks to both economics and technology, it's going to continue to exist.

In both cases, the argument is over whether to close the barn door after the horse has already escaped. Instead, sane people must look not at the revolution which has occurred but at the *post*-revolutionary state as it is. The question to be asked and addressed is what will we do with the revolutionary change in our lives and our world, not whether or not we like it. We've got it and we're stuck with it. How we deal with it and who we let shape the post-revolutionary period determines whether we have a world whose leaders make Hitler pale in comparison because their revolutionary technological tools are more advanced or whether those same new tools and methods are used in a positive manner. The situation is far worse now because we are in an age where such revolutions happen every day. And the tendency of even the well-educated and well-meaning is to reach for simplistic Dick-and-Jane solutions to problems that are infinitely complex. It is far easier to go for the cheap slogan than to have to do real work, yet what groups one gives time or money to, what politicians and political movements one supports, where one's tax dollars are spent, all count.

Nor does anyone have to understand how something works to make moral decisions about it. I don't really understand exactly how today's computers do their work, but I certainly know what I do not want human beings to do with them. The potential for better, more efficient work, for microprocessor control of the common things, can very easily be turned into control of human populations. I don't need to know what AI means or how to design integrated circuits to understand choices like that. There exists now a massive data bank, as yet unorganized, that can track a person from cradle to grave and into which any knowledgeable person can tap, including the government. It doesn't take Big

Brother's TV camera in every home to control people; just a smart fellow with a CRT and a modem. So do we try and wipe out such advances, turn back the clock?

My mother had a heart attack in 1975 so serious that she died on the operating table and was brought back to life by 1975 technology. At that time she had at best a reasonable hope of living five more years. Technology advanced. I am writing this in the final third of 1987 and she is still alive and living her own life in her own home. She has, in fact, outlived her first heart specialist. She is no better, but she is no worse—technology is keeping an even pace with her damaged heart. Much of this advance came from space medicine. I live in a very rural area with no public fire department, water department, and the like, and my county doesn't even *have* a police department. But if I have an attack, my wife can dial 911 and have here in minutes a mobile cardiac intensive care unit with telemetry going right to the heart specialist.

Hooray for technology! But that same technology has its own dark side. The chemical blockers that help my mother survive are okay for heart problems, but that whole field is now open for chemical blockers in other parts of brain chemistry. How about a redo of your cranial biochemistry? Intelligence, aggression, creativity, submission, sex, love, hate... Depends on who's doing the redo, doesn't it? And who's reading what data, data with the potential for the state to monitor people even behind closed doors and in the privacy of their own homes?

A great deal of radicalism, both right and left, is really reactionary. The left tends to look at the Rousseauistic ideal, natural and nontechnological, a state of grace as it were (gods not necessary). John Lennon's *Imagine* is the theme here. Okay, but even if we get the right human nature (which I doubt), nobody's telling Mother Nature. Wipe out modern medicine, and we return to an average lifespan of between twenty-seven and forty. We're also going to be wiping out mass communications, mass transportation, and inexpensive power, including the ability to get the food surplus from where it is to where it's needed. Modern technology, mass communications, and research and development are expensive and can't come out of a vacuum.

Emphysema and lung cancer were the scourges of ancient Eskimos. Huh? In that clean air and ideal state of nature? You bet—they had to be constantly burning stuff inside those mud lodges and igloos and then be all hunched up inside to keep warm. They breathed carcinogens so automatically and regularly that they died from it. Of course, we can move lots of folks to the tropics, the breeding grounds of everything from malaria to AIDS. Uh huh . . . Sorry about that, but I "imagined," and, on the whole, I'd rather be where I am.

Political revolutions rarely change anything except the faces of the rulers. Technological and economic revolutions change everything. There are countless added examples, but the point is made, and that's what my books are about. They are basically models: one takes a look at a revolutionary change, a single concept in many cases, and then all the logical consequences of that revolutionary discovery or idea are explored. Logic sometimes dictates a different book than drama might want, but I am at heart a social scientist cursed with a logical mind.

Quite naturally, the books tend to be about how such revolutionary discoveries and ideas might be perverted and misused. Utopias tend to be dull subjects, and one does not need to be warned about the use of something but its misuse. We will use these discoveries in a positive manner (as in the heart problem above), but sooner or later somebody will have other ideas. It's the murder mystery syndrome. Which is more interesting and likely to be read beyond the lead sentence: "He tightened a screw on his bike with a screwdriver," or "He was stabbed through the heart with a screwdriver"?

The critical complaint leveled most often at my work is from ideologues. How dare I show women in other than a perfect superhuman light? How dare I have men who are scared or chauvinistic or divorced or whatever? How dare I show people who are dumb or easily led or who are sometimes idiots? Why do so many of my characters come from backgrounds that are so *seamy*?

Well, that's the masses, baby. Those're the people I grew up with and the people I taught in school and the people who lived in the neighborhoods I hung around in. I don't care about the insular *bourgeois* world that's open to only a few where vitamin therapy and food allergies are big deals, and don't wave your stint in VISTA at me, Marie.

Besides, who's being nationalistic here? Eighty-five percent of the world's people live under dictatorships. What about the status of women in Saudi Arabia or dozens of other non-Western cultures? What about the vast number of people in non-Western traditionalist or tribal societies? Or don't they count? Well, maybe they don't . . .

Pol Pot's Cambodia massacred as many people as Hitler's Germany and with equal ruthlessness and efficiency. The left was conspicuously silent on it and remains so, taking as the last word leftist lawyer and social critic William Kunstler's comment, "I don't criticize socialist countries." Well, after all, they were yellow and they weren't Americans or Europeans, right? And one wonders how Hitler could murder twelve million in gas chambers and concentration camps while we ignored it? The implication here that I find most horrible is that if Hitler had proclaimed himself a revolutionary socialist and explained his actions in Marxist terms while still doing it all the same way, it would somehow be okay to those of the left in the Western world—they'd cheer and defend it.

Ready to send me nasty letters? I just saw a Black Marxist radical who was well-known at that time talking to the Black Student's Union at the University of Maryland. He's still for socialism, anti-imperialism, and utopia, and one of the first things he told his listeners they had to do was arm themselves and get rid of all the Jews. That's right, kill them. Exterminate them. He said they were a lower form of creation and that world socialism and an end to imperialism and racism could not exist until every last Jew was slaughtered. And he got cheered (and, it might be added, demonstrated against as well by the Jewish Students' Union looking and sounding for all the world like black civil rights demonstrators in the sixties).

In other words, the Marxist utopia can't come about until, among many other things, all of the descendants of Karl Marx (and Bill Kunstler) are exterminated. One would love to see Kunstler support this guy on this point. From old Bill's point of view, though, all the socialists should just keep quiet and ignore it when radicals in the name of socialism kill all the Kunstlers in the name of socialism and anti-imperialism. Right, Bill?

In Cambodia/Kampuchea they are still unearthing mounds of skeletons, some as large as good-size hills, where hordes of people were massacred and dumped and burned. But it was all done in the name of socialism and progress so it's all right, huh? And it was done by Cambodians to Cambodians so it's none of our concern, moral or otherwise, right? No? I just look around and paint what I see...

The more things change, the more they stay the same. That's why I keep writing about these things.

Still, I have to wonder and maybe be a little smug about my writings. I mean, people are sending me *outraged* letters complaining about what I did to poor Cassie and Suzl—and those two people do not exist. Their world does not exist. Even their villains don't exist. I made them up. They have no more reality than Tinker Bell or Babar the Elephant. If they've become real enough in the minds of people hundreds or thousands of miles away from me whom I don't know and have never met to cause letters of outrage at what I do to them— damn, if that ain't art I don't know what is. Thanks, folks, for the compliment.

Of course, all of my characters are composites of people I observe, and all those villains have real-life counterparts, and all revolutions are Pandora's boxes, two-edged swords that not only might cut in unexpected and nasty directions in spite of the motives of the revolutionary discoverers but *will* go that way—if we aren't very, very careful. Whatever can be used by a Pasteur or

an Einstein can also be used by a Hitler or Napoleon—
and will. Pasteurize food inside bottles or cans and it can
be stored and transported wherever needed. Wonderful!
A cure of starvation and many other ills! And without
that discovery Napoleon's armies and all the armies after
it could not have conquered and killed so efficiently.

And, perhaps, *that* is why you get so mad at me when
I create these very nasty characters and let them do horrible things to my nicer characters. It means I'm getting
through to you. It means that somewhere deep down you
have recognized your own world, and your friends and
neighbors and maybe yourself, and it's disquieted you.
It's only relevant at all if you see in yourself or your
friends a Cassie or a Suzl or a Misty or a China or a Sam.
If you don't, then what difference is it what I do to
them?

But many of you, particularly the current crop of
critics, can take only the first step and not see beyond;
not see that the forces I employ to do those terrible
things are real and are here now—always were, always
will be. The only difference is, my characters generally
beat the system in the end—that's what the books are
about. Neither Orwell nor Disch in his own stories
allow their characters to win. But history shows that
you *can* beat evil, albeit at a terrible price sometimes,
if you really want to. Only in *The Identity Matrix* did I
show a failure, and that's a warning; the system *could*
have been beaten there, but wasn't because of the
flaws of the victims.

The problem is, if the villain isn't as real to you as the
victims, then we *are* in trouble. The difference between
New Eden and Gor is that New Eden is real, just like
Cassie and Suzl are real, and it has to be fought.

Consider the implications ...

And that's why I'll continue to suck you in with fantasies and wish fulfillment and all sorts of romantic what
ifs ... Because you're just as vulnerable as the poor and
helpless and ignorant, but you're different. Yes, that's
important to note. You—EVERY ONE OF YOU
READING THIS NOW—rich or poor; yellow, black,

white, or red; male or female: you are superior human beings no matter what—yes, you are.

You are superior human beings who read this because you *can* read this and *are* reading this. I don't care if you're a Ph.D., a janitor, a prison inmate, a computer engineer, or whatever. I don't care if you have degrees as long as your arm or never finished grade school. You're special. You read, voluntarily and for pleasure. You are the superior human beings—and the targets. You see, they can always get the rest, but if they hook *you*—and you're too bright and clever to get hooked, right?—then they've hooked everybody who can stop them. It doesn't even matter who "they" are, or might turn out to be. Don't take anything for granted, not in my stories. And not outside of them, either. Don't get too comfortable, too smug, too complacent. They're only fantasies, right? Escapism, nothing more. You can always return to the real world, but perhaps just a little less smug, a tiny bit less comfortable.

So I don't want you to look for magic solutions, and I don't want you to turn back the clock or bury your head in the sand. I want you to confront the transformations and learn to deal with them. I am a strong activist, and the only thing I detest as much as pop cults and radical leftist movements are radical right movements. Show me *any* dogmatic ideologue, and I see only the true ancient enemy of the human race.

Yes, that's right. I am a militant, activist centrist.

The *Titanic* was not only a real ship and a real tragedy, it was also a metaphor and that's what keeps it endlessly fascinating. The super rich, the middle class, and the poorest of the poor were all there and all equalized, just like a miniature Earth. Open your eyes. Look at the news, read the papers. The whole *world* is the *Titanic*, rushing headlong into the night trying to ignore the icebergs and feeling itself unsinkable. I can't save her—no single human being or political system or religious idea can. But fate and talent have put me in the dance band, to do the best I can to keep us from going under and doing something positive until we do. It's what all us mere entertainers should do. While that last performance ended tragically for the artists of the *Titanic*, it was one hell of a performance. It calmed those who would live, and gave them an anchor, it comforted those who would not, and set a standard of courage. Their program wasn't very original but it was the kind of performance artists dream about and you couldn't ask for a better audience.

Yeah, I have good reason to write transformation stories.

Besides, transformation is a cheap trick that works every time.

And now you know the truth. Perhaps ten years from now I'll have a sufficient number of short pieces to do another of these. Perhaps, ten years from now, you all will still want to read them.

Perhaps, just perhaps, ten years from now there will still be enough of you *capable* of reading them. It would be nice to think that the commentaries and fears expressed in this book would date like the social references will, but they won't. Only the names and faces and the latest examples of true revolution will change. The enemy will remain the same, which is why it must be constantly fought.

And now you've got my number. Chalker's revealed his true self. Make of it what you will. In general, like most artists, I dislike explaining myself and probably won't do it again soon, but it was worth saying at least once, not so much for your benefit as for the benefit of those pseudo-intellectuals out there who call themselves critics and who tend to dismiss those writers of multi-volume novels and popular fiction that might just be a little more complex than the critics want you to think. We are the dangerous writers. We march to no drummer but our own, and we have respect, not contempt, for our readership.

And now this work is done, but we're not finished, you and I. We're a team. It's a wonderful, even fun thing to be blessed with the talent or art to create people who never were and places that will never be, and to make people from a variety of places and a number of nations laugh once in a while, cry once in a while, get angry once in a while, *think* once in a while, and all the while entertain. It's a form of magic, but magic is nothing without an audience to do it for. I hope that some of my tricks did that for you and that we'll continue to be a team, if only because I need to work the magic far more than you need to experience it, so thank you.

So long as you remain in the audience, I will remain on the deck, performing to the last, praying that you, at least, make it into the lifeboats, inadequate as they are. I will try to work the magic as best I know how, and it is enough.

THE OFFICIAL JACK L. CHALKER HANDOUT BIBLIOGRAPHY

A SHORT EXPLANATION FROM THE AUTHOR

What follows is an edited down version of what you get if you send me a fan letter. Not a long, or involved, or complex letter requiring a reply, but the usual "I read all your books and I love your stuff" type letter that I love to get. The one you get from me is more detailed and also has many comments found elsewhere in this book, and it's continually updated, but this is given as a basic record of thirteen years of writing fiction and twenty-eight years of doing other things in it and I think it belongs here.

Until recently, I answered every single letter from a reader (who wasn't nasty) personally. It's something I would love to do, but the volume is getting so great that between writing the books and answering the mail, my son was beginning to ask his mother who I was, and she was having trouble remembering herself. As a result, I've been forced to this, which contains the answers to many of the most asked questions. So, unless you asked something unique that requires a personal answer, here's what you get: an autographed copy of this thing. Sorry —but what can I do?

THE MOST-ASKED QUESTION:

(1) *Where do you get your ideas?* A: K Mart Idea Sales. (2) *Why do you live in Maryland when you could live in southern California or Florida?* A: How can anyone live in regions where you can't get Old Bay Seasoning, crab soup, and fresh oysters off the dock? (3) *Will there be more [a]* Well World *novels [b]* Four Lords *novels [c]* Dancing Gods *novels?* A: Probably no, definitely no, and see #40 under NOVELS. (4) *What do you do for a living?* A: I write novels. (5) *Can you get me copies of books of yours that are out of print?* A: No. For first editions, try the SF/F out-of-print booksellers and prepare to part with at least one arm and one leg. I do not have surplus copies lying about. If you just want to read them, all of my book-length fiction is in print anyway no matter what your bookstore tells you. (6) *Which SF writers do you particularly like to read?* A: Eric Frank Russell, James White, some Phil Farmer, early Raymond F. Jones, early Heinlein, Jack Vance, and others too numerous to mention. I do not read SF as much as I used to. It's too much like a busman's holiday. (7) *Do you play role-playing games?* A: No. Why should I spend my free time doing for nothing what I get paid to do? (8) *What SF movies do you like?* A: *Forbidden Planet, This Island Earth*, the second and fourth Star Trek movies, several George Pals, Quatermass, and the first two Star Wars. Okay? (9) *Will you read my manuscript or help me with my writing?* A: And you also get free doctor advice, free legal advice, etc.? Do you know how much they charge you at Clarion? And, yes, I am also a professional editor, but I accept no unsolicited manuscripts. I have no incentive, economic or otherwise, to collaborate with anyone, either. If you got what it takes, you'll make it. If you don't, a Shakespeare

couldn't help you. (10) *You write so much. Is there a list of all you've done?* A: Glad you asked that question . . .

NOVELS

All of the works below are listed in order of publication as a form of checklist. Data on current editions is given if and when available.

1. **A JUNGLE OF STARS**, Ballantine/Del Rey, 1976, *et al*. Also Editions Albin Michel, Paris, 1979 (in French). Some German fans insist there was a German edition circa 1978 but if there was I never saw it. Of course, nobody sent me the French one, either. I got it because Somtow Sucharitkul spotted it in the Paris airport and bought it for me as a gift.

2. **MIDNIGHT AT THE WELL OF SOULS**, Del Rey, 1977, *et al*. also Penguin Books, U.K., 1981; Goldmann, Munich, 1978 (in German). Danish and Dutch editions now appearing, more to come. Series sold to Italy in 1987, my first seven-figure advance. Unfortunately it's lira . . .

3. **THE WEB OF THE CHOZEN**, Del Rey, 1978, *et al*. Also Wilhelm Hein Verlag, Munich, 1981 (in German); also in a highly rewritten Hebrew edition (Tel Aviv, 1981).

4. **EXILES AT THE WELL OF SOULS**, Del Rey, 1978, *et al*. Also Penguin Books, U.K., 1982; Goldmann, Munich, 1979 (in German). Danish, Dutch, Italian editions now appearing.

5. **QUEST FOR THE WELL OF SOULS**, Del Rey, 1978, *et al*. Foreign editions as above.

6. **AND THE DEVIL WILL DRAG YOU UNDER**,

Del Rey, 1979, *et al*. German edition, Goldman, 1983, with same cover French edition 1987 with new cover in large-size trade paperback format. Optioned to the movies.

7. **A WAR OF SHADOWS**, Ace: An Analog Book, 1979. Reprinted with new (good) cover and packaged like a mainstream thriller, Ace, October, 1984. Optioned off and on to the movies.

8. **DANCERS IN THE AFTERGLOW**, Del Rey, 1979, 1982. Also Goldmann, Munich, 1982 (in German as *Der Tourister Planet*).

9. **THE RETURN OF NATHAN BRAZIL**, Del Rey, 1980, *et al*. Foreign editions as above (see *Midnight*.)

10. **THE DEVIL'S VOYAGE**, Doubleday, 1980, in hardcover. Japanese rights were sold, but no book produced so far in Japanese. Out of print at Doubleday, after two printings. After a long dispute with me over paperback rights, Doubleday found a loophole and sold it at the last minute to Critic's Choice paperbacks, a new company in NYC formed by former Pinnacle execs who first tried for cheap works by well-known SF authors but who no longer do SF at all. Unfortunately, they published the Doubleday version, not the one I wrote; 1985, with a great cover. Book is a WWII novel, not SF, although John W. Campbell is a minor character. Someday my complete original version will be published, I hope. Still, if you want to know a main attraction of SF over mainstream, not a single SF character has ever threatened to sue me or taken offense at what I wrote; one in this book did. Groundless, but it makes a point.

11. **TWILIGHT AT THE WELL OF SOULS**, Del Rey, 1980 *et al*. Foreign editions as per *Midnight*.

12. **LILITH: A SNAKE IN THE GRASS**, Del Rey, 1981 *et al*. Also Goldmann, Munich, 1982 (in German). British edition pending.

13. **CERBERUS: A WOLF IN THE FOLD**, Del Rey,

1982 *et al.* Also Goldmann, Munich, 1983 (in German). British edition pending.

14. **THE IDENTITY MATRIX**, Timescape: Pocket Books, 1982. Reprinted, with new cover and fresh typesetting, by Baen Books, January, 1986. Sold to Goldmann, Germany, other foreign sales pending. Although #14 in publication, this was written #3, immediately after *Midnight at the Well of Souls*.

15. **CHARON: A DRAGON AT THE GATE**, Del Rey, 1982 *et al.* German edition (Goldmann), 1984. British edition pending.

16. **THE FOUR LORDS OF THE DIAMOND**, The Science Fiction Book Club, 1983, March main selection. Contains all four "Diamond" books (#s 12, 13, 15, and 17) although slightly rewritten by me to eliminate some recap that was needed in the four but unnecessary in a single volume edition. Original cover by Richard Powers for this book. British and other foreign sales are pending; there is suddenly a lot of interest in it abroad.

17. **MEDUSA: A TIGER BY THE TAIL**, Del Rey, 1983. Also Goldmann, Munich (in German), 1985. British edition pending.

18. **THE RIVER OF DANCING GODS**, Del Rey, delivered in March of 1982 but Del Rey did not publish it until February, 1984. British edition, Futura, 1985,

19. **DEMONS OF THE DANCING GODS**, Del Rey, delivered in October, 1982; published May 24, 1984. British edition, Futura, 1986.

20. **SPIRITS OF FLUX AND ANCHOR**, Tor Books, 1984. First of a large novel eventually split by economics, sheer size, and greed into five books. Delivered in February, 1983. Series was also sold to Holland and Denmark for 1987–88 publication.

21. **EMPIRES OF FLUX AND ANCHOR**, Tor Books, 1984. Second in the Soul Rider books, delivered in May, 1983 and written continuously with #20 above. Mar-

keted as *Soul Rider: Book Two* with the title off to one side.

22. **DOWNTIMING THE NIGHT SIDE**, Tor Books, May, 1985. A complex time travel novel not connected to a series or other words. Delivered December, 1983.

23. **MASTERS OF FLUX AND ANCHOR**, Tor Books, January, 1985. Third but not last in the Soul Rider saga, although it completes the original novel as outlined. Delivered January 25, 1984. Copies were received in November, 1984. The Dutch edition of this one will be abridged, they tell me, and not by me.

24. **VENGEANCE OF THE DANCING GODS**, Del Rey, July, 1985. Third but not the last of the *Dancing Gods* series, although the last written to date. Delivered April, 1984. Futura, U.K., 1986.

25. **THE MESSIAH CHOICE**, St. Martin's/Blue Jay, May, 1985 in hardcover. Mass market paperback, Tor Books, May 1985. A horror novel with SF overtones, should appeal to my regular readers who don't like horror. Delivered August 1, 1984. Blue Jay is technically bankrupt (not my doing!) and the copies were remaindered by St. Martin's and may be available cheap somewhere. The Tor paperback is still in print, though.

26. **THE BIRTH OF FLUX AND ANCHOR**, Tor Books, 1985. A "prequel" to #s 20, 21, and 23 above, set 2600 years earlier. Delivered January 15, 1985, copies received November 14, 1985. No, they called it *Soul Rider: Book 4*, not *Book O*.

27. **CHILDREN OF FLUX AND ANCHOR**, Tor Books, September, 1986. Not a sequel, as originally intended, but actually the last part of the mega-novel I thought I could cover in Three but ran out of room to do.

28. **LORDS OF THE MIDDLE DARK**, Del Rey, June, 1986. First volume in a new mega-novel, *The Rings of the Master*, which was not my series title (I called it *The Malebolge Rings*). Delivered July 15, 1985. Entire series

sold to Hodder/NEL in Great Britain for publication starting late in 1987 and going through late 1988. Series recently sold to Italy as well, no publication data yet.

29. PIRATES OF THE THUNDER, Del Rey, March, 1987. Continuation of the *Rings of the Master* series begun with #28 above. Delivered March 27, 1986. British edition from Hodder/NEL; Italian edition coming.

30. THE LABYRINTH OF DREAMS, Tor Books, March, 1987. First in an open-ended series of at least three stand-alone novels with the same lead characters and premise. The series overtitle is *G.O.D., Inc.* Originally intended as a mega-novel, this turned out to be a true series, each book complete. I had so much fun with the first one, I wrote it in near record time and delivered it on August 10, 1985, five months before it was due. It sort of does to parallel worlds and thirties' detective fiction what the *Dancing Gods* does for Conan. Rescheduled because of the St. Martin's buyout of Tor, so while I had no books come out for nine months, this came out the same month as *Pirates*. I don't control those things, which is why I put the delivery dates in this. This book and its sequels have been banned in parts of Alabama, Tennessee, and the Carolinas because distributors considered the overtitle sacrilegious. Chain book stores there will have it, though.

31. THE SHADOW DANCERS, Tor Books, July, 1987. Second of the *G.O.D., Inc.* books. The first was sort of Raymond Chandler; this one is more like *Alternate World Vice* although it has a fun parody of *The Thin Man* at the end. More serious than #29 but still fun. Delivered December 15, 1985, copies received June 17, 1987. See banning notice on #30 above.

32. WARRIORS OF THE STORM, Del Rey, August 1987. Third in the *Rings of the Master* series begun with #28 and #31 above. Delivered May 25, 1986 at Disclave. British: Hodder/NEL; Italian edition coming.

33. WHEN THE CHANGEWINDS BLOW, Ace/Putnam, September, 1987. After three books from three publishers in three consecutive months people are going to think I have Clark Kent's typing speed. First in a projected trilogy that is one long continuous novel and is a totally continuous narrative. It is fantasy, not terribly comedic although it is satire of a different sort, but it has all the elements you've come to expect from me. Delivered October 20, 1986. The book has a really fine wrap-around Darrell Sweet cover. British edition pending.

34. **MASKS OF THE MARTYRS**, Del Rey, February, 1988. Last of the *Rings of the Master* series, delivered February 24, 1987. British: Hodder/NEL; Italian edition coming.

35. **RIDERS OF THE WINDS**, Ace, May, 1988. Second book in the *Changewinds* series (see #33 above) for Ace/Putnam. Delivered May 22, 1987. British edition pending.

36. **DANCE BAND ON THE *TITANIC***, Del Rey, July, 1988. The book you're holding now.

WRITTEN AND DELIVERED BUT NOT YET PUBLISHED

37. **THE MAZE IN THE MIRROR**, Tor Books, 1988. Third and probably (but not definitely) last in the *G.O.D., Inc.* series begun with #29 above. It was a tough book to write and not delivered until fall 1987, late.

38. **THE WAR OF THE MAELSTROM**, Ace/Putnam, September, 1988. The climactic and final *Changewinds* book. British rights pending.

39. **THE DEMONS AT RAINBOW BRIDGE**, Ace/Putnam, 1989. *The Quintara Marathon* is the overtitle for this, the first of a projected three-book series I am probably just starting to write as *Dance Band* is being published(!) It will be issued first in hardcover as part

of the deal, so it might be 1990 before the paperback of the first volume appears. All I'll tell you is that it's absolutely SF, multi-galactic in setting, and right now I don't see anybody being physically transformed into something else, but you never know. With twenty-seven characters to juggle, I may need some transforming.

40. SWORDS OF THE DANCING GODS, Del Rey, 1989. This may—or may not—be the last book, but considering what the series satirizes there was no way I could leave it at a clichéd trilogy. Be warned: this involves a massive frozen battleground, the Master of the Dead, the Baron, both Irvings, and a strange and epic fantasy quest involving *Gilligan's Island*. Although not due until November '88 I will probably write it earlier, to let *Quintara* percolate a while after the first book of that series is finished.

SHORT FICTION

Since you're reading this in a collection of my short fiction, you already know the stories and their history. A list of titles is included here for the sake of completeness.

1. **NO HIDING PLACE**
2. **FORTY DAYS AND NIGHTS IN THE WILDERNESS**
3. **DANCE BAND ON THE *TITANIC***
4. **STORMSONG RUNNER**
5. **IN THE DOWAII CHAMBERS**
6. **ADRIFT AMONG THE GHOSTS**
7. **MOTHS AND CANDLE**

NOVELTIES

1. **THE NECRONOMICON: A STUDY**, Mirage Press, 1967, as by Mark Owings. Because of this book, "Mark Owings," a very real person, has been listed as a pen name of mine and in a sense really was. Actually he was to do the book, then could not, and I did it for him. He got the billing and I got paid. However, Owings, the field's leading bibliographer, has other books in his own right on his own and and with me. All books, articles, etc. bylined by him alone other than this one are in fact his alone and not mine. Long out of print and a major collector's item these days.

2. **AN INFORMAL BIOGRAPHY OF $CROOGE McDUCK**, Mirage Press, 1974. Done with the cooperation of McDuck creator Carl Barks, I have never given up hope of illustrating an edition with Barks panels in spite of Disney's refusals to date. Out of print and one of my rarest books.

RELEVANT NONFICTION

Actually, I've written quite a lot over the years, including much not in the SF or related fields, much in other works, etc. both credited and uncredited. But is anyone fanatical enough to want to know that I wrote the course of study for high school geography for the Baltimore City Public Schools, for example? Those below are both major and minor material, but all relate to SF/fantasy.

1. **THE *NEW* H.P. LOVECRAFT BIBLIOGRAPHY**, Anthem, 1961. Compiler. Out of print. An updating of George Wetzel's 1952 bibliography authorized by Arkham House but not Wetzel. Long story. Printed and financed by Don "Jon DeCles" Studebaker.

2. (*editor*) **IN MEMORIAM: CLARK ASHTON SMITH**, Anthem, 1963. There is talk of a new edition of this excellent anthology, but don't hold your breath. Contains some Smith material never published anywhere else, including a complete play in blank verse set in Zothique; appreciations by Fritz Leiber, L. Sprague deCamp, and many of Smith's closest friends; a memorial poem (also never published elsewhere) by Theodore Sturgeon; Introduction by Ray Bradbury; etc. In case you haven't guessed, I grew up in this field and there are few in it past or present I don't or didn't know. Financed by Bob Madle, printed by me with assistance from Mark Owings, who bound ten copies in hardcover. Out of print.

3. (*editor*) **MIRAGE ON LOVECRAFT**, Anthem, 1964. Out of print. I also wrote the long introduction to this small collection of articles by August Derleth and David H. Keller, plus some obscure Lovecraft writings, mostly from the pages of *Mirage* magazine. Financed with profits from #2 above.

4. (*with Mark Owings*) **THE INDEX TO THE SCIENCE-FANTASY PUBLISHERS**, Mirage Press, 1966, two editions. We have been working on a monster update and revision of this for over ten years now, and we hope and pray to get it out sooner or later. My problem has been a lack of time for labors of love, and Owings has been having the kind of luck best described by example: he was hit by a truck while on his way to his chemotherapy session. This is a history and bibliography of the specialty presses, with commentary and analysis. In the meantime, abbreviated parts were serialized with expanded personal commentary by me as the column, *On Specialty Publishing* in the excellent *Fantasy Review*, starting with the January, 1983 issue until the magazine's demise in the summer of 1987. All text by me, bibliographic info from my data base and Mark's copious file cards (he refuses to trust computers—he works for the government). Time permitting, we will get the third edition out in 1989 or 1990 from Mirage Press.

5. **H.P. LOVECRAFT: A BIBLIOGRAPHY**, in *The Dark Brotherhood And Other Pieces*, Arkham House, 1965. Out of print. Reprinted (in French) in *L'Herne*, 1967. An attempt to do it new rather than from old bibliographies, Derleth reformatted this to the Wetzel style without my knowledge or permission.

6. (*with Mark Owings*) **THE *REVISED* H.P. LOVECRAFT BIBLIOGRAPHY**, Mirage Press, 1971, Out of print. Almost all Owings, really, but based on my original 1965 bibliography for Arkham House (see above) which Derleth did not use.

PERIODICALS

1. **MIRAGE**, an amateur magazine of fantasy, 1960–1971. Ten issues. My only Hugo nomination was for this magazine, which produced some major work by top names, both fiction and scholarship, and inspired all of today's fan interest in fantasy/horror. For example, this contained the first published stories by Ramsey Campbell and Edward Bryant, and Seabury Quinn's last. Never officially folded, I occasionally get the urge to do another, but sanity prevails. Still, who knows what might emerge in playing with the laser printer?

2. **INTERJECTION**, a small magazine that usually appears in February of each year in the mailings of the Fantasy Amateur Press Association, 1968–present. Essays and commentary on various subjects, mostly not SF or fantasy related. Available only to FAPA members. Please don't ask for a copy, but if you publish a fanzine you might consider applying to FAPA for membership. If you don't, or don't know what a fanzine is, forget it.

GAMES

TAG Industries, which specializes in miniatures for war games, has done a Well World role-playing game, released in fall, 1985. I do not play role-playing games for fun; I get paid to do that, so I don't even understand the rules and I am not responsible for the descriptions of some of the races used in the game. The game is available from game stores and wholesalers; the box is a large reproduction of the cover of the U.S. edition of *Midnight*. At least all of you who keep pleading for more Well World books can act out your own script. There is a lot of interest in a Soul Rider game for computers right now, and talk as well of a *Four Lords* adventure game, but nothing firm yet. Again, we'll see. I am neither writing nor doing anything more than licensing these. TAG, by the way, does a lot of miniatures for other companies' role-playing games and is considering doing miniatures of the Well World creatures. I am promised some say in their design, but that's what they always tell you. The game did okay but TAG suffered from distribution problems.

COLUMNS

I wrote a regular column on SF/fantasy small press for *Fantasy Review* as referred to elsewhere here, and I also am writing a computer column for *Supermicro*, a quarterly of interest only to those with S-100 and other odd busses computers and CDOS/Flexdox/Turbodos users. But if you want to be a completist, I mention it here. I might well continue an SF oriented column somewhere but I haven't had many offers yet.

ODDBALL MISCELLANY

In addition to the above, I wrote almost all of the uncredited text of Progress Reports #3 and 4 and the Program Book of Discon II, the 1974 World Science Fiction Convention. I also wrote almost all the uncredited text for all progress reports and the Program Book for Suncon, the 1977 World Science Fiction Convention. I have columns in all four of the progress reports of Con-Stellation, the 1983 World Science Fiction Convention (all bylined, for a change) at which I was Toastmaster, and have a very tongue in cheek "biography" of 1988 worldcon toastmaster Mike Resnick in the Nolacon II Progress Report #2 getting even for what Resnick did to me in 1983. I also did an appreciation of Ron Goulart for the 1979 Lunacon Program Book (bylined) and another (shorter) *depreciation* of Resnick in the Lunacon Program Book for 1987 where he was the Roastmaster and they "roasted" me. I still occasionally appear in fanzines as the mood and time strikes me, always nonfiction. I also just wrote the entry for "Small Presses" in Jim Gunn's forthcoming SF Encyclopedia, and participated in a "round robin" novelette being written by a number of SF writers for charity under the auspices of the 1988 World SF Convention in New Orleans.

For the record, a book once listed in the colophon of one of my other books titled *War Game* was changed by Doubleday to *The Devil's Voyage*. Another, listed *Ripsaw*, I intended to write that year but suddenly got too busy to do so. It is yet to be written, but one of these days I'll get to it. It's not SF/fantasy, anyway, but a rather bizarre murder mystery set in Arizona in the 1880s. I occasionally review computer software and hardware; I used to do it for *Advanced Computing* on a regular basis until it folded, now I do it for various magazines on an irregular basis. I have electronic mail addresses on Delphi and several private and public BBSs and have done on-line interviews for most of the commercial services who have SF SiGs. I check Delphi regularly, though; the others may go for a month or more between message checks, so just because you might see I'm a member of some service doesn't mean I actually call them up.

ERIC FRANK RUSSELL REISSUES

In 1985–1986, Del Rey Books, at my urging, reprinted five of the best novels of the late Eric Frank Russell. Anyone who likes me and has never read Russell is urged to do so. These include the first complete publication in the U.S. of *Wasp* and *Next of Kin* (a.k.a. *The Space Willies*). Also included are new printings of *Sinister Barrier*, *Three to Conquer*, and *Sentinels From Space*. All have introductions by me. If you can read *The Space Willies* without cracking up you're not my kind of person, and *Sentinels* was one of my primary influences as a budding writer.

SUMMING UP

I have not missed a World SF convention since the 1965 LonCon, so if you want to make sure and see me I'll always be where the worldcon is. (In 1988 it's in New Orleans, 1989 Boston, both Labor Day weekend, and in 1990 it's in The Hague, Netherlands, a week before Labor Day). As Bob Silverberg says, you do something for twenty, twenty-five years, it gets to be a habit. I like conventions and go to a lot of them. If there's an SF con near you but you've never seen me there, the odds are I was never asked or the Powers That Be don't want me or it always conflicts with one of my regular gigs. I don't go where I'm not wanted. Exception: I generally turn down cons with a strong media bias (Star Trek, etc.) or ones that are heavy on non-reading or non-SF print media, not because I disapprove of them but because I just don't have fun at them myself. I like conventions filled with people who buy and read books.

The data used in this abbreviated version of the Handout was compiled in November, 1987, and is more or less complete up to that time. Thanks to you all, and keep reading, and enjoy!

BRIEF BIOGRAPHICAL NOTES
FOR THE INTERESTED

BORN: 12/17/44, Baltimore, MD (although all bios and even *Who's Who* say Norfolk, so who am I to argue with *Who's Who*?). It's a self-perpetuating error that has grown too large to be worth correcting. I really don't mind since I have roots and tons of family in Norfolk, anyway.

EDUCATION: Baltimore city public schools, Towson State College (B.S.), graduate degrees from Johns Hopkins University. Although I have a strong science background, my degrees are in history and English. My graduate speciality is "History of Ideas" which is to say I'm a certified expert on *-isms* and *-ologies*. I have taught history on the high school and college levels, and am or have been a lecturer at the Smithsonian, The National Institutes of Health, and numerous colleges and universities.

OCCUPATIONS: Aside from the usual kid occupations, I've been a professional typesetter, a sound engineer for rock concerts, an audio and computer reviewer, freelance editor, a publisher (founder and now sole owner of The Mirage Pres, Ltd.), a book packager, an Air National Guard Information Director, new and used book

dealer, and teacher as mentioned above. I was a special
forces Air Commando during the Vietnam war period
but never served west of Amarillo (note, however, that
no Viet Cong penetrated east of Albuquerque while I
was there). My TDY duty tour in Vietnam lasted a bit
over four hours. Since 1978 I have made my living solely
by writing, although Mirage Press continues in business
and plans to produce at least two more books before
folding its tent, both announced almost two decades ago
but delayed by all sorts of horror factors.

FAMILY: Married Eva C. Whitley on the ferryboat *Roaring Bull* in the middle of the Susquehanna River in 1978;
one child, a son, David Whitley Chalker, b. 1981. Also
inhabiting the house is a nearly human Pekingese named
Hoy Ping Pong and Stonewall J. Alleycat, one of the
dumbest cats in history and a strong argument against
evolution.

MEMBERSHIPS: Author's Guild, Sierra Club, National
Parks & Monuments Association, Amnesty International, The National Aquarium, Maryland Academy of
Sciences, Smithsonian, Maryland Historical Society,
Washington Science Fiction Association, American Film
Institute, many others, with varying degrees of activism.
I have long been active in and supportive of conservation
and historical preservation causes. I'm also the past
three-term treasurer of the Science Fiction Writers of
America but because of disagreements with the current
guild I am no longer a member. I am a registered Democrat (there are only two Republicans in Maryland and
they're both in office) and two-time unsuccessful candidate for office myself.

CONTINUING INTERESTS AND AVOCATIONS: Ferryboats,
travel, national parks and monuments, consumer electronics, politics, history, space program, printing and
publishing, book collecting, auctioneering, old time radio
and classic TV, computers.

The computer this is composed on is an S-100 bus
CompuPro 816C HD running concurrent PC-DOS 5.1 if

you care, and I also have a Toshiba T-3100 AT clone
laptop that I take with me when I travel. My son has a
Commodore 128. The recent addition of a Compaq
386/20 earned me a Junior Pournelle merit badge. Printing is courtesy of the Apple LaserWriter Plus. My novels
are written and spell checked with a text editor called
FinalWord II, from Mark of the Unicorn, Inc., which I
strongly commend to anybody doing long documents or
who has bad electric service (it rescues unsaved text
from power outages and even some operator blunders).
Yes, I know how to program but consider it in the same
thrilling vein as being asked to inventory sand grains in
Libya. I am frequently on CompuPro-related and Mark
of the Unicorn BBSes, occasionally on BIX and Compu-
serve, but if you have a specific question for me the best
way (if you have a computer) is to ask it on Delphi's SF
SiG, where I tend to hang out regularly. Any EMail for
me should be sent there, or to the SF SiG Forum. Many
SF writers hang out on Delphi's SF conference, occasionally including me.

An Epic Tetralogy from and

Jack Chalker
THE
FOUR LORDS
OF THE
DIAMOND